Brian Brown

A Novel

Crown Publishers
New York

Published by Crown Publishers, New York, New York.
Member of the Crown Publishing Group.

Random House, Inc. New York, Toronto, London, Sydney, Auckland
www.randomhouse.com

CROWN is a trademark and the Crown colophon is a registered trademark of Random House, Inc.

Printed in the United States of America

Design by Elina D. Nudelman

Library of Congress Cataloging-in-Publication Data

Brown, Brian.
    TV: a novel / by Brian Brown.
      1. Television broadcasting—Fiction. 2. Television broadcasting of sports—Fiction.
    3. Live television programs—Fiction. 4. Unemployed—Fiction. I. Title.

  PS3602.R68 T8 2001
  813'.6—dc21

                                                                    2001028298

ISBN 0-609-60615-8

10 9 8 7 6 5 4 3 2 1

First Edition

Author's Note

About the time I turned thirty, I changed careers, switching from newspapers to television. I assumed, incorrectly, that I was going into a closely related field. I assumed, incorrectly, that I was trading one high-pressure world for another. In the newspaper business, there always seemed time for simple civilities. In TV, you could work on shows for hours in a cocoon of frenzy, where even a trip to the rest room was a luxury. Membership in a cult would have been less consuming.

The reward for working on these intense productions, especially live broadcasts watched by millions, was an incomparable moment-to-moment high. But operating for hours one second away from catastrophe can fray the nerves of even those with the best of intentions. Often, the operative management technique was creative tension times two: That is, it was the abusive and asocial who survived. And that's where the motivation for writing this book began: I had come across men and women who had become monsters, a whole race of seemingly unredeemable creatures, and wondered where they came from, why so many thrived, wondered why they were tolerated for so long.

At the same time, during a decade of debating whether the value of the product was worth the blood and guts spilled in the effort, there were moments of great satisfaction—great fun. I've also known people who while under fire were in fact able to summon immense talent *and* substantial goodwill. So there is love with hate in the story you are about to read.

At this point, I would be expected to write the standard disclaimer, telling you that this is a work of fiction, and any resemblance to actual persons, living or dead, is entirely coincidental. As everyone knows, writers of fiction tend to create characters that resemble persons living or dead. Just like painters and sculptors, we often find it helpful to begin our formulations with a human model in mind. Even science fiction writers tend to rely on Homo sapiens. In the interest of disclaiming, I think it better to explain how much resembling I am guilty of.

My central character, a TV director, will bear some resemblance to several people in the world of television, but he is not based on any one man. He is a composite, and at the same time a work of the imagination, and also, to paraphrase Flaubert, a piece of him is partly me. Further, for the sake of drama and authenticity, this character is credited with directing many major events that were, in real life, the notable achievements of others. At the conclusion of this novel, you will see that I have made a small attempt to remedy this distortion of history.

Nothing in this book happened exactly this way. And much of what you will read is entirely made up. But, as noted, I bring to this story my own experiences in television, and in preparing to write this book, I also begged my colleagues to share their fondest stories and educated impressions. For those who work in live TV, where most shows fade instantly in the collective memory, there remains a body of anecdotes that everyone understands is important to preserve and supplement. In a way, sometimes that is all that is left. Call it a modern kind of oral storytelling. And it is a tradition I have been able to exploit.

Nothing in this century, perhaps nothing in our history, has had the impact of TV. It has linked us together and, at the same time, insulated us from one another. On the same night, it can show us classic entertainment and utter trash. TV can be both a force for positive change and a poisonous influence. I would like to think that the character you are about to meet, a man as flawed as he is brilliant, seduced by excess and ambition, defines the nature of the medium and his time.

Prelude

*"I fought because I understood, and could not bear to under-
stand, that it was my destiny . . . to sit in the stands with
most men and acclaim others. It was my fate, my destiny, my
end, to be a fan."*
    —FRED EXLEY, *A Fan's Notes*

"Swish!"
    —MARTY GLICKMAN

Super Bowl

The most watched event in the history of American television was about to end. The people responsible for televising it were huddled inside a converted truck, a darkened, loud, cramped mobile control room.

"What are we doing?"

This was a fair question. The broadcast was coming back from its last commercial break and Caesar Fortunato wanted to know what to do with the seventy pieces of equipment at his disposal. To differentiate between all this hardware, there was a code: His cameras were numbered, tape machines were identified by color, the top-end toys that did special effects were lettered. Caesar wanted to know if he would be using numbers or colors or letters, or perhaps a combination.

"What the FUCK are we doing?"

"I don't know," the producer replied.

"What do you mean?"

"I've lost track."

"JESUS CHRIST!"

"It's a blimp pop or a promo or billboards. I don't know which one. Sorry, Caesar, I'm totally fried."

"Coming back from commercial in thirty," the associate director noted.

"You're an idiot. We'll do a blimp pop."

"Fine, fuck it."

As director, Caesar Fortunato was the person most responsible for what America had been seeing. He'd been writing an improvisational narrative with pictures, composing each and every shot, determining the pace, rapidly and artistically: cut, cut, cut . . . or cut, *dissolve, dissolve.* It was Caesar who had decided when America would see a wide shot, when America would see a close-up, when America would see a replay, when, in some cases, America could go to the toilet. But, as usual, this being a Super Bowl, he hadn't been able to make much of a movie. In another NFL championship game swiftly sapped of drama, Buffalo's forever hapless Bills had been outscored 24–0 in the second half by the Cowboys of Dallas.

Through fifty years of TV history, Super Bowls dominated the top-ten list of most watched shows. But maybe one out of every five were worthy competitions. That last-minute touchdown pass by Joe Montana against the Bengals was one example of the few and far between, and Scott Norwood's missed field goal that could have won it for the Bills, and somewhere in the 1970s, the Cowboys and the Steelers were in a good one. Most of the rest: awful, soporific: Broncos busted, Vikings falling flat, and here he was in the middle of another foregone conclusion. The water cooler summits on Monday wouldn't even review his work. As usual, they'd be forums for chatting about the best commercials: talking frogs, snappy beer ads, soda spots with million-dollar budgets.

"I don't see it!"

"Caesar, we may be out of blimp shots."

"Here we come in ten . . ."

"I don't see it!"

"Caesar, we're still rewinding!"

The tape operator at the red machine was stationed in another part of the truck. His hand was trembling, the right index finger poised inches from the play button, disposed as Adam's crooked finger on the ceiling of the Sistine Chapel.

"Nine . . ."

The man's name was Larry Swenson, and his heart was beating at about ninety-six percent of its capacity.

"Eight . . ."

"Where is the fucking blimp shot?"

"WE'RE REWINDING!"

"JESUS, SOMEONE ANSWER ME!"

Caesar knew that his tape operator had provided him with an adequate response more than once.

"Seven . . ."

But as the associate director dipped under double digits in his count back from break, and though Caesar knew Larry was surely scrambling, he kept asking for the shot anyway, and he couldn't resist uttering the most commonly used phrase in live television.

"You're killing me! . . . YOU GUYS ARE KILLING ME!"

It didn't make the tape machine rewind any faster, but it allowed Caesar to vent, which was almost justifiable after seven hours of directing the most-watched telecast of the year, where a missed commercial or a screwed-up blimp pop was an unforgivable mistake. Every second of the Super Bowl that could be sold had been sold. Nowhere else, and never before, did time cost this much.

"Six . . ."

The log said there was a nighttime aerial from the blimp at 12:00:00. The counter on the Japanese-made BVW 78 was whizzing downward, 12:04:21 . . . :20 . . . :19, but Larry Swenson couldn't be certain it would reach the desired destination when America would be rejoining the broadcast.

"Five . . ."

Weather properly British, wet and nasty, had grounded the blimp, so throughout the broadcast the gang in tape had been helping the network fake it, frantically rummaging all game through old reels for previous blimp appearances at the Georgia Dome. The Pinestar company had long been one of the network's leading advertisers, and CEO Thaddeus Hutchinson relished hearing the boilerplate promotional copy about his beloved airship. In fact, he had phoned the network sports president just before kickoff and demanded that mention be made of his blimp, even though the sissy-ass pilot had refused to put it in the air and the network was only obligated to promote a blimp that was verifiably airborne. Since the blimp would have been present for the entire game, and since the game stretched from late afternoon to early evening, this increased the degree of difficulty to Olympic proportions: Caesar's tape people needed both day and night shots, all of them showing a city in the midst of a soaking.

Atlanta would get these sort of events with a kind of bait-and-switch, pretending to be the lone cosmopolitan destination in the Deep South, where ostensibly winters were a rumor. The truth was, it had been frigid and gray much of the week, as it often was during Atlanta's Januarys. This only substantiated Caesar's low opinion of the city, which he compared to Tokyo and Dresden, other disheartening, war-victimized concrete enclaves that looked as though they had been built on top of parking lots. As Caesar understood it, Atlanta had virtually no architectural history because it had been obliterated twice in its young life: first famously by Sherman's thousand points of flaming light, then more recently and unannounced by the city's second black mayor, Andrew Young, who used any excuse to knock down structures associated with lingering white imperialism.

"Do we have the blimp copy?"

For the fifth time since the start of the second half, Henry Kapp entered the truck to remind his production staff about a sponsorship obligation. Kapp had all the right qualifications to run a TV sports division. After getting his MBA, he had become a breakfast cereal executive. For some two years, Caesar Fortunato and Henry Kapp had been circling each other in a kind of operatic boxing match, repeated verbal jabs and counters, but as yet no knockout blow.

"Three . . ."

"Mr. Fortunato, we've got to do the blimp!"

In the months leading up to the Super Bowl, Henry Kapp had assiduously and fearlessly degraded the editorial content of the broadcast and inflated business opportunities, packing the program with a scandalous feast of commercials, billboards, on-air mentions, in-house promotions, and blimp pops. The kickoff was sponsored and the scoring replays had a sponsor and the injury report had a sponsor and the announcers were wearing clothes provided by a sponsor, and there was a blimp provided by a sponsor, though the game was being played indoors, and therefore invisible to flying objects, and, anyway, there was no blimp. Amidst this storm of shilling, it was unclear if the sporting competition between the Cowboys and the Bills to decide the best team in pro football was even the point of the broadcast, or just filler between the ads.

"WHERE'S THE TAPE! WHERE THE FUCK IS IT!"

Kapp versus Fortunato wasn't exactly a fair fight. Though Caesar Fortunato was the inventor of the instant replay and had probably done more major live TV events than anyone, and was certainly a big name inside the business, he was viewed as a dying breed. Even if he could slay Henry Kapp, Caesar understood there'd be another clone right behind, another bottom-liner, another coldhearted, white-shirted, narrow-brained accountant type sent from the home office of the behemoth that owned half of the entertainment business, another who would walk into the building with not one second of television experience, not one creative bone in his all-too-starched body, another without any fucking business doing TV.

"Two . . ."

The $60,000 Japanese-made BVW 78 had just reached 12:00:00, the correct starting point for rainy, nighttime aerials of the Georgia Dome photographed by a hovering Pinestar blimp some three years earlier.

"RED MACHINE! COME ON . . . WHERE IS IT?"

A production assistant working back in tape noticed that Larry Swenson was staring perplexed at his trembling right index finger. The gap between his finger and the play button was certainly not about to be traversed in the next two seconds.

"One . . ."

"ROLL RED!"

Only members of the United Television and Radio Workers, such as Larry Swenson, were permitted to operate the tape machines. The production assistant was nonunion, at the bottom of the food chain: overworked, underpaid, immensely vulnerable.

"ROLL, GODDAMMIT! . . . ROLL!"

But the wrath of the union did not compare to Caesar's. The production assistant hit play.

"And," said the associate director, "we're back."

"Go, Kevin," the producer said to the announcer.

Tonight's aerial views provided by the people at Pinestar. We thank them for all their fine work this season on our football telecasts.

"Ready two . . . Dissolve . . . Cue . . . All right, let's get this fucking game over with."

Once a master at managing his body chemistry, Caesar Fortunato had turned himself into a flammable cocktail: caffeine on top of adrenaline, rage on top of caffeine. He had risen throbbing with a semi-migraine from four beers too many the night before and then knocked his latest solution to everything, a vial of benzedrine, into the toilet at the finish of a robust flush. Chain-smoking, with its less potent but relatively effective nicotine buzz, was no longer an option in the new era of smoke-free environments, so he resorted, reluctantly, to coffee as his reserve upper, ten cups in three hours, which, inevitably, saddled him with a bladder screaming and swollen by the second quarter, except he couldn't leave the truck to pee, not even at halftime, because he had to direct the league's bloated entertainment extravaganza, this one featuring a gigantic white-suited, love-and-harmony singing, borderline-spastic young people's chorus that might have made even Lawrence Welk puke.

"A reminder everyone: The game isn't over. IT'S NOT FUCKING OVER!"

Caesar's choices were arrayed before him along a wall of stacked monitors, an electronic gallery of human motion. Camera 1, front and center, was the main coverage shot at the 50-yard line. Camera 41, lower left, was a small, unmanned, point-of-view device affixed to the peak of the Georgia Dome, a fish-eye lens with a bird's-eye view. With the game having just ended, Caesar was relying on a small squadron of handhelds, the hardware most appropriate to document the thrill of victory and the agony of defeat.

"Get me a shot of Levy, that fucking loser! HEY, MARV, THIS JUST IN. THE GAME IS FOUR QUARTERS!"

Prior to kickoff, Caesar had decided that Marv Levy and his Ballerina Conference team were overdue. This horribly rash judgment, backed by an irresponsible wager, stoked his peevishness and ensured that his Philadelphia bookie would be able to maintain a lifestyle of Cadillacs, power boats, and fur coats. Levy, Harvard-educated, had just become the first NFL head coach to lose four straight Super Bowls. Like Levy, Caesar Fortunato was a bright man who knew a lot about football. But that, by itself, did not make either of them winners. Caesar Fortunato's grasp of the sport was professorial. He knew its history, sensed when games would turn, often correctly anticipated the next play. This quality enhanced his directing and had utterly no effect on his ability to handicap.

"Ready seven. Take seven! Awful shot. Ready ten. Take ten! Another loser. Ready six. Frame it up, six! Take six! F-u-u-u-c-k . . . Listen . . . All of you . . . all of you cripples, all of you fucking alleged professionals, please wake the fuck up."

It was acceptable for a director to be abrupt, for his voice to be emphatic, but Caesar Fortunato on this lousy Sunday had werewolfed into the much-despised category of screamer. By definition, a screamer wasn't just loud. He was abusive for the sake of being abusive.

"Tape, are you ready? Have you figured out what the fuck you're doing back there? . . . I want blue . . . Stand by blue . . . Roll blue . . . Come on! While I'm still breathing!"

Caesar wanted a replay of the winning quarterback celebrating the victory, about to announce an impending trip to a popular Florida theme park. What America saw was a meaningless play from the first quarter, a run up the middle for no gain.

"SHIT! . . . You know what, you guys? You know what? And this isn't a threat. It's fucking real. Next year, we won't need you. We won't fucking need you. You won't be able to fuck up my games. Next year, automation. It's here, baby. I'll be talking directly to the machines. Machines with brains!"

Whack.

Whack.

Whack.

Caesar slapped the narrow table he shared with the producer and technical director. Since everyone outside the truck was wearing double-muff headphones sensitive enough to let them hear Caesar breathing, his attack on the table caused a universal, momentary hearing loss.

The punishing treatment of the crew did not match their alleged crimes. Overall, they were solid and often enough excelled. Except Caesar had lost touch, lost touch with these men and women who had for so long surrendered their best efforts for him, lost touch with the very nature of the medium. He was becoming more and more intolerant of even the smallest mistakes. It was as if he was searching for the perfect broadcast, though he knew that to be another lost cause. There was no script in live sports. No second takes. Error was inherent in its making. He hated live TV for this, and because it was the lowest of art forms, because it had trapped him, because he knew he should have gotten out long before, because Caesar Fortunato was meant for bigger and better things.

He had done some of the good, but too much of the ugly, and though the quality wavered, the cost did not. Everyone, from the guys in tape to the geezers in transmission, were shortening their lives, really, bruising their insides. The math never worked. There wasn't enough time to edit that feature on the quarterback. Not enough time to write the script for the pregame show, to distill the fifty story lines and mountain of minutia created by the big game, not enough time to debug a technical operation that had almost as many cameras and tape machines and miles of cable as the network's New York headquarters.

Once, even scabby locations and putrid events and his crabby nature could be soothed by the network's enlightened, liberal travel policy: Don't ask, don't tell. But with sports president Henry Kapp having swiftly concluded the belle époque of limos and Learjets, hotel suites and company-paid credit cards, Caesar's entire business life had been bumped back from first-class to coach. The flight to Atlanta from his home in Rancho Mirage departed at a stomach-turning 5:45 A.M. and included connections in Salt Lake City and Pittsburgh. He could have flown to Paris faster. Accustomed to ground transportation by other means, he was driving a midsize two-door rental, before it was towed for lack of an official parking pass, which forced Caesar onto the plodding media shuttle bus. The league had given the network a sufficient allotment of proper parking passes, three hundred in all, but Henry Kapp distributed just ten to production and the remaining two hundred and ninety to the families and friends of key sponsors. One of the network's catered dinners, the worst in Caesar's memory, summarized the new order: stale nachos with nuked cheese.

"Closing credits in two minutes," the associate director noted.

"Credits, what a fucking joke!"

"You listen to me, Mr. Fortunato," said the hovering Henry Kapp, undeterred by Caesar's evident disgust with his very presence, "we want these people to know that we value them."

"I need security. We have an intruder in the truck."

"Credits in ninety, assuming we're going to credits."

"Excuse me, I want credits!"

"This broadcast has been one long fucking embarrassment. No credits."

"I WANT CREDITS! IS THAT CLEAR!" Henry Kapp bellowed with a force that seemed to make his closely cropped hair stand at attention and his droopy eyelids bolt awake. Since coming to the sports division, Kapp had largely maintained his composure, cognizant that having a burly six-foot-four, football-sized body, an inscrutable expression, and a reputation for merciless cost cutting was intimidating enough. Caesar had instigated a display of rage only Mrs. Kapp had ever seen.

"I need security. We've got a man out of control in here."

"EXCUSE ME. THIS IS MY TRUCK!"

"No, Mr. Rice Krispies, this is my truck, and I would appreciate it if you would get the fuck out of it."

"Mr. Kapp," said the game producer, "could we just get this thing off the air. Huh?"

Sometimes in sports, it's not so much that a team has lost, but that another has won. . . . And tonight, the Cowboys were simply the better team. It was not a lack of effort that beat the Bills, but a team with better talent. You know, at the beginning of the season, I picked these Bills to win it all, and you know, they got there and they fought and just ran out of gas. We salute them both, Bills and Cowboys. Great teams, one just a little greater.

9

"Those have to be the most moronic closing comments I have ever heard. And he's making excuses for this shitty, shitty team that has lost me a lot of money."

The play-by-play announcer in question had previously spent all of his professional life in cable television and was doing his first major show on the network. In cable, Kevin Barrett addressed a desirable but limited demographic: young men in a kind of perpetual boyhood who loved sports, beer, and swimsuit models with big tits. On network TV, Barrett's limitations were evident. He came across as a chronological inversion, a shallow, know-it-all fourteen-year-old somehow residing in a forty-year-old's body. In Barrett, Kapp was getting what he paid for: half the talent at half the price.

"CHECK THE SCORE, ASSHOLE."

The final was 30–13.

"That's just such bullshit, Mr. Fortunato," said Kapp, arms folded in a false appearance of repose. He had taken two steps back, and was bouncing nervously, sensing Caesar might be inclined to violence.

"One minute."

"Give me another blimp shot," Caesar ordered. "Best work I've had all day. Shots from a floating bag of helium recorded eight years ago."

"Mr. Fortunato, we don't need to do any more blimp pops."

"Restraint, Mr. Kapp? No more blow jobs? It can't be! There must be something we can promote."

"No, we're done."

"I'm sure there must be at least one more way to compromise our-selves. There must be some show we can promote. Some kind of pig-fuck piece of synergy. I know what we can do. We can officially sell our integrity. *Integrity sponsored by our friends who make that Rocky Mountain swill they call beer.*"

"Thirty seconds to credits, assuming we're going to credits."

"Credits, Mr. Fortunato! Or there'll be hell to pay. I swear."

"You make everyone fly through Alaska to get here, put them up in the fucking Best Western, and make them eat cheese and crackers all week. Rolling credits doesn't get you off the hook, big guy. . . . Stand by green. America, tonight, I officially pronounce TV dead."

"Ten to credits . . . nine . . . eight . . . seven . . ."

"What a fucking embarrassment. Ready green. Roll green, *dissolve.*"

The New Boss

The English muffins were just emerging from the toaster, the bacon crackling, the eggs simmering, the glasses and plates being assembled with a familiar clinking. His cup of espresso, freshly ground, Italian, was as yet undisturbed. It was a saintly winter morning in Rancho Mirage: temperature seventy-two, sky blue, humidity zero. At his poolside patio table, Caesar Fortunato was at last in full leisure mode, liberated in cotton pullover and nylon sweats, awaiting the imminent delivery of breakfast from his live-in maid, Marisol. He was reading the sports TV column of *USA Journal,* January 31, 1994.

The game may have been a rout, but the coverage was compelling, thanks to the work of Emmy-lauded director **Caesar Fortunato.** In his 14th Super Bowl, Fortunato was typically well prepared. He showed how, early on, the Dallas offensive line was outmuscling Buffalo's defenders. Later, with one close-up after another, he effectively documented the gathering gloom in the faces of the Buffalo players and coaches. Known for his innovations, Fortunato had Godzilla-sized camera cranes flown in from Japan. Stationed behind each end zone, the dramatic high angle was able to show how plays developed, and also added to the "big game" feel. It was a welcome Hollywood touch from the California-based director.

Back on the East Coast, on a rainy, dispiriting afternoon, twenty-five floors above Sixth Avenue, the suits were assembled to resolve the dilemma that was Caesar Fortunato. They sat opposite each other on two couches, sports division president on one, executive producer and head of business affairs doubled up on the other.

"As I recall, the idea for putting the big cranes in the end zones was my idea," said Henry Kapp.

"You definitely approved the idea," said executive producer Geoff Simms.

"Geoff, I didn't just approve the idea. It was *my* idea."

"I guess you're right, Henry. Yes, you're right."

"Oh, Chaaad."

"Yes, Henry."

Chad Goodman was the head of business affairs.

"I didn't know the equipment came from Japan."

"It doesn't, sir."

"Why did the paper say it came from Japan?"

"I don't know."

"It's probably his new press agent," said Simms.

"He has a press agent?"

"Yup."

"You know, I got a call from the old man. He wanted to know why the fuck we had to be flying equipment across the Pacific Ocean. Shit."

"Apparently," said Simms, "Caesar's decided he is not getting enough attention."

Though Simms was the executive producer, he understood that his job security was contingent upon having no public profile whatsoever. If a reporter was on the phone, Simms didn't hesitate, didn't dare even offer a "no comment." He immediately had the call transferred upstairs to Kapp's assistant. To the extent it was possible, Henry Kapp wanted to make sure every success was somehow attributable to him. It was why he took the stage to accept each and every Emmy award at the annual banquet. This additional form of gluttony was naturally detested by his top creative people, who had been leaving at the rate of almost one a month since the start of Kapp's reign, now in its third year of improving revenues and diminishing quality.

"Roland will print anything, won't he?"

Nick Roland was the sports TV columnist for *USA Journal.* As a rule, he was favorably inclined to producers and directors who bought him a good meal and splurged on the wine. During Super Bowl week, Caesar's new press agent had introduced Roland to a delectable French white from the Sancerre vineyards of a highly regarded winemaker named Boda.

"Geoff, I want you to call my friend and tell him that he's cut off. No more scoops from me."

"Okay, Henry."

Roland did little more than wait for the network executives to call him with scoops. Because his paper reached three million readers, the TV industry used his column like a bulletin board. Roland merely provided the tacks. When Simms called and threatened a boycott, it was likely he would whimper, apologize six times, and promise to write a column the next day revealing Kapp's vital role in the production.

"Now, Chad, to the more serious matter. What was our boy doing in that limo?"

"Sir, I've warned him."

"That's just outright subordination. He's going to regret it, I assure you. He is going to regret it."

For Caesar, it was essential that he be able to leave the game immediately and catch the first flight out of Atlanta. This was one tradition he would never forsake, and with his rental car missing in action, he needed a ride. In the interest of maddening Kapp further, Caesar made sure the vehicle was a limo. The first of Kapp's commandments when he took over was *Thou shalt not be conveyed by limousine.*

"It was probably best for his safety," said Chad Goodman.

"Yeah, after the game, I can't tell you how many people said they'd never work with Caesar again," said Simms. "More than one person used the phrase 'that insane motherfucker.' "

"Forget all that other stuff. Did you hear how he was addressing me?" said Henry Kapp.

"Yes, sir. It was like the guy was fucking possessed."

"All right, we've got to do something about this problem."

"Yes, sir."

"Do you want to talk about some kind of buyout?"

"NO, GOODMAN! We're not making a charitable contribution to the Fortunato fund. That's exactly what he wants. We're not buying him out. He's not going to be playing golf on our money. No . . . fucking . . . way."

When United Systems Inc. purchased the network, Caesar had a guaranteed, long-term contract worth millions of dollars. Kapp could have bought out the contract at any time, let Caesar walk with his sacks of cash, cut out the cancer immediately. But that was not company policy. The executives at United Systems made people quit. For more than two years, Henry Kapp had been waging a war of attrition against his pampered, dissolute lead director, wanting him to crawl and weep and surrender, so that Caesar Fortunato would quit, therefore making his contract, one of the last reminders of a contemptibly irresponsible regime, null and void. Out the door, no money owed.

"I think our esteemed chairman had a good suggestion," said Kapp. "After Mr. Makem expressed his displeasure with me for importing extravagant TV equipment from Japan, we talked a little about Mr. Fortunato. Apparently, entertainment needs a director for this Disney special coming up."

"Oh, Caesar's not going to want to do that. He hasn't had a break in seven or eight months."

"Exactly, Geoff. Would you call him?"

"Right now?"

"Yeah, right now. With the time difference, he's probably still asleep. Get his ass out of bed. Let him know how much we love him. That prick."

* * *

Henry Kapp was infamous for his first speech as the division president, delivered in the spring of 1992. It came to be known as the "Marine Speech."

"Good morning, ladies and gentlemen. I am here to tell you that it is a new day at our network."

It was a little after eight. Everyone in the sports division was in attendance, almost two hundred people. Weeks before, the network had been sold to a company best known as the makers of Fruity Flakes and antiballistic missiles. Kapp had risen through the ranks by demonstrating a kind of benign ruthlessness; that is, he had been neither sued nor assaulted. He also could hold his liquor, a quality greatly admired by Chairman Ed Makem. Kapp had come to New York after being head of the company's famous food division: breakfast cereals, soups, cookies, carbonated and noncarbonated beverages. He knew as much about making Fruity Flakes and Chips Aplenty and Green Tango as he did about TV: zip. That wasn't the point.

"Ladies and gentlemen, you have cheated on your last expense report. Is that understood?"

This stirred Caesar Fortunato, who had been napping at the back of the large conference room, sitting in the last row of chairs, virtually concealed. He had just flown into New York on the red-eye. His secretary, Bonnie Tedesco, had called and said she was worried about the new guy, heard he was going to fire everyone. Caesar would have blown off the meeting, but he wanted Bonnie protected. The reasons were more selfish than altruistic.

The ghostwriter of his many, many fictitious expense reports, Bonnie Tedesco almost never phoned. More than that, he had never heard fear in her voice before. In fifteen years with Caesar, she had probably produced a thousand phony dinner receipts, named hundreds of men and women associated with the industry who attended business meals that actually never occurred, made convincing horticultural, medicinal, psychological, and meteorological arguments for odd on-location costs, money in fact used mostly for illicit reasons. Caesar had something better than American Express. With Bonnie Tedesco's loyalty and imagination, he had carte blanche.

There was a notorious expense report from golf's British Open.

Network accountant: "Bonnie, this one is too much."

Bonnie: "What do you mean, Phil?"

Network accountant: "I watched the tournament on television."

Bonnie: "As you should, Phil."

Network accountant: "Well, on Caesar's expenses, I see five thousand bucks in the miscellaneous column for tree trimming."

Bonnie: "It was the usual stuff, Phil. Clearing the sightlines for the cameras. Tree cutting. That sort of thing. Okay?"

Network accountant: "Well, not really, Bonnie. There are no trees on that golf course."

Bonnie (after a short pause): "Well, Phil, obviously the people Caesar hired did a very good job."

"I know you think you're all God's gift to television. I know you think you have the right to be the little arrogant sons of bitches that you are. Well, none of it means squat to me. I don't care about the Emmys. I don't care about your reputations. The candy store is now closed."

A mumbling could be heard in the room. Caesar felt a tightening in his chest, a brewing headache, a wave of nauseating dread.

"I am here to run a business, and I am not going to allow you to abuse this company any longer. Just because you are self-proclaimed geniuses doesn't mean that we are going to subsidize your drinking and your drug habits and your hookers."

Kapp had found Fortunato in the room and was looking right at him. Tapping the index finger on his right hand to the pinky on his left, he began to list some of the known offenses:

"You will not . . . fabricate expenses . . . steal petty cash from unit managers . . . use our courier service to ship plants to your loved ones . . . concoct taxi rides that never happened . . . sell your credentials . . . scalp our private stock of tickets for your personal financial gain . . . put nonexistent humans on the payroll and have the checks sent to your home. You will not be flying first class . . . sleeping at five-star hotels . . . dining on champagne and caviar . . . traveling anywhere at any time under any circumstances by limousine. Understood?"

Fortunato returned the glare.

"The days of wine and roses that you charged to us are hereby ended. Understand? The dance hall is closed, ladies and gentlemen. I've sent the waiters home. The ice sculpture has melted. . . .

"And listen, I'm not making promises. If you play by the rules, maybe we'll get along. Maybe. If you don't play by the rules, you'll be out of here. OUT. My new policy is simple: zero tolerance."

Kapp's next statement was the one most often repeated.

"Ladies and gentlemen, I have been privileged to serve with the United States Marines. I believe in the old-fashioned concepts of duty, honor, country. And, standing in front of this room today, I know this: I would not want to be stuck in a foxhole with any one of you."

"Likewise, dickwad."

Caesar had mumbled this response, not expecting it to be heard. But Kapp was like everyone's fifth-grade teacher. His ears were somehow attuned to back talk, no matter how quietly it was uttered.

"Mr. Fortunato, I appreciate the input. And I have two things I want to tell you, since you've spoken up. First, if Jimmy Carter had as many helicopters at his disposal as you seem to have every weekend, we would have saved the fucking hostages in Iran. And secondly, just so I'm on the record with everyone here, I consider you, by far, this division's biggest embarrassment."

Caesar sensed he had probably sealed Bonnie Tedesco's fate. Any wiggle room with Kapp, the possibility of negotiating, of establishing an uneasy truce—that was gone. Already, the first shots had been fired.

Even before the meeting, Henry Kapp had put Caesar Fortunato at the top of his most-wanted list. He'd been briefed, knew Caesar Fortunato had been traveling like a sheik, abusing illegal narcotics, socializing extensively with prostitutes, indulging his formidable temper, and . . . gambling, daily, recklessly, compulsively. Kapp heard that Caesar had once been kidnapped by mobsters over an unpaid gambling debt, that he had driven production assistants to suicide, that, incredibly, just before the start of the 1988 Seoul Olympics, he had chartered a jet home in an eleventh-hour effort to mend a collapsing affair with a young coworker. It seemed that the network even paid for his one foray into the film world: a soft-core feature he produced and directed while covering the Indy 500. Network personnel and facilities had been used in the making of *Love or Lust,* and the star was a nineteen-year-old college student who logged tapes by day and played a naughty nun by night.

"Hi, Mr. Kapp, I'm Bonnie Tedesco."

It was a few hours after the Marine Speech. Here was Caesar's secretary suddenly standing in front of the new division president.

"Correction," Henry Kapp replied, about to utter another line that would be much quoted, "you *were* Bonnie Tedesco. Ma'am, please clean out your desk. You're not needed here any longer."

Upon hearing the news from a sniffling Miss Tedesco, Caesar Fortunato understood that a formal declaration of war had been declared. At the time, he didn't see the need for an exit strategy. He was sure that a guy who made Fruity Flakes couldn't last.

Mount San Jacinto

In 1977, by a pond beneath the Eisenhower Cabin, one of the founders of the Masters shot himself in the head. The death confounded all who knew him. Cliff Roberts, who started the world's most famous golf tournament along with the revered Bobby Jones, was a difficult but effective autocrat whose life seemed to be as steady, as meticulous, as radically traditional as the tournament over which he presided for some four decades. That he went and splattered his brains under a tree by a pond in the Georgian paradise he had made seemed far too poetic for someone of little style and no humor who famously banished one of Caesar's announcer friends for audaciously describing the Masters gallery as an unruly mob.

On a Tuesday, the first day of April, 1997, three years after being forced out at the network, inspired in part by the example of Mr. Roberts, Caesar Fortunato decided he would end his life with a gun amidst a picturesque setting, at the summit of precipitously inclined Mount San Jacinto, 10,831 jagged feet above his beloved Rancho Mirage. The specific location was picked for the deepest of emotional reasons. This was the mountain, at the time assaulted by high winds and heavy rains, that had claimed the propeller-driven twenty-seater carrying Maria Fortunato.

Until the death of his mother, two months before, he had not ever considered the hand of God in his slow, steady demise, that he might be cursed, scheduled by a greater power to have his life unravel piece by piece until his last breath. And if it was going to continue this way, if there was not to be another windfall in Vegas, another night of unexamined lust, of irresponsible drinking with his good friend Charles Beck, another great professional success, if this was going to be a world run by Henry Kapps, if there was not to be anyone else who understood him, understood him like his mother and Beck and his old boss at the network, Omar Hawas, if he was only going to be a pariah to his children, if his life's work was not even going to be acknowledged, then indeed it was better not to be.

If there was a curse, he knew exactly the day it began, the day when he went to see Omar Hawas during the Seoul Olympics and saw for the first time full disappointment in Omar's eyes, when he knew immediately that he had horribly betrayed a trust, and even more, betrayed a promise to himself never to take the work for granted, never to let anything he did while playing affect his commitment to professionalism. He had been able to forgive himself many things because he had long observed the essence of his own constitution, short as it was. Caesar Fortunato, no matter what his misgivings about his job through the years, no matter how much he indulged himself, always maintained that work was a privilege and that all men and women were required to pursue excellence with unwavering vigilance.

After Omar Hawas made him patently aware of violating those articles, it didn't just rain on Caesar's parade; there was a relentless monsoon. As a hopeless gambler, he was by nature optimistic, so it took Caesar Fortunato a long time to recognize that winning wasn't inevitable. He believed, truly believed, that the losing would stop as

20

long as he kept playing. For a very smart man, this was stupidity of the highest order, but there were millions of millions like Caesar Fortunato who believed big scores were somehow their destiny—if not on the next roll of the dice, then on the one after that. Like most gamblers, he was blind to the cause of his destruction. He wasn't really playing to win something. He was playing to risk something. The more, the better. It had actually taken a very long time for the odds to catch up with Caesar Fortunato.

Around St. Patrick's Day in that spring of 1997, with the identity of the person or persons who had shotgunned his house still unknown, he had gone to Chico and bartered a relatively new Sony twenty-six-inch monitor for the gun, which replaced his second wife as his nightly bedroom companion. Originally acquired for the purpose of self-preservation, the weapon was now conveniently his means of earthly dispatch. Caesar was headed north, to the aerial tramway. To that point, it had been a wholly unattractive tourist spot, but he had persuaded some of his egregiously tiresome visitors through the years to give it a try and they had returned sufficiently pleased by the singularity of the experience, being whisked skyward from perpetual summer to perpetual winter in fourteen minutes by a generously sized cable car imported from Bern, Switzerland.

He puttered along Palm Canyon Drive at the wheel of the only automobile obeying the thirty-five-mile-per-hour speed limit. He was taking a long last look, unless he chickened out at the moment of truth, or blew off only half his face and lived, which was a nagging concern. The next morning, Caesar Fortunato was supposed to surrender himself to an assistant district attorney in Beverly Hills. He was being charged with assault. His former agent, Palmer Nash, proposed the services of a newly minted but reportedly razor-sharp Harvard-trained attorney and Palmer was willing to post bail, but he had also prepared Caesar, as gently as possible, for the prospect of Thanksgiving and Christmas dinners in prison. There was also a letter he left at home unopened from the Internal Revenue Service.

The dreadful prospects of jail and an audit weren't driving him to suicide, however. While he was taking an unplanned vacation in Mexico after slugging Academy Award winner Johnny Ray Thompson on the grounds of a Hollywood studio, Bob Gilmartin had left a truly disturbing message on his answering machine.

"Hey, Caesar . . . how about this HBO show? If you didn't see it, Vaughn's still taking credit for the replay."

As it was, Caesar was in a state of nagging distress, battling motion sickness and caked with a film of grunge after a twenty-three-stop, fourteen-hour international bus trip from Rosarito Beach.

"We should really beat the crap out of him once and for all. Call me."

The HBO show was called *The Greatest Moments in Sports Television*. In it, Caesar's longtime rival Tommy Vaughn was credited with doing the first instant replay. Vaughn's breakthrough, according to the show, occurred on the same day Bob and Caesar ripped a one-thousand-pound, two-inch tape machine out of a wall and trucked it to the 1963 Army-Navy game.

He delayed a much-coveted shower and returned Gilmartin's call.

"It's the same shit, Caesar. The old napkin story. He says he was in L.A., at some burger place, and drew up the specs on a napkin covered with ketchup."

"You know, the last time he did this, I said I would sue him."

"Really? You know, my brother-in-law was at the house, and he's such a putz. A bunch of people are watching the show and he turns to me and says: 'Oh Bob, do you have something to tell us?' Margaret got so mad she asked him to leave."

The BMW crossed Frank Sinatra Drive. There was never going to be a Caesar Fortunato Drive in Rancho Mirage, and he would be little remembered if that fucking HBO show became the last word on instant replay. Sinatra was beyond the reach of any assholes. He was essential to American music for fifty years, and he never surrendered to the nonsense of his indulgent personal life, or repeated and sometimes devastating professional setbacks. While the man may have been compromised, the artist aspired to godly standards. Caesar imitated Sinatra's ironclad swagger and presumed infallibility, but he had much less to show for it, and virtually nothing if he wasn't going to get credit for changing sports television.

Motivated by the talk with Gilmartin, Caesar decided to launch a final, all-out cellular assault on the way to his suicide. He would call as many people as possible to sct the record straight. The first was that cocksucker Tommy Vaughn.

"Hello, you've reached the Vaughn residence. Liz and Tommy aren't home at the moment. But we'd love to return your call. Please leave a detailed message after the beep." *Beep.*

"Mr. Vaughn, this is Mr. Fortunato. You know what you did. And you know it is not right to take credit for other people's work. Tommy, I have a good friend in the mob. No kidding. And I am calling him today, and I am asking him how much it will cost me to have you killed. . . . Have a nice day. You too, Liz."

His bookie was next.

"Caesar, I'm so sorry to hear of your troubles."

"And I'm sorry I blamed you for shooting up my house."

"It's all right. Of all people, you should know that we're not in the business of shooting people. Dead people can't pay us. You know? . . . So you've called to tell me that the check is in the mail."

"Dominic, actually I need a favor."

"Speak."

"Director named Tommy Vaughn. He's caused me some problems. I need to shake him up."

"What are we talking about? Rock through the window? That kind of thing?"

"Yeah, something like that."

"That's no problem. You've been a good customer for many years. Glad to help."

"It just needs to happen soon."

"All right. Two, three days, the guy will be shitting in his pants. Okay? Maybe I'll ask Fred to do one of his mailbox jobs. Small explosive, blow the thing to bits. Very disturbing, you know? One of my best methods of securing overdue payments. Anything else?"

"Sooner the better."

"Right. Listen, Caesar. I want you to know that I understand the position you're in. And if you do go to jail, I won't charge you any interest on the fifty grand you owe me."

"You're a sweetheart, Dominic."

On his left, up a winding road, was Bob Hope's shah-like compound.

23

Caesar had done a couple of specials with him, this an older Hope who couldn't memorize anything and had his daughter read him entire scripts through a well-concealed earpiece. But what a run, what a fabulous chameleon, to survive an entire century in businesses for which no textbook was provided, to win the loyalty of audiences decade after decade, in vaudeville, then radio, then films, then TV. Like the man it was named after, Bob Hope Drive had a broad reach, stretching from one end of town to the other, starting on the main drag and ending at the freeway, crossing streets named for some of the town's other heavyweights: Sinatra, Dinah Shore, Gerald Ford. Like Caesar, all had searched for a place to depressurize and discovered this sanctuary with dry, heated air and daily sunshine and like-minded companions, people who needed people who would leave them alone.

Caesar dialed Steve Greengold, the producer of *The Greatest Moments in Sports Television.*

"You're getting sued."

"Excuse me?"

"My attorney will be talking to your attorney today, Steve. Tommy Vaughn did not do the first instant replay. Everybody knows I did it."

"I trust our producer."

"Who's that?"

"Andy Kushner. You might know him."

"Shit, the guy has it out for me."

"What do you mean?"

"I worked with him years ago. He spent all his time doing stuff not related to the broadcast, and he wanted me to get him promoted."

"You mean, he arranged the escapes."

"Yeah, stuff like that."

"Caesar, I started in network television twenty years ago. That's all you guys ever cared about, and I know for a fact that Andy was the best there ever was at escapes. Am I correct?"

"Is the show running again?"

"Yup, later this week."

"I want you to fix it."

"I'm not going to do that, Caesar."

"I did the first instant replay, Mr. Greengold. Tommy Vaughn was a wuss and tried something lame at halftime. Bullshit. Total bullshit."

"Yeah, Andy explained all that to me. And that's why Tommy gets the credit. He did his thing at halftime, and yours happened in the fourth quarter. I understand you guys were working on the same thing at the same time, but the guy who's first gets the credit."

"His wasn't an instant replay. That's the whole point."

"Caesar, listen, can you send me an e-mail about this? You know, I'll take a look and, you know, see if there is something we can do."

"I don't do e-mail, you little scumbag. Look, I know your boss, and I will be making a case that you should be fired for extreme incompetence. How's that?"

"And how about you eat shit and die, Caesar?"

He ducked into the drive-thru lane at McDonald's, was back on Palm Canyon Drive less than ten minutes later. His last meal was going to be a Big Mac, medium Coke, large fries. There were five or six more calls and then he would go up the mountain.

He left another message for Vaughn.

"I'm holding off on having you killed. This is what I want you to do. I want you to write a letter to the Director's Guild. Okay? I want you to apologize for any misunderstanding regarding the first instant replay. Make sure the letter is published in the next DGA newsletter. By the way, if you have some property damage soon, let me assure you: I'm responsible."

He doubted his threatening phone calls would make much of a difference. Caesar Fortunato never had proof of his greatest day. It had been electronically cremated. The reels of two-inch videotape used to record the 1963 Army-Navy game, expensive and in short supply, were immediately recycled for an episode of *Captain Kangaroo*.

Caesar was approaching the turn for the tram parking lot, this after stop-and-go plodding through downtown Rancho Mirage and downtown Palm Springs, passing a succession of businesses catering to women of infinite income: eye-catching facades; shops for jewelry, antiques, interior design, makeup, nails, clothes from New York and Milan and Paris without need of price tags, shoes; hair salons; specialty stores for pastas and cheeses; galleries for sculptures and paintings; cafés with cozy interiors and astounding prices.

Caesar's favorite place was Billy Ray's, an upscale diner that had a tremendous French dip. It was also at Billy Ray's that civilization ended abruptly, as if there had been a swift scene change on a movie sound-stage. One block was people and sidewalks and commerce. The next was desert wilderness, cactus and sagebrush and dunes. He drove by the surreal San Gorgonio wind farms, four thousand wind-turbine generators, the largest a hundred and fifty feet high and topped by blades half the size of a football field. Together, these stationary propellers acted like a vast catcher's mitt for a fastball of wind that began a hundred and twenty miles away in Los Angeles and then rolled down a natural tunnel formed by a long chain of opposing mountains. At times, there would be hundreds of propellers in sync, the huge blades spinning much more slowly than their aircraft counterparts, and it would remind Caesar of a morning in Beijing when he saw hundreds of old men and women in the public parks moving in premeditated slow motion, doing their daily tai chi.

Before heading into the mountains, where the cell phone probably wouldn't work, he wanted to get in touch with Larry Kessler, the press agent he hired before Super Bowl XXVIII.

"Who is this?"

"Caesar Fortunato."

"Caesar who?"

"Larry, I asked you to get me some ink when I was working for the network a few years ago."

"Right, right. So sorry, Caesar. Of course, the world's finest TV director. Where you been?"

"Listen, there was an HBO show that had a big mistake in it."

"Right, right."

"Didn't credit me with doing the first instant replay."

"The what? I'm having trouble hearing you."

"I'm driving up a mountain. Listen, I need you to call some of your print buddies and get them to write about this."

"Caesar, are you there?"

"Larry, can you hear me?"

"Caesar, I think I've lost you."

"Shit."

He downshifted and sent the BMW uphill. The tram parking lot was at two thousand feet. Out of the car, he was instantly winded and huffed his way to the Valley Station. The tram, half-filled, slid up the mountain, issuing a low hum, a tape-recorded message informing the passengers that there were few places on earth where one could be so speedily transported between such contrasting climatic zones. The voice compared it to driving from Mexico to Alaska. After five minutes, slivers of snow were evident. Goats stood on short ledges and stared. The cable-car operator talked about the rare spotting of a ringtail, a racoonlike creature once used by the miners in the area as an early warning sign of a dwindling oxygen supply, à la canaries in coal mines. Two riders had brought cross-country skis. His gun was holstered and concealed.

At the top, he climbed some more. Before him was the eastern half of California, golden desert alternating with an archipelago of golf courses. If he had had a pair of binoculars, he would have been able to spot Las Vegas at the edge of the horizon. His leather jacket wasn't sufficient covering. It was forty-five degrees, minus the windchill. Jets landed below him at the Palm Springs airport, appearing to descend in an almost frozen, feathery fall, his view from above belying their true air speed. It looked as if a giant hand was cupping each flight and guiding it gently to the ground. Long estranged from his father, having never established a genuine bond of devotion with either of his wives, he shared his triumphs first and foremost with his mother. They never found her body in the fifty miles of forests behind him.

In the distance, he heard it announced that the next tram would be leaving in about fifteen minutes.

He was fifty-eight years old and as he folded his arms and stared at his adopted home from these heavens, he totaled the damage. Long gone was the job that made for him a very comfortable living and caused him to be respected, honored, even feared, the job that had taken him from a suffocating nowhere to an outpost of the rich and famous. He had failed in two marriages, neglected his son and daughter as children, harmed them as adults. He had preyed upon the vulnerable. Again and again, he had betrayed himself. He was in debt with no immediate means of repayment, about to lose his freedom, and they were even taking away that December afternoon in 1963 when he risked so much and made TV history.

Caesar Fortunato walked away from the chalet-style summit restaurant and down a path between the Jeffrey pines and the black maple.

He came to an opening, another hypnotic panorama, this one facing north. The ground he was standing on, at the edge of the San Andreas Fault, was slowly moving toward Northern California, in the midst of a million-year-old geologic event that would someday end with the whole state tumbling into the sea. Caesar took the gun and put it to his temple. With his fate in his own hands, there was a chirping sound from inside his jacket. Maybe it was that asshole Vaughn. He'd take the call, then kill himself.

Introduction

"It's Señor Simms," said Marisol. "You want to talk now?"

"Yeah," he grumbled, and found a towel.

"Hello."

"Caesar, Geoff. How are you?"

"Well, the sun is shining. Jacuzzi is warm. Football season is over. How are you going to fuck my day up, Geoff?"

"Well, Caesar, we do need your help with something."

"No, you don't."

"It's not something you have to do right away."

"Geoff, I don't have anything to do until the Kentucky Derby."

"This is an important project. We need you to do this Disney special."

"What?"

"Yeah, entertainment is short on producers and directors. Everybody else is assigned."

"What?"

"Yeah, it's your turn, fella. Sorry. I know you're exhausted."

"I'm calling my agent, Geoff. This is total bullshit. I've been working since last July."

"Sorry, but Henry's going to insist, Caesar."

It was three years before he'd decide life had no meaning, the day after the 1994 Super Bowl. When the call came, Caesar Fortunato had finished breakfast, roasted in the Jacuzzi, popped into the pool for a cooling dunk, and was about to make his first frosty mimosa, about to establish a long, mellow buzz and anesthetize a battered cerebral cortex in serious need of pleasing. Sam Cooke was singing "Change Is Gonna Come."

"This isn't going to happen."

"Caesar, go ahead, talk to your agent, but I think he'll tell you that you don't have an option here. Either you do this job, or you're in violation of your contract."

"Okay, I see. . . . Well, aren't you Henry's little buttboy?"

"Nice talking to you, Mr. Fortunato."

"GEOFF!"

"*Yeess*, Caesar."

"You don't want to do this. I'm toast. You know I'm toast."

"Caesar, like this was my decision."

"Come on, Geoff. What's going on? This is, like, fucking criminal."

"A determined executive, backed by one of the world's largest capitalized companies, is waiting for your resignation, and he and they are prepared to wait for a very long time. I might add that you don't help by hiring press agents and telling the boss to fuck off."

"I've been provoked."

"Well, you now have Mr. Kapp's complete, undivided attention. Congratulations."

"You guys won't talk about a buyout."

"At this point? Not under any circumstance I could possibly imagine."

"If I don't do this show, I'm totally fucked."

"Yup."

"You know what happens when animals are backed into a corner?"

"Yeah," said Geoff Simms, "the hunter slaughters them."

Caesar Anthony Fortunato never tired of the notion that he was a descendant of people who once ruled the world. As he was so often advised by his father, he wasn't Italian; he was a Roman.

When the boy became a man, he was able to confirm his ancestry by looking in the mirror. Caesar had a patrician's face, a pleasing, balanced composite in which no feature was more noticeable than another. Thick black hair, warm brown eyes, svelte, he begged attention. At a party, people gravitated his way. It was not just the looks, but a bearing reminiscent of a certain genre of elegantly aging leads, guys with a compelling, studied insouciance, perceptibly masculine but stylish: George Peppard, James Garner, Robert Wagner. Caesar dressed like them, too, casual but costly: muted colors, double-breasted blazers, dress slacks, silk shirts, expensive loafers. Around wiseguys all his life, he also adopted one of their essential fashion sentiments: Ties and jeans were unwelcome in his closet.

He had happily fled the East and found shelter in a man-made oasis anointed an enclave for the ridiculously rich and celebrated. Life in Rancho Mirage was no illusion. Mr. Happy Sun, the little weather icon atop the local paper, was a daily fixture. Rain, that dreadful inconvenience, happened to other people. The temperature might hit triple digits, but it had to be the dead of summer and 115 degrees or so before it became really uncomfortable. And even if the days were occasionally torrid, the nights were rendered tolerable by the vast, heat-sponging Mojave Desert.

His multimillion-dollar home had been carefully positioned to best take advantage of the geography. From the fifteen-foot, floor-to-ceiling windows of his living room, he could see gatherings of well-groomed palm trees dotting a carpet of green, the fairway of the fifteenth hole of his private community's lightly trafficked golf course. And beyond the burnt orange of the tiled rooftops of all these multimillion-dollar Americanized haciendas was a Kodak shot, a bedazzling horizon of soaring, shapely peaks topped by snow most of the year.

31

There was serenity to be discovered here, where the air could be so still, so sweetly scented, and even Caesar Fortunato found an occasional release from his usual pedal-to-the-floor existence. This was where he crashed, repaired himself, exercised some semblance of moderation. In the afternoons, he'd crank up his customized oldies tape, conjure a pitcher of mimosas, settle into the Jacuzzi, idle away, Buddy Holly and Sam Cooke and Bobby Vinton providing the soundtrack as he baked in a gentle alcohol-induced fog and periodically admired his snowcapped horizon.

Other than a weakness for fast food, an ability to subsist for long stretches on Big Macs, KFC, and Pizza Hut, he bled green. The vodka had to be Stolichnaya, the chardonnay from a South African vineyard, the beer supplied by a trendy Seattle microbrewery. His pills, energy inducing, sleep enhancing, mood altering, were obtained at extortionist sums from a local physician without a conscience. He had a full-time maid, part-time cleaning lady, and a driver on call, who was also his source of first-class pot—vintage Hawaiian, gourmet Humboldt hemp. There was a fat monthly fee for the expert agronomists who gardened his Eden and carefully, constantly clipped the spectacular golf course he had used six times. One of his monthly phone bills tallied up 1,432 calls.

Lynette, wife number two, was a former stewardess. They had a symbiotic relationship: Caesar enjoyed traveling and philandering and didn't want a full-time wife, and Lynette, at least in the beginning, tolerated a six-month husband who signed off on her spa existence: massages, facials, body wraps, aerobics, personal trainers, golf lessons, enough spandex to open a sporting goods store, and, when she got bored with the local spots, the occasional getaway to Liz Taylor's favorite Swiss resort, a destination decidedly out of reach when she was employed by American Airlines.

Caesar also had the most famous gambling problem in TV.

He would give the new kids the same instructions.

"If the phone rings during the game, do not disturb me. Understand? Unless it's the Green Hornet."

Caesar and the Green Hornet always had business. What surprised the kids was that the Green Hornet had the voice of an older woman.

"Let me talk to Caesar," she'd demand.

And he'd take the call immediately, and the director and caller would talk in this code. The Green Hornet placed all his bets, which everyone knew, though they found it very, very strange that this person involved with his feeble attempt at clandestine wagering was female and, it seemed, a senior citizen. No one ever put two and two together because no one even dared let his imagination consider such a notion.

Maxine, his first wife, was never able to reconcile this arrangement, how his mother could conspire in the ruination of not only her son but their marriage and the lives of their two children. Nights at home, the nights when he was home, could turn into this frightening spectacle. Her husband would be watching TV, having bet money on a game, and she knew sometimes he had bet thousands of dollars and it really mattered to him who won, and sometimes, the winner didn't just have to win, they had to win by a certain number of points.

There was a basketball game in the middle of one winter. The young Fortunato family was residing in Manhattan: Apartment 8H, Fifth Avenue, view of the park, all the trappings of a privileged existence.

"Shit, you motherfucker!"

That was for the guy who missed the free throw, and his daughter, Cynthia, was on the couch, staying up past her bedtime to be with her daddy, who was just back from another trip but was very angry about something she didn't understand.

"Caesar, come on. How many times do we have to talk about this? Not around the children!"

"Put her to bed."

"She wanted you to read her one story. Just one story."

"Tomorrow night. This is unbelievable. How can he miss two free throws? Shit."

"Cynthia, we have to go to sleep."

"Nooooooo. I want Daddy to read me a story."

"Go to sleep, little girl. Right now! Daddy will read to you tomorrow. They're going to blow this fucking game. Shit."

"Cynthia, come on, Mommy will read you the story. Let's go to your room."

In the early sixties, he was in Los Angeles for a Lakers game. He found out Jerry West, the star of the team, was going to be scratched from the lineup with a minor injury. This was extraordinary inside information. As the TV director, he was able to walk into the Lakers locker room twenty minutes before tipoff and find out that the star player was all of a sudden not playing. So he changed his bet. The line had the Lakers favored by twelve points. There was no way the Lakers were going to cover the spread without Jerry West, their leading scorer. No way they were going to beat the Warriors by twelve points. He called the Green Hornet.

"You gotta change the Lakers bet, Ma."

"Why, hon?"

"West's not playing."

"Who's West?"

"Jerry West, their best player."

"Okay. So you're taking the Warriors and twelve."

"Right."

"Ten thousand, honey, just like before, right?"

"No, Ma, this is going to be a big score, here."

"All right. How much, dear?"

"Thirty."

"Are you sure? You've never bet that much before."

"Trust me."

"Okay, dear. Warriors and the points. Thirty thousand."

"Hurry."

"Okay. You'll have it."

Maria Fortunato, the Green Hornet, called Manny, a runner for a Philadelphia bookie named Dominic Santangelo, who was backed up by one of the leading organized crime families on the East Coast. Smart bettors always used bookies backed by the mob; the mob always paid up; they never ran out of money or bolted town like some of the little operations. But smart bettors also knew that teams who lost their star players tended to overachieve. The Lakers, minus West, still won by thirteen.

* * *

34

"Sam, I need fifty thousand."

"Caesar, you know there are significant penalties, and you'll get killed on the taxes."

"I don't care, Sam."

"I can't do it today."

"Why not?"

"Can't get the paperwork done. I have to have your signature."

"Sam, whose money is this? Is it yours or mine?"

Because he had a decent, difficult broker who made it almost impossible for him to liquidate any of his holdings, Caesar was not broke. In the early eighties, in a moment of unusual clarity, he had given Sam Cordano a chunk of his money. Now, on the last Monday in January, a day after the 1994 Super Bowl, once again mystified by how little was left in his checking account, his three-month vacation having evaporated, Caesar got frantic. The first meeting for the Disney show was a week away. He needed a place to think. Figure out this mess. By the next morning, he wanted to be speeding toward Las Vegas with a respectable amount of cash.

"Sam, I'm not going to live forever. I don't want to be buried with my money."

"Caesar, can you hold on just a minute? I have this other client who's been trying to reach me."

"Sam, don't put me on hold. Don't you fucking put me on hold!"

"Hold on, Caesar."

In times such as these, when it seemed there existed a vast conspiracy to keep him from well-deserved fun, Caesar called Beck.

"You've been working for the Man too long. How many times have I told you that?"

Charles Beck was one of the greatest running backs in football history, a Heisman Trophy winner who, unlike most Heisman Trophy winners, was actually a terrific pro. He was football's answer to Joe DiMaggio, an athlete who performed with a dancer's élan. Beck side-stepped hulking defenders intent on his destruction with an inexplicable effortlessness. This quality he carried into life after football. He accumulated women and money and product endorsements with the same kind of ease. In fact, he was the first major black athlete who truly transcended race. As a running back, he had learned how to move in restrictive spaces and trust his remarkable intuition. These qualities he carried with him into life after sports.

"I don't want the speech again. Let's talk specifics. How do I get out of this fucking contract?"

"Are you serious? Or do you just want to bullshit me some more? Because I'm happy bullshitting with you."

"Fuck you."

"Okay. What's this next show, again?"

"Anniversary for Disney World."

"The Great Caucasian Paradise, where the magic is everywhere, for those who can afford it."

"Yeah, right."

"Well, don't give them the show they want. Give them just the opposite. And spend a shitload of money."

"I make it so bad they can't air it."

"There you go. And there's nothing these pricks hate more than people spending lots of their money. And, on top of that, something really expensive that they can't fucking fix."

"Where do you learn all this stuff?"

"Excuse me. As a former athlete now in the film business, I am an expert on massaging contracts."

About the only place Beck hadn't achieved raging success was the movies. As an actor, Beck's work didn't seem effortless so much as totally without effort. On the big screen, he was exposed as an ex-jock whose range was limited: He could only play ex-jocks.

"So I give them this horrible show that cost too much money. And then they give me two million bucks to go away."

"Right."

"Look, this is the kind of language they understand. You're operating like a terrorist. Now they have to worry about the next event you do. Like, you're directing the Kentucky Derby, and you decide to take a shot of some gorgeous chick just as the winning horse is crossing the finish line. That's a big problem for them. Whole broadcast gets fucked up. Sponsors won't like that. You can't have a director who could blow up the telecast at any moment. See?"

"But can't they fire me for doing bad work? I'm sure that's in the contract."

"How do you define bad work? I'm a shitty actor, but I always get paid. Look, if you finish this Disney show, and it's done professionally—you know, the show looks good—then we're talking about artistic differences."

"Artistic differences?"

"Yeah, you can't be fired over artistic differences. Check with your agent. And even if they wanted to fire you, you say you'll take them to court. First Amendment rights. That stuff. They'll cave and you'll get your money."

"Kind of risky."

"And," said Beck to Caesar, "that's a problem for you?"

Mr. Nice Guy

As a younger man, still fortified by a palpable spirit and able to adequately wrestle his own demons, he typically orated during "The Star-Spangled Banner," the accompanying, interwoven, absurdly hyperbolic rhetoric delivered with a classic Gospel flourish. In a separate tradition, the associate director, who counted into and out of commercials and otherwise coordinated all things that needed clocking, would always time the anthem for Caesar.

Oh say can you see

"Boys and girls, take a deep breath. . . ."

By the dawn's early light

"Consider the importance of this day."

What so proudly we hailed

"You are broadcasting the most important college football game of the century to all of America."

At the twilight's last gleaming

"The nation is counting on you. Your families and friends . . ."

Whose broad stripes and bright stars

"Listen to me, all of you."

Through the perilous fight

"You will tell your children about this day."

O-er the ramparts we watched

"And your children's children."

Were so gallantly streaming

"Cameras, audio, tech managers . . ."

And the rockets' red glare

"PAs, ADs, our beloved talent . . ."

The bombs bursting in air

"Hear me now!"

Gave proof through the night

"We must embrace our destiny!"

That our flag was still there

"Do not shrink from it!"

Oh say does that Star-Spangled Banner yet wave

"We are the privileged. . . ."

O-er the land of the free

"We are . . . the chosen."

And the home of the

"We are TV all-stars. . . ."

. . . braaaave?

"What do you have, Gary? That was brutal."

"Two-fourteen."

"I thought she had a chance at the turn."

"She did."

"Too bad."

In the first half of his TV existence, stretching from the late fifties to the mid-seventies, there was a wall between his work and the circus that was his personal life. The work was his oasis, inadvertent therapy, and inside a TV truck he'd exhibit a welcome playfulness, an uncommon sense of justice, and an admirable understanding of human nature. As the big broadcasting events approached and the collective anxiety level became almost palpable, he understood the prevailing need for levity.

In the setup phase, the show didn't require any central guidance: The producers were building content, the engineers creating a mini–TV station, Caesar backing everyone up, something like a pilot doing a routine check before takeoff, though TV had a much higher incidence of crashes. A common phrase in the business was: "Shit happens." By game time, Caesar usually took charge, prepared for turbulence, aware there was a need for a soothing presence.

"I thought we might have been witnessing history."

The record for slowest national anthem, which had been challenged that day by country-western star Bobby Ann Temple, was the glacial 2:38 rendition by jazz giant Pearl Bailey. At the halfway point, or the turn, as Caesar called it, Bobby Ann was at 1:33 and looked to be challenging Bailey.

"But once she got to 'rockets' red glare,' Bobby Ann really got rolling."

"She became," said Caesar, "a regular Silvia Rambeau."

Everyone knew that the fastest anthem in history, Caesar's history, was a fifty-eight-second sprint by then eight-year-old Silvia Rambeau—that performance taking place in Montreal at a baseball game between the Expos and the Cubs. Little Silvia, who spoke French but had to sing in English, had more interest in completing this odd bit of musical homework than in getting any of the words right. While she sang and stumbled and sang faster and faster, she glared at her mother, Marie, who had threatened a total ice cream embargo if Silvia refused to perform. The young French Canadian's record hadn't faced a serious threat in years.

"Silvia still rules."

"Gary," Caesar said to his AD, "her incomprehensible 'Star-Spangled Banner' at polka speed may remain unsurpassed in my lifetime. I truly believe that. Yet, as you may not know, Silvia's version is really truest to the original composition. 'The Star-Spangled Banner' is based on an old English drinking song, and it is meant to be sung allegro, not adagio."

After Bobby Ann left the field, the game before them, on October 27, 1973, was number-one ranked Notre Dame and second-ranked Nebraska State. The papers were describing it as the

Game of the Century. For Caesar, it was his sixth Game of the Century in ten years of TV. Because he was dealing that day with a producer who could turn a game of checkers into an apocalyptic struggle between good and evil, a man with a curiously erratic sense of perspective, Caesar was intent on being more jovial than usual.

Bill McBride was twenty-eight but aging prematurely. He was sickly looking: bleached, bony. All of his shirts seemed a size too big, his neck swimming in the collars. His large aviator-style glasses made it seem as if he had a windshield on his long, narrow face. McBride also had a very big secret, which explained almost everything: He was manic depressive and, what's more, typically altered his medication schedule. For a really big game such as this one, requiring his full creative powers, McBride would take half the amount of prescribed lithium. At full strength, the drug succeeded in eliminating his spells of Napoleonic ambition, but it also left him battling a fog of apathy. Being in a fog of any kind was a problem for live TV.

As of kickoff that afternoon in South Bend, McBride's chemical gamble was succeeding, his brain humming but not overheating, and he believed himself to be fully prepared, which was also important to stabilizing his mood. The night before, as per custom, McBride had created a small but complex library of index cards: green cards with player anecdotes, blue with historical nuggets, yellow for statistics, red for emergency scenarios. In the truck, the cards, alphabetized and numbered, rested before him in four tidy piles.

This was not the first time McBride had fudged his lithium intake. In fact, the strategy failed most of the time. By game day, McBride's brain would be starved for its balancing potion and on the verge of combusting. However, in live TV, McBride had discovered a home where his disturbed, frightening, manic state hardly seemed inappropriate. Caesar suspected something might be wrong the first time they worked together and McBride insisted that all of the production meetings take place in a sauna at six A.M. Later, McBride proposed to two women during a single commercial break. So Caesar had a clue, though at the time he didn't actually know he was working with a chemically unbalanced human being.

* * *

"What's going on, Rusty?"

"I can't hear you, Bill!"

"Stop the jets! I'm not ready for them."

"What?"

"STOP THE JETS, YOU IDIOT."

"Did you say stop the jets?"

"Yes! Stop the flyby. Tell someone to stop the jets. . . . Oh, forget it. It's too late. Just cue the Big Red Band."

"Wait a minute, Bill. The homecoming queens are coming out."

"I don't give a fuck. Tell the band director to play the fight song. I want to hear the fucking fight song!"

"He won't do it. He's shaking his head at me."

"Bill," Caesar interjected, sensing the need for an immediate distraction, "look at the homecoming queens. Look at those tits! It's better than the fucking band."

"Caesar, shut up! I rehearsed this with everyone! . . . I want the broadcast to start with the Nebraska State fight song. Rusty, what's happening?"

"I'm talking to the guy."

"Yes or no, Rusty! Is that fucker going to play the fucking song?"

"Sorry, Bill, no go."

"Rusty, you have ruined my show. Ruined it. We rehearsed this. Band. Jets. Homecoming queens. That was the order and that was your job and you failed to do it. You're fired. Do not come back to the trucks. I don't want to ever see your fucking face ever again."

"Bill, you can't fire him," Caesar interjected. "He's doing the graphics. Score, down, yardage . . . you know, him. That guy. We're fucked without him."

"Shut up, Caesar."

"Okay, Billy . . . do you want me to leave the stadium, too?"

"Go ahead."

Caesar took off his headset, rolled to within inches of McBride, grabbed the producer's right arm just below the shoulder, and then, within inches of McBride's ear, reiterated his threat in a biting hush.

"Billy . . . If you don't calm down, I am going to quit, you got that? And I'm not Rusty the production assistant. I'm the director. You can't produce and direct this game by yourself, okay? Not this game. This is a big, big game. Okay? Got that? Now, let's get ready for kickoff."

42

As Caesar slid back to his position, McBride remained quiet for a couple of seconds, then blurted, "Everyone's against me. You all want to see me fail. I swear."

During the first commercial break, McBride walked out of the truck in search of someone to scream at. Innocent or guilty, it didn't matter. It would help calm him down.

Rusty was rehired just before halftime. But McBride had since fired the runner who spilled coffee on his index cards. She stayed fired. He also fired the audio guy for playing a cut of Rolling Stones music over billboards. McBride only wanted music originating in America to be played during college football broadcasts; he thought everyone knew that. The fired audio guy got his job back a few minutes later when his assistant mistakenly added a Halloweenesque reverb to the voices of the announcers. For a moment, Roger Simpson, doing play by play, sounded like Vincent Price on speed.

In the third quarter, it got ugly. Pat Peterson, the Nebraska State coach, had a habit of losing his temper in public. Like McBride, he was manic depressive. Unlike McBride, he had never been diagnosed. A college football coach was permitted to have profound mood swings and fully indulge his manias and depressions. It meant he cared. Pat Peterson cared. In a career that was more or less one long tantrum, he had won eight conference championships and two national championships. Yet, on this very important afternoon, in a close and decisive game against the legendary Fighting Irish, the old coach learned something new. He found out that slugging an opposing player during a game was considered unacceptable.

"Did you see that?" Caesar shouted, astonished.

"He hit the kid!" McBride shouted, astonished.

"I can't fucking believe it!" Caesar said.

"Roger, Roger," McBride said, almost spitting to his announcer. "He hit him . . . he hit him. He hit the Notre Dame DB."

These editorial messages were delivered to Simpson via earpiece. While he was on the air, Simpson couldn't respond directly to McBride, otherwise the whole nation would hear half of a conversation. If the producer was telling him something he didn't know, something he needed to know, something he needed to say on the air, Roger Simpson usually repeated the information from the producer immediately, with the kind of compliance expected of a ventriloquist's puppet. It didn't matter whether he had seen or understood the event being described by the producer sitting in the production truck parked outside the stadium. Most of the time, the announcer simply trusted the producer, and if the producer said the Nebraska State coach had hit someone, the producer expected his announcer to say so on the air, immediately. He expected him to say something like, *Folks, at the center of the disturbance on the Nebraska State sideline is head coach Pat Peterson. Apparently, he has hit an opposing player.*

But Simpson didn't say it. He was ignoring this scene of mayhem, a concentration of bobbing gold and red helmets, intermittent shoving, and, at the center, his trademark baseball cap gone, the rarely seen bald head of Nebraska State coach Pat Peterson. It begged for explanation. A huge national television audience thought they had seen Peterson take a whack at the Notre Dame defensive player who had just intercepted an NSU pass. But it had happened so quickly. Maybe it didn't happen. That's what a lot of viewers were thinking. Maybe it didn't happen. Roger Simpson wasn't talking about it. He was ignoring that mess of angry bodies being shown to America by director Caesar Fortunato.

"What's wrong with our boy?" said Caesar, turning toward McBride.

"I don't know. Goddamn it, Roger, you've got to say something!"

"The story right now," said Caesar, "is the riot that has erupted on the Nebraska State sideline. And my cameras are covering that story."

"Go to commercial!" McBride ordered. "Go to commercial, goddamn it! Jesus, what the fuck is Roger doing?"

"Gentlemen, where is the replay?"

At last, as the commercial break began, Roger broke his silence on the matter at hand.

"Roger," said McBride, "didn't you see Peterson hit him?"

"Nope."

"What do you mean?"

"Didn't see it. Show me the replay."

Bill McBride had one minute and forty seconds to compel Roger Simpson into telling America about the brazen daylight assault by an

American coaching legend. McBride had a strong suspicion that Roger had seen the act and decided he would try to protect Peterson if at all possible. Announcer and coach were friends, traded Christmas cards, had been blind drunk together more than once. To Roger Simpson, who grew up around the corner from Main Street in a Kansas farming town of white picket fences, Pat Peterson was everything that was right with a disintegrating 1973 America, this country where draft dodging and pot smoking and free love and nonsensical loud music were tolerated, even celebrated, where there was no longer the proper respect for authority.

In fact, Simpson had seen the punch and indeed feared that Peterson's many enemies would quickly trumpet this indiscretion and get him canned.

"Here you go, Roger," said Bill McBride.

But the one replay angle didn't show it. The isolated camera, handheld, at field level, didn't get it. After the interception, the operator trained his lens on the NSU quarterback, then swiveled around when he sensed the commotion—but two seconds too late. Shooting the quarterback was the right move, the correct instinct. That's where the drama was, awaiting the reaction of this senior who had just thrown the interception, made the biggest mistake of his life in the biggest game of his life.

"I don't see it, Bill."

"Caesar, why don't we have it?"

"Camera was doing what it's supposed to be doing. Covering the quarterback."

"Is it on the line cut?"

"We're not recording the line cut."

"What?!"

"We never record the line cut, Mr. Shithead. They do it back in New York. For archive purposes. As you should know."

There was usually no reason to record the line cut. It was the show itself, the combination of cameras chosen by Caesar to cover the event in real time. Any necessary elucidation was provided by the replay cameras. But not on this day, during this very big game.

"And Mr. Instant Replay doesn't have an instant replay?"

"Nope."

Replays showed angles not seen in the line cut—from the so-called isolated cameras, or isos. These cameras had very specific duties. They were usually focused on a specific marquee actor; in the case of a football game, a quarterback or running back or receiver, a player throwing or running or catching. Never before had game action included a coach assaulting an opposing player out of bounds. Later, as sports TV coverage became ever more comprehensive, there would be an iso on everyone short of the water boy.

"You're all against me, I swear to God!" Bill McBride screamed, repeating an earlier sentiment.

America had seen the punch from a camera stationed in the stadium's upper deck, above the fifty-yard line. But that had occurred live, in a flash, a second and a half. America awaited the replay. Since its invention, first done in 1963 by either Caesar Fortunato or Tommy Vaughn, America had come to rely on this production device to confirm all moments of interest at a sporting event. If something important couldn't be replayed, it was almost as if it hadn't happened.

"We don't have it, Roger," said a crestfallen Bill McBride.

"Then I'm not talking about it."

"Roger, I know you saw it."

"Bill, if you have a replay confirming that Coach Pat Peterson, the most revered coach in America, did in fact strike a player on the opposing team, I will announce it. Short of that kind of conclusive evidence, you're not getting shit from me."

"Roger, you'll just have to trust me."

"Ha, ha!"

Division president Omar Hawas was watching back in New York.

"Bill McBride. Phone."

"Who is it?"

"It's Mr. Hawas," said the local college student at the back of the truck: female, blond, big-eyed, endowed, the usual qualifications. "He says he must speak to you at this moment."

"Not right now."

"Sir . . . uh, Mr. Hawas says you better get your ass on the phone."

Caesar took the call. He could see that McBride's entire body was quivering.

"No, the prick's not gonna talk about it. Why? Because we don't have the replay. Why? Because we don't. That's it. It's no one's fault, Omar."

Caesar cupped the phone.

"Mr. Hawas would like to speak to Mr. Simpson directly. What's the phone number in the booth?"

"Roger," McBride told Simpson in his earpiece, "Omar is calling you."

In thirty seconds, they'd be out of commercial.

"No, Omar, I will not. I don't care."

In the truck, they could hear half of the conversation between the network's lead college football play-by-play announcer and the network sports president.

"I'll quit. That's right, I'll walk out of the booth. . . . Embarrassing? What's embarrassing is that the people in your production truck have no replay. . . . Don't call me a liar, you little Arab shit. I didn't see it, and I'm not going to fucking say anything about it. You got that, pardner? . . . Fine, fire me. Go ahead. Fire me after the game, you little towel head."

The year before, Roger Simpson had expected to be named Olympic prime-time host. Instead, Hawas gave Simpson his usual assignment, the rowing and equestrian events. Hawas meant it to be a kind of punishment for the announcer's increasingly tiresome behavior. Simpson was still upset about not getting the top Olympic job, and no less tiresome.

Another no-doubt-about-it disaster followed. In the fourth quarter, they missed the winning field goal. America was watching commercials.

"They're kicking!"

"Yup."

"Caesar, we've got to cover this."

"I'm covering it, Bill. See? It's right there. My cameras are covering it."

"Punch out! Punch out!"

"Can't do it," the AD told McBride. "We're in the local."

In TV parlance, they had taken a station break. That is, after a national ad paid for by a large, well-known corporation, the network's

228 affiliated stations were running 228 different commercials, local merchants selling local goods. For that one minute, the network didn't control its own network. There was no way to tell 228 stations to stop rolling their commercials because the college football national championship was being decided and everyone was missing it.

"Shoot it."

"I am shooting it," Caesar told Bill.

"Hold 'em! Hold 'em!"

"There's the snap," said Caesar.

"It's fifty yards. It's too far. He won't make it."

"The kick is up. . . ."

"Oh, Jesus Christ!"

"And the kick is good."

"Are you covering it?"

"Yes, Bill, see up there on the monitors? . . . the players running on the field, celebrating. Those are my cameras and they are covering it."

"I'm going out there."

"What do you mean you're going out there?"

"HE CAN'T DO THIS TO ME!"

Late in this very big game, when it seemed as if Notre Dame was too far away from attempting a field goal and would instead try to run the ball, McBride called for the station break. The referees had been told the network needed a TV timeout, and there was a go-ahead from the field, and then, all of a sudden, Notre Dame was trying to kick it. Lou Radley, the head coach, had rushed his kicking team into position, hoping to surprise Nebraska State. He had used only twenty seconds of his two-minute timeout. He had fucked them, everyone.

Finally back from commercial, America saw Notre Dame players high-fiving each other and had no idea why. Roger Simpson, attempting to supress his rage, said, *Moments ago, Notre Dame took the lead on a long, fifty-one-yard field goal—the move surprising Nebraska State, which did not even have enough players on the field to defend against it . . . just moments ago. Here's the replay.*

Hawas was on the phone again. Again, Caesar had to take the call.

"What do you mean we didn't cover it, Omar? We covered it. Did you see the replay? Yeah, that was my replay. Oh, you want to know what happened? Okay, then I guess you want to talk to the producer. Where is he? Look at your TV. You see that disturbance on the sideline? The guy going after Lou Radley? Yup, that guy. Does he look familiar? Yup, that's him. Your producer."

That Monday, Hawas was at work early. So was Caesar, reluctantly, at Omar's request. As expected, the newspapers were slamming McBride, wondering if Simpson was covering up. There were phone calls to return and phone calls to be made, and in times such as these, Hawas had come to rely on the counsel of his talented, usually levelheaded young director.

"Caesar, the man is so wound up. He can never have any fun. You know? The conditions are not easy. TV is a fucking pain in the ass. That's why the people in charge have to make it fun. You have to bring some level of enjoyment. Otherwise, what's the point? You'll have everyone killing themselves and being miserable. If it's going to be like that, then we should all go and work in a fucking coal mine."

"Omar, the guy needs to see a doctor. He's got some kind of condition. Get him to go see someone."

"It won't matter. Every week, this McBride thinks he's producing *Gone With the Wind*. It's only TV. He's trying too hard. He has to be told people only care about the game. Was it a good game? Was it a shitty game? It's sports, for God's sake! Caesar, you have the right approach. You're probably high half the time you direct."

"Omar, I admire him for trying. You know, some of his other producer buddies, all they do is buy the chips and pretzels."

"All right, I won't fire him yet. Listen, next time you work with him, I'm serious, get him to have a beer before kickoff."

"You're kidding."

"No. Do something. Get him a joint."

"I wouldn't know where to get something like that."

"Caesar, what a funny man you are."

"What about Simpson?"

"Don't say anything. I'll keep him until the end of college football. Then he's out. I'll negotiate something. I can't have people like that around. Just openly defying me. That's not good for the department . . . now, Mr. McBride, that's something else."

Two weeks later, in his last assignment with the network, McBride again left the truck and ran out on the field. The opening kickoff of a game between the Giants and Cardinals had occurred while the broadcast was still in commercial.

"Did I tell you to kick off? Did I?" McBride said to the head referee while snatching the ball away and putting a finger to his face. "What are you doing? What the fuck are you doing? I'm the producer. We're running the show here. Do you understand? You don't do anything, you don't take a pee, you don't fart, you don't pick your nose unless I tell you it's okay. Now do this fucking kickoff over again."

Bill McBride then handed the ball back to the stunned sixty-three-year-old official, off the field a highly respected attorney with a prestigious Washington, D.C., law firm. Though the man had counseled Kennedy during the Cuban missile crisis and was in the midst of navigating Nixon through Watergate, he could not recall an equivalent scene of unraveling in his lifetime.

The Magic Exposed

Work on the Disney special concluded with the network's top director and his friend, a living legend, emptying their bladders above defenseless petunias at the edge of Lake Epcot. The flowers were arranged in the shape of Mickey Mouse's head. Beck targeted Mickey's left ear; Caesar laughed at having this beaming icon appear to swallow his fulsome shower. Security, alerted by one of the park's hundreds of hidden cameras, arrived as the men were zipping up. After sampling the indigenous alcoholic beverages of England, France, Germany, Italy, Japan, China, Mexico, Morocco, and Norway, drinking their way through the entire World Showcase, the prospect of enjoying an alfresco piss seemed worth the risk of getting busted.

"Gentlemen, would you mind coming with us?"

"Evenin', fellas," said Beck.

"Let's go, guys . . . let's make this easy on everyone."

"We're with the fuuuucking network, you fuuuuucking fake cops," said Caesar. "So . . . why . . . don't . . . you . . . just . . . fuuuuck off!"

Ordinarily, Matt and Joe would have radioed for the Orlando police and then escorted the offending urinators with all due diligence and little regard for comfort to a designated holding area. But this was press night at Epcot, Disney World having arranged a far-reaching happy hour for the global media to promote its upcoming twenty-fifth anniversary. Thus, Matt and Joe exercised an uncommon amount of restraint.

"Sir, you know you can't be taking a piss anywhere you want."

"Who can find a fuuucking bathroom in this place? . . . Did you people ever hear of porta-johns? Or did Walt want everyone peeing in their pants?"

"Let me please *esplain*," Beck explained. "My friend . . . my friend, he has kidney troubles. . . . Normally, he would have a . . . a special, su su su-per absorbent diaper. But . . . but . . . he-he . . . he forgot."

"Beck, fuuuck off! . . . And, look, we're . . . we're leaving any . . . anyway. Where's the fuuucking monorail?"

"Gentleman, how about we get a golf cart to take you there?"

"Exactly . . . that's . . . that's the kind of treatment we should be getting at this place."

"Charles Beck?" said Matt, raising his flashlight. "Mr. Beck, you're not supposed to be here anymore. You could be in a little trouble."

Beck would have been instantly recognizable for any number of reasons. He was a Hall of Fame football player, minor film star, and leading spokesperson for several big companies. On top of that, his picture had been circulated at one of the daily security meetings: Someone had accused Beck of wrecking a vessel at Pirates of the Caribbean.

"Gentlemen, I am . . . I am absolutely innocent of all charges. But if you're going to take me in, I will first need to contact my attorney. And he will then fucking sue all your asses."

Next, Caesar threw up all over Mickey's left eye. The security guards—correctly sensing that this was a highly volatile situation inconsistent with their level of experience—nodded to each other.

"Listen, guys, we're going to have to leave you," said Matt. "It looks like we've got an urgent situation."

"Yeah," said Joe, "but we strongly suggest you get back to your hotel as soon as possible."

Unlike the millions and millions of children and adults who come to experience the magic at the happiest place on earth, Caesar arrived at Disney World in the spring of 1994 intending to spend a galling amount of money for a wholly objectionable program. The show was already over budget before any of the twenty-four contracted cameras had recorded a frame. For this one-hour special, he had enough people and equipment to do a five-part series on the history of earth.

Caesar had point-of-view cameras, and steadicams, and he was going to put cameras on small cranes and large cranes, and he had hundreds of feet of dolly track, straight and curved, and special low-riding camera trucks, and he was going to shoot in both video and film, and he had enough lighting equipment to turn night into day, and he had rented two helicopters and the Pinestar blimp. Had he not wanted out of his contract, had he not wanted a fat buyout, had he instead been a good soldier interested in a credible product at or under budget, three handhelds and six guys would have been sufficient. Caesar's catering bill alone put him over budget.

Being the author of this devious plan, Caesar thought it only fair that Beck come along. Beck's presence also ensured a subversive style of fun, Caesar's favorite. On day one at the Magic Kingdom, Beck took a souvenir from It's a Small World. While the guided boat was puttering past a miniature alpine village, he swiped the arm of a yodeling Swiss Miss. He carried the arm with him the rest of the week, sometimes letting it hang from his half-open fly in a wholly juvenile gesture. No one believed in the souvenir's authenticity, despite Beck's protests. At the various nightclubs on Pleasure Island, he would engage young sightly women in conversation, the appendage of the Swiss Miss saying hello from below.

"I swear."

"C'mon . . ."

"Really!"

"You did not . . . and take that thing out of your pants."

Beck and Caesar also were involved in the first sea rescue at Pirates of the Caribbean. Caesar insisted the boats were unsinkable, a theory Beck, dubious, put to the test. As it turned out, Caesar was largely correct. After Beck punched a hole near the bow of the rowboat, it stayed the course, though all the passengers were eventually submerged up to their waists. The rescue was necessary because a fifty-two-year-old woman visiting from Argentina panicked and attempted to swim to a nearby, pirate-infested shore. Her foot got snagged in an underwater cable.

Later, asked to explain the incident, Caesar confided to a park vice president that Beck had an unusual problem.

"They're just starting to understand it now."

"Uh-huh."

"You know Beck played pro football for about ten years."

"Yes, yes. I saw him play. Terrific running back."

"Well, you know, they're calling it Collision Stress Syndrome."

"Right . . . uh-huh."

"You know, he was taking stuff during his playing days. And apparently, all that excess testosterone leaves a residue of sorts in the brain. Beck has these flashbacks where he suddenly thinks he's on the football field with a tackler in front of him."

"So that's what happened on the ride."

"Apparently."

"That's a little far-fetched, Mr. Fortunato, don't you think?"

"It's not what I think. You can ask the guy who's the expert on this thing at UCLA. You want his number?"

"No, no, that's not necessary. . . . Let me tell you what I need, all right? I need Mr. Beck to leave the grounds—pronto. Mr. Fortunato, as you can appreciate, we have a potential lawsuit here, and it wouldn't look good if we had a man who caused an emergency situation at Pirates of the Caribbean still walking about Disney World. You understand?"

"Of course, I'll talk to him and see what I can do. But, you know, he's in a bit of a fragile state right now . . . these flashbacks are pretty scary."

"Mr. Fortunato, he has twenty-four hours to be out of here. . . . Listen, Universal has a nice park, too. I can send over some free passes, if you'd like."

"Beck could get you a great deal with the cruise line he sponsors."

"We have our own boat. It's free to employees."

"I see. How about fifty cases of beer? Beck's a spokesman for one of those guys."

"I'm a wine drinker."

"Right."

"Mr. Fortunato, I want him off the grounds by tomorrow."

The centerpiece of Caesar's budget-busting plans was pop star Melissa Divinity. Under normal circumstances, she was pricey and objectionable, a prototypical pop star whose looks and lyrics were borderline pornographic. He kept telling everyone that Gloria Estefan, reasonably priced and unobjectionable, would be the headline act. He was always going to approach Estefan, but only with premeditated sabotage in mind. By sprinkling the negotiations with insulting propositions, he'd ultimately get Estefan's people to back out, then hastily produce Divinity as a better-than-nothing, last-minute substitute. The network would be so happy about this apparent rescue, they wouldn't bother to ask how much she cost. At least not right away.

"I'm sorry, we can't afford to fly everyone."

"From Miami to Orlando?"

"All right, we'll fly Gloria and her husband."

"And the band members are supposed to drive?"

"Yeah, but if they need to get lunch or something, we'll pick that up."

"Okay . . . you're trying to be funny, Mr. Fortunato, right?"

"Well . . . no."

"So you're serious about everyone staying at the Best Western."

"We get a really good rate there."

"So does everyone else in America. Are you fucking insane?"

"I mean, my budget is insane. I'm just trying to do the best I can. I mean, we *are* giving Gloria network exposure."

"She's sold millions of albums, toured the world over and over, and has more money than she will ever be able to spend. She does not really need network exposure, Mr. Fortunato."

"Okay, we'll put everyone up in the Holiday Inn. We get a good rate there, too, and they've got a Jacuzzi in the pool area."

"When you want to get serious, we'll talk. But if I don't hear any-thing that makes sense in the next couple of days, this is dead, okay?"

"Please, we want to make this happen. Let me see what I can do. You know, it's not me, it's the pricks on the business side."

"Well, maybe you need to look elsewhere for musical talent. Why don't you see who's booked in the nightclub at that Holiday Inn, Mr. Fortunato? Then you wouldn't have to worry about travel costs at all."

As expected, the negotiations with Melissa Divinity's contact included many extravagant conditions.

"No commercial airlines. It has to be a charter."

"Fine."

"And you're going to need a big plane. She prefers an Airbus. Doesn't like Boeing."

"Okay."

"Her normal traveling party is thirty-five people."

"With the band, that's not so bad."

"That doesn't include the band."

"I'm just curious, what do these other thirty-five nonmusicians do?"

"You know, makeup, wardrobe, public relations, security, food prepa-ration, driver, trainer, nurse, traveling secretary, agents, business man-ager, her cousin Sarah . . . I mean, thirty-five is like the bare minimum, just so you know. We'd like to help you out."

"Okay. Well, I think we can work with this. What else?"

A month later, on a pleasant winter morning in Los Angeles, the network's top entertainment executives and chairman Ed Makem gathered in a conference room expecting to see a tame pro-gram suitable for family viewing that celebrated the most popular theme park in America. Caesar's first bogus format, circulated a couple of weeks before in L.A., indicated a show that included two perfor-mances by Gloria Estefan, an emotional tribute to Walt Disney, and a tour of the park by a well-known comic. When Estefan was suddenly unavailable, everyone thought Caesar amazing for landing Melissa Divinity so quickly. As a result, they had started thinking of the show for sweeps: There was star power and they figured Caesar would be producing the caliber of work that had put sixteen Emmys on his resume.

The running length of this one-hour show was actually forty-eight minutes, allowing for twelve minutes of commercials. After fifteen minutes of viewing, Makem asked somebody to stop the tape and, in full boil, demanded that Henry Kapp be found.

The first feature was an exposé on the tunnel system beneath the Magic Kingdom. It was Caesar's intention to show that the wholesomeness exhibited above was suspended in the catacombs below. The piece showed Mickey and Donald headless, flirting, each with a smoldering cigarette at their sides. Dopey, also headless, admitted to having sex in a closet directly below Cinderella's castle.

Melissa Divinity recorded two songs for the show. The first was the title track from her new album.

Before I wake
There is one last dance
One last chance
Your eyes burn my soul
Your body makes me bold
You're my perfect lover
There is no other
My wet fantasy.

The song was elaborately staged. Steadicams tracked Melissa as she made her way around Frontierland, from a perch atop the Mark Twain steamer to Splash Mountain. She was technically naked. Philippe, an avant-garde French fashion designer, was flown in via Concorde to cover her with a layer of body paint. When this special paint dried, it hardened into a durable rubbery layer, appearing to be something of a customized raincoat, albeit one leaving nothing to the imagination. Melissa wanted a lost-tribe look, and she ended up with a pleasing yet busy combination of earth tones convincing enough to get her on the cover of *National Geographic*. As the song concluded, just as she sang the final lines, the flume ride reached its final splashdown, washing away Melissa's paint. Before anything could be revealed, there was a cut to a wide shot.

Makem stopped the tape in the middle of the next feature. It was a profile of Walt Disney. At a strip club in downtown Orlando, Caesar had met a professor from a local junior college. He had enjoyed the professor's deconstruction of Disney's film mythology and decided to interview him for the show.

"Disney's genius is that he attacks the subconscious. His real intention is to make horror films for children. But the horror comes later, when the kids go to sleep. You know, in these stories, the mothers are always dying or absent. Snow White is an orphan, Bambi's mom is killed, Mowgli in the *Jungle Book* is raised by a portly bear and an erudite panther. And in *Mary Poppins,* the parents are clueless. So what happens is, when the kids go to sleep, their subconscious minds start thinking about a world without mommy . . . and, of course, that's a terrifying concept for a four-year-old."

When the lights came on, Makem was in for another stunner. He was told the preliminary budget figures: Caesar had spent in the area of four million, which put him over budget by three hundred percent.

"When was someone going to tell me about this? HUH?"

"Sir, we haven't confirmed the numbers. It's what we're hearing from New York."

"All right, ladies and gentlemen, a certain employee of this network has just delivered a big fuck-you to us. Well, fuck him. Rodney, I want legal on this right now. I know this man is hardly pure. Let's start digging. And you know what? If you can figure out a way to put this guy in jail, that would be delightful. . . . Now, can someone get Kapp on the phone for me? I want to know how he let this happen."

Kapp's eyes and ears on the project was Mark Kreidler. Caesar had kept this former food division accountant up in the air for the entire week of production. Kreidler was told he had to shoot the aerials. This was highly appealing to Kreidler, because none of the other producers or directors had ever allowed him to do any real TV.

"Again?" Kreidler asked Caesar day after day.

"Yeah, get back up there. Your shots suck."

"You're not messing with me, are you?"

"Oh no, Mark, come on. We need everyone pitching in and doing good work. Let's make this show a winner, okay?"

Virgin in the Forest

Caesar was already directing shows at one of the local affiliates by age nineteen, a savvy, charming, handsome kid who found a business younger than he was and still writing its rules. He began his ascent in the summer of 1958, when he borrowed a cameraman with a big heart on a lazy Saturday and went back to his neighborhood. The hula hoop had descended upon South Philly.

Caesar had to cut the film quickly. He found out news director Stu Clifton was on a search-and-destroy mission, outraged by the brazenness of the swarthy-looking kid who fetched the coffee. But it was a story with ready-made pictures, there was sound from a couple of giggling kids, and it was somehow quintessentially American: Dumb invention galvanizes nation's youth. Stu briefly berated the boy but gave the piece two minutes at the end of the newscast. It was a seasonally appropriate sign-off for a muggy August Sunday, when viewers were too tired to think. The station director, Larry Gates, was watching at home.

"Hey, Stu, nice way to close the show."

"Yeah, that worked, didn't it?"

"Your idea?"

"No, it was the Italian kid . . . Caesar something."

"You assigned him?"

"Ummm . . . he assigned himself."

Caesar was excessively competent and, unlike most his age, not afraid to mix with his superiors. In particular, he knew where to spend his sycophancy and he didn't waste his energies on Stu Clifton. After the hula hoop story, Caesar won promotion to the assignment desk, listening to the police radio, fielding phone calls, reading the wires. He knew Stu preferred stories that engendered civic pride, such as the construction of the Schuylkill Expressway, while station director Larry Gates was awaiting the next Paul Petrillo, an infamous local tailor who had a side business showing unhappy wives how they could collect big insurance settlements by killing off their husbands with a poisonous pasta sauce.

"He was just at my dad's bar."

Caesar's source on his first big story was his well-connected girlfriend.

Not long after his promotion, Jerry Doyle became the most wanted man in Philadelphia, and the most beloved. He had been riding behind an armored truck when its doors opened and deposited $1.2 million on the street. Doyle then turned Robin Hood, appearing at South Philly bars and homes, buying drinks, distributing crisp hundreds to friends out of work, families with medical issues, the old, the lame, drunks on the street. The police were being hindered by an uncooperative populace.

"My dad said he came in for about fifteen minutes last night, and he bought everyone a round. Can you believe it?"

By providing this information, Catherine O'Hara was placing her boyfriend's best interests over her father's gag order.

"I'm going to have a crew go out there, okay?"

"Dad will be upset, but then he'll think about the publicity."

As Catherine suspected, her father enjoyed the attention and even granted an interview. Actually, it was Caesar's dad, a Philadelphia cop, who was horribly bothered: His son was consorting with the daughter of an Irish barkeep who permitted fugitives to loiter in his establishment.

"He's trying to leave the country."

A few days later, Catherine was eavesdropping on one of her dad's calls. Doyle had told a fellow longshoreman, a bar regular, about his escape plan.

"I think he's headed to Mexico."

"He's got to fly out of New York."

"Probably."

City cops tailed Caesar and his camera team all the way up the New Jersey Turnpike to New York's Idlewild Airport. Philadelphia viewers saw Jerry Doyle being handcuffed minutes before he was about to board an Acapulco-bound DC-8, one hundred thousand dollars stuffed in his work boots. When, six months later, Larry Gates fired grumpy, bald Phil because he asked for a raise, Caesar became the director of the station's Saturday morning children's show. The host was Susie Gold, who played a Peter Pan–like character named Billie Piper, though she seemed better suited for a Las Vegas chorus line, which was, in fact, among her previous occupations.

All right now, *children, listen up. My next guest comes to the Magic Forest all the way from a reservation in Oklahoma. He is chief of the Naka-homee Indians . . . please welcome my old buddy, Running Deer.*

Running Deer was Lou Stillitano, one of Susie's drinking pals. The closest he had been to Oklahoma was Pittsburgh.

How are you, Running Deer?

The spirits are taking good care of me, Billie Piper, thank you.

I'll bet they are. Do you pray to the spirits often?

Yes, they fill me with warm feelings.

What are you going to do for us, today, big fella?

A rain dance, Billie Piper, so that in our days and nights, we may never be dry and thirsty.

Caesar was in the control room, nominally in charge. He was cutting three cameras, hulking things anchored by platforms on steel wheels. Each weighed about a thousand pounds. If any of these cameras ever fell over, the result would have been a crater ten feet deep. Paul, one of Caesar's camera operators, was at the back of the bleachers, behind an audience of enraptured, hair-sprayed kids in brutally starched, twice-worn outfits. Paul was the wide shot. Jimmy and Frank had the cameras on the floor, angled right and left. Caesar's basic directing challenge was when to be close and when to be wide.

"Frank, can you pan over to the kids for a reaction?"

"No, Caesar."

"What do you mean, 'No'?"

"It's stuck, I can't swivel."

"Jimmy, how about you? . . . Jimmy? . . . Jimmy, can you hear me? Why can't Jimmy hear me? Come on, people!"

The job was really little more than a conference call between the three camera guys and the director. There were no tape rolls, because there was no such thing as videotape. Titles at the top and bottom of the show were written carefully with a paintbrush and placed on an easel for Jimmy or Frank to shoot, live. Also on the easel was a card that viewers saw almost every week: WE ARE HAVING TECHNICAL DIFFICULTIES, PLEASE STAND BY. The cameras were always crapping out, which is why a fourth camera, the sacrificial camera, was placed nearby, ready to be cannibalized for spare parts.

Ten minutes into the show, everyone was wilting, as if they had begun a trek through the Sahara. At the time, TV studios weren't meant for the living. The monstrous cameras had pathetic optics, sort of small-brained dinosaurs with shitty vision. To produce a reasonable image, they required a forest of hulking, blazing lights. Otherwise, Billie Piper and Chief Running Deer would have looked like Rembrandt portraits, shadowy and mysterious. The temperature could have been vastly moderated with air-conditioning, but the AC unit had to be shut off before the show began because it clanked and hummed and banged at a decibel level that made conversation difficult. In the commercial breaks, Susie needed to grab three towels to mop her dripping makeup. Guests, including Running Deer, had collapsed during the show.

"Why can't I talk to Jimmy? Why doesn't Frank's camera work?"

"Caesar, you should pay attention to Running Deer," said a voice in the control room.

"Why?"

"He's probably going to fall over."

"Fall over?"

"Happened three weeks ago."

"Mark . . . Mark? Shit, Mark can't hear me, either."

Mark was the stage manager. Actually, Mark could hear him. And so could Jimmy. And there was nothing wrong with Frank's camera. They were bored. The show was far more interesting when things became chaotic. Besides, the director had pimples and a funny name.

"I'm going out there," said Caesar, imagining the old drunk breaking his head in a bloody, scandalous mess. "Stay with Frank's camera."

He ran out of the control room on his way to Susie Gold, weaving through smiling parents. The star of the show was backstage undergoing damage control, sitting inches from a large fan, a pile of discarded towels at her feet, a makeup woman working in haste, like a boxer's cutman between rounds.

"Susie?"

"Who's directing my show, honey?"

"Susie, please hurry over to Lou. It looks like he's in trouble."

"Sure, sure, listen, would you stop by after the show? I'd like to talk to you about a few things. I have a few ideas. Okay?"

"Okay."

Susie, half-repaired, went to rescue her Indian friend.

Thank you so much, Running Deer. I'm sure we'll get some refreshment from the spirits after that wonderful dance. And now, let's gallop over to Bob, who has a message from our sponsor, Franklin Dairy.

The commercials had to be live as well. Bob followed cue cards held beside Jimmy's camera. He was about to conclude and drink the glass of Franklin Dairy milk set before him on a small table, unaware the son of the guy who handled the props drank the real milk before the show, and the white liquid in the glass was actually water stirred with chalk.

Assuming the milk was there to be seen, not swallowed, the prop guy, Larry Anderson, thought himself clever for improvising a last-second substitution.

Franklin Dairy, with the most delicious milk on earth . . .

Bob imbibed without hesitation, finishing in four gulps. The water Larry Anderson had spiked with chalk went all the way down, then swiftly came all the way back up. He vomited powerfully, spraying the camera and Jimmy and even some of the kids in the front row. The total damage was not apparent to viewers at home, whose TV sets were suddenly clouded with a thin, dripping filmy substance that included the remains of a turkey sandwich.

At first, Susie Gold viewed the hiring of the nineteen-year-old as an insult. Near the frightening dawn of forty, within months of the day when no amount of makeup could hide the wrinkles and drooping and weathering, after five homes and two husbands and failing in New York and Los Angeles, and even that shithole Las Vegas, getting this little boy as director seemed like a very bad sign. It meant the station didn't give a shit about her. Any minute, they were going to replace her with a cowboy or a clown or a puppeteer. Or Larry Gates would just find a woman with bigger tits. But after a couple of weeks, after Caesar proved to be a lot sweeter than grumpy, bald Phil, Susie got over it.

She was alone in Philadelphia, parents in Illinois, sister in Cincinnati, not finding anyone at the station who had traveled common ground. They were all so . . . *childish* . . . so *provincial.* Her assumption about the essential decency of mankind had long been obliterated from making the rounds of casting calls at the Hollywood studios, where it seemed each audition, each interview with some producer or director involved a request, never overtly stated but clearly implied, that she humiliate herself: not even to get the job, but just to be considered for the job. That she was now playing a fairy for children was a concession statement, though not yet a complete surrender. She still harbored a notion that something big could happen to her in this new thing, television. She had started to think that maybe she could help this darkly fetching young thing . . . and maybe he could help her.

"Come in."

"Hi. Good show."

"Yeah. Drunk Indian, twelve annoying banjo players, barfing Bob, and I get bitten by that nasty chipmunk. Did they hear me say 'shit' on the air?"

"Uh, think so . . ."

Susie Gold was sitting down at a makeup table, wiping a mask of glop off her face. She was in a bathrobe, like something Caesar had seen geishas wearing in those World War II movies. It appeared to him that she was naked underneath the robe. Her breasts had fallen, as if unsupported. But he wasn't sure. Breasts as large as these were wholly new territory.

"Been up to New York?"

"Couple of times."

"We should go. I'll introduce you to some of my friends."

"Okay."

"One's a pretty important executive. You should see the view he has of Central Park. Big shot at the network."

"Great."

"Maybe next week . . . in the meantime, would you mind rubbing my shoulders? They're a little tight."

Caesar hesitated. His twelve grades' worth of Catholic school conscience told him that rubbing Susie Gold's shoulders was a beginning, not an end. So did his equipment below, which was not entirely reliable. His nineteen-year-old penis, untested, was excited by bra ads.

"Come on, I won't bite."

Unlike Catherine O'Hara, Susie Gold had the aroma, the voice, the presence, the saunter, the body of a woman. He had never gotten this close to a woman. At the station, the Saturday morning children's star, in spite of a boyish haircut, was the leading object of desire. "Oh boy!" was the most common of the predictably juvenile exclamations uttered repeatedly in the all-male control room when Susie would move in a way that highlighted her attributes. Her ample, outward-curving breasts were clearly outlined by the tight green leotard she wore, as were her narrow waist and wide hips. Above her boots were trim, athletic legs, and her eyes and cheeks radiated a healthy, outdoorsy glow. It wasn't the makeup. A local riding club had made her an honorary member, and she drove into the Philadelphia suburbs a few days a week for vigorous afternoon gallops with her affluent sponsors.

"Is that good?"

"A little more, keep going."

Susie's eyes were closed and she was leaning back, leaning against him. Some nineteen-year-olds, all too tender, would have made an excuse and left. Caesar continued the hesitant but heartfelt massage, on the verge of a great awakening.

"Lock the door, would you?"

After the click, Susie Gold turned and looked up at him for a moment and then looked back at his waist and opened his belt. She lowered his zipper, then slowly lowered his pants, just a little. Caesar was exposed and rising. Susie Gold took his hard-on in her mouth and began lovingly sucking and moving, back and forth, moist sucking and moving, back and forth, with a seductive groan sucking and moving, back and forth. Caesar lasted about ten seconds, and she swallowed as he moaned in a hush because he didn't want anyone to hear.

"Simmer down! Simmer down!"

They met, like so many from South Philly, at the Bishop Neumann dance. It was Friday nights from eight to eleven. Twenty-five cents. Catherine was from St. Maria Goretti.

"Jimmy Jones in the back, shut up!"

This was Father Cox. When he wanted to get everyone's attention, he always told Jimmy Jones to shut up. There would be a thousand kids at the dance, and none of them had ever met this kid. For that matter, neither had Father Cox.

"All right, most of you know the rules," he'd bellow from the stage without a microphone, having just halted the band. "I want separation. At least this much."

As he said this, Father Cox positioned his hands a foot apart.

"You get a little too friendly, you'll be out of here. No buts about it. Now go enjoy yourself."

He caught them about ten minutes later.

"What did I tell you, my children? I am very, very much in favor of Christian conception, but not on the dance floor."

66

Caesar Fortunato and Catherine O'Hara unlocked. This was their third date, and the boy was more than pleased with his progress. He was not, however, able to build on these early gains, which initiated his dopey misgivings about Catherine, the girl he should have married.

The next summer, he was invited to the shore, Wildwood. Mr. O'Hara was always inside, stained undershirt with flopping suspenders, the receiver to his ear, mopping himself with a handkerchief while the ceiling fan and the floor fans were whirring futilely. It could be ninety-five degrees, but Mr. O'Hara would still be inside on the phone talking about the Phillies, horses, point spreads.

Gambling was the difference between mere survival and making a living. The patrons of the bar provided for the O'Hara family by drinking boilermakers, playing the numbers, and betting on horses. Gambling on the ponies resulted occasionally in payouts to the customers. Playing the numbers and flushing money down the toilet were in effect the same thing. The bar patrons who played the numbers were hoping that the three digits they would pick out of the air would be the same as the last three numbers of the handle on the fifth race at a distant Florida racetrack. The smart customers knew that drinking always had the biggest payoff. You drank, you got drunk. That was guaranteed.

Caesar was at the bar on a hot afternoon when Catherine thought her father would be merciful and provide them with cold Cokes and allow them to bask in the air-conditioning. He remembered hearing the laughter as he came in and then how it stopped. Out of the bright sun, it took time for his eyes to adjust. He thought he saw all of them look up from their drinks and issue glances laced with disgust, these men with burly forearms, watery eyes, another species. He didn't feel like a Roman that day. He was Catherine's little dago boyfriend.

At the back wall, the door was half-open, and inside was a man talking on the phone and writing on a table with a pencil.

"You won't tell your dad," Catherine began, after he asked her about the curious activity in the back room. They were outside, headed back to the park, her father having politely thrown them out, but with Cokes in hand.

"No, of course not."

"The guys in Dad's bar make bets on the horses. And the guy in the back keeps all the bets straight, and then, as soon as a race is over, he erases everything off the table, so no one gets in any trouble. Pretty neat, huh? You know what my dad calls him? . . . Pencil."

"That is pretty neat," said Caesar, who had already dismissed the hostile greeting at the bar and found himself thrilled at being so close to a real live conspiracy.

Weeks later, near Labor Day, after dinner, the moon nearly full, Caesar guided Brendan O'Hara's third daughter to the hollow of a Wildwood dune and produced a bottle of Chianti. There was shared sipping and then foreplay that had long been stalled at French kissing. He felt emboldened by the wine and slid his left hand to her breasts. Catherine O'Hara recoiled.

"It's getting late, don't you think?"

"No."

"Well, I'm tired."

They had yet to sleep on the first day of 1959. Like half the city, Caesar Fortunato and Catherine O'Hara arrived at Broad Street too drunk to know they were exhausted. The Mummers Parade was Philadelphia's Mardi Gras, a momentary respite of misrule when, some might say, the city's true nature was exposed. Philadelphia on New Year's Day was a town of highly skeptical, slightly perverse, semienlightened alcoholics. The O'Haras, like other Second Streeters, were the guiding spirit of the Mummers Parade. On New Year's Eve, they opened their home and through the night served pepper pot stew and whisky of every origin to the serenading string bands. The music was dreadful, badly performed and repetitive, but that was beside the point, which was all-out, nonstop boozing—or at least that's how it seemed to Caesar. He was having trouble remembering much of the night, except for a general sense that he was among a large, loving family that bore no resemblance to his own.

Not long after sunrise, the Comics opened the parade, rambunctious Charlie Chaplins, Abe Lincolns, Joseph Stalins. Their job was cut-rate broad satire, the costumes amateurish, the work of overserved men new to sewing needles. Those unable to summon specific identities settled for cross-dressing. The crew of the Hammond Club was smeared in blackface, though they knew this was offensive to the city's Negro residents. The Fancies followed, distinguished by their gargantuan frame suits of circus colors, elaborate constructions of lumber and wire that turned men into floats—overtaxed and puffing but proud. The captains of the Fancies were the most lavishly overdressed, outfitted with capes that had enough fabric for ten Supermans. The best club won a cash prize, but more importantly, bragging rights. In the early days, there were kidnappings, captains drugged.

The String Bands were the last to march, banjos in the lead, backed by saxophones, accordions, and glockenspiels, producing in sum barely palatable sounds from yesteryear that deserved to be performed in such an element: with the musicians wobbling, frozen, desperate to pee. Jim Durning of the Durning String Band once told a prospective member, "I don't care how well you play. How loud can you play?"

Susie Gold, shitfaced, was waving to Caesar.

"Hey, honey bunch. Who's the wench?"

Philadelphia's leading children's star, dressed in her Peter Pan outfit, was playing a glockenspiel for the Lionel Ferpo String Band, one of the most famous of all the string bands in the Mummers Parade. It was a risky move. Women were forbidden to march, though in 1929 a female reporter dressed as an Eskimo and billing herself as Admiral Byrd's girlfriend had worked herself into the parade.

"Hi, I'm Susie!" she shouted in the direction of Catherine O'Hara, waving the hammer of the glockenspiel. "What's your name?"

Catherine looked at Caesar with raised eyebrows.

"Yes, I know him, dearie," she said, moving on. "I suck his cock all the time."

There was a story in the next day's paper, front page of the *Philadelphia Chronicle*'s City section.

Susie Gold, the star of the city's most popular children's show, was arrested on New Year's afternoon at the Ramapo Riding Club in Weymouth Falls. Gold and nine others were charged with indecent conduct. Police were vague when pressed for more information. A spokesman said the activity occurred inside a barn on club property. Four of those charged are members of the Lionel Ferpo String Band. Gold was marching with the band during the Parade, despite a long ban on female participation.

There was only one direct quote in the article. It was from Larry Gates:

"Susie Gold has already been replaced. I find it deplorable that someone in her position, the host of a children's show, has so terribly violated the trust of Philadelphia's children."

With Susie the reigning fantasy and leading topic of gossip, people at the station freely speculated about the nature of her indecency, some wondering if horses were involved. A trial would have clarified matters, which is why some were disappointed when the charges were dropped. The prominent husbands of the implicated Ramapo Clubbers hired top-rate legal talent.

Caesar last saw her on a windy night with the hurt of winter. As he was leaving the station, Susie was getting out of her car, on a surreptitious mission to gather her belongings. She walked quickly, her head turtled inside her coat.

"Hey, honey bunch," she said suddenly, coming out of her trance. "How are you? Can you come back in, help me out? I'll just be a few minutes."

"Sure."

In the dressing room, she was apologetic. With each moment, their affair became more and more unreal to him. It was as if their gaping age difference had become suddenly apparent. She was going. It was all over.

"I said something to your girlfriend, didn't I? I was just so irresponsible. . . . Let me tell you. I've been to some out-of-control parties. But these rich horse broads, I mean, when they want to have a party, they don't mess around. Of course, that's no excuse for all the crap I got into."

Well before the dawn of the Age of Aquarius, the odometer on her sex life had already passed two hundred associates, and perhaps the most appreciative was the nineteen-year-old standing before her. To Caesar, Susie Gold might as well have been from Mars. He was still flabbergasted by it all, by the revelation that sex could be delicious and spontaneous. He was bothered but not bereft that Catherine wasn't taking his calls. He had been calculating her unreciprocated devotion for a while: two proms, three years, hundreds of wasted erections. Caesar had predictably chosen instant gratification over devotion, and it took him thirty years to realize how horrible a choice that was. There were more Susie Golds to come, but there would not be another Catherine O'Hara.

"I want to give you the number of the guy I told you about. The one in TV."

"In New York . . ."

"I don't think we'll be making that trip together . . . I'll write it down."

"Thanks. Thanks a lot. I'll call."

"Really, do it. You've got a lot of poise. You're very comfortable doing this. This is your kind of thing."

"You're not staying in Philadelphia?"

"No, time to go, really, really time to go . . . but we'll see each other again. Huh?"

Caesar waited as Susie Gold filled up two shopping bags. He couldn't bring himself to ask her and she didn't volunteer any more of the much-coveted details. If there was going to be full disclosure, a total stranger was going to be the one to hear it, in a bar, in another city, at two in the morning.

Out in the parking lot, she put an arm around his waist and gave him a wonderful, delicious farewell kiss, not too long, not too short.

"We should be having a drink. At least one drink. But my picture's been in the paper, so I'm afraid some parent might take a whack at me. I've already gotten some nasty phone calls. Like their kids read the papers, you know? Anyway, I'm driving out West in the morning."

She looked in his eyes, smiled. Caesar was quiet for a few moments.

"I'll miss you," she said.

"I want to tell you how much . . ."

"Hush."

Hands in his pocket, he watched the car, the brake lights flashing as Susie Gold waited impatiently to join the humming stream of traffic.

Pissed Off

"I won't pay."

"Mr. Fortunato, you will pay."

In the lobby of the Starlight Grand, two red-blazered hulks had excused their way to the front of the checkout line and stopped about a foot behind him and blocked his exit. They had that familiar bouncer look: chest puffed out, hands clasped together at belt level, feet planted and evenly spaced—all in all, a menacing still life. Caesar and the clerk were in minute six of their dispute. Penny and Latitia, or whatever their real names were, had been on a truly magnificent spending spree and had charged all of it to his room. He had been at the hotel for three nights and the bill was forty-seven pages long.

"They're fucking hookers, do you understand?"

"Please, Mr. Fortunato."

"You supplied them, my man. This is your pussy we're talking about."

"And this is your credit card that's been charged. If you want, sir, call American Express and try to explain the situation."

"Wait a fucking minute, these guys are on your dime. That's the deal."

"As one of our valued customers, we pay for services provided, yes. We absorb the, ah, escort expenses. But wardrobe costs are on you. We're not a department store."

After finishing the edit of the Disney show in New York, five days of nasty grease and constant sugar injections and the normal property destruction, in this case a monitor shattered by a soda can during the course of a creative discussion, Caesar Fortunato did not go straight home. He was convinced, though he needed little convincing, to stop in Las Vegas and lay the groundwork for his life after TV. In another brainstorm, Beck had assured him that Hollywood was waiting. All it required was the commitment of an A-list actor, whereupon they'd be producing and directing a big-budget film.

Johnny Ray Thompson was the strong, silent type, a taciturn Texan with the weather-beaten but classic look and manner of a cowboy, which he was in real life, when he wasn't off shooting a picture and being paid astonishing sums of money. Once, Beck and Thompson had been in the same backfield on the Cornell University football team. In the interest of wooing his fellow alumnus, Beck arranged an all-expense-paid weekend in Las Vegas, which Caesar agreed to finance because he was expecting a windfall at any moment.

"How about half?"

"How about this? We'll take two thousand off the bill. And all the minibar charges."

"How generous . . . those fucking hookers."

"Mr. Fortunato, some of the people behind you in line are now fully traumatized, okay? Please, let's finish this up. Two grand off the bill, and we'll try to make it up to you when you come back."

"Shit. Fine . . . and like I'd come back to this fucking dump."

Three days before, he had lifted off from JFK on a pleasing two-beer buzz, not certain but hopeful that he had won his freedom, hopeful that when his employers saw this grossly overbudget, subversive piece of television on sacred Disney they would at last see the urgent need to be rid of him and cut a very, very big check, as his contract called for in such an event.

"Got you good, sir, did they? I'm very sorry."

"Oh fuck off, Richard."

His driver had been waiting patiently in the lobby, at a safe distance, while Caesar was drawing a crowd during his fit about contracted working girls who had seriously abused his credit card.

"Have you back in a jiffy, sir."

"They bought coats made out of Afghan yaks and charged them to my room, Richard. It's unbelievable."

"If I may ask, sir, were they generous?"

"Richard," he said proudly and credibly, "it was a sexual Olympics. Multiple rounds. A veritable decathlon."

That was about as close to the truth as the Warren Commission report. Caesar wasn't the main course. Penny and Latitia were instructed to satisfy Johnny Ray Thompson, but then the whole thing turned into room service booty, which was why the women felt entitled to extra compensation. After giving their all with the Hollywood actor, they were summoned unexpectedly by the Heisman Trophy winner, and after that by the TV director guy, who was the most obnoxious. Acquiescing, but barely, Penny soaped up Caesar's dick once and made him come, and there was a ten-second fuck with Latitia. Caesar also had a memory of waking up in the middle of the night and finding them encoiled and purring, or perhaps that was just the remains of cannabis and Champagne combining in his brain.

"What about lady luck, sir? Was she also generous?"

"So-so, Richard. I had a big run going, then my new actor friend showed up, total Maloik."

"Maloik?"

"You know, someone who ruins your luck."

"Johnny Ray Thompson was a Maloik?"

"Fucked everything up."

The two-time Academy Award winner, who was without a doubt one of the richest entertainers in the world, had bet a long

74

shot with all of Caesar's chips, and in ten seconds, hours of play and a sizable profit were history. Johnny Ray had joined the scene just as a vivacious older woman, able to pull off an ensemble of red silk blouse and black leather pants, was riding a confident twenty-minute roll at the craps table, often predicting exactly how the dice would tumble.

"Coming up, boys, little Joe from Kokomo."

"What's she talking about?"

"She's going to roll four the hard way, I think."

"Dear, is that correct?"

"Yes, indeed, Mr. Thompson. Two and two, big money for you."

"Do it."

"It's a ridiculous bet, and she's very drunk."

"Do I look stupid to you, Caesar?"

"All right, Johnny Ray."

"I'm feeling it. I'm tellin' you."

Moments later, the table roared when, as forecast, there were two spots up when each die was cast, which paid off at lovely odds of eight to one. Caesar knew this was the worst thing that could have happened. It was suddenly amateur hour.

"Give me some more chips," Johnny Ray demanded, the tenor of the voice suggesting Caesar had to comply immediately, without question.

"Come on, boy, give me some of those damn chips."

"Fuck. All right."

"Real money, my man, some real money."

Before Caesar could stop him, Johnny Ray Thompson moved an unwieldy pile of plastic, thousands of dollars, toward the middle of the table.

"Aces," he muttered, curtly, motioning to one of the dealers. The chips, once put in place, wholly concealed the box showing snake eyes, thirty-to-one odds. It was a million bucks for Caesar or nothing.

"Can you help me out, darling?"

The saucy sixty-something winked at Johnny Ray Thompson, but when the dice settled, she wasn't able to show him the look he wanted, instead crapping out with a seven.

"Great, Johnny."

"Give me some more."

"There is no more. You just bet it."

"Easy come, easy go. Right, my friend?"

"I was up fifty grand, amigo."

"Come on. That's piss."

There was a body pushing against him. Already fuming, Caesar turned with harmful intent, which vanished as soon as he saw the smile of the man with the most recognizable face on the planet. Muhammad Ali was in town for a heavyweight fight and stopped when he saw his old friend.

"Let me give you some advice," Ali whispered in Caesar's ear.

"Yes, Muhammad?"

"Stop gambling, chump. It's against Allah's laws."

Ali raised a fist to Caesar's face, a crowd that was getting ever larger laughed heartily. Then the three-time heavyweight champion and two-time Academy Award winner, arms around each other, headed off, hijacking the palpable buzz that had only moments before engulfed the table, leaving a vacuum of dead air behind, with Caesar flushed out.

"Caesar," said Johnny Ray Thompson upon departing, "lighten up. This is merely a temporary setback. I'm going to make you a rich man. Trust me."

"There was a message for you at the house," said Richard. "Mr. Simms telephoned. I'm told it's urgent."

The drive from Las Vegas to Rancho Mirage was two hundred miles but a straight shot, an unwavering line through the sand that encouraged high speeds. Richard, who used to race motorcycles, would have him home in a couple of hours. Caesar would make the call to Simms, and Simms would tell him that the network was at last ready to push him out of the plane with a golden parachute worth several million dollars. He dialed on the cell.

"Please hold on, Mr. Fortunato."

"Caesar, Geoff . . . ah, we have some big problems."

"Okay."

"We're going to have to terminate your contract."

"Why is that, Geoff?"

"You can't be surprised."

"Geoff, you want to get rid of me, fine. I just want to know the terms."

"Terms?"

"How much, Geoff? I've got two years left. How much?"

"Nothing, Caesar."

"Whoa. I have two years left. You owe me a couple of million."

"That would be correct, if you hadn't violated the morals clause, among other issues."

"What?"

"You need me to lay it all out?"

"Oh, you fucking dick. Yeah, I want to hear this."

"Sexual harassment, fraud involving your expense statements, and urinating in public."

"Bullshit, bullshit, and bullshit. Anyone I fucked wanted to be fucked. You approved all my expense statements, Mr. Shithead. And urinating in public? What the fuck are you talking about?"

"I'm afraid the Disney security guys wrote up a report, Caesar . . . also, there are a number of people here who think your behavior during the Super Bowl was far too abusive."

"That's fucking ridiculous."

"There's also an issue of repayment."

"What?!"

"Chad Goodman estimates you owe the company about a hundred grand."

"That little prick!"

"You've been taking cash advances from unit managers for a number of years, and there's no evidence of repayment on your part."

"Oh, you hypocritical piece of trash . . . Does Henry know the company sent the wife, the kids, and the secretary you're banging to Hawaii for the Pro Bowl?"

"Oh, come on, Caesar. Let's get real here. You spent four million dollars for something that can't be fixed. You fucked us. What do you expect?"

"This is not going to happen."

"I don't think you're getting it, big guy. This is happening. And you know what? You gave them the smoking gun. Or should I say, the smoking dick."

Caesar dialed his agent, who didn't answer. He left a message: "PALMER, WHAT THE FUCK IS GOING ON?! WHAT THE FUCK IS A MORALS CLAUSE?! AND WHY DO I HAVE IT? CALL ME. NOW!"

He asked Richard to pull over. Caesar was having trouble breathing. He walked into the vast nothingness and looked up at a sky that had no ceiling, hues of blue upon blue. It calmed him. His cell chirped.

"How can you let this happen?"

"You're kidding?"

"Palmer, this stuff is make-believe."

"Are you composed now? Or should I wait another thirty minutes?"

"When did you get all sensitive?"

"Look, we could make the sexual harassment thing go away. The pricks there have a few secrets they wouldn't want distributed. It's true you have been stealing from them for years, but so have the unit managers. I'll ask for depositions and those guys will drop all that crap, too. But the peeing incident is a problem. I know it sounds silly, but they've got paper. And you do have a standard morals clause in your contract."

"Why do I have a morals clause?"

"Because everyone has a morals clause. I would have gotten it dropped if I had known you were planning to commit criminal acts."

"You're fired."

"If there's anyone you should be angry with, it's your buddy Beck, the co-urinator."

"Lay off Beck. We were just having fun."

"Fun that's going to cost you a couple of million bucks."

"What can you get me?"

"Well, after I get them to drop sexual harassment, and theft, and desecrating Disney's holy ground, maybe two hundred grand."

"That's it?"

"Caesar, right now, these guys in L.A. think they can figure out a way to send you to jail. Embezzlement. Unreported income. Shit like that. They'll try to find out if you've ever had sex with a minor. You know, full-court press. I'm hoping I can get you some money, and if I indeed get you some money, it's because I'm a fucking great agent. You understand, Mr. Pinhead? A lot of people need good directors. Let me get on the phone."

"I can't fucking believe this."

"Caesar, these are not TV people. They make bombs and nuclear reactors. You don't mean shit to them."

"Two hundred grand. That's it?"

"Maybe."

"I need two million."

"I'll get you another job. Are you going to be okay?"

"Yeah, yeah."

"How's Lynette?"

"Mexico . . . Cancun. She's back tonight."

"Don't worry, we'll figure this out."

"Palmer, I don't deserve this."

"That's debatable. Caesar, I'll have another job for you in two days. Do not drive back to Las Vegas and spend the rest of your money."

"Fuck off."

"Right, nice talking to you, too."

Caesar snapped the cell phone shut. They had been driving only thirty minutes but were already almost fifty miles from the Nevada border. If they'd been closer, Caesar would have had Richard turn the car around.

"Are you all right, sir?"

"Usual, Richard. Nonsense from the network. Palmer will sort it out."

"He usually does, doesn't he?"

"He's the best."

"Would you like a joint, sir?"

"That sounds perfect, Richard."

As they pushed on across the Mojave cactus fields, the reality of being removed from his job far short of the remuneration he antici-pated was deferred by Richard's potent, brain-clouding Maui Wowie. As the pot took hold, and he began staring longer and longer outside the window of the Mercedes, he decided Palmer was lowballing it. He'd get more than two hundred. Palmer would do better. Fuck them all anyway, he said to himself. He was going into the movie business.

Teacher

Those who encountered Caesar Fortunato as an adult would find something about him profoundly unsettling. It seemed he had no point of origin. Nothing in his conversation or manner provided a clue about his beginnings. Even those who knew him best never heard him speak of his parents, or school, or the old neighborhood. It was as if he emerged from the womb as a twenty-one-year-old. In truth, he wished he had a deep allegiance to a spot on the map, a place from which to view the rest of the world, a bed where he could always sleep the deepest sleep: home.

As it was, he lived a life conducive to utter disorientation. Caesar was among the first guinea pigs of the jet age, when propeller-driven DC-8s were exchanged for continent-leaping 707s, big jets easily able to outrace the sun and confound the senses. And before he abused anything else, he was first and foremost a junkie of the electrified moment, the rollicking, nerve-wracking, can't-stop, don't-want-to-stop high of live TV. Who needed a warm, fuzzy past when you were one of the special people with an almost eternal, heightened present?

When he remembered home, when he looked back, it was always late afternoon, the shadows stretching, the colors desaturating, twilight approaching on an uninspiring sameness, unending blocks of functional, indistinct, two-story row houses, squeezed ninety-six to a block, largely treeless with laughable lawns, horizontal housing projects, spit into being during a long epoch of architectural apathy that persisted even after the Second World War. Little of substance had changed since Charles Dickens complained that Philadelphia was "distractingly regular."

This flat, square city on the Delaware River was chauvinistically content with the status quo, a worker's paradise of simple pleasures delivered without excessive fanfare. It was a day at the public pool, a night at the amusement park, a local ale chased by an obscure whisky at the corner bar, a hot, soft pretzel topped with mustard. And it was cheesesteak, a famous, delicious, amply seasoned, artery-clogging melt of meat and dairy served on a wedge of fresh bread, lightly toasted. Dangerously good, dependable, always satisfying, cheesesteak, by itself, ruined the palate for bolder adventures.

With so much concrete, so little green, an inert topography, Caesar Fortunato, searching and suffocated, peered north and south, somewhere west beyond the numbing Pennsylvania plains. In Rancho Mirage, the California desert haven he eventually discovered, the days were painted in shades of gold. Back in Philadelphia, where so many mornings bloomed drab, the weather forecasters were always hopelessly overmatched. The winters were usually cold and wet, the summers hot and stupidly humid, and what came in between might be an unpleasant mix of both—a biting spring, perhaps, or an unseasonably bitter, rainy fall.

Others, many, many others, all the many who never thought of life on the other side of the Ben Franklin Bridge, would defend this nasty inconstancy as pleasing variety. But in Caesar's mind, nearby cities compensated for this cruel sort of climate with an appealing identity, something that formed a bond. Philadelphia was being turned inside out during his boyhood, the vexing but energetic collision of peoples evaporating while the Irish and Italians and Jews migrated to nearby suburbs, leaving in their wake a reduced metropolis, suddenly monochromatic. There were two cities created, one where the vanilla power brokers resided, setting standards of self-imposed decorum, reasonable ambitions, insisting upon preservation of all things familiar. *American Bandstand,* the local hit show, was broadcasting to America from a downtown Philadelphia studio, but it wasn't playing the sound of the surrounding streets. Rock 'n' roll was too subversive. Colored music.

Maybe under other circumstances the perceived drawbacks of his place of birth would have been virtues, its urban grit and unwavering, chesty attitude an antidote to the prevailing fatuousness. Instead, Caesar Fortunato was struck by what was wrong. His city's in-your-face climate and mostly forgettable architecture and unseen culture were what he remembered from a long stumble into manhood that began when his parents let the music leave their lives.

"You are right-handed, yes?"

"Yes."

"The right hand is now your enemy."

"My enemy?"

"Yes, I want you to ignore your right hand for the next three days."

"But how will I do my homework?"

"Okay. You can use it for writing. But nothing else. Do you have a basketball?"

"In the basement."

"Please get it."

At almost any hour, he was likely to recall some aspect of Mr. Palumbo's irresistible, unorthodox musicology. The short, stooped, hatted figure who came shuffling up his steps and tapped at his door for hundreds of afternoons did more to feed his brain than any other man or woman in his life. He taught Caesar how to play the piano by proposing he dribble a basketball and learn how to type. He taught Caesar by connecting music to the rest of art and all of life. He showed the boy how big a world there was on the other side of Philadelphia.

"Dribble only with your left hand."

This was how his first music lesson began, in the alley behind the house.

"I'm not so good with my left."

"Get better."

"I don't understand."

"This will make you a better musician and a terrific point guard. You'll see."

The old man's inviting eyes put him at ease. They were a soothing olive green and they sparkled.

"Keep going?"

"Five more minutes."

On that first day the aging Sergio Palumbo came to the Fortunato residence at 25 Bullock, a two-story row house painted red and white, the new pupil, face freshly wiped and hair spit-combed, tiptoed close to the kitchen so he might hear. Before he started, Mr. Palumbo wanted a word with Caesar's mother.

"Mrs. Fortunato, I want to make sure that my methods are acceptable to you. I don't believe in music books. I don't ask the children to practice. And I don't believe in having a regular lesson schedule. All right? Please let me know if you are uncomfortable with any of this."

"No practice, Mr. Palumbo?"

"I have been teaching for almost forty years, and I have come to discover that children never practice. In the beginning, it is up to me to teach the child. The child should not be obligated to teach himself."

"And no books?"

"At this age, the pages of notes look like impossible mathematics."

"But you will teach him to read music."

"Oh yes, in time. Trust me."

"And the other . . ."

"What I said about the lesson schedule?"

"Yes."

"If it is all right with you, some weeks I would like to come more than once."

"I don't know if we can afford that, Mr. Palumbo."

"It will be the same price, Mrs. Fortunato."

"Oh."

"Also, Mrs. Fortunato, there is something else . . . and you may not want to hear this. Music lessons are usually a waste of time. Most children don't have either the aptitude or desire. Often, they continue only because their parents insist upon it. I will not teach under those circumstances. If your boy does not show a certain amount of progress after six months or so, I will have to stop."

"Please give Caesar a chance."

"I will, Mrs. Fortunato. I will."

"Mr. Palumbo . . ."

"Yes?"

"That piano cost us a bit of money, you realize."

"I have every hope that your boy will come to love and respect music the way I do."

Sergio Palumbo went to school on his own schooling. In turn-of-the-century Milan, where Puccini's *Madame Butterfly* had just debuted at the city's world-famous opera house, he survived one lazy, abusive teacher after another. It was as if they had entered into a conspiracy to rid the world of aspiring musicians. His last instructor was the most famous and the worst of all.

"The way you butchered that piece would be all right for your auntie or your mother," the esteemed but embittered Giuseppe Marucci offered more than once, without sufficient reason. Unable to repeat the success of his one great work, the B-flat Piano Concerto, Marucci was coming to fear he would be thought neither a Puccini nor even a Paderewski. Sixteen-year-old Sergio Palumbo, with all his zest and hunger, was about as welcome as a visitor from hell, a reminder of the glowing hopes he once harbored for himself and could not retrieve.

"I think you should consider playing with your nose, boy," he sneered another time. "It could be no less effective than your fingering."

Often, Marucci's critiques were accompanied by childlike twittering from an auspiciously developed teenaged girl sitting to the side. The faces changed, the bodies were all distractingly alike.

"Is it possible to ever have these lessons in private?" Palumbo soon impudently inquired, on the verge of fury.

"Ask such a question again," the maestro snapped back, "and I will make sure you flunk out of the conservatory."

One session, Marucci demanded that his student balance coins on the back of his hands, alleging he was not keeping them properly horizontal. When he wanted a special stress placed on a certain note, he gouged the young Palumbo's left shoulder until the piano yelped. Marucci's vitriolic moments were sometimes followed by short naps, student continuing while teacher snored.

"I have told you all that I know, boy," he announced one month before semester's end, "and if you don't know it yet, I suspect you never will."

In order to attach melody to rhythm, shift from forte to piano, staccato to legato, a peace had to be made between right and left. Before his student depressed one key, before the mention of scales or tempo, Mr. Palumbo set about to join Caesar's hands in harmony. After the dribbling exercise in the alley, he brought a portable typewriter to the house and had his new pupil hunt and peck with only the fingers of his left hand. He asked him to open doors lefty, read lefty, brush lefty. And when it came to the music, it was always bass clef before treble clef, left before right, rhythm before melody. In this way were the preludes and fugues in Bach's *Well-Tempered Clavier* eventually conquered—counterpoint mastered first, the hands married later, their independent workings blending suddenly into a satisfying, somewhat surprising communion of effort.

Mr. Palumbo's bag of tricks was deep indeed. To quell the boy's periodic despair with the need for numbing repetition, he used Milanese Zen.

"Every time you take a bath, Caesar, is it the same?"

"Kind of."

"All right, listen. Every morning you walk to school, is it the same?"

"Sometimes the weather changes."

"That's right. Now, every time you throw a baseball, do you throw it exactly the same way?"

"I guess not."

"So, define practice."

"Doing something over and over."

"Wrong."

"Mr. Palumbo, you're giving me a headache again."

"There really is no such thing as practice, is there?"

"Mr. Palumbo!"

"You cannot do the same thing over and over. You can do something only once. As you told me, every time you throw a baseball, you do not throw it the same way. Just like every time you play a piece for me, you will do it a little differently. But you will have the chance to do it better. Each time, you have the chance to do it a little better. Can you imagine, being able to do something better and better and better? How marvelous, don't you think?"

"You'd like my fingers to bleed, wouldn't you?"

"Your fingers won't bleed if you keep doing the dribbling exercises, like I told you."

He labored to have Caesar bring a newness to every moment at the keyboard. With a pen always in hand, a notebook on his lap, Mr. Palumbo graded the first and fiftieth imperfect rendition of a knuckle-busting Chopin étude. Only when Caesar was awarded ten straight A's was the piece thought to be mastered.

"It's still practice."

"There is no such thing as practice. There is only improvement. That is why God put us on this earth. To improve. We wake up every day with a chance to improve. Isn't that marvelous?"

"No."

"Let's go outside."

"I'm tired of dribbling."

"Okay, then it's time for shooting. A point guard must know how to score with both hands, as well."

Almost every musical notion that Mr. Palumbo introduced was accompanied by a corollary from another subject. A crescendo, Caesar learned, was something like a baseball game decided by a ninth-inning home run. The famous motif of Beethoven's Fifth was Democracy versus Communism, with Truman defeating Stalin. Mr. Palumbo used the written word to convey the essence and art of rhythm, playing the march of Shakespeare's iambic pentameter against the linguistic river of Seuss:

hearing of Brutus the assassin warning of lost ventures, Horton the steadfast elephant meaning what he said and saying what he meant.

Structure, the beauty and intent of design, was made more tangible in the confines of the Barnes Foundation, an astounding private art collection: one hundred and eighty Renoirs, sixty-nine Cézannes, and forty-four Picassos reached by a twenty-minute bus ride. One Saturday, Mr. Palumbo's piano student was present for an address by the founder.

"We do not teach students how to paint, for that would be like teaching an injured person how to scream. We teach them to learn how to see."

Dr. Albert Barnes, physician, entrepreneur, collector extraordinaire, certified eccentric, made a fortune by age forty selling a popular antiseptic, and then spent the remainder of his life indulging his bliss. He bought his first Picasso from a Paris dealer for twenty dollars and there followed a shopping spree of amazingly prescient taste. He all but hijacked Impressionism from France. On a Saturday morning in 1950, a year before his death, this prophet without honor in his own city, derided by local critics for importing horribly debased, unpleasant pictures, was teaching a seminar in the central room of his very own gallery, underneath a wall painting he had commissioned from Henri Matisse.

"We try to eradicate the almost universal, bad, confusing habit of looking at a painting for what it was not intended to be. We endeavor to create new habits of perception by objective analysis of pictures. That is, by objective observation of the relationship of line, light, color, and space that constitutes form. We study the artist's language and how it has been affected by environments. In other words, we study the great traditions."

As he spoke to the students—handpicked, of all ages, with international representation—Dr. Barnes was seated, legs crossed, petting his sleeping cocker spaniel, Fidel. Mr. Palumbo had warned Caesar that he should be careful of saying anything critical while at the gallery. Years before, Dr. Barnes asked his so-called humble factory workers to enjoy the pleasures of his collection. As they roamed through the rooms, where the paintings had been carefully arranged, bordered by antique furniture, ceramics, hand-wrought iron pieces, Dr. Barnes would often be sauntering among them, disguised. Those who were heard to take issue with some aspect of the gallery were never allowed to return.

"Well, I understand that you are a fine musician."

Caesar shuddered. The seminar concluded, the students having disbursed throughout the gallery's twenty rooms, Dr. Barnes was suddenly behind him.

"If you see the way the artist's hand moved, it's almost like an orchestra in action."

Before them was Matisse's *Blue Still Life*, painted in 1907. To the boy of eleven, the picture of a vase of many-colored flowers was vastly appealing, though he could not explain why.

"Look at the brush strokes," Barnes said gently to Mr. Palumbo's pupil, "there is an immense range and diversity, the way the hand has to move, the way the wrist is holding the brush: left, right, up and down, slow, quick, thick and thin. How would you put it musically, this contrast?"

"Adagio and allegro," said Caesar.

"Right. Slow and fast."

Mr. Palumbo smiled.

This was the moment in his childhood when a door opened and let the future in. Caesar was among his own, the composers, those who could make something new and beautiful and true. He saw how, even in a hasty pencil sketch, Picasso built a compelling frame. As music was an attempt to merge elements in opposition, melody and rhythm, forte and piano, harmony and discord, so art was also about achieving a balance, manipulating foreground and background, blending form and substance, making something ordered from the noise of existence. On that Saturday, in the presence of the masters, in a self-built gallery on 300 North Latches Lane displaying works eventually valued at a total of ten billion dollars, Caesar Fortunato found one place in Philadelphia, for one afternoon, that seemed like home.

* * *

With each new piece, Mr. Palumbo attached flesh and blood to the sheets of intimidating black-and-white notations. He told Caesar that Beethoven once got so carried away, he snapped the strings of his delicate Viennese piano. He noted that Brahms played in a tavern before drunken sailors because he needed the money. Mentioned proudly that he, Sergio Palumbo, had once played on the same stage as Mozart.

There was nationalistic chest-thumping, but it, too, had a purpose. He reminded Caesar Anthony Fortunato of his connection with a proud Italian tradition. Who invented the first piano? Why, of course, an Italian, Bartolomeo Cristofori. And what an all-star team: Scarlatti, Vivaldi, Clementi, Rossini, Verdi, Puccini—and soon, Fortunato.

If Caesar's parents only knew how dangerous the short, stooped, hatted figure really was. How he changed the boy's days and nights, sent his mind soaring beyond the sidewalks of South Philadelphia, filled his slumber with possibility. Ruined him.

"It is a good thing to be able to copy reality," he told the boy, quoting his fellow Milano Giuseppe Verdi. "But to invent reality is better."

Kapped Out

It arrived in a box, delivered by UPS, Emmy number seventeen—the first one someone else had touched before he had. He almost wanted to send it back.

The Emmy Awards for 1994 were presented in the spring of 1995, at a banquet in New York that Caesar Fortunato was not invited to attend. The Super Bowl XXVIII broadcast, his final show for the sports division, was judged Outstanding Live Sports Special. It was traditional for each network to invite every nominee, but Henry Kapp would rather have had a fork stuck in his eye than be responsible for summoning great Caesar's ghost.

When Caesar's name was called, Kapp walked up to the podium and made the shortest acceptance speech of the night, five words: "Caesar Fortunato thanks the

Academy." It was the only Emmy won by Kapp's sports division, which had a total of three nominations, the least by far among the competition. Further, the other nominations were in minor categories, one being Tech Team Remote, the other Promotion, or as Caesar renamed the category, "in-house blow jobs."

Kapp was expecting a win in Promotion, one of his self-described specialties, along with client relations, and he had prepared a long acceptance speech in first-person singular, on five carefully penned index cards. The campaign under consideration, a series of cartoons that spiked the interest of the highly valued eighteen-to-thirty-five demo, was conceived and executed wholly and unequivocally by an underappreciated twenty-eight-year-old associate producer living across the Hudson in Hoboken: one-bedroom with two roommates. Like Caesar, he was among the missing at the banquet, having recently left the network for a job in advertising that paid him five times as much. When the Promotion Emmy went elsewhere, Kapp's "SHIT!" was audible amidst the applause.

In Rancho Mirage, three weeks after the banquet, Caesar opened the UPS delivery with a small degree of trepidation. There was no indication of its origin. Given Caesar's ability to accumulate enemies as his TV career progressed, it was not ridiculous for him to think the box was going to explode. After dislodging the bubble wrap, he saw a familiar object and read the inscription:

1994 Emmy Award
Outstanding Live Sports Special
Super Bowl XXVIII
Caesar Fortunato: Director

Of the three major awards, the Tony, Oscar, and Emmy, the Emmy was the tallest, at fifteen inches. Back in 1948, after the Academy had settled on a design, they wanted to call it an Ike, after war hero and yet-to-be-president Dwight Eisenhower. That didn't float, however, and the Ike then became an Immy, a term commonly used for the image orthicon cameras. The name was later modified to Emmy because of the statuette's gender.

The four and three-quarter pounds of copper, nickel, silver, and gold in Caesar's hands formed a winged woman holding an orbiting atom, muse and molecule meant to symbolize the Academy's goal of uplifting the arts and sciences of television. The sixteen sisters in Caesar's house were displayed with care in the den, illuminated by track lighting with telescopic low-voltage heads. Number seventeen would not be accorded such an honor. It had been touched by Henry Kapp, Enemy Number One.

Caesar returned Outstanding Live Sports Special Emmy to her box and put her in the garage to rot.

"In all honesty, I have wondered at times if all the work was worth the kind of sacrifices we make . . . and the kind of sacrifices made by our families. Sports and television are often trivial. Diversions. Entertainment. By themselves, not really important. But when they are combined, they can be very important, as I discovered."

It was never as good as the first time, the first time when his name was called and he weaved his way among the bunched circular tables and walked to the stage, thirty seconds out of time, instantly sorted to a cubbyhole in the brain for top-ten moments. On the stage, he first thought of his last-second living room rehearsal, already late for the cocktail party, speeding through his victory speech as he fidgeted with his cuff links, Maxine on the couch critiquing as she absentmindedly rubbed the bulge in her belly, in the homestretch of her second pregnancy and in full glow. He turned to her first when they said he won and it seemed she was as jarred and as pleased as he was.

It was 1966, when an American passport was virtually worthless in half the world, the half that allegedly based its economic and political philosophy on the writings of a *New York Tribune* freelancer named Karl Marx. There were no Bermuda shorts and soft-soled-shoe-wearing, buffet-eating, loud and proud, just-raised-the-kids Mr. and Mrs. USAs cavorting around the Communist strongholds. This was long before tour groups were getting bused to the Great Wall or shopping at GUM after getting a peek at the chemically preserved Lenin just next store. The world on the night that Caesar Fortunato won his first Emmy was red . . . or red, white, and blue. We were good. They were evil. And the only ones getting to Moscow or Prague or Shanghai were spies, or the scattering of antiwar college kids supplied with super visas, or the very occasional American TV sports crew. Caesar Fortunato had directed a track meet in Moscow that for one afternoon made sports and television seem important. For this work, he was gripping his first Emmy and actually using the speech he had rehearsed that night in his living room and at least thirty times before that.

"Boris Voronesh was trying to break the world record in the high jump. And up in the chairman's box at Lenin Stadium were the Soviet and American diplomats who were in Moscow that week, trying to negotiate an arms agreement—the first serious arms agreement between our countries. They had come out to see this extraordinary track meet and these extraordinary athletes. It was getting dark and a light rain had started to fall. Our cameras were able to make out the raindrops gathering on the nose and chin of this great Soviet high jumper. He was down to his last attempt. There were ninety thousand people in the stadium. Voronesh had come close on the previous two jumps, each time barely grazing the bar. It teetered and then fell, teetered and then fell, and the whole crowd moaned in disappointment."

Just days before the meet, the Soviet mission in New York had yet to yield the required paperwork. It started to look as if the whole show was going to come apart. Still hopeful but with no tangible reason for having that feeling, Omar Hawas sent fifty technicians and twenty tons of equipment to West Berlin, as far east as they could go on a U.S. passport, because otherwise they wouldn't arrive with enough time to set up. He liked crapshoots as much as Caesar. The paperwork was finished on a Thursday. Hawas's crew landed in Moscow on a Friday morning, a day to spare.

The high-tech American TV equipment provided an additional attraction for the spectators at Lenin Stadium. The Soviets may have gotten a head start in the space race, but videotape was as mystifying to those Muscovites as a magic act. Leaning over the railings, the Americans having been told to place their equipment in full view, the fans marveled at seeing their first instant replays. In watching Voronesh do it all over again, they were able to appreciate more fully how wondrous and intricate this simple athletic act really was, able to truly grasp how high their champion athlete soared and how ably he adjusted his spindly body in midair.

"In the fading light," Caesar recounted to his peers in the still nascent business of live TV, "he sprinted to the bar, and he took off, and he made it. Jumped higher than anyone ever had before. And it was like the whole city erupted. And I took a shot of the chairman's box, and there were these old men, Russians and Americans, hugging each other, jumping up and down and screaming, and hugging each other. It was the single most important image I have ever broadcast. They were enemies who spoke different languages and couldn't even agree on a way to prevent the world from blowing itself up. Yet, there they were, embracing like brothers on world television at the simple act of a man jumping over a bar."

He was ushered backstage and guided to a small conference room at the hotel, where a photographer was flashing the parade of victors. Returning to his table, he hugged Maxine and as soon as they sat, she almost grabbed the trophy, anxious to touch this object that made her reevaluate, for that one night anyway, the all too many missed holidays and birthdays and anniversaries.

1966 Emmy Award

Program Achievement

U.S.-Soviet Union track meet

Caesar Fortunato: Director

More golden muses with molecules followed, almost annually, and in their new Fifth Avenue apartment, Maxine eventually centralized them in a customized bookcase. The Emmys had been getting scattered. One had found a home in Cynthia's room and was usually attired in an evening dress or nurse's outfit borrowed from her Barbie collection.

To his children the statues were odd, but they sensed their importance, sensed that they made their father important, and this fact gave them a certain comfort, made their father seem like the princes and knights of their storybooks. A hero. For a while, the Emmys bought time for Caesar with his family. Made it somehow okay in his children's world that he was the only dad always absent on weekends, who never made their ballet recitals or baseball games, the dad who was always taking naps and often really cranky.

It was almost enough that he brought home exotic souvenirs from faraway lands, Petrushka dolls and Arabian tom-toms and robotic teddy bears from Japan. It was almost enough that he brought them to Hawaii when he was doing a football game, and let them pretend to be announcers before a ski race in Colorado, and took them for steaks at 21 and Toots Shor's and Mike Manuche's. Mark loved to load the huge, steaming baked potatoes with butter. Cynthia anxiously awaited the triple-scoop chocolate sundaes. It was when they left their apartment that their dad became this regal entity respectfully addressed by the doorman, and the waiters, and the deli guy, and the guy at the dry cleaners, and the stewardesses, and the ushers at the ball games. And they benefited by being the heirs to Mr. Fortunato's throne.

Eventually, the plating on the Emmys regressed from a gleaming gold to a shiny silver to a flat bronze. And Mark and Cynthia, about the time the gifts from foreign lands started collecting dust, began to find flaws in the fairy tale. Though their father often accorded many strangers his undivided attention, they were mostly told not to interrupt.

"Mr. Fortunato. Henry Kapp."

"I didn't think you'd have the guts to call."

"You fucking son of a bitch."

"Takes one to know one, shithead."

"I'm going to be brief, Mr. Fortunato. I am calling to tell you that in light of your ridiculous and insulting letter, I am going to make it one of my top priorities to ensure that you never ever work in this fucking business ever again."

After getting the boxed Emmy, Caesar was moved to send Henry Kapp a message. It was not in his constitution to pass up an opportunity to abuse a state-of-the-art corporate tool like Henry Kapp.

Mr. Kapp,

I just received my Emmy. That's MY Emmy, in case you need reminding, you cocksucker. I knew you weren't man enough to face

95

me at the dinner. But I also heard about your eloquent speech on my behalf. I mean, how small can we be? You are the first Marine I have met who is truly a cunt, a bitchy, spiteful, small-minded cocksucking cunt. May you soon eat shit and die.

"Hey, listen, tough guy. Next time you're in the neighborhood, why don't you come over, and I'll kick your little fairy ass."

"You just don't get it."

"I get it. Oh, I get it. You've spent your life beating up people for blood money. That's what you do. So someone pays you an obscene bonus and you can build another room on your Connecticut mansion. Believe me, I get it."

"That Disney show hurt a lot of people."

"Oh, piss off . . . you knew I was exhausted."

What galled Caesar the most was that Kapp had utterly no concept of the history they had made, the millions of miles and absurd sacrifices. It seemed this noxious jarhead was purging everyone closely connected with him, blithely terminating people Caesar knew to be the best there ever was in television. Kapp had dumped the ever loyal Rope, Caesar's best handheld guy, who was on his fourth marriage and in need of a new liver; and Lou Beekman, a portly, conscientious production assistant who had spent much of his young life sitting in front of TV monitors and who hadn't eaten a vegetable in a decade and who had chalked up his first heart attack at age thirty-six; and Sid Zweibel, the network's top engineer, who had missed his mother's funeral because he was stuck at a fogged-in Romanian airport. Sally O'Brien, a gifted producer Caesar had bedded and Kapp deemed too pricey, had postponed her search for a committed partner until she began to see indifference in the faces of men she would eye and knew she had waited too long. For all of them, it was never about the money. The evidence was in their biographies: stories of horrible compromises, misbegotten devotion, supreme loyalty to their craft. Hawas had paid all of them well, allowed them to enjoy superior comforts when they traveled, encouraged their creative efforts, and in return, they gave the network the better part of their lives. That was the trade-off. Kapp, on the other hand, would have let Tiny Tim croak.

"Mr. Fortunato, you are a fucking degenerate. A gambler, a drunk, a philanderer, a man who seems to take pleasure in abusing those beneath him. And, of course, you are an ingrate. I think it fair to say that you practically killed poor Mr. Hawas with your behavior in Seoul. How do you fucking live with yourself?"

"Like you're some fucking saint, asshole. Do you remember what you did to me after the New York Marathon last year?"

"Excuse me?"

"Yeah, like you forget. I miss the fucking Tanzanian crossing the line and when everyone's calling me a racist, the TV director who's too busy paying attention to the white chick leading the women's race, were you a stand-up guy? Did you tell the press that maybe I had been beat to shit? That I was almost blind after working seven months in a row under your abusive regime? Oh, no. You relished the whole thing. Loved seeing me twisting. Yeah, what a stand-up guy."

"That, sir, is typical. Blame others for your own failings. That would seem to be the story of your life. When you were down in Orlando, did someone make you take your dick out of your pants?"

"You will never be able to do the things that I have done. And no one will remember who the fuck you were, or that your ass ever warmed a chair at that network. In two or three years, you'll be running the light-bulb division and making everyone's life there a living fucking hell, too. And that, my friend, is not a legacy."

"Listen, Mr. Fortunato, let me assure you of this: You're going to have plenty of time to work on your golf game out there in California. I'll make sure no one hires your sorry ass ever again."

"My friend, you are a pimple on someone's butt . . . an ugly fucking bag of pus . . . and what you don't know is that you are a terrible joke, a horrible joke, an incompetent boob who's chief management skill is taking something worthy and turning it into a pile of shit. Congratulations."

Inventing Reality

Though Caesar Fortunato would find himself in the midst of many major events, and though he would apply many creative flourishes to the coverage of sports and entertainment, the highlight of his career occurred in 1963, on a mild, late autumn afternoon at Philadelphia's Municipal Stadium, when he was weeks shy of his twenty-fifth birthday.

It was a year that foretold much of what was to come. In 1963, George Wallace became governor of Alabama and Martin Luther King made the most famous speech of his life; the Beach Boys would be overtaken on the AM playlists by a sharp backbeat from Liverpool; Betty Friedan deconstructed the feminine mystique and a New York housewife founded Weight Watchers; and, on a weekend in late November, the new Telstar satellite sent pictures of John F. Kennedy's funeral live to the world.

That same year, Caesar Fortunato invented the instant replay. It happened, by great coincidence, in his hometown, Philadelphia, while he was directing the Army-Navy game. He had hijacked a tape machine from New York, made some ingenious adjustments, and, after several failed attempts, replayed a fourth-quarter touchdown by the Army quarterback. The announcer felt compelled to tell the audience that they were not seeing Army score again.

There was no postgame celebration, and though this revolutionary addition to sports coverage was televised to a huge national audience, America didn't really notice. And Caesar at that point didn't really care, because he was fixated on getting this two-ton tape machine back to New York before anyone important knew it was gone. His production manager, Bob Gilmartin, had made up a story about the machine needing repairs, and in an early morning raid two days before, they had virtually pulled this thing out of the wall. They wheeled it slowly and unsteadily through the maze of hallways at the broadcast center and in their wake left a shattered window, a broken picture frame, and a number of badly bruised walls. Gilmartin broke a toe when the refrigerator-sized, decidedly unportable piece of equipment slipped off a sagging, creaking dolly. On the way out, the security guard's silence was purchased for ten bucks.

Not for a second did Caesar consider getting approval for this venture. He knew, correctly, that his idea would have been greeted with a condescending chortle and instant rejection. Harry Kaufman, the executive producer, a creepy radio veteran whose toupee only magnified his apparent decay, linked his prospects for promotion to remaining comfortably under budget, and to this end he had shed people from his department without hesitation. He dumped Billy Smith, an aging, average cameraman, while his wife was dying of leukemia. Harry had also wanted to ax this lippy, impetuous, and fiscally imprudent kid from Philly, but Caesar Fortunato had been hired by Omar Hawas, one of the most important executives at the network and, once, Susie Gold's lover.

Even had Caesar Fortunato been working for a more enlightened supervisor, the timing of his experiment would have seemed at best inappropriate. For one thing, the Army-Navy game was a big, big deal—not a time to be fucking around with the broadcast. Before America's appetite for sports reached gluttony and millionaire athletes became commonplace, Army-Navy was, in a way, the epitome of athletics, a virtuous encounter between the nation's officers-to-be who also happened to be extraordinary football players. On the eve of a fundamental shift in American life, just before the outbreak of a feverish contempt for the temples of authority, Army and Navy attracted the best players: speedy, intuitive, universally desired athletes who chose West Point and Annapolis even with the chilling knowledge that there was a very good chance they'd be somewhere dodging bullets soon after graduation.

At the time, college sports shared the spotlight only with baseball. And, in college football, only Notre Dame could approach the mystique of Army and Navy. When the service academies met at the end of their seasons, they were replenishing an antagonism that had been stoked for decades not only at West Point and Annapolis but on countless battlefields and bars around the globe. It was understood that the game would live on, for better or for worse, for each of its participants. The season, their college careers, important bragging rights, in perpetuity, hinged upon this one day. The broadcast, on radio and TV, would be heard inside the cockpits of jets flying near the speed of sound, on aircraft carriers and destroyers, on bases that stretched from one pole to the other. This was an event that resonated across the country, over the seas. America had been spending much of the century applying its military might, and even those who never had to endure basic training were attuned to the rich back story. At the time, almost every family in America had some connection to the military.

The president would always be in attendance, along with one hundred thousand fans. They'd enjoy the pageantry preceding the game, the Brigade of Midshipmen and the Corps of Cadets, the entire schools marching carefully, confidently out of the stadium tunnels, vigorous young men in gray and blue stepping in precision, all of American history suddenly on parade. When the game began, the pregame pomp and reserve was shed for incessant hat-waving and well-organized, back-and-forth taunts and chants between the academies. At halftime, the commander in chief would demonstrate his neutrality by switching sides, taking an anything-but-casual stroll across the fifty-yard line. It was the most famous walk in sports.

That meaty majesty and meaning should have been enough of a reason for Caesar Fortunato to think twice about experimenting. Everyone watched this game. But in 1963, there was much more. The narrative was as thick as it had ever been. Navy was in contention for the national championship, and its quarterback had just won the Heisman Trophy, and two weeks before, the leader of the Free World, a decorated Navy veteran, had gotten his head blown off in Dallas.

Caesar Fortunato reacted to the coverage of the Kennedy assassination with awe and envy. That late November weekend, television's power was demonstrated as never before. From that Friday afternoon to midnight Monday, from the first ominous bulletins until the final what-have-we-learned commentaries, the nation, the whole nation, was linked by this unscheduled telethon. Nielsen was reporting that ninety percent of the country's TV sets were in use. And between the president's death and burial, in the midst of these hours and hours of coverage uninterrupted by commercials or regular programming, Caesar recognized something else remarkable.

It was Sunday afternoon, and just as the voices of the announcers settled into a somber, dutiful recitation of the funeral arrangements, there was a completely unforeseen aftershock: Oswald had been shot. Caesar was watching as the network anchor was handed a piece of paper, put on his glasses, took them off, dramatically raised his head, and attempted to suppress his excitement. *This just in . . . moments ago.* Then the videotape rolled, Jack Ruby rushing into frame, pressing a gun into Lee Harvey Oswald's side, one popping sound, then a mass of bodies obscuring them both. Later, it was speculated that the guards had been distracted by the presence of the TV cameras.

In his apartment, Caesar muttered to himself, "Son of a bitch . . . son of a bitch." As the rest of America was dumbstruck with the broadcast of a nonfiction homicide, Caesar broke into a smile and shook his head. Everything about the first videotape machines was impossibly difficult: The tape itself was two inches wide, the reels fifty pounds apiece, and there was nothing precise about any of the functions. Hit play and for the first five or six seconds, the picture would attempt to assemble itself, a smear of squiggles and colors in search of coherence. Half the time you had to rewind and try again. To be able to record the shooting of Lee Harvey Oswald and play it back cleanly within a few minutes was not so much remarkable as divine.

The Army-Navy game, scheduled to take place a week after the assassination, was immediately postponed. Then it looked as if the game wouldn't be held at all. According to reports, the usual frivolities at the academies, mascot kidnappings and the like, were absent. President Kennedy, the famous P-T boat hero from World War II, was something of an older brother. There wasn't such a gaping distance between these boys and the man who ran the country: Jack Kennedy was just on the other side of forty the day he was gunned down, a president who was once serenaded by Marilyn Monroe in public, a guy who could still get it up. Eisenhower was a round of golf at Augusta and Kennedy was touch football at Hyannisport. One was a five-star general, the other a lieutenant, and actually not a very good one at that.

Kennedy had attended the last two games, more fan than president really, as jolly as the thousands who took rollicking, beer-riddled trains from Boston and New York and Washington. Kennedy took part in the pregame coin toss both years, spent a few moments chatting with the team captains, warmly acknowledged, in that disarming way he had, the swelling applause as he changed seats at halftime. This wasn't in any way an obligation of his office. In the end, the game was played because Jackie made a special request, said that's what her husband would have wanted, and Army-Navy 1963 was rescheduled for Saturday, December 7, the anniversary of a different sort of ambush.

On that day, with a whole nation numb from the murder of their young president, when everyone was ready to sleepwalk into the holidays, Caesar Fortunato, made oblivious by his raging ambition, was prepared to ruin his career. The instant replay was not really an idea whose time had come. The kind of tape machine sufficient for Caesar's needs hadn't been invented yet. On the way to the stadium, he told his announcer of this new thing he'd be trying.

"If this somehow makes me look like a total moron," said Roger Simpson, "I will find you after the game and beat the shit out of you, okay, Caesar?"

To solve the problem of the utterly inexact, virtually useless rewind function, the director once tutored by a devoted music teacher found a way to make use of audio. Caesar had a technician record beeps on the tape: one beep when Army or Navy came out of the huddle, two beeps when the play began. When rewinding, the tape operator would stop as soon as he heard two beeps. Without this inspired little trick, rewinding would have been TV roulette. The other nagging issue was unresolved. Though Caesar had a way of rewinding to the right spot on the tape, his imagination had no answer for what followed after hitting the play button, which was usually nothing. No picture. Just crap on the screen. But late in the fourth quarter, after a touchdown by the Army quarterback lifted the one hundred thousand from their seats, it worked. It worked. The picture locked, and, oblivious to its significance, America saw the Army quarterback rewrite history.

"Go, Roger!"

"What?"

"We got it, damn it! We got it. It's working."

"What? What?"

"The replay. Look on your monitor. It's the touchdown! The same play! We're playing it over. Tell the audience. Explain it."

Ladies and gentlemen, you are not seeing Army's quarterback score another touchdown. That's a replay of the same score. The first instant replay in television history. How about that?

The first instant replay, afterward little noticed nor long remembered, would arguably have a greater impact on the country than the horrible assassination of a young president. By introducing this device, Caesar Fortunato was making the television broadcast better, allowing the viewer at home to see something not available at the game. And Caesar Fortunato would be followed by many other impetuous, free-spending, lippy young men who thought of inventive ways to enhance sports broadcasts. They added more cameras, smaller cameras, high-powered lenses, parabolic microphones, slow motion, super slow motion, blimp shots, three-dimensional graphics; encouraged lively, opinionated commentary; hired garrulous, famous ex-jocks to dissect the action with multiple replays from multiple angles; artfully deified the performers with cinematic framing and music. Their work, more than anything else, ignited a sports explosion. More and more people watched the games, which meant the advertisers paid the networks more money, which meant the leagues could ask the networks for more money to televise the games, and that meant the leagues had more money and the players, following instrumental labor unrest, had more money, which spurred an ever larger pool of pubescent dreamers who were willing to sacrifice much of their existence throwing a football, or shooting a jump shot, or swinging a bat. And even if they couldn't play, they still watched. Blame Caesar Fortunato for crafty merchandising and legions of agents and league expansion and all-sports cable TV. When his tape operator hit play in a TV truck parked outside Philadelphia's Municipal Stadium, and for the first time a moment of a sports event was seen over again, it caused a ripple that begat a wave that produced globally popular athletes, sneakers more expensive than shoes, and games as important for some as life itself.

On that same day in 1963, on the other side of the country, Tommy Vaughn had performed a similar though less audacious experiment. Both Tommy and Caesar readily saw the possibilities of using videotape as a tool to improve the broadcast. And both weren't about to wait for the tape machines to shrink into manageable sizes. They were always tempted to jump-start history, and, as would happen throughout their careers, they would find themselves in a neck-and-neck competition.

Vaughn procured the refrigerator-sized, two-inch tape machine minus subterfuge, by getting fifty-yard-line seats for the executives of the manufacturer, and he ended up replaying a touchdown in an appealing, atypical Saturday pro game between Vince Lombardi's two-time champion Green Bay Packers, the league's new juggernaut, and the Los Angeles Rams. However, Vaughn's replay was delayed, not instant. He postponed his experimenting until halftime, so there'd be no chance of interrupting the game coverage. As it was, viewers only saw half the play, ugly fuzz finally resolving into a picture showing a ball spiraling into the hands of Max McGee.

Like Caesar Fortunato, Tommy Vaughn felt a need to express himself in television, try new things, push the dopey machinery until it gave you what you wanted or blew up. But Vaughn also wanted to keep his job. He liked having a sense of security. That's why he was in sports. There'd always be sports. Everyone loved sports. When he started, in 1947, pulling cable, literally tugging and dragging these weighty, rubber-coated wads of wire, as wide as a boa constrictor, the young Tommy Vaughn saw what happened to people who worked on game shows and dramas. The shows would get canned, some in months or even weeks, and everyone would be fired. But sports was eternal. Sports was TV's top salesman. And TV was the best thing that ever happened to sports.

When Don Larsen of the New York Yankees pitched a perfect game in the 1956 World Series, and the whole nation and every one of Tommy's camera guys were glued to every pitch in those final innings— waiting to see if Larsen could really do it, really shut down the Dodgers on no runs and no hits and surrender not even one walk, not one base runner, become the only man ever to reach pitching perfection in the World Series—Tommy knew TV and sports were a sure thing. And after eating too much Spam during the Depression and experiencing a few too many near misses in the war, Tommy Vaughn liked the idea of a safety net. He remembered when his dad and his uncles were out of work until Roosevelt put the whole country on welfare. And during the Greatest and Most Dangerous Adventure of the Twentieth Century, World War II, Tommy Vaughn was piloting bombers and in four almost hallucinatory years experienced more than a sufficient amount of debauchery and risk-taking. Enough, in his mind, for ten lifetimes. This was how Tommy Vaughn differed from the younger Caesar Fortunato, who never truly faced the prospect of his own mortality, had never seen people lose jobs, starve, had never calculated the cost of losing real gambles with long-shot odds. In the air above France and Germany during World War II, Tommy Vaughn saw too many cocky pilots needlessly crash and burn and knew that he was almost one of them.

"What are you doing?"

"What does it look like I'm doing?"

"It looks like you're going to fly under the Eiffel Tower."

In the summer of 1945, when it was all over, Tommy Vaughn was flying a C-46 cargo plane back to the States, his final assignment. They had just dropped off a general and his girlfriend in the Italian Alps and the general had repaid the gesture with a case of Champagne.

"You're not serious," said Tommy's copilot.

"This izz . . . no sweat."

"Pull up."

"Ah, come on."

"Do it."

"Fhuck you."

"Fhuck me? . . . Tommy, we're drunk."

"Thas not a good enough reason. We can make it."

"I'll shoot you. I swear to God. You're going to kill us, you asshole."

"You're not gonna . . . shoo me."

"Yes I fhucking am. . . . The most fu-famous structure in the world is still standing after this entire ridiculous war and now you're going to fhucking knock it over and kill several thousand Parisians, not to mention the crew we have managed to keep alive for fifty fhucking missions."

"Hold on! Here we go."

"I'm not holding on! I'm going to fhucking shoot you."

"Are you going to help me fly this thing or not, you pussy."

"I gave you a chance."

"Owwwww!"

The copilot, whose unsteady aim ended up only grazing Tommy Vaughn's left thigh, would soon be taking the vows of priesthood in the Roman Catholic Church.

In their rush to return the tape machine, Caesar Fortunato and Bob Gilmartin did twice as much damage to the broadcast center. On that Monday, Caesar was summoned by Harry Kaufman.

"The guard confessed."

"Mr. Kaufman, it worked. Isn't that the point?"

"But you destroyed a very, very expensive piece of equipment."

"Come on, it's not destroyed."

"That's not what they're telling me, Caesar. Look, we just can't have this sort of thing going on. I'm sorry, but we're going to have to let you go."

The windows on the twenty-fifth floor of the Sixth Avenue office were trembling from a whistling wind. Caesar was looking north to a forest of naked trees in Central Park, the tip of his nose still defrosting from the chill.

"You're still missing the point."

"There is no point."

"Every little boy remembers the time he hit the home run, or scored the winning touchdown. You replay the memory over and over again. In sports, you always want to see it again. This could make our product better than being there."

"So for a couple of seconds, we saw the Army quarterback go into the end zone again. Actually, I think it was rather confusing. Also, don't be thinking you did something special. I'm told Tommy Vaughn did a replay out in Los Angeles."

"What?"

"Yup. At the Packers game."

"That can't be true."

Caesar couldn't stop the welling at the corner of his eyes. This was his claim to fame, his piece of art, his inventing of reality. He was fully aware of Tommy Vaughn, knew of him as this revered, even adored figure. He thought of Vaughn as his chief competition, but no one in the business was talking about doing a remote instant replay, or even wondering how it could possibly be done. No one. How many people could have thought it sensible to rip a machine out of the wall, as he had just done? Vaughn was a dad with kids. It didn't sound like Vaughn. Vaughn wasn't going to beat him on something like this.

Mr. Palumbo had once told him how the classic composers were forced into a certain simplicity. Their audiences had to understand their music immediately. There was no such thing as hearing it again on a vinyl disc or radio broadcast. Once, all music was live music. As a result, composers were largely ignorant of the work of their contemporaries.

The only way to listen to the other masters was to travel. But once that changed, once music could be reproduced, like books, copied again and again, so did the nature of listening and composition. Complexity could be tolerated. Music evolved at a much faster rate because the leading talents would build upon the achievements of others, synthesize once foreign sounds into their own stylistic impulses.

After the Second World War, Caesar knew that Bing Crosby discovered a sound engineer, an ex-GI who had updated another bit of audacious technology spawned by the Nazis: magnetic tape. For thirty years, radio was live, but this new recording tape was of such a high quality, there was no way to discern the difference between a show broadcast live and one recorded days or weeks before. The first tape-delayed, edited radio program was Bing Crosby's *Philco Radio Time*, October 1, 1947, during which Crosby crooned, among other tunes, "My Heart Is a Hobo." Crosby had personal reasons to push this innovation: He was finally the master of his schedule. By clustering his radio work, taping several shows at once, he had time to indulge his other passions: golf and horse racing. But, in the larger scheme, radio was removed from the tyranny of the present tense. There was now an element of control. Tape allowed editing, editing elevated quality.

And before videotape, Lucille Ball and Desi Arnaz discovered the virtues of using film to enrich TV. When they proposed starring in a show based on their Mr. and Mrs. Vaudeville act, they were told it would have to be done in New York. That's where all the shows were done, and where all the shows were done one way, the only way: live. By using film, rolling three cameras at once, performing before a live audience, then cutting it later, Lucille Ball and Desi Arnaz were able to shoot *I Love Lucy* where, when, and how they wanted: in Los Angeles, but with the energy of Broadway theater and the look of a polished Hollywood feature.

Privately, Caesar had some misgivings about his instant replay, wondered at first if this new production device would diminish the broadcast. He likened athletes to magicians. If athletes were doing supernatural things, as it seemed, perhaps it was better not to examine their bag of tricks. That's what a replay did. It allowed the viewers to examine more closely these extraordinary mortals. As it would turn out, having the chance to fully examine the beauty and power and rare talent of the athletically gifted, in replay after replay, didn't flatten the viewing experience. It made it that much more compelling.

"I know you were highly regarded at the station in Philadelphia," Harry Kaufman concluded. "I'm sure they'd love to have you back. Listen, if anyone asks me, I'll say you resigned for personal reasons. Leave it at that. Okay?"

In a few days, his studio apartment was overtaken by newsprint and the stench of takeout grease. Drinking would have been slightly better medication than the steady ingesting of Chinese food and cheeseburgers, which produced a disputatious stomach. In his heart, he was hoping for a reprieve, which is why, even almost paralyzed by a committed lassitude, Caesar was still taking calls. So he was disappointed when he heard from his girlfriend, Maxine. She scheduled a date, which was odd, wanted it to happen as soon as possible, which was odd, and her voice was almost businesslike, that odd as well. These irregularities were noted by Caesar but dismissed a few minutes after he hung up. He had hurried Maxine off the phone in case someone from the office was trying to reach him.

Against his will, fortified by Pepto-Bismol, the next night he went to see her, plunging into a city directly at odds with his mood. He was assaulted by New York at Christmas, the clanging bells being swung demonstrably by the Salvation Army Santa Clauses; reclining, bunched Scotch pines awaiting buyers; sidewalks made more treacherous by overburdened shoppers. Outside the coffee shop, Maxine gave him a hug, but there was a kiss only on the cheek. They met while she was waiting tables at a cavernous German restaurant in Greenwich Village. Caesar had known Maxine Sanders for five months. She wanted to be an actress.

"I have to tell you something," she said, interrupting Caesar before he could elaborate on his career in crisis.

"I . . ."

"Yes . . ."

The next morning, Omar Hawas would call Caesar Fortunato and reverse Mr. Kaufman's decision. He apologized to the network's youngest director, told him the instant replay was the work of genius, informed

Caesar that Mr. Kaufman had been fired, and then offered a stunning series of inducements in order to win him back and clearly convey the network's appreciation for his profound creativity. Caesar's salary would be doubled, a personal secretary would be provided, and the company would pay for his apartment and any necessary business entertaining. None of this, however, did Caesar know the night before, as he sat across from Maxine Sanders, dispirited and dyspeptic, about to hear of her own brewing crisis.

"Caesar, I'm pregnant."

Turnabout

12

"I'm putting you in Berkshire Hathaway, exclusively."

"Wait a minute. I want you selling, not buying. This is my money, Sam!"

Selling the Mercedes would leave him with just one car, and that was unacceptable for so many reasons. It would be bad for appearances. It would be bad for Richard, who didn't like driving the BMW. It would be bad for his marriage. The BMW was Lynette's car. Sharing was not an option. It might compromise her opinion of him. In a bad sign, she had already volunteered to economize, which prompted an ugly scene that concluded with Caesar smashing a glass and two plates. And there was no such thing as a proletarian alternative, like getting around by bicycle. Rancho Mirage was like the inverse of Beijing. No one rode a bicycle for any reason, ever. As for public transportation, the buses ran morning, noon, and night: that is, three times a day. Faced with the prospect of becoming the first person in his municipality to downgrade from four wheels to two, he decided it was better to simply liquidate his holdings with broker Sam.

"What are you now, Caesar, mid-fifties? It's time to be thinking of immediate, steady growth. Warren's the man for you."

Broker Sam had just come back from Omaha, where he and fifteen thousand others attended the annual Berkshire Hathaway stockholders meeting, which was really more of a pilgrimage than a business event. Sam and the multitude had journeyed to the very middle of Middle America, at least a thousand miles from anything that could be described as a resort, to hear the mahatma of capitalism, a profoundly unassuming, bespectacled Nebraskan who looked as if he had stepped out of a Grant Wood painting. Warren Buffet drove his own Lincoln town car, lived in the house he bought for thirty grand in 1958, and was the world's second-richest man. By listening to him, investing with his stock fund, many who had come to Omaha that weekend, dentists and factory workers and teachers and janitors, were the only millionaires on their block.

"I am going to fucking kill you."

"Class A shares. You've got thirty. It'll be great."

"What did you do with the rest of my money?"

"It's all with Warren now."

"You said you only bought thirty shares."

"Right, they're about fifty grand each."

"This is the most fucked-up thing I've ever heard."

"Listen, Caesar. If you had given Warren ten grand in 1965, and don't we all wish we had, it would be worth about sixty million today. He's a big brand guy, proven brands: Coke, Gillette, Disney. That's where he's been putting the money. You know what he says this weekend? He's a big Dairy Queen guy, too. He says the Dilly Bar is more certain to be around in ten years than any single software application."

"I am going to fly to New York and cut your throat out, Mr. Dilly Bar. You are no longer my broker. Okay? And I want the rest of my money. Not next week. Not next month. Right now!"

"Caesar, you just drained a half million out of the account. What are you going to do for retirement? As your financial advisor, I must strongly object."

"Are you listening? You're not my financial advisor anymore!"

"Caesar, can I put you on hold?"

"Don't fucking put me on hold!"

"Caesar, hold on."

In the summer of 1995, some eighteen months after directing Super Bowl XXVIII, Caesar Fortunato, the inventor of the instant replay, remained not so much unemployed as unemployable. In a way, Caesar did have a job. He had become a full-time gambler. He had announced his career change, in a manner of speaking, by losing $250,000 one long night in Las Vegas, ridiculously stubborn at the blackjack table. Smaller but still stunning losses followed on subsequent trips. It was too easy to get there. He'd give Richard a call, and stocked with junk food, dope, and oldies, they'd take off on a two-and-a-half-hour dash through the desert in the comfortable, able Mercedes. Other mornings would start with a trek to one of the horse tracks in L.A. just up the freeway. The damage there was not quite as stupendous.

He did get something in return. The gambling, which he did daily and with devotion, offered some kind of shape to his life, a purpose. Every day at the track could be made pleasingly the same. Arriving around noon, he'd first examine *The Racing Form* over an espresso. The surge of caffeine always elevated his mood, activated his ridiculously optimistic nature. Before each race, he'd walk down from his seat and assess the entries as they were led to the post. All his life, he needed visual confirmation. Didn't matter if the athlete was two- or four-legged. If a horse seemed too jumpy, or there was a dull look in the eyes, or the animal was slicked by sweat, he'd revert to his second or third choice. The horse's appearance was more important to him than the other variables to consider, such as owner, trainer, jockey, age, sex, breeding, win-loss record, recent workouts, track condition. Some players considered as many as twenty-five distinctive pieces of information before making a determination. Caesar was a look guy. He wanted to make sure the horse looked ready. In the grandstand, having made his wager, he'd await his fix of adrenaline. Race after race, as the horses rumbled down the stretch, the tingling would flow from the toes to the scalp, electrifying the whole body as reliably as any drug.

In Las Vegas, Caesar received the preferential treatment accorded players who bet copiously, without reserve. At first, it was a welcome flashback to his former life of absolute power and subsidized luxury. He could have a ringside seat among the celebrated at a major fight, phone to have a five-course meal wheeled into his Jacuzzi-equipped suite, request the company of compliant, silicon-breasted Barbie dolls. In his more recent sojourns, however, he had made less and less use of these diversions. In order to stem his sizable losses, he decided to apply some self-control. So he doubled his time at the tables.

On the night he lost $250,000 at blackjack, he was paying close attention to the dealers. He'd been told they would usually lean away from a table when they had a bad hand. Caesar found credence in this tip. It was like evaluating a horse before a race and looking for some telltale sign. At first, he was up, which encouraged him to make it a long night. The losing became catastrophic after he'd been at the same table for fourteen hours, eleven different dealers, and eight vodkas. The advice on the blackjack dealers was worthy but belated. Ten years before, a consulting firm that worked with the casinos on so-called game protection had cautioned all of them about this incriminating habit.

"You said you'd have another job for me in two days. That was like two years ago. Hello?"

"We've got to talk."

"You're dumping me."

"Not exactly. I think I might be able to get you a music video. It looks pretty good, but give me a couple of days."

His client had spent at least half his career burning bridges, or not even bothering to build them. Even so, Palmer Nash didn't think he'd have that much trouble getting Caesar's career back in motion. The television universe was expanding rapidly, new networks coming into being almost daily, and the demand for anybody with experience, anybody, far exceeded supply. All of his other clients, even those with suspect ability and multiple rehabs, were getting work.

"I'm selling one of my cars, Palmer. Selling it. Understand? I have serious cash-flow problems. I'm ready to work. RIGHT NOW."

"What you have is a serious affection for the tables at the Starlight Grand and the ponies at Hollywood Park."

"And you are the world's most worthless agent. Fucking Bill McBride. Nut case. Medicated nut case. He's working."

"Let me be straight with you."

"What?"

"I can't help you right now. And I'll tell you why. It's a new world out there. Half the people I call won't even deal with agents. To them, an agent means expensive. They think they can't afford you."

Palmer Nash was lying. His story was credible. No one was paying what Caesar Fortunato got anymore, which Caesar knew. But money wasn't the reason no one wanted him. After his client literally pissed away a top-dollar contract unequaled in the industry, a contract that was a testament to his agenting skills, Nash had made a good-faith effort to find his famous and famously tempestuous director another job. Though most of the executive producers and their like didn't return his calls or his follow-ups . . . and his follow-ups of his follow-ups, he had had enough conversations of unprecedented candor in the preceding months to realize the futility of his efforts. Apparently, almost everyone was pleased, even tickled by Caesar's misfortune and thought it inadvisable to hire a bottomless pit of evil. There also were stories going around that he had molested Minnie Mouse and was undergoing shock treatment. Palmer Nash assumed Henry Kapp was behind that dirty work.

"So you're dumping me."

"No. But you need to make some calls on your own. Guys who really owe you."

"So I have to beg."

"Call it what you want. But, look, I'm still trying. I think I can get a couple of new things for you. Stuff outside sports. The sports guys are all fucked-up. They've spent it all on the rights fees. They have nothing left for people like you. They'd rather hire some young kid to do a half-ass job."

"Why is Bill McBride working?"

"I don't know."

"It's because he has a real agent."

"Hello, asshole? What happened to that two-million-dollar movie deal?"

"It's gonna happen. You know Hollywood. Everything's in development hell."

"So you think Johnny Ray Thompson is going to come through for you?"

"He better. His lawyer calls me every week so I can send Johnny Ray more of my pot. Apparently, he loves the stuff Richard gets me."

"Can you spell the word 'fool'?"

"Oh, fuck off."

"Don't count on this guy. I'm telling you."

"You're just jealous that I'm hanging with the big boys."

"Right. Let's see what kind of job you do as your own agent."

"Can't do much worse than you."

"Remember, my friend . . . first rule: Don't sound like you're too desperate."

"Hey, Steve, Caesar Fortunato."

"How are you, Caesar?"

"Okay. Okay. I hear you need some directors."

"Well . . . well, we might."

Steve Webb was a senior producer at the all-sports cable network. Once upon a time, when he was gainfully employed, Caesar viewed the operation with total disdain. Too many insipid, minor events: sailing, rugby, billiards, dog shows. Little boys operating the equipment. A procession of crappy look-alike, sound-alike announcers. Six people watching. It wasn't quite that way anymore, though he knew the pay was still awful, and most everyone involved was under forty and overworked. He thought of it as the world's first air-conditioned sweat shop. Little girls making sneakers in Malaysia had better hours.

"It's not easy for me, Steve . . . I'm not very good at . . . at . . . you know, I'm looking."

116

"Caesar, I don't think we're in your territory, as far as the money goes."

"Steve, I need to work, you know?"

"Of course."

"What about the college football? I know you just expanded the package."

"Well, actually, I think we're in pretty good shape there."

"How about a little later, the basketball?"

"Caesar, how about this? I've got a meeting in five minutes, let me get your number."

"Okay, Steve. You know, I'm out here in the desert, but if paying for travel is a problem, I'll find a way to get there. Maybe I could work out some kind of per diem."

"All right, Caesar. Let me take a look at our situation, and I'll try to get back to you in the next few weeks."

"Okay, okay, Steve . . . But if you could get back to me sooner, that'd be great."

Steve Webb needed directors, and he could have used someone with Caesar's tremendous experience. But as it happened, Andy Kushner and Steve Webb had been college roommates. And one night, over five beers, Steve had heard the whole story.

"If Caesar Fortunato calls again," he told his secretary, "I'm either busy or deathly ill."

Escape Artist

Andy Kushner, the architect of some of the greatest escapes in sports television history, was living reluctantly with his parents in White Plains at age twenty-five. His job at the network and the daily commute were viciously incompatible. He was always missing the 12:51 train, the last one out, so he'd end up going back to work and sleeping on a fashionable but brutally uncomfortable couch in the executive producer's corner office. The first light of day poured unhindered through the wall-to-wall windows, making further sleep utterly impossible. In a stupor, he'd brush, shave, shampoo in a men's-room sink, using a towel provided by the overnight cleaning ladies, all of whom he knew on a first-name basis.

Andy, despite his fame and competence, was as yet a freelance production assistant, and though some weeks he'd work every day, he was only paid for two: the day before a game and the day of the game. He endured this, a salary that made him eligible for food stamps, and he packed a lunch and ironed his own shirts and tolerated Mom and Dad because he operated on the assumption that very soon, in a year or two, he'd be rewarded with a staff job, on the way to making real money. Caesar Fortunato kind of money.

It was unclear if anyone at any of the networks understood or cared that their entry-level employees were receiving very little training in the fine art of television. The production assistants were magnets for every task that everyone else didn't want to do. Some secretaries were able to delegate much of their work to the Andy Kushners. One claimed she had gone years without photocopying. In medicine and the military, there seemed a purpose in getting new recruits accustomed to severe sleep deficits. But TV never required the saving or taking of lives. Andy Kushner didn't sleep because of a great collective selfishness, in order that everyone else would be able to do less: so the network president could make the 5:12 to Larchmont, so Caesar Fortunato would have everything he could possibly need delivered to his door in Rancho Mirage, so Trish Pardo, the secretary who hadn't copied since the Stone Age, would be able to shop, get her nails done, schedule a massage, enjoy extended lunches with her dates, leave two hours early on Fridays.

On a fall Friday in 1982, as Trish Pardo caught the getaway subway to Flushing and a weekend of vegetating, Andy Kushner was already on the ground in Lincoln, Nebraska, once again bracing for the final push. He had booked travel for some thirty people—airfare, hotels, and transportation—divided the crew by privilege or lack thereof, first class or coach, suite or single, limo or rental. He had hired a small brigade of local gofers, mostly college students familiar with the area, to fetch with the relish of retrievers, lead the network's employees through the stadium's catacombs with the savvy of Saint Bernards, copy, collate, and staple with the speed of greyhounds. He had purchased a high level of goodwill in the home city with hundreds of hats and T-shirts sent by overnight mail.

The show began in earnest at the Friday night production meeting. Andy was responsible for reserving a large conference room and stocking it with the required elements: forty media guides, twenty from each team, a stack of press releases, legal pads and pencils, tape decks, VHS and Beta, pretzels, potato chips (with ridges, if possible), soda (regular and diet), one big-ass bowl of ice, two dozen beers (domestic and imported), one scotch, one rye. The meeting would conclude with a discussion of the escape plan, such as who was assigned to which escape vehicle, and Andy would be asked to organize everyone's wake-up calls.

On game day, he'd have three gofers help him transport two cargo trunks to the game. Inside would be enough office paraphernalia to open a stationery store and enough videotape to start a small TV station. During the week, Andy also had accumulated every pertinent professional and personal detail of each athlete involved in the game, including favorite color, shoe size, and last book read. This information, carefully arranged so as not to be in the least bit confusing, was distributed to the announcers and typed into the graphics generator. Before, during, and after the game, Andy could expect to have a conversation of some substance with virtually every network employee on-site. On any given Saturday or Sunday, they'd want food, information, another ticket, another rental, a different limo driver, a different flight home, money, another media guide for the two they'd lost, another credential for the one they'd secretly sold, a souvenir for their little boy.

Caesar held Andy in great esteem. He was setting one record after another for escapes. Thirteen minutes from the Georgia Dome to Hartsfield. Twelve minutes from Texas Stadium to DFW. Six minutes from the Vet to Philadelphia International. Andy would ride shotgun with one of the local cops, at the head of the pack, siren wailing, half his body out the window, shouting at sluggish, departing fans about to be run over. Escapes were very important, almost as important as anything else that happened during the weekend, including the broadcast. It was essential to bolt out of the parking lot ahead of the fans, drive recklessly, and catch the plane just as the flight attendants were about to shut the door.

One of Andy's crowning achievements was the 1978 PGA Championship. While the golfers were in the midst of a playoff, competition was delayed as two helicopters landed beside the green. The golfers and tournament officials were incensed. But that wasn't important. What mattered was that everyone made their flights, including analyst Ken Baker, who kept some four hundred people waiting sixty-four minutes on a British Airways 747 to London. Andy had called ahead and asked them to hold the flight. He identified himself as Elton John's agent and told them the Rocket Man was on his way.

Custer could have used Andy at Little Bighorn. One announcer was so impressed with Andy's work, he even mentioned it on the air.

Ladies and gentlemen, said Roger Simpson, *I would not be with you tonight except for the imaginative work of Andy Kushner. Just hours ago, I was a thousand miles away at Legion Field in Birmingham, Alabama. Then my improbable journey began. First, a police escort to the airport, private jet to New York . . . and then a waiting ambulance.*

The New York cops didn't do escorts. Simpson had to get from a Southeastern Conference football game in Alabama to Game One of the World Series at Yankee Stadium, from one soldout stadium to another, in a matter of hours. The network switchboard was inundated with viewers irate about this misuse of an emergency vehicle. New York politicians voiced their objections. Andy was appalled.

"You're supposed to keep those things to yourself," he said later.

Then came the starched shirt incident that weekend in Nebraska, which solidified Andy's greatness in Caesar's eyes.

Fred Boyle was the coach at Texas State for seventeen years before joining the network as a college analyst. Andy had been warned that Boyle treated the production assistants as veritable butlers. It was decided he was caught in some kind of Southern time warp, when there were plantations and cheap labor, people to pour drinks, wave big bwana-style cooling fans incessantly through muggy afternoons, do everything but wipe one's butt. After the Friday production meeting, Boyle handed Andy a soiled, rumpled white dress shirt.

"Son, make sure this is cleaned by first thing tomorrow morning and I don't want any starch. NO starch. Is that clear?"

"You're kidding?"

"No, son. I am not kidding. First thing tomorrow, or I'll have your ass."

Early the next morning, as Boyle opened his door to retrieve the local newspaper, the shirt was waiting, not only starched but petrified. It was standing without support. During the game, Boyle could be heard complaining repeatedly about the chafing of his neck and nipples. Down in the truck, each expression of discomfort was followed by a roar. Everyone knew about the super-starching. Andy was now enshrined in the PA Hall of Fame.

Though Caesar's respect for his PA had reached new highs after the Boyle incident, it did not preclude him from having Andy fetch him a gram of coke at two in the morning. This extracurricular pickup happened at a greasy spoon in the very middle of Middle America, where the only game in town was college football and at least half the dealers were undercover cops. Caesar told Andy he was picking up some special medicine. Andy suspected otherwise but went anyway. It was not very dangerous to irritate talent like Fred Boyle, who was far too self-consumed to help a PA's career, even a PA who correctly laundered his shirts. With very few exceptions, talent never helped anyone, ever. But Caesar Fortunato's opinion of him did matter. Caesar could help him, liberate him from Mom's dry meat loaf and Dad's deep disapproval of a job that had his son working seven days and getting paid for two.

"No, I don't know him."

A representative of the Lincoln, Nebraska, police force was on the phone asking Caesar if he knew Andy Kushner.

"You're sure, sir?"

"Do you know I'm here directing tomorrow's game?"

"I understand that. So you don't know this young man? He told us you'd be able to explain everything."

"That's incorrect. Can I go back to sleep, officer?"

"This kid's in a lot of trouble, sir."

"Good night, officer."

This was Andy Kushner's third trip to Lincoln, Nebraska. From organizing escapes, he had gotten to know many of the people in local law enforcement. Just that week, he had sent the cops not only a big box of pins, T-shirts, and hats, but also two banners with the network's logo. Banners were as good as gold. No one else in Lincoln had banners. The police also knew of Caesar Fortunato. This was his second trip to Lincoln, Nebraska. On his first visit, Mr. Fortunato had shifted his rental car into reverse while moving forward at about sixty miles per hour. The police found his car hugging a telephone pole, with Mr. Fortunato drunk and somehow uninjured.

Andy Kushner was released on his own recognizance.

Not long after New Year's, 1983, Caesar Fortunato was in an elevator with Andy Kushner, going down. Caesar's favorite production assistant had been calling him, repeatedly, asking for a recommendation. Andy was being considered for one of the precious staff jobs. Caesar winced when he saw the kid step into the elevator. He wasn't in a generous mood. He had been forced to New York by another grievance hearing, an incident with a camera guy who got hit by lightning during a golf tournament. Caesar hadn't returned any of Andy's phone calls.

Over the next twenty-five floors and six stops, Andy wavered, thinking to himself, Why bother? But, in the lobby, as Caesar speed-walked his way to the revolving doors, Andy thought of being stuck with his parents for another year . . . of missing trains and sleeping on that fucking couch and trying to shampoo his hair in the men's room sink. He interrupted Caesar just as he was about to hail a cab.

"I can't do anything for you, kid," Caesar said, stepping off the curb onto Sixth Avenue. "I just don't do those things for anyone. You understand? If I do it for you, I have to do it for six other people. I learned my lesson a while ago. Look, I think you did a great job, but I'm not the guy to talk to. Okay?"

Andy persisted. His tolerance for ham-and-cheese had been maximized.

"I did everything you asked, Caesar. Not just for the games. Uh, I'mmm . . . I'm not just anyone."

"Are you threatening me, young man? Are you threatening me? Are you telling me I owe you? I don't owe you. And, you know what? I'm going to do you a favor and forget this fucking conversation."

Caesar was a live director as a teenager. He was never able to sympathize with the ones who came after him, all so unattractively desperate. He denied the presence of the hand of fate in his rise: the disgraced Saturday morning TV star who was his ticket out of Philadelphia. He had mentors as a child and as a man, but never grew capable of playing such a role for another. Worse, others were being pulled into the swirl of his woeful vortex.

"And if you ever . . . if you ever talk about me to anyone, I will make sure you never work in this business. Anywhere."

"Jesus, Caesar, I didn't deserve that. I just need a staff job."

Andy Kushner had committed body and soul, performed a mountain of tasks that had little to do with the actual process of making TV, and once, in Lincoln, Nebraska, put himself in ridiculous peril. He did it all because he believed there existed at the network an unspoken but enforceable contract. One day, there'd be dignity. A clear future.

After Caesar dove into a cab without another word, the widely esteemed but as yet part-time production assistant walked in a daze to Grand Central and caught the 7:16 back to White Plains.

Days in the Life

Not long after bolting from Andy Kushner, still attempting to work up a plausible justification for the wholly evil curbside scene with this decent and devoted young coworker, the cab stopped at a light and provoked a memory he understood immediately to be cruel in its coincidence. They were on Lenny's block, two doors down from the apartment, and so his brain began to rewind, against his will, back to the first time he walked through the door, back when he was a steely, cocksure twentysomething certain he could do anything he wanted with the rest of his life.

"What's his name again? The Beatles' producer?"

In the spring of 1967, one month before the Summer of Love, Caesar had been asked to Leonard Bernstein's thirteen-room Park Avenue duplex for a script conference. The man who epitomized classical music to all of America was going to dissect the rock revolution, at the time viewed by much of the country as loud, electric hippie garbage. Caesar was at a table in a large living room, which featured two grand pianos, each topped with an orderly platoon of family photos. A children's author and young composer were there to help with questions of clarity and musicology. An associate director was clicking a stopwatch, timing Bernstein's readings. Caesar had been asked to sub for the regular director, who was ill.

"He's the one responsible for the high Bach trumpet in 'Penny Lane' . . . that haunting string quartet in 'Eleanor Rigby.'"

"George Martin."

"Right. Thank you . . . Jason, why does our new recruit have this information and you do not?"

Bernstein was ribbing his young composer friend.

"Because you have me here for questions about music history, Lenny, and this is not music history."

"All right then, Jason, how about some Beethoven questions. Name the year in which he penned the famous love letter to his obscure object of desire?"

Caesar beat Jason to the punch.

"1812."

"Who was the love of his life?"

"Antonia Brentano, wife of an Austrian aristocrat. Very married. Very unavailable. Very depressing for Ludwig."

"Jason, our new man is kicking your butt. One more. In what twentieth-century novel does a central character claim Beethoven's music proves God's existence?"

"Aldous Huxley. *Point Counter Point.*"

"Oh, Lenny," said Jason, "I'm not in the mood. I mean, this new stuff. Don't you think this new stuff is trash? I can't believe we're doing a show about it."

"Well, sure, ninety-five percent of it is trash. But the other five percent is actually quite good, particularly the Beatles."

Bernstein wrote every word of the show's first draft, penciling it on a yellow legal pad. This fact alone impressed Caesar, accustomed to talent who couldn't say hello and good-bye unless someone wrote it for them. The revising went on and on, intensely, at successive script sessions. He watched Bernstein challenge himself and everyone else in the room to find language that was at once economical, illuminating, and lyrical. This persisted until the night before the show's taping.

In watching Bernstein work, he thought of a story about Henri Matisse. Sometime in the thirties, Matisse delivered a painting to Dr. Alfred Barnes and was there to see Barnes place it on the wall of his private gallery, whereupon Matisse made a fairly startling request: He wanted to do a touch-up. According to the story that Barnes told Caesar and Mr. Palumbo, Matisse was ready to open up his box of paints, find a stool, and start up again, right in the middle of the day, while people were sauntering about. Barnes succeeded in stopping the artist and in his mind kept him from ruining a masterpiece, by telling Matisse that he was likely to miss the dinner being lovingly prepared by Mrs. Barnes, which would hurt her feelings. There was no such thing as a true deadline for such people, for a Matisse, or a Leonard Bernstein—just an inconvenient stopping point.

"Beethoven was always probing and rejecting," Bernstein was saying one night. "He was dedicated to the principle of inevitability. For reasons unknown to him, he gave away his life and energies just to make sure that one note followed another with complete inevitability."

When the staff met for the fifth or sixth time to review the *Rock Revolution* script, Caesar made the mistake of asking Bernstein why he was spending so much time on a TV show. Caesar understood his own work ethic to be admirable, but this was devotion of a different order.

"Caesar, we strive to do things so they seem as right as rain. It may be an odd way to spend one's life. But you want something to check out . . . maintain a worthy consistency. We should leave our audience with the feeling that we've worked hard to earn their attention and trust."

By his thirtieth birthday, Leonard Bernstein had conducted the New York Philharmonic and composed a ballet, a musical comedy, and two orchestral works. In 1954, he made his first major television appearance, dissecting Beethoven's Fifth. Understanding the potential of putting his audience to sleep in seconds, of the expectation that this new medium was supposed to entertain, he had the entire floor of a television studio painted with the first page of the score, which contained the most famous opening phrase in classical music: three Gs and an E flat. Managing to convey his erudition in a charming fashion, his voice invitingly aristocratic, not pretentious, his manner dripping with enthusiasm, Bernstein would tell the audience how Beethoven had written fourteen different versions of that four-note sequence over eight years until it sounded as right as rain. Twelve musicians, one for each principal instrument used in the piece, were introduced by a spotlight and they took their place in a row, at their appropriate notation, dwarfed by the score. Bernstein showed how Beethoven at first planned to use the vast range of all twelve instruments. After the audience heard flute, oboe, clarinet, bassoon, horn, trumpet, timpani, two violins, viola, cello, and double bass combine, Bernstein told them what they already knew. With this musical dozen, the sound had been somehow feminized. In his words: "It was as if a delicate lady had intruded in a club smoker." He noted that the flute was the leading culprit. This instrument and four others were dismissed, the musicians taking a giant step to their right, off the page. The seven that remained then produced the utterly "masculine utterance" Beethoven took eight years to find.

In the subsequent Young People's Concerts, an incredible fifty-three shows over fourteen years, and with a vast assortment of other musical programming, concluding with the performance of Beethoven's Ninth in Berlin months after the wall tumbled and just months before his death, Bernstein would display not only his genius but his generosity of spirit, which did not go unnoticed by Caesar Fortunato in the sessions at the Park Avenue living room. Bernstein was playing composer, conductor, and teacher, occupying three vocations when there wasn't enough time in his all-too-examined life for one, and bringing to each the same fresh insights, the same uncompromising will, a forcefulness few could match. He was attacking his life at a sprint, blind to the possibility of running out of breath.

In 1961, television was described as a vast wasteland by Newton Minow, chairman of the Federal Communications Commission. This scathing critique had the networks in full knee-jerk mode. One of the beneficiaries was Leonard Bernstein and his televised Young People's

Concerts. An oasis in that vast wasteland, Bernstein's show was moved from Saturday afternoons to prime time. For several years, while the FCC made an issue of bad TV, a mass audience was given a chance to view the young medium's greatest educator. As soon as the FCC looked the other way, however, Bernstein was booted back to public TV.

Many who entered Bernstein's world remained. Caesar Fortunato never broke free of sports television, fattened by the money, seduced by the knowledge that his shows were being watched by millions and millions of people. In truth, a deeper truth Caesar managed to suppress most of the time, broadcasting the really big sports events required a suspension of common sense. They would inevitably become death marches, long days and weeks of elaborate, titanic preparation, adrenaline substituted for sleep, so many blindly falling on their swords, so much yelling and cursing and bad food, so much importance placed upon the coverage of a sport, of an event that had absurdly little effect on that which mattered in life. Having been in the business of big events since its inception, Caesar Fortunato was probably among the first to see the twisted purpose underlying all of it. By the time he was in his forties, frazzled and desensitized, he had spent too much of his life engaged in masturbation on a grand scale, serving in these slightly demented, artificially stimulated, masochistic armies squeezing every possible ounce of entertainment out of games that too often left no mark at all in the collective imagination.

Bernstein liked working with the fill-in director and offered him a steady gig, but it would have meant cutting back on his sports work. Caesar, as much as anyone, understood the virtues of working with Bernstein, a wise man prepared to share, a deeply creative thinker who was going to leave the best kind of legacy, not just his music, but a creed. Every day of his life was a creative act and Leonard Bernstein was showing everyone else how to milk the divine aspects of their humanity. Every day, he was giving to others every man's most precious resource: his time. And Bernstein's time, in several respects, was highly precious. In 1967, Caesar instead chose the new deal Hawas was offering, which allowed the Fortunatos to move east and up, Fifth Avenue, six rooms, seventh floor. It was not far from Lenny's place geographically, but was spiritually in another universe.

The Learning Curved 15

"No, son," his mother said.

He had just sliced into an inviting, still steaming chicken parmigiana.

"Mom, I can't miss practice."

"Well, dear, then you can't play baseball."

Summer and puberty distracted him, days of bursting sunshine that went into night and the chance to see what he could do with this new body. He had just survived the tryouts for the church team, which played a fifty-game, citywide schedule with other parishes. It forced him into a decision he was not ready to make: baseball or piano. It was the allure of the unknown, the camaraderie of peers, simple fun, versus a musical journey of subtle gratifications without an end in sight: more and more intense, insulated afternoons spent on a bench in the Fortunato living room. He had begun to steal glances through the lace curtains. The neighborhood was alive again with the sound of play—homework and school suspended until faraway September.

"I've never missed a lesson. It's just for the season, a couple of months."

"Talk to your coach. I'm sure he'll understand."

"No, he won't."

Caesar's father had been hiding behind an outstretched *Philadelphia Bulletin*.

"Come on, son. The piano is more important right now."

"Dad, it's just for a couple of months."

"You'll have other chances to play baseball."

"Dad, it's a big honor. A lot of kids didn't make it. These are all the best kids. And if I don't play now, they'll get ahead of me."

He was a better-than-average second baseman, an extraordinary pianist aborning, and the music had no chance, especially since just two years before, the Whiz Kids had inflamed the imaginations of every boy in Philadelphia. The summer of 1950 was the longest, happiest summer of his childhood, when the radio was as vital as food and shelter, when the long-futile Phillies went on to win the pennant on the last day of the season, in Brooklyn, at Ebbets Field, against the mythical Dodgers.

This gang of Whiz Kids had nicknames suitable for a team of baseball children, guys called Puddinhead, Putsy, and Swish, but they actually were no babes. They supplemented their athletic achievements with succulent tabloid fodder appropriate for more mature audiences. And being less than innocent made them that much more attractive. Pitcher Russ Meyer, the Mad Monk, had a nose permanently scarred from a bite delivered in a Chicago bar by an offended blonde. Shortstop Granny Hamner, a pro by age seventeen, never reached proper maturity as far as the team was concerned. Once, Granny called the cops on an all-too-obvious private investigator hired by the Phillies, a Charles Leland, who was arrested in front of Hamner's house while traveling with his objectively attractive wife and two loaded revolvers. And then there was first baseman Eddie Waitkus, who had been shot by a lovesick nineteen-year-old named Ruth Ann Steinhagen. She had left

131

him a message at the front desk of the Edgewater Beach Hotel, where the Phillies stayed in Chicago when they played the Cubs. After Waitkus walked into her room, 1279-A, highly curious about this stranger who claimed to have something extremely important to discuss, Steinhagen took a rifle from the closet and shot him once in the stomach. "Oh, baby," he said, widely quoted, "what did you do that for?"

Steinhagen was placed in a mental institution. Waitkus made a hasty recovery and was named Comeback Player of the Year in 1950, helping the Whiz Kids to the pennant.

"I'll practice with you," his father said during that dinner summit to determine the future of Caesar's burgeoning baseball career.

"You never have the time."

"Caesar, don't you think we know what's best for you?"

"Mom, what about what I want?"

"What you want! . . . Do you consider all we've done for you?"

He set down his silverware and engulfed his head in his hands.

"Look at your mother when she speaks to you."

"They're my friends," he said, his words muffled. "I just want to be with my friends."

"Son, Mr. Palumbo is not going to wait around while you go off playing ball with your friends."

"Yes, he will."

"No, I spoke with him. He told me he's spent a lot of time with you and he would be very hurt if you stopped now."

"Mom, you're making that up."

"Excuse me?"

"Mr. Palumbo wouldn't say that."

"Caesar, I don't like your tone."

"I don't like your tone, either."

"After supper, you just go up to your room."

"Bastards."

Caesar was flat on the kitchen floor almost as soon as the word left his mouth. He saw his father preparing to deliver another blow and he instinctively covered his eyes. He heard his mother sobbing and then the back door slamming. His father had never hit him like that before, and he never would again.

Maria Fortunato knew that her son had a genuine attachment to the music and it would have been sensible to let him indulge his athletic crush. She and her husband had turned the issue into a test of will, and the boy, in the first major confrontation of his adolescence, wanted victory at any price. The situation called for patience by the adults, of which there was far too little. Her guilt never subsided after she saw her son knocked to the floor by his father. Afterward, their marriage faltered and she came to apologize to the boy in her own way, by treating him like a prince, even when he became a man.

Sal Fortunato, a cop who brought the job home, also harbored an unspoken dread about the growing conflagration. He couldn't bring himself to tell his thirteen-year-old boy just how much pleasure his music provided after a day too full of broken people explaining the unexplainable. Sal Fortunato would be sitting in the kitchen, coffee after dinner, two spoons into a dish of comforting ice cream, the sports section spread before him, and he'd smile, soften, relax while his son somehow made sense of another incomprehensible squiggle of notes.

One of the pieces Caesar had recently learned was the gorgeous and lush *Fountains of Rome*. Sal Fortunato had seen pictures of Rome, and the Respighi symphony made him think of the crinkled, yellowing black-and-white photos of his aunts and uncles, and the postcards he had seen of the Spanish Steps, the Trevi Fountains, St. Peter's, and the Sistine Chapel. The music—his son's music—took him to a better place. After fucking with the scum of the earth, wearied by the rage required to keep the peace, this was more than a small blessing.

Even at thirteen, even though he was blinded by baseball, Caesar sensed that he might be giving away something he couldn't reclaim. He had spent half his life training his hands. One week away from the piano required two weeks of recovery to restore what the hands had learned. This he knew from breaks during the holidays. In a way, it was a continuing athletic test, developing a fitness, a memory for your fingers, so that they could be ready for anything, so that they could dance with Chopin, plunge into Joplin, soar with Ravel.

There was this, too: The piano, unlike most other instruments, allowed you to see a very big picture, scary but grand. A drum and a trumpet and a saxophone, and the rest of the strings and brass and winds, were accessories. The piano allowed an unmatched freedom of expression. It was the composer's starting point, the means to make a sound complete, articulate the essence of a creative vision. Until he started fielding grounders with a precocious alacrity and swatting balls over the heads of outfielders, until the metamorphosis of puberty, the boy foresaw the man in a concert hall, praised for producing a sound never heard before. Then the cuffs of his pants began rising, T-shirts tightening . . . five inches, twenty-five pounds.

He recalled his visits to Shibe Park, home of the Phillies, that separate world, a swath of emerald green, so unexpected and so welcome, set as it was in the midst of the city's lifeless, relentless concrete. For the typical American boy in the middle of the century, no piece of architecture had the power of a ballpark. Further, his stadium was occupied by Whiz Kids. Caesar lied to himself: The piano could wait.

A few weeks into the standoff, he walked into his teacher at the neighborhood grocery store. Mr. Palumbo spoke first.

"Will you wait for a moment? I'm just getting a few things."

Caesar nodded. By this point, it was instinct to do as Mr. Palumbo commanded. For almost five years, they had been engaged in an undeclared joint project to make him a great musician. Caesar waited, pacing outside the store, hands in his pockets, fearful his friends might spy him.

"So I've lost you to baseball."

"Uh, this doesn't have anything to do with you, Mr. Palumbo. I mean, you're not the reason I quit. I mean, I didn't want to quit."

"No, this isn't about me. And it isn't about your parents, although I'm sure they have expressed their disappointment emphatically."

Caesar chuckled.

"I haven't praised you very often, and maybe I should have. But I thought I would be with you a long time, at least a few more years. I thought there would be time for all that. But maybe there isn't. And I don't want this to sound like you have to come back to me. . . ."

134

This quelled Caesar's fidgeting. He had never heard an adult so clearly confess to a shortcoming.

"You're one of the best students I've ever had, because you give something of yourself to the music. This is very rare for someone your age. You take risks all the time, exposing yourself, showing through the music who you are. . . . If you need a break, good. Take a break. But don't wait too long, please. Play without me. Just play. Or come over to my house. We can keep it a secret from your parents. Remember, this is just about you. This is something you do for yourself. All right?"

Mr. Palumbo paused and tried to find Caesar's eyes, but the boy's head remained tilted to the sidewalk. Mr. Palumbo was not going to have another like him, this he knew. His wife, so weary of the winters, was all but packed for Florida. She had been begging for years. And there was a younger teacher at the high school who was soon going to replace him.

"So much will change, Caesar, I swear, listen to me. So much will change, people will always be disappointing you. But, listen, the music is a friend, a loyal friend. And it will be with you always, and it will nourish your heart. It's a gift, that's what you have, and I know you must know it. And my wish is that you will nurture this gift all your life. Capisce?"

Sensing his teacher had concluded his appeal, Caesar raised his head.

"Okay . . . okay, Mr. Palumbo."

He wished he had heard more conviction in Caesar's voice. It was too much to expect one so young to have the twenty-twenty foresight of an old man who had spent a life judging musical ability.

"By the way, you've very close on the Scarlatti. Watch the sixteenths, and you still need a little more work on your fourth and fifth fingers, all right? They're still not strong enough. Grip that rubber ball I gave you. Remember, the piano is not just a mental activity."

"Thanks, Mr. Palumbo. It's nice, what you've said."

"What position are you playing on the church team?"

"Second base."

"Be careful of those hands. . . . And, Caesar, please, wear a batting glove, okay?"

* * *

135

Caesar was made to desire an elevated legacy as a child, when Mr. Palumbo gently preached the value of art and leaps of faith. Later, he'd work with a composer who had very much incorporated those notions into his personal creed. Christos sought mental clarity the way Caesar courted distraction. He made his music in a barely furnished cottage well below his means on a squiggly street in the Hollywood Hills. To compose, he became a hermit. He had learned how to work fourteen hours a day, day after day, month after month. He told Caesar that he didn't always get things done, that there were many frustrating days with little production, but he stayed put. The inspiration eventually materialized. Christos would lose weight, ignore his appearance, watch his easily bronzed Mediterranean skin whiten, subsist on cigarettes, coffee, and Cheerios, cut off contact with friends and family. This was what he needed to do to make something out of nothing.

They were together on one amazing night in Istanbul. Christos asked Caesar to set up the show. It was a ridiculously dangerous enterprise, certain to stir regional enmity as deep as the irrational divide that separated Catholics and Protestants in Northern Ireland, Muslims and Hindus on the Indian subcontinent, Jews and Arabs in Israel, Serbs and everyone else occupying the explosive peninsula once known as Yugoslavia.

After leaving Greece as a teenager, and writing his own version of the American success story, Christos decided to stage the first-ever concert at Hagia Sophia, the Church of Divine Wisdom, an ancient Greek Orthodox cathedral built in the fifth century by Emperor Justinian. To Greeks, especially the devout, the site was an old wound: The Turks had desecrated the holiest of their holy sites by turning it into a mosque. Christos himself was from a town in southern Greece famous for having resisted the Turks during the nation's successful battle for independence in the nineteenth century. But his music was built on the framework of rhythms and textures shared across the Middle East by many a warring clan, and Christos knew he was immensely popular in Turkey, despite his heritage, and this fact confirmed his deep-seated belief in music's unifying power. Christos sincerely believed he could go to Turkey and be a healing force and live to tell about it.

136

Caesar went into the project with the notion that his temerity was unchallenged. Two weeks before the show, when the promoter in Turkey said the required permit wouldn't be forthcoming unless he received an additional fee of $100,000, Christos told Caesar to fire the fucking thief. Unbowed, Christos retreated to his hotel suite and worked the phones. The ashtray became a heap of cigarettes. A bottle of Finnish vodka was drained. As Caesar watched, Christos journeyed into a jungle of red tape. He contacted an influential local travel agent, a sympathetic reporter, a former Cabinet official. The foreign minister's office became involved. Two unidentified males telephoned death threats. By nightfall, Christos had his permit.

One week before the show, when Christos decided the orchestra he had hired was unsatisfactory, he told Caesar to find him another. Fortunately, the London Symphony wasn't doing anything that weekend.

On the night it finally came together, in his accustomed position cutting cameras before a wall of monitors, Fortunato was helping a talented friend who had been able to summon a supreme level of courage and faith in his music and this project, and he was deeply jealous. This was once his own firmly held ambition: to originate, perform, not to be the timid soul watching others claim their destinies. Even as a celebrated TV producer and director, he was yet a spectator. Always the one watching, not the doer.

Christos was justifiably proud. He was in the land of his enemies, a star, playing with one of the world's revered architectural masterpieces as his backdrop, his mother and father and sister and brother there to applaud his mission and his gumption, applaud what he had made of himself, to listen, along with ten thousand Turks, to music that cleverly incorporated and modernized an ancient sound familiar to the sons and daughters of Istanbul and Athens. The whole night seemed like a long standing ovation.

For Christos, art was about order, on several levels. They had many conversations about this—about how difficult it was to unscramble the imagination, about the difficulty of separating the many unfruitful beginnings from the rare plum of a great notion. And for Christos, the pursuit of his own creativity imbued his days with a kind of moral imperative. Getting started was the hard part. Then, once an idea had promise, it became a companion, a jealous companion demanding attention, insisting on nourishment. It was like having an intense conversation with someone who never tired.

On the way back from Turkey, he spent a few days relaxing with Christos in Greece. He had already heard about the father who bought a piano when the family had nothing, the father who had denied himself so much in doing so, even sacrificing his regular visit to the café for a five-cent cup of espresso. Dmitri Katakalidis did not expect his children to make a life in music, only that they would somehow be better for having had the experience. Together, during long afternoons on the balcony of the beach house Christos had proudly, gratefully bought for his parents, they played poker and backgammon and relished slow sunsets over a wide bay.

"You need more rest."

"Papa, enough."

"Caesar, what did you do to my son?"

"Papa, leave us alone."

"Look at both of you. I'm eighty years old and I could kick your ass."

In Greece, Caesar saw a son and father who were each other's best friend. He saw why Christos was able to trust his imagination, compose something out of nothing, why he possessed such a formidable will, such indomitable confidence. This was a boy who had been loved unconditionally.

"Don't get up from the table."

The boy froze.

In that essential summer at the Fortunato residence, 25 Bullock, it was week five of the standoff. And with reason still in retreat, there was a final groundbreaking dinner.

"This is what's going to happen," said the father. "Look at me. I will go with you to baseball and tell the coach you are leaving the team."

The boy's head dropped, mostly so his parents wouldn't see his tears and hear his sniffling.

"Then you're going back to the piano. There's no discussion about this. Understand? . . ."

The boy remained silent.

"UNDERSTAND?"

"No, I don't understand."

"You WILL get smacked. All I want to hear is the word 'yes.'"

The boy didn't respond.

"EXCUSE ME?"

"This is just such bullshit," he said, head down, barely audible.

Sal Fortunato raised his right hand to strike but dropped it quickly, splattering his coffee cup against the wall.

By the end of that week, the piano had been sold.

Live to Tape

His affection for Sinatra swelled as his money, self-respect, and well-being were vanishing. After another dark Saturday, after another toe-to-toe with Lynette, he'd turn to Frank for a reason to keep going. It was the summer of 1996, on the eve of the conventions, the eve of another Olympics, another football season, and no one had asked him to take part in any of it. Maybe they heard about his little incident. That's what he tried to make himself believe. That's why the phone wasn't ringing.

Caesar Fortunato was under house arrest, not so much by doctor's orders but his wife's. He was recuperating from a self-inflicted coronary event, which alerted him to the astonishing fact of his mortality. Instead of Las Vegas therapy, complimentary fellating for every fortune lost, he had to settle for crooning at the stars, Sinatra recordings being sent out into the twinkling night sky on the outdoor speakers while he lounged and stared heavenward during long, slow drunks, courtesy of vodka made in Russia.

By this point, the big networks and newspapers around the country were readying their Sinatra obituaries. Like Caesar Fortunato, Frank Sinatra was ailing. Neither had worked regularly in two years. About the same time as Caesar's Disney debacle, the spring of 1994, Sinatra fell on a stage in Richmond, Virginia. Everyone wanted to put him in a hospital, but he successfully protested, told them all no fucking way, and got on his private jet, longing for the comfort of a cigarette and a waiting glass of whisky made in America and the peace he had long found at his home in the desert. That flight back to Rancho Mirage turned out to be the last leg of his final road trip. Sinatra became a pampered prisoner, finding that his once indomitable will was at last surrendering to the effort, to the hours, to the all too many nights of smoking and drinking and incurable restlessness.

Director and legend lived two miles apart, one inside a gated compound, the other with a compound all to his own. Aside from a memorable chance encounter, they were not in similar social universes, not really fellow travelers, not really made of the same thing, but in Caesar's mind, he and Frank were the same guy. They took the blows and did it their way.

Born with his own scarlet letter, a name that ended in a vowel, later a comet that was grounded at thirty-four, Frank Sinatra's voice was enriched by indignation and lessons learned. And unlike the vast majority of pop acts in the latter half of the twentieth century, he sang with a writer's reverence for language, worked it with the same verve he applied to chasing the most coveted objects of the opposite sex. There was a story behind every song and they made sense, wonderful sense. It was more like narration put to music. Sinatra's keyboard was the alphabet. Every sentence, every word, every letter was an opportunity to tell the story better, to make the connection between his voice and your world. And it was delivered with a devotion to diction that, once upon a time, Catholic school nuns preaching the fundamentals figuratively— and literally—beat into the unwilling souls of first-graders everywhere.

Frank Sinatra was talking about lost loves, and late-night drinking, and celebrating life lived without regret. He sang like he knew, which he did. Caesar Fortunato knew that in 1950 Frank opened his mouth at the Copa and nothing came out, and then he got divorced by his first wife . . . and by his record label and movie studio. After repairing his throat with a forty-day vow of silence, Sinatra retraced his steps, rebuilt his career small gig by small gig, and in two years was working with Nelson Riddle and shooting *From Here to Eternity* in Hawaii, a movie that produced an Oscar for Best Supporting Actor and certified his comeback.

By the second Stoli, he would be prepared to receive any form of encouragement, and the voice of Sinatra would produce, at his best summoning for Caesar the nights when there was just enough of everything: wine, conversation, lovemaking. Caesar never felt any better about tomorrow, or a rash of bad yesterdays, but Frank made the moment bearable, and the next, and the one after that. And if he kept drinking, he never got past the moments. The wreckage was building and Caesar had to find ways to forgive himself, or at the very least forget.

After months of promising, Palmer Nash had managed to get him a couple of high-paying jobs. Though they had enabled Caesar to rescue his standard of living from fast-approaching bankruptcy, each experience had its drawbacks. These were some of the memories Sinatra was successfully keeping in the rearview mirror. For the first time, Caesar directed a commercial and a music video. Both jobs were killers, one sapping his reason to live, the other ending prematurely with a famous rap producer kneeling on his chest, performing cardiopulmonary resuscitation.

He got the commercial because Palmer Nash was so good at shading the truth.

"You're Antonio."

"What?"

"That's your middle name, right?"

"No, it's Anthony."

"Right, but that doesn't sound as sexy as Antonio."

"I will not do this."

"Then you will not get this job. I'm sorry, but it's got to be this way."

"No. No fucking way."

"You're getting fifteen thousand dollars a day."

"Okay."

So he was just off the boat, Antonio, an alleged Milan-based director who had won at Cannes. Caesar did have a trophy with the word "Cannes" inscribed on it and, underneath, the vague addition of "Grand Prix." The intertwining couple on top was a little suspicious, but this wasn't an Oscar or Emmy, which was a good thing. No one knew what a trophy from Cannes looked like, or, for that matter, if there even was one. Palmer Johnson assumed with a high measure of confidence that no one would ever probe far enough to find out that his Antonio was an American citizen living two hours outside of Los Angeles and that his trophy from Cannes classified him as a one-time successful soft-core porn director, a winner at the X d'Or, which took place a week after the famous film festival. The event honored the world's best erotic and pornographic work. Caesar's film was called *Love or Lust*. It was the one he had made using company money and personnel while working at the Indy 500.

After a run of acclaimed Hollywood films were shot or directed by men born elsewhere, by guys named Milos and Janusz and Vittorio, it had come to be assumed that foreigners were essentially more artistic. When they pointed a camera, the film came out looking as if it should be hanging on the wall of a museum. There was only one Milos and one Janusz and one Vittorio, but suddenly their fellow expatriates were benefiting from a kind of halo effect. Several of Palmer's clients had changed their names after watching foreigners of equal or lesser talent gain greater employment and command higher salaries.

"Add an 'o' to the end of your name," one told Palmer, "and add a zero to the end of your paycheck."

So Caesar Antonio Fortunato went to work, in a very foreign world. The product in question was a new entry in the cola wars. Gem was slightly sweeter than Pepsi and not as fizzy as Coke. It made Caesar think of the flat taste of cans left opened in the fridge, buried behind the butter, carbonation ebbing away. Palmer had convinced the soda people they were fortunate to have Antonio, who normally didn't do such things, which was true, and who had agreed to work at a discount: six figures, not the usual six zeroes.

At first, it seemed absurd. He was going to make half a year's salary for one 30-second commercial. Caesar was accustomed to producing volume, to getting beat up. He was used to decathlons, punishing workloads. He'd done fifteen hours of TV a day for seventeen days at several Olympics; shot *Love or Lust* in two weeks, at night. He had been in the directing chair, aggravating his hemorrhoids, from sunrise to sunset, day after day, week after week. He was capable of making a thousand creative decisions in the space of an hour. And here was this nutty job, where they were giving him a month to shoot a couple of kids playing beach volleyball and drinking soda.

"Who cut my bagel? Why are the bagels cut?"

As soon as shooting began, he had trouble keeping track of all the hovering, self-important people. All of them made suggestions. None of them was in charge. All were experts at making semi-valid proposals. All were able to deftly defer when it was time to make a decision. Caesar constantly felt as if he was playing a kind of hellish tennis game where no points were ever scored. It was just serve and return. He'd serve, they'd return. Then he'd serve again, and they'd return. There was no resolution in this surreal game of back and forth.

"I assume you guys want to shoot at sunset. Right?"

"It's a good idea. Let's talk about that."

"Well, we need to know by tomorrow."

"Sure. Who else have you spoken with?"

Some worked for the manufacturer. Some for the ad agency. Some for the production company that had been hired by the agency. Some were freelancers of no clear association. They all carried themselves with an air of importance. They all looked as if they were in charge. Three weeks into the project, new faces were still showing up, like this woman who was having the fit about the bagels, a display that Caesar secretly admired, given his own history of exploding over inadequate food preparation. Perhaps the bagel lady, dressed in tasteful, tailored gray flannel, was really in charge, though a guy named Bob told him it was a guy named Phil.

"I need to speak to someone about these bagels, right now!"

"You don't want them cut? Doesn't that make it easier for you?"

"Who are you?"

"I'm the director."

"Oh, hi. I'm Susan Smith, public relations. Your name again?"

"Antonio."

"Oh, yes . . . right. You know, you don't sound Italian."

"I spent some time in the States."

"Right. The problem with cutting the bagels is they start to get stale right away. I mean, feel this one. It's already getting kind of hard and crusty. Do you know who I can speak to about this?"

On day two of the principal photography, three weeks earlier, they had to do everything all over. Roberto, the DP, was shooting out of focus. Roberto was, in a former life, Robby Vesco from Brooklyn. He needed glasses, had known it since he casually ran over a raccoon and found out later it was the neighbor's cat. But Roberto, the *artista* from Italy, couldn't possibly ever need glasses. After the first day fuckup, Roberto allowed Antonio to check each shot in the viewfinder before they rolled film.

They spent two days shooting the actors, three days shooting the bottle of Gem, which was the real star. At sunset, everyone would be ready for the closing product shot, Gem perched on a boulder being washed by waves and, it was hoped, framed by a golden hue. The problem was the soda's transparency. In the fading light, Gem looked more like chocolate syrup or molasses, not a refreshing drink for a busy day at the beach. Kit, the density expert, had brought several bottles of diluted Gem. On day three, after experimenting with ninety-percent Gem and sixty-percent Gem, they found a winner in Kit's seventy-five-percent Gem: three parts soda, one part water. Just before another day was lost, in the twilight's last gleaming, Roberto was able to roll off ten solid minutes of this version of water-diluted Gem, the now modified liquid inside the bottle being favorably enhanced by the sun's glistening rays—the counterfeit the more worthy in close-up, more inviting than the real thing.

"I don't like the blue."

It wasn't the bagel lady, who after getting her bagels whole said nothing else. And it wasn't one of five other people who had made suggestions, not decisions, during the edit. The voice asking about blue hadn't said anything before. Until then, he had just watched, sunk in a couch at the back, rolling something incessantly in his right hand, à la Queeg from *The Caine Mutiny*.

"Can we do something about the blue. It looks like Pepsi blue."

"Well," said Caesar, and paused. It was a safety measure. He wished he could scream at this son of a bitch in full roar the way he had screamed at so many others in almost forty years of television, most of them not anywhere near the level of imbecility of this pasty-looking fart in the back of the room. But in this situation, he was meant to serve, whoever that was. "Sir, um, the water is blue, and all water is blue, and you can't make water any other color than blue, or it will not look like water."

"But it looks like Pepsi blue."

"Excuse me, sir. Who are you?"

"Phil. Phil Bennett."

"Oh . . . so you're the guy in charge."

"I suppose."

"I tell you what, Mr. Bennett. We can bleach it a little, okay?"

"Okay."

Hours later, Phil had another comment.

"That girl looks Japanese."

"Well, Phil, I can assure you she's an American."

"No, I don't mean that. I mean she looks like she could be from Japan."

"And . . ."

"Well, that's a big, big problem."

"Why is that?"

"Well, the Chinese hate the Japanese. We won't be able to show this commercial in China. And that's a pretty big market to alienate, you know?"

"And Phil, somebody is telling me about this now?"

"Well, can't we fix it?"

"What, take the slant out of her eyes?"

"Yeah."

"No, Phil, we can't do that. But we can reshoot the whole fucking commercial. We can do that. Bring everyone back, except our Japanese girl, and shoot the whole thing over. And while we're at it, Phil, we can spend another week trying to get the fucking bottle just right, and maybe we can dye the ocean, so it's not Pepsi blue."

"Uh-uh-uh . . . umm . . . excuse me, please."

About a half hour later, Phil's absence was noted by one of the junior suggestion makers. The edit facility organized a small search team and found him in a supply closet, his face almost flat against a corner. Caesar later learned that Phil, the guy who was truly in charge, the one paying the bills, hadn't been in the office for almost six months. Until his appearance at the Gem edit, he had been afraid to leave his home. Phil Bennett, senior vice president for creative affairs at Global Commerce, the makers of Gem, had recently produced a very expensive but unsuccessful Super Bowl ad. He had sent a team to the top of Everest, where they were to be shown live drinking the company's answer to Gatorade. Everyone loved the idea until two of the climbers threw up. The fallout caused Phil to develop agoraphobia, and Caesar's minor tantrum had swiftly undone the progress made in therapy and plunged Phil into his abject fear of being helpless in an embarrassing or inescapable situation. Phil was still there, being counseled by a psychologist, when the bloated edit suite emptied out, the commercial put to bed. There were no more suggestions.

"Rewind, muthafucka!"

This was how it ended, or at least what he remembered of it. Ahmad Rachman, part of Fred D. Lite's posse and executive producer of the music video, was screaming at the editor, demanding that he rewind the tape faster. This was not possible.

"Big guy, that's as fast as this thing goes."

"You fucking with me?"

"No."

"Don't be fucking with me!"

Rachman was deep into a bottle of Bacardi and not interested in logic. He pulled out his nine-millimeter Smith & Wesson and put a bullet through a monitor.

"If you don't rewind faster, Mr. Editor, there's going to be a bullet through your head!"

The editor wet his pants, dropped to the floor, and rolled underneath the console.

"Oh, I'm only kidding. Come on, muthafucka, let's get back to work."

Caesar was also on the floor, right hand squeezing left nipple.

"What's wrong with you?" Rachman asked a shuddering Caesar.

"I think this muthafucka is having a muthafuckin' heart attack," a posse member offered.

"Call 911!" Rachman ordered. "Shit, shit. We cannot have this man dying right here. Someone will blame us."

Ahmad Rachman, who had been a lifeguard and was versed in the various life-saving techniques, straddled the man he believed to be named Antonio, checked his carotid pulse, found nothing, began rescue breathing, a little clumsily at first, then locked his hands as prescribed and began pumping, with meaning, fifteen chest compressions for every two full breaths.

"You gonna break all of the muthafucka's ribs, Ahmad."

"Shut the fuck up."

"Your breath is gonna kill this old white man."

"Listen, muthafucka, after I kill him, I'm going to kill you. Did you call 911, like I told you?"

"Yes, nigga. The ambulance is on the way. But all they gonna find is one super dead Italian guy."

Like most everyone else in the entertainment world, Caesar Fortunato was coked out by the mid-eighties, in search of a less problematic high. Of course, it had to reach epidemic proportions for people like Caesar Fortunato, and eventually the body count was noticeable; cocaine was the ultimate fatal attraction. In response, the leading South American producers courted a new generation of users by increasing the supply and improving the product. The business plan worked. Crack, the new super-high-test premium cocaine, was made absurdly affordable. It could be had for the cost of two draft beers. The short but intense rush of pleasure was unequaled by any other drug.

Inadvertently, Caesar experienced this high. One of the posse had given him a seriously boosted homemade cigarette, the tobacco snow-capped with the shavings of an immensely potent crack cookie, the coke having been baked into a small uneven block. Years before, Caesar had been a champion snorter, but in the seventies, it was truly buyer beware. The cocaine was always cut with other foreign substances: baking soda, flour mix, a dealer's dandruff, anything that was white and fluffy. One night, Caesar had put nothing but baby powder up his nose. He suspected the cigarette from his hip-hop buddies might have been altered, but as yet his body had not proven vulnerable to any substance made by man. So he took a puff. In the first instant, he was the king of the world, omnipotent, infallible, supremely delighted. Then his heart went on a gallop, like a thoroughbred being whipped to the finish.

Until he slipped off the couch in the edit suite and slumped to the floor and lost consciousness, he had been having a good time, which was no small surprise. Rap was beneath his contempt and beyond his understanding. The songs, as far as he knew, described a fundamentally corrupt world without hope, where the black man was an endangered species, the target of a vast white conspiracy. Caesar had played with black athletes, become friendly with black entertainers in his work, had come to believe in the essential righteousness of the civil rights movement, of the need to recognize America's sorry racist past and the need to rectify it. But this music he found insanely counterproductive. In his mind, it preached hate and materialism, said that it was the duty of all young brothers to accumulate luxury automobiles, ostentatious jewelry, and large-bottomed bitches until that one inevitable day when a cop shot them in the back. Caesar Fortunato agreed to become a participant in the promotion of this music, which he considered ugly and degenerate, because without money he could not do that ugly and degenerate thing that had come to be the point of his existence: gambling.

"Caesar, the lynching isn't over. You know the story of Adam and Eve. Well, let me remind you about Clarence and Anita."

Fred D. Lite was phoning, being heard over a speaker. He was unable to attend the edit because he had just begun a two-year sentence for assault and was now residing at the Sing Sing Correctional Facility in Ossining, New York. With Fred D., it wasn't a case of art imitating life. They were really one and the same. He had more war stories than most vets. Bullet fragments that floated yet in his right shoulder and left leg set off metal detectors everywhere.

"It's okay for the black man to be a performing minstrel, to entertain the white man with his skills. It's okay for him to be dunking and making dance music. But we don't want a nigga with any power on the Supreme Court. No, that shit's too funky. So, we'll let Clarence have the job, but in the meantime, we'll have some 'ho show up and say he peppered Coke cans with his long, black pubic hairs. That he was just another nigga with only one thing on his mind: pussy. Because that's all the nigga's brain can really focus on: pussy. But there's no way the U-nited States Congress would ever do that to a white man, ever allow some 'ho to show up complaining that some white man was rapping with her about some porno video and shit. Fuck no! All white men are entitled to be pussy-hoppers because their brains are different. They can walk and think about pussy at the same time. Know what I mean?"

By this time, by the time Fred D. Lite was sharing another tidbit of his worldview with Caesar, they had bonded. It started on a basketball court in Washington, D.C., where the video was being filmed. Fred D. was a few weeks from his sentence hearing. He challenged Caesar to a shooting contest, unaware that this ostensible Italian-born director was actually once a college basketball star in the USA. Ten shots from the top of the key.

Fred D. fashioned himself a pretty good basketballer. He mentioned frequently that he had once blocked a shot by Dennis Rodman during a celebrity game, though he usually did not talk of the postscript, how Rodman provided subsequent unsolicited dental work, a well-placed elbow that dislodged one of the rapper's front teeth. Fred D. made seven of ten shots from the top of the key and assumed he had the competition won. They had bet a thousand dollars, or as Fred D. put it, "ten Benjamins." Caesar shot quickly, using a style long gone: two hands on the ball, feet never leaving the ground. The set shot passed away about the same time as Caesar's stillborn career, back in the fifties, and he was never a set shooter himself. But he had adopted the technique for one-on-one shooting contests like these, which he often solicited and always welcomed, had used this unfashionable, ungainly method to attract the overconfident, the classic suckers—an old hoops

150

shark who would again and again separate the all too presumptuous from a pocketful of cash. Fred D. became another astonished victim, even more so because of Antonio's ostensible point of origin.

"I didn't know they could shoot like that in fucking Italy. Shit, if the guineas had a few more guys like you, they could beat the fucking Dream Team! Are you sure you're I-talian?"

He won a total of ten thousand dollars from Fred D. Lite. The venue for the final competition was a Georgetown bar with a pop-a-shot machine. The film crew and posse were in attendance, loaded and loud, and they looked on in wonder as Caesar scored ninety-six points, which was thirty-eight baskets in sixty seconds, each basket being worth a bonus three points in the last twenty seconds. When Fred D. Lite took his turn and saw there was no chance of matching the performance, he began playing pop-a-shot with the nearby furniture.

Caesar came to decide that Fred D.'s life was not any more adventurous or dysfunctional than most of the pop artists he had known or read about. Bing Crosby, the first recording superstar, was a lousy father, abused his kids, went to make a picture in France while his first wife was dying, and in that hysterical era of Prohibition, spent thirty days in jail for possession of alcohol. Elvis Presley's first great love was a child and his relentless pill popping was the cause of his premature death. The Beatles admitted that hallucinogens played an important role in their magical mystery tour. And his beloved Sinatra was often the definition of belligerence.

Caesar found out that Fred D. was more worried about being capped by one of his own than any whitey, did not always sing about killing cops or big-bottomed bitches, and that some of his music was tolerable, if not authentically creative. The music video was for a new song, "Increase the Peace." It was filmed at night, against the floodlight-bathed Capitol, White House, and monuments to Washington, Jefferson, and Lincoln. The musical foundation was a sample from Steely Dan's "Do It Again," a top-ten hit from the seventies that employed entrancing, exotic-sounding percussion and an electric sitar that rocked out. Fred D. Lite had reached a stage where he was looking for an escape from the carnage. All rappers died young, and he feared that he'd never see his children grow up.

You could be . . .
one for hi-story . . .
Increase the peace
erase the hate . . .
make your world . . .
a loving place.

One besotted night, after another private performance under the stars by Frank, he went to the cabinet containing his
old tapes and shuttled them in and out of the VHS. The commercial he
had just done didn't belong to him, and it would never find its way into
the cabinet. Nor would the music video. Too many others had shaped
those recent jobs. The music video wasn't his idea. He just helped exe-
cute it. The commercial was a typical horror show of creativity by committee, which was an oxymoron. Creativity by committee was a process
whereby people of lesser abilities took one person's idea and perverted
it, smothered it with self-aggrandizing opinions of no merit, and, in
total, produced something half-baked that looked as undistinguished, as
forgettable as the thousands of other products produced by committee.
Though most of the best work in film and TV and theater and music
was the result of one mind working alone, or a very small group of creative equals, business executives and their associates all too often chose
to insert themselves and their associates into work that they could never
summon from their inadequate brains and only made worse. They
couldn't have cared less that this made good work all but impossible. But
they should have figured out that it was bad for business.

Among Caesar's favorite tapes was the opening tease to the 1992
Barcelona Olympics. After the fiasco in 1988 at Seoul, where he was
given the coordinating producer job but imploded like a collapsing
supernova, he was back to being only a director and was also given the
inglorious task of cutting features for the preview show, a program that
required a great deal of labor but did not generate a large viewership,
or any sort of appraisal from the press. Having Caesar do the preview
show was Kapp's idea, another salvo in the scheme to convince his
most expensive employee to up and quit.

The preview show, an excuse to sell commercials, was scheduled two days before the Opening Ceremony, before America was really ready to watch the Games. Caesar was left alone, and he enjoyed this increasingly rare run of freedom. Barcelona was the Olympics of the New World Order. Since Seoul, global politics had been in a welcome free fall. The bad guys were out. The good guys were in. He went to his friend Christos, whose bold orchestrations often enhanced images of athletes in action, and he asked him to write an original piece of music to capture the smiling strut of this new liberated world. A high-end production house in Los Angeles constructed the opening scene using the latest special effects software, the earth spinning in space and steadily approaching the viewer, a spectacular splash of color in the consuming deep black.

IN THE HEAVENS, IT IS JUST A SPECK . . .
BUT OUT HERE IN THE COLD AND DARK, IT'S ALSO AN OASIS . . .
THE GREEN AND BLUE A SIGN THAT HERE'S A PLACE INVIGORATED BY
    LIFE . . .
A PLACE WHERE DEATH IS ALWAYS FOLLOWED BY BIRTH . . .
A PLACE THEN OF UNENDING CHANGE.

ON OCTOBER 2, 1988, THE OLYMPIC FLAME WAS EXTINGUISHED IN
    SEOUL.
ON THAT DAY, AS THE GAMES CONCLUDED, THERE WAS NO SUGGESTION,
    NOT A HINT OF WHAT WAS TO COME . . .

WHO COULD HAVE SEEN HOW QUICKLY THE SOVIET STATES WOULD
    COME APART . . .
HOW ABRUPTLY GERMANY WOULD REUNITE . . .
HOW IT WOULD COME TO PASS THAT A VERY TENTATIVE HEALING
    WOULD BEGIN IN SOUTH AFRICA . . .
HOW SO MANY BORDERS ELSEWHERE WOULD BE ERASED OR
    REDRAWN . . .
HOW SO MANY PEOPLE WOULD SEEK TO ASSERT AND REDEFINE THEM-
    SELVES.

NOW IN THE SUMMER OF 1992, IN THIS WORLD WHERE NATIONS RISE
AND FALL IN A MATTER OF WEEKS, THERE IS—AT LEAST IN THIS
SPOT—A BRIEF RESPITE FROM THE TURMOIL . . .
IT IS TIME AGAIN TO CONVENE THE WORLD'S YOUTH . . .
THE OLYMPICS HAVE COME TO . . .
BARCELONA . . .

From the 3-D graphics of a spinning earth, the tease shifted into audacious aerial photography. Caesar had gone up in a helicopter and shamed
his Spanish pilot into getting perilously close to the mountains along the
country's northern coast. The shots made it look as if the bottom of the
helicopter had almost grazed the peaks, which was not an illusion.

ALONG THE COSTA BRAVA . . .
IN A SETTING OF CENTURIES-OLD LANDMARKS AND ENDURING
BELIEFS . . .
THE WORLD WILL GATHER FOR SIXTEEN DAYS . . .
AND ANOTHER CITY WILL BE TOUCHED BY THE ENCHANTMENT ONLY AN
OLYMPICS CAN PROVIDE . . .
BARCELONA . . .

Next, Caesar inserted some of the best film from Olympics past,
clips from Leni Riefenstahl's ode to the bodies beautiful in Berlin, the
teenage decathlete Bob Mathias posed to throw the javelin, an event
that hearkened back to the ancient Games, and Taiwan's C. K. Yang,
in Kodachrome, cutting the tape in the 100-meter sprint, his head moving furiously left and right, the whole body in complete exertion.

IN ATHENS AND PARIS, LONDON AND LOS ANGELES, THE OLYMPICS HAVE
ALWAYS DRAWN THOSE WHO DARE TO DREAM . . . WHO DARE TO TRY . . .

He insisted that his production assistants find the best iso shots of the
current Olympic stars. He wanted brilliant close-ups. Exultation. Despair.
Tears of joy. He wanted great live photography. And his young brigade,
inspired into diligence, found Mike Powell, arms windmilling after breaking Bob Beamon's forbidding, twenty-year-old long jump record . . . and

pole vaulter Sergei Bubka, a study in power and composure catapulting himself twenty feet in the air . . . and sprinter Michael Johnson shedding a fulsome droplet after winning his first world championship.

AND NOW, IN BARCELONA, THE NEXT GENERATION HAS ASSEMBLED . . .
THEIR MOMENT IS HERE . . .
THEIR PIECE OF HISTORY AWAITS . . .

The news footage was the easiest. He asked for the sledgehammers in Berlin, Mandela released from prison, Lenin dismounted and pulverized.

AS WALLS CRUMBLE . . .
AS PEOPLE CRY FOR FREEDOM . . .
AS EMPIRES COLLAPSE . . .
IT IS A VASTLY CHANGED WORLD THAT COMES TO . . .
BARCELONA . . .

A tease could be judged objectively, by how many chills it produced. In Barcelona, after this magnum opus was finally finished, one of the associate producers counted. There were a dozen. And four years later, with his heart weakened, his future never so uncertain, the chills were still there for Caesar. He had more of the same left in him, more award-winning work, more of the kind of stuff that would shake viewers, cut through the volumes of lame crap, of all too much work slobbered upon by too many fools.

Like rappers, TV producers and directors generally died young. On top of being old and thought at best impolite, he was now seriously damaged goods. He needed someone to believe in him. He needed to know there was a next thing. Frank may have been waiting to die a few blocks away. Caesar Fortunato wanted one more shot. At least one more succulent project.

"Can you come down to my ranch?"

"When?"

"Next week, we're rounding up the cattle. I'll have all my boys here. Real cowboys, my friend. How about that, huh? Next Wednesday, is that good?"

"Where I am going?"

"Texas, son."

"I know it's Texas, Johnny Ray. Can you be more specific?"

"Fly to El Paso. Take a left. Drive exactly two hundred and twenty-one miles. That's my place. Can't miss it. It's about one hundred thousand acres, give or take a few thousand."

"I'll be there. Sounds great."

"We'll talk about that picture you're going to direct for me."

"So we're ready?"

"Total green light. And, Caesar, will you do me a favor? Bring some of that wacky weed you got, all right? It'll be useful for our creative discussions."

Italian Stallion

When they got to the airport in El Paso, Johnny Ray
Thompson told them to rent a four-wheel drive. The
ranch didn't have a foot of paved roads. Beck and
Caesar ended up, as promised, in the middle of
nowhere, a nowhere owned entirely by a very wealthy
Hollywood actor who more than anything else
wished he could go back to being a cowboy and doing
simple cowboy things.

From the central house on the WT Ranch, at a rise
in the property, there was a view that encompassed
much of what Johnny Ray Thompson had bought,
which seemed like all of Southwest Texas: an ocean of
rolling arid plains flowing between smallish bookend
mountain ranges. Johnny Ray's father had nothing,
was only called a farmer instead of a sharecropper

because he wasn't a Mexican. His daddy's dream was to someday own a decent piece of land. It was a dream deferred and, in the skipping of a generation, vastly improved in scope. The son's capacity for rapaciousness knew no bounds.

This was a cattle ranch, Texas style: a thousand head on a hundred thousand acres. His beef needed space because their home was a borderline desert. The kind of grass able to subsist in these conditions, brittle, almost colorless, and all but dead, did not make for great eating, unless you were able to eat one hundred thousand acres of it. With a one-week rainy season that produced about a foot of accumulation, everything that lived did not so much prosper as connive, toads and snakes and goats and hardy vegetation that earned a living by some kind of guile. There were no large trees to provide shelter from a sizzling sun rarely obscured by clouds. At sundown, it was as if the season had changed instantly, from the height of summer to the brink of winter, blazing hot days becoming nippy nights with cutting winds.

"A little bit of farming and a little bit of oil and a little bit of cattle, that's what you got here, fellas."

Beck and Caesar and Johnny Ray and Johnny Ray's ten cowboys were circled around a small fire warming a pot of coffee. Johnny Ray had his visitors up before dawn, up with his boys who were completing the cattle drive. Beck and Caesar were careful to bring enough warming layers but were still shivering. The gauchos, Johnny Ray's Argentinian imports who doubled as his polo team, looked wholly comfortable covered by their indigenous woolen ponchos. They were notably handsome men, dark hair and tanned skins and gentle features, and when they saddled a horse, the picture was almost too ridiculous—so poetic, a bloody painting in motion.

"Y'all come eat," said the cook, who worked out of a chuck wagon. "It's ready! It's hot! Otherwise, I'm gonna throw it out!"

The eggs and bacon and biscuits had just appeared, but Johnny Ray's cook was acting as if he had a troublesome group of children who couldn't be bothered with breakfast. In fact, the reverse was true. The cowboys leaped to their feet at the sound of his voice, and the food was soon to be inhaled.

"Hey, cookie," said one of the local cowboys with a grin, "you don't have to tell me more than once."

When they all went out to find the cattle, dispersing over Johnny Ray's vast property, it was another moment of life imitating art, at least for Caesar and Beck, for whom these images were terribly familiar but until then only seen on film. Each of the riders went searching for pockets of cattle, and within an hour, Johnny Ray's scattered herd had been unified into a dutiful, slow-moving pack. The animals were being funneled into a pen, snorting and braying all the while, prodded along by the shouts of a small surrounding cavalry and enticed by a trail of food pellets, tasty vitamin cookies that were being dropped from a pickup at the head of the herd. With his skilled Texans and Argentinians, the sons of cowboys who were the sons of cowboys, plus walkie-talkies and a food truck for rolling beef, the roundup was almost too efficient. Even the bulls, with their air of menace, were obedient. It was a totally pro effort, and Johnny Ray Thompson was in its midst, guiding an imposing, confident, brown-speckled horse, directing traffic, in charge. This was not an act.

The rest of work involved medicating, tagging, and branding. And there was the matter of castrating the new calves. That was the part that was inevitably the most compelling and the most unsettling. Johnny Ray's herd didn't need more than a few bulls for repopulating. They were some of the great sluts of the animal kingdom. On the flip side, a creature with a full tank of testosterone does not lead much of an examined life. Therefore, in the interest of peace and quiet, virtually all the male calves in Johnny Ray's herd were not going to grow up with balls.

The vet cut and pulled almost in a single motion, blood-drenched scissors in the right hand doing the emasculation of the exterior, the left hand then pulling out the milky-white vascular plumbing. In the final step, Johnny Ray branded. The whole process was done in less than thirty seconds. The disengaged testicles were roasted on a flat metal plate resting above the branding flame. Beck sampled a slice, Caesar did not.

As a reward to his crew, Johnny Ray organized a late-afternoon polo game. The cattle rustling that was expected to take a week had been done in four days and Johnny Ray was immensely pleased to be running ahead of schedule. Several coolers of beer were procured, not a trivial matter with the nearest town some forty miles away. Caesar, only weeks removed from a heart attack, thought it best to remain a spectator. Beck was put on a stock horse: gray, burly, slow. When Johnny Ray and Beck played for the Cornell Big Red, one was a smallish offensive lineman with an outsized heart, the other the most talented halfback in the history of Ivy League football. Johnny Ray knew that Beck shared a certain quality with his bulls, having also been born with enough testosterone to spare. Had Beck been given a strong, speedy thoroughbred, there was the strong likelihood of calamity.

"Beck, do you know whose side you're on?"

"The side that will be doing the castrating, I expect."

"That's right. You're on my team."

"Johnny Ray, we gonna burn the town."

"Beck, you try to stay behind me. I am going to play three. The two gentlemen from Argentina, being ten-goal players, will be up front. All of these numbers mean nothing to you, but you will understand this: It costs me some two hundred thousand dollars a month to rent these Argentines. Okay? All you need to know is that they have played the game before and are much better than you. Therefore, you are in the four position."

"You're hurting my feelings."

"No, I am trying to keep you in one piece. Play defense. That's all you have to worry about."

"I'm a scorer, Johnny Ray."

"One more thing. Unlike football, a sissy game, fouls in polo can cause injury to a man or horse. Or death. So, Beck, if you are going to ride somebody off the ball, do it at the same relative speed. Collisions are not welcomed in this sport. All right? You have to play this game in safety, or you will die."

It hadn't rained for more than ten minutes in almost a year, so the field of play was a dustbowl waiting to happen. Eight horses changing directions moment to moment created a thick roving cloud of airborne dirt that followed the play and obscured the riders. Beck was largely capable in his polo debut, though he was called several times for intimidation. Johnny Ray's team was victorious.

"Beck, nobody was going to get by you!" said Johnny Ray, can of beer in hand, filthy but radiant.

"What's this bullshit about intimidation? They were calling these fouls on me when I was thirty yards away."

"It is truly hard to understand. Why should anyone be afraid of a homicidal maniac who never played the game before? It's ridiculous. Sir, you have earned this beer. We have at least five cases to drink. Let's get started."

The party moved to a corner of the field, which sat in the shadow of one of Johnny Ray's two mountain ranges. The chuck wagon had been pulled over, horse-powered. Everyone was on metal folding chairs with a view of the sunset.

"Let's fucking do it, Caesar."

"I'm ready, Johnny Ray. What's next?"

"We'll get you a contract. I'll have my lawyer take care of it."

"If you don't mind, I would like to hire someone I know at NFL Films as the DP. He hasn't done a big feature, but I think he'll be the right guy for what you need. Westerner, like yourself. Played for the Raiders. You'd like him."

"An outsider. That's fine. Anyone except those frauds in Hollywood."

The movie in question, which for three years Caesar Fortunato had been waiting to direct, was a sequel. The original, starring Johnny Ray and a young, rising talent, told the story of two intrepid commercial jet pilots who saved the world from alien invasion.

"This is not the picture I want to make, Caesar. But it's money in the bank. That's how I can afford to have my own sunsets. You will do well, share in this bounty, and then we will do some real work together."

Caesar was banking on a million-dollar directing fee, plus a point. Johnny Ray insisted the sequel would gross one hundred million in the first couple of weeks.

"Mr. Fortunato, did you bring that slice of paradise from Hawaii?"

"Yes, sir," said Caesar, pulling out a cigarette holder with a dozen joints.

After dinner, the cook pulled a violin out of a battered case, and in the sinking sun capped a splendid day with a classic cowboy song. For Beck and Caesar, it was a movie that never ended.

"An old fiddler," said the cook, starting up, "once told me that fiddling is like politics. If you keep it short enough, they will love it."

Well, my foot's in the stirrup, my reins in my hand
Goodbye, little darling, my pony can't stand.
The country's so wide, my back is so sore
Goodbye, little darling, see you next fall.

"Sure."

Cindy Lenihan's audition was wrapping up.

"We can meet at the bar of the Westwood Marquis."

"Are you staying there?"

"Uh-huh."

"Wow, that's a nice hotel."

"I should be done here around eight. Let's say nine. Okay?"

"Great. So, do I have the job?"

"I can't say officially, Miss Lenihan, but I'll put it this way: You're not going to be watching the Oscars on television. Okay?"

"Okay. O-kay! Well, see you at nine."

As Cindy Lenihan departed, Caesar Fortunato found himself hypnotized by her delicious ass, which was exquisitely framed by jeans that had reached a state of perfection, in that happy medium of washed and worn: comfortable, still presentable, and virtually formfitting. In a landmark decision notable for its audacity, Caesar became the first director ever to insist on interviewing the so-called Oscar bearers, the young women who were supposed to saunter onstage and present the statuettes to the winners. This less than essential production issue was normally handled by the talent coordinator.

On that Monday morning, as preparation for the 1977 Academy Awards began in earnest, he was at the center of the entertainment universe and someone who mattered, or so he thought. He had walked out of the hotel into a gentle sun and blue sky, into an extraordinary Los Angeles day where the curtain of smog had risen and revealed the surrounding, snow-sprinkled mountains and oh-my-gosh views in virtually every direction. After a room-service breakfast that turned up at his door five minutes after he phoned, a record, he enjoyed pancakes that were still steaming and coffee that was almost tongue-stinging hot. A stretch limousine was waiting with the requested gram of cocaine; Todd the Driver had already exceeded his expectations. Twenty minutes later, sequestered in the mezzanine of the Dorothy Chandler Pavilion, he was chatting with the latest generation of aspiring starlets. They arrived in disarming casual wear that accentuated the best of what God had designed, prepared to please, suppressing their desperation, hoping this stranger was going to provide, at long last, their first big break.

Until that Thursday sundown at Johnny Ray's ranch, he had looked back upon that Monday morning, upon the retreat of Cindy's beauteous behind, as the last glimpse of a promised land he would never reach. The Academy Awards was not, as he anticipated, the exit from his serial misgivings about who he was and what he did.

"I-i-is anyone out there?"

Caesar's interviews with the Oscar bearers had strayed into the afternoon rehearsal. Jimmy Stewart was onstage, his right hand above his eyebrows, searching for someone in charge.

An announcement was made over the public-address system.

"Would Mr. Fortunato please come to the truck."

"Is that our man?" said Jimmy Stewart to no one in particular. "Is that who we're waiting for? Y-y-you know, Capra never made me wait."

As he walked out of the auditorium, Caesar's brain tried to reconstruct the morning. He had conducted eighteen interviews, and as he paged through the mental album, the candidates were framed in pieces: snapshots of firm, rangy legs; bulging cleavage; sultry eyes; wide, inviting smiles. He mentally undressed all of them. There was even a chance that he'd be able to compare his imagination with reality. He had made dates with five of the eighteen.

"You're fired."

"What?"

"You heard me. You're fucking fired."

"Now why I am fired?"

"Because you've kept George Bailey waiting. Jesus, Caesar! The guy is the icon of goodness. Jimmy fucking Stewart. And you keep him waiting because you want to get your dick sucked."

"So?"

"I mean, come on."

"Am I still fired?"

"I guess not."

Caleb Solomon was famous for firing people. He made it a habit to fire at least one person the first day on any job. He believed it set the right tone. He had fired one assistant director for highlighting a format in yellow magic marker instead of blue. He had also fired people for not bringing fortune cookies with the takeout and having bad haircuts. Caleb couldn't bring himself to fire Caesar for being a pig, because that would have been truly hypocritical.

"You can't have them all."

"Yes I can."

"So you're seeing that Cindy chick tonight, huh?"

"How did you know?"

"Hey, come on. . . . Listen, I want in."

"Find your own."

"My man, I'm too busy doing the actual work here to find my own. I want some of yours."

Caleb Solomon was among a new wave of young American directors making all sorts of statement films. They made serious pictures, good pictures, and were liberated in the ways of narcotics and sex. The studio bosses, whom the mavericks loathed, had allowed these disrespectful young shits a long leash because their work was making money for everyone. Caleb Solomon was the most defiant of the lot. Summoned by the suits to hear notes on his most recent film, he arrived at the designated restaurant wearing stained overalls and immediately ordered tequila. An entire bottle. It took him fifteen minutes to inhale five shots and keel forward. He didn't have to change one frame of his movie. Having Caleb Solomon in charge of the Oscars was an indication of how strangely submissive the film establishment had become. It was like asking an atheist to give the Sunday sermon. Caleb Solomon believed ninety percent of everyone in the business was absolutely full of shit. That was why he picked Caesar Fortunato to direct. Fortunato was a guy who did real stuff, like sports.

"I have a plan."

"Yeah?"

"If you want to get laid all week, you'll listen to me. We'll tell the girls they can sit in the audience after they do their walk-ons, and we'll put them behind the big nominees."

"Uh-huh."

"Like, you can tell your Cindy that she'll be sitting near William Holden. He's a lock to win Best Actor. She'll be guaranteed lots of camera time."

"You're a genius."

"I know. So where are you meeting that Cindy chick tonight? My insight does not come free."

Caleb was seen crying during his last film, and it was regarded as the most remarkable event in the four months of shooting. The story was cynical boy meets idealistic girl during a Central American Revolution, where the evil, portly CIA-backed generals were fending off the Communist insurgents. Solomon was terminating crew members with Stalin-like efficiency, associates he had known for years, young people who had had their sunny illusions nuked. Shooting was taking place around a small town south of Guadalajara, Mexico. The personnel merry-go-round was a bonanza for the local cab company. Its two vehicles were making twice-daily airport runs, supplying replacements off the morning flights for the souls of the less than dearly departed from the night before. Near the end, by which time Montezuma's famous revenge had downed all the gringos, one of the cabs ran over a goat in front of the lobby of the production hotel. Caleb Solomon, not quite recovered from his own mano a mano with Montezuma, which had him vomiting, shitting, shivering, and sweating all at once, witnessed the accident. The goat was sent some ten feet in the air and splashed down. Solomon walked over to the scrawny dying animal, convulsing in a growing pool of red, and he erupted in a big heaving cry. It was noted immediately that he had more feeling for this pathetic creature than any human he had ever worked with.

Caleb Solomon and Caesar Fortunato were kindred spirits. Neither needed confessors. They freely excused themselves. Since they were subjected to ungodly pressure in every project, as everyone could see, they thought themselves entitled to indulge their whims without question. Caesar had become a classic screamer. Solomon slugged. The film director had, on more than one occasion, punched an actor to draw a better performance. One replied with an uppercut. Another, badly shaken, produced a take that contributed to his Oscar nomination.

At first, when he finally became a premeditated prick, Caesar's suspended morality was confined to the broadcasts. Afterward, as if emerging from some trance, he'd search the production compound for those he had wronged and ask forgiveness. Flowers or chocolates or Champagne often followed. One year, Caesar's secretary, Bonnie Tedesco, was ordering a dozen roses every week from one of Manhattan's top florists. Eventually, the man inside the truck took over and corrupted all of his life, and there weren't enough flowers in the world to repair his litany of transgressions.

It was a shock when people learned that these men were uncommonly close to their mothers. Caleb and Caesar were anything but nurturing. In fact, they were poster boys for male chauvinism. For their entire adult lives, their mothers had treated them like infants, feeding, consoling, pampering, with no expectation that their devotion should be repaid in any form. Caleb Solomon's mother was still buying him socks and underwear. Caesar's mom gladly administered his life in gambling.

"Ma, who do you think for Best Actor?"

"Holden or Finch, honey. The two guys in that movie about TV."

"Which one? I got to get back."

"The Finch guy is English and he's dead. I'd go with Holden."

"All right, two on Holden. What about Best Picture?"

"Let's see . . . *Network* is three to one and *Rocky* is five to one. I like *Rocky*, honey."

"It looked cheap, you know what I mean? Kind of grainy. Let's go with *Network*."

"Are you sure, dear? I think the Academy likes the feel-good stuff. Really."

"Stallone's a show-off, and he's too new. Put the money on *Network*."

"Okay. Let's cross our fingers, dear."

It was one of the easiest jobs Caesar ever had. They had rehearsed everything six times. He knew exactly where each of the nominees was seated. If the script mentioned the movie *Network*, his assistant director noted in his script binder that he should take a shot of William Holden or Faye Dunaway. By the time of the broadcast, he had been reduced to a puppet. Caesar decided that he preferred the anarchy of big sports events, where the future was yet to be made. At the Oscars, even the one alleged moment of suspense, the one alleged unscripted moment, the announcement, was made simple. In the interest of reducing the margin of error to zero, he was told the names of the winners when the show began.

Caleb Solomon's chief innovation was eliminating the scourge of presenting pairs, which effectively eliminated patter. Patter was the name for the insipid cross talk between two celebrities asked to present one award. For one thing, patter required too much thought. Days would be spent building the pairs. Since duplicity was the town's principal activity, in business and in bed, it was always hard to know who was or wasn't talking to whom. For some reason, it had also been decided that patter should be funny. Once these pairings were established, a gaggle of comedy writers would overwork their funny bones trying to construct a simple joke for people without timing.

Instead of patter, Solomon had a victim of Hollywood's famous blacklist flown in by private jet from Martha's Vineyard. Before presenting Best Documentary, Lillian Hellman reminded everyone that the film community had confronted the McCarthy era with the force and courage of mashed potatoes. Hellman had just published a memoir of the McCarthy era, entitled *Scoundrel Time*.

Caesar admired Solomon's balls. The night was a long fuck-you. The other hosts were Jane Fonda, a Communist sympathizer; Warren Beatty, who was about to make a film about the Communist Revolution; and Ellen Burstyn, who was dressed like a Communist in a tuxedo and blue ruffled shirt.

Caleb also didn't want any gushing sentimentality. He vetoed a plan to have Peter Finch's widow accept for Best Actor. Only two months before, after appearing on *Good Morning America*, Finch had died of a heart attack in the lobby of the Beverly Hills Hotel. Given the circumstances, the appearance of Finch's widow would in all likelihood make people weep, and though he had once bawled over a deceased Mexican goat and therefore had some discernible amount of sentimentality, Caleb Solomon held a low opinion of actors and he certainly did not want any tears shed for a used-up Brit. Not in his show. Not on the night when he was showing Hollywood a new, smarter, honest way to do the Oscars.

When the late Peter Finch won, everything began as planned. The film's screenwriter, Paddy Chayevsky, went to the podium as requested.

For some obscure reason, I'm up here accepting an award for Peter Finch, or Finchie, as everybody who knew him called him. There's no reason for me to be up here. There's only one person who should be up here, and that's the person Finch wanted to accept his award. Are you in the house, Eletha? C'mon up and get your award.

Caleb Solomon yelled at Caesar.

"Don't cut to her. Don't do it. Shit. Shiiiit!"

Caesar hesitated, then defied Solomon.

"What are you doing? That fucker lied to me. I don't want this old hag on my telecast. Go to black! Go to black!"

Caesar was unruffled. He had spent a career coping with producers in the midst of total meltdowns.

"Caleb, he fucked you. Now shut up and sit down. Besides, listen, she's going to make everyone cry. It'll be nice."

"I don't want people crying. I don't want dead people mentioned on my show. How could they pick a dead guy? Those fuckers! Caesar, you're fired."

"Oh stop it."

Todd, driver and supplier of Colombian marching powder, was missing. Thirty minutes after the show, Caesar was the last one without a limo. Of course, this was the worst thing of all. Caesar was accustomed to intricate *and* successful escapes, slaloming around vehicles in vast parking lots flooded by the emptied contents of hundred-thousand-seat stadiums. The Oscars were small-time compared with the postmortem obstacles presented by a Rose Bowl or Masters or a college football Saturday in Ann Arbor, Michigan, or Lincoln, Nebraska, or Tallahassee, Florida.

The problem was compounded because Caesar had dawdled. On the way out, he gaped at Streisand, Nicholson, Norman Mailer. He watched Caleb Solomon screaming at Paddy Chayevsky. He heard William Holden tell someone: "If that son of a bitch hadn't died, I could have had my second Oscar."

Caesar's date was trailing the Stallone bandwagon.

"Where are you going?" he asked Cindy Lenihan.

"Um."

"So you're not coming with me?"

"Well, you told me Holden was going to win. I was sitting right near him and I was going to give him a big kiss or something. You know, I told my mom to watch. I mean, you kind of embarrassed me."

"Your mom saw you. I was taking shots of Holden all night."

"It's not the same. I was counting on him winning. You lied to me."

"I don't pick the winners, Cindy."

"You know what? I can't believe anything you say. I've got to go."

As Maria Fortunato had predicted, the Academy had gone for the feel-good story over Chayevsky's dark satire of the television business. Though he expected *Network* to win, Caesar thought it laughable. He had never met a high-ranking female executive like the one played by Faye Dunaway, nor a principled suit like Holden's character, nor an anchorman with a British accent. In truth, Chayevsky's vision was a little premature. In the next few years, Caesar Fortunato would indeed find himself faced with ruthless women who made the rules and a climate where an unstoppable ratings decline and dearth of imagination led to the green lighting of unconscionable shows that exploited terribly sad, mentally ill people. At the time, however, it was the Age of Innocence, the Age of Hawas, who cherished his top creative people, showered them with money, and tolerated all manner of bad behavior.

In the meantime, Caesar Fortunato was mad as hell, still waiting for Todd. At the time, his driver was snoring. Todd had parked in a designated underground garage nearby and went to the backseat with the intention of taking a short nap. The high volume of drug deliveries had made him weary. Caesar went back inside to call a cab. He decided to go straight back to the hotel, bypass the big parties. He had begun the week with his ego wonderfully inflated and in the end decided he was no more significant than Cindy Lenihan. That week, he was just another bit player, a laborer in Hollywood's greeting card to itself. The show would be defined, remembered, by one man's creation, by the name of a fictional boxer from the landscape of Caesar's childhood.

Like Caesar Fortunato, Sylvester Stallone had found Philadelphia too small for his ambition. Unlike Caesar, Stallone did not settle for half a dream. He had a hundred bucks in the bank, a pregnant wife, a starving dog, and he said no. Told the studio he wouldn't sell them *Rocky* unless he could be the star. The studio grudgingly agreed but forced the producers to mortgage their houses; the film was shot in twenty-eight days, and the Philadelphia Board of Health shut down the less-than-savory, cost-conscious, on-location commissary. Stallone could have taken a hundred and fifty thousand dollars to give it up and walk away, more than enough to feed the dog, but he fought to play the lead and accepted six hundred bucks a week. The *New York Times* hated it, the rest of America cheered long and loudly.

Stallone was only the third man in movie history to be nominated for Best Screenplay and Best Actor. The others were Chaplin and Welles. He did not win in either category, but his director did, and so did the producers who mortgaged their homes.

I guess Rocky gave a lot of people hope, said the film's director, John Avildsen, in his acceptance speech.

The sentiment was surely shared among the millions who had seen the film and were making it one of the most profitable ever. That Monday night in March, Caesar Fortunato was not among them. Hollywood had become a bad dream, made worse because he so much wanted it to be real.

A Taste of Spring

Approaching winter, waiting for Johnny Ray's lawyer to call, cash dwindling, he was more often than not idle and outdoors at his desert home, doped and topless. Caesar Fortunato became self-conscious about the hint of flab around his waist, and he paid closer attention to the small rivulets around his eyes and the thinning patch of hair at the top of his scalp, and he was feeling every bit as castrated as Johnny Ray's predestined eunuchs. The heart attack had made him soft. Suddenly, he was an old man married to a perfect ten.

Lynette looked like many of the trophy wives collected in the Coachella Valley: tall, tanned, athletic, and superbly coifed. She had rubbed the remaining cellulite off her thighs with a smart, varied regimen of weights, StairMaster, and three-mile jogs, had trimmed back her intake of pizza, beer, and Klondike bars, started every day with yoga. She was about as fit, as inviting as a man could reasonably desire. This was not what he wanted.

In the beginning, Caesar Fortunato was truly impressed with Lynette's dignified manner of partying. She got hammered without getting sloppy. He had met so many women who became spectacles, particularly the English, who would be seen in public falling-down drunk, stumbling and stupefied. He suspected that Lynette, being Irish, had an inbred tolerance for alcohol and other stimulants. What really surprised him was the sex. She was not plagued by the voice of an inner nun, like so many of the Irish girls he had dated. Not since Susie Gold had he been with a lover as inventive, as ravenous . . . with a woman who made sexual fulfillment, hers and his, such a priority.

Soon, Lynette Kelly progressed for the better. After reading *The Great Gatsby* while exfoliating during a facial, she decided it was more prudent to experience ruination vicariously. So she checked into the nearby Betty Ford Clinic and graduated with honors. The rehabbed Lynette was willing to hang tough during the trials of her unreformed husband. But secretly jealous and disturbed by her success, Caesar could not bring himself to lean on this fast-maturing woman who had loved him at first sight.

She woke him with a swift, soft kiss, some seven miles above the earth. It was a guerrilla kiss, a recent practice of the bored and horny stewardesses in the first-class cabin on the Paris–New York crossing. After the movie started and the lights dimmed, with the freshly fed passengers fighting a creeping drowsiness, it was agreed Caesar Fortunato should be the designated target. He fit the specs: male, relatively attractive, not likely to make a fuss in the event of catastrophe. They had the sense that Caesar wasn't going to make a fuss because he had started to flirt with them from the time he walked on the plane.

By failing, by waking Caesar, Lynette Kelly would now be obligated to buy a round of drinks, not long after landing, for Jane and Mary

Ann, the other conspirators. Until that moment, the designated penalty had yet to be enforced. All targeted men had remained unconscious, and they had mostly forgotten that this kind of behavior could conclude their airborne careers.

Mary Ann and Jane were trying to restrain giggles as Lynette dashed back to the galley, hoping the guy in 3B would decide that he had dreamed this horrifying violation of his privacy.

"Lynette!" Mary Ann exclaimed while maintaining a whisper.

"What's he doing now?" Lynette asked.

"Let me take a look."

Jane stuck her head out and glanced up the row.

"He's coming back here!" Jane exclaimed while maintaining a whisper.

"Fuck!"

"Shit!"

"Double shit!"

"We'll tell him he must have been dreaming."

"Who's idea was this thing?" Lynette asked.

"Yours!" said Mary Ann and Jane.

As Caesar arrived, they all had their backs turned, cleaning without purpose: clanking empty tin pots, opening latches, stuffing time sheets into plastic pouches.

"Excuse me."

Mary Ann and Jane fled for coach, complete cowards.

"Yes, sir."

"Hello," Caesar said with a warming smile that put Lynette at ease.

"I'm very sorry. We're getting a little carried away here . . ."

"I really . . . really didn't mind."

"You're not angry."

"Nope."

"Can I get you something?"

"How about some wine? Now that I'm suddenly awake, I think I need something to get me back to sleep."

"Okay."

"Where's home?"

"New York. You?"

"Rancho Mirage . . . ever get out that way?"

"Whenever I want, I suppose."

"You know, I wouldn't mind an encore."

"My name's Lynette."

In 1986, he was on Lynette's flight returning from a taste of spring in France, a decidedly mixed interlude. He had directed a show about supermodels produced by a former Buddhist monk, won at Cannes, and nearly killed Pascal.

"Usine à merde."

"Usine du merde?"

"No, zat would be a factory made of sheet. You say *usine à merde*. A factory that makes sheet."

"Right . . . was that so bad?"

"I zink I would have liked better to eat real sheet."

Caesar had spent a week at home with Pascal, in Sancerre, about two hours south of Paris. Hurrying to catch his flight out of DeGaulle, they stopped at a McDonald's. It was the first time for Pascal. At long last, his curiosity had overcome his outrage.

"I'm so sorry," Caesar said, having taken the wheel from Pascal, who was grimacing.

"I zink the sheet factory has dee-stroyed my stomach."

"Are you going to be okay?"

"Je ne sais pas."

"Seriously?"

"Yeah. I zink I have a big problem."

He envisioned Pascal's death and how unsuitable the reason, via the least original cuisine in the history of mankind. Further, in his work, Pascal had been so casual about his mortality. He was the most daring cameraman Caesar had ever known. This Big Mac attack was doubly ironic.

Pascal went to civil wars and flew more than once on Aeroflot, Murder Incorporated of the skies, and he had hung from a harness high in the Alps for a better view of semi-suicidal rock climbers, and he once crawled inside a pyramid unopened for three millennia, and he had

174

reached a speed of one hundred thirty miles per hour in a Chrysler minivan while trying to make last call at a favored bar, and he survived a decade of the Tour de France, shooting from the back of a motorcycle. His tombstone was meant to contain words like "daring" or "courage" or "brave." It was life in the fast lane, not fast food, that was meant to be his undoing.

He was nearly killed so many times on the Tour, a race as dangerous for the cameramen as it was for the riders, particularly in the mountain phase, with so many successive, dizzying switchbacks made additionally hazardous by rain, fog, and unreliable drivers. One year, Remy, his moto driver, was distracted by marital problems. He had taken his visiting wife to dinner, then kicked her out of the car after a big argument and left her on the highway, many, many miles from the hotel. The following morning, with the wife having not returned, the husband was conjuring images of rape and homicide, considering his culpability, while driving and turning and turning some more on narrow roads made slick by a night of showers. This was why they crashed and why the kneecap in Pascal's left leg was made of plastic.

He had been up and over the Alps ten times, had chronicled the Tour with an intimacy never before known because he worked without fear and because he thought of his profession as an art, and now Pascal was folded into a fetal position in Caesar's rented Peugeot and moaning, dying of hamburger poisoning.

"*Hôpital,* Caesar. *Hôpital.* I am zo seek."

"What?"

"Seek."

"Oh, you're so sick."

"*Oui.* Very seek."

Pascal had just spent the week providing Caesar with a backstage pass to the world of supreme gastronomy. They had made a visit to a notable local winemaker. His name was Boda and his product was desired on every continent. But he only sold it to people he liked, and they had to visit his wine cellar, and they could never ever ask to buy his famous white wine, described as full, intense, elegant. It was said to have a hint of the famous, sweet Alsatian grapes, but the taste was not as one-dimensional. The wine's reputation flowered because Boda made it so precious, so particular was he about picking only the most perfect fruit and confining the purchasing process to firsthand encounters. He didn't care how many bottles he sold. He wanted the right sort of people enjoying his wine, and he insisted upon witnessing their pleasure.

"He knows why you are there," Pascal had told Caesar. "So don't zay anything. Okay? Or no wine."

Pascal was part of the team that harvested Boda's grapes every fall. The workers, Boda's acquaintances—lawyers and doctors, butchers and bakers, a Tour de France cameraman—assembled just after dawn, most having chased their breakfast with two aspirin. Boda gave them a pair of special scissors to separate the grapes from the vines. The work stopped an hour later when Boda opened a few bottles. And then the work stopped again at eleven, and at one, and at three, and finally, about thirty minutes before sunset, when Boda summoned his hands from the fields for good.

By this time, he had shared his best vintages, not only his own but extraordinary wines and Champagnes from all of France. At the end of the picking, Pascal and the team would have sampled a Montrachet, a Château d'Yquem, a Pol Roger. At dusk, when the feasting began, the rookies not bombproofed by aspirin were rocked by thundering headaches. Dinner included all the essential small animals: *escargot, grenouille, lapin,* and *canard,* in order of size: snail, frog, rabbit, and duck. Boda believed his sponsored day of indulgence, his grapes being harvested by drunken, unskilled help, added a kind of soul to his product. His wine had personality, not to mention a very tiny residue of minced leaves and twigs, the result of careless cutting by the trembling hands of Sancerre's unpaid, shitfaced citizenry. Sometimes, if there was a little bit too much joie de vivre, he'd have a small, sober group of wine pros clean up the loose ends.

"Monsieur Fortunato, Pascal tells me you are in TV. This does not seem like a honorable way to make a living."

"Excuse me?"

"Wine making, it has purpose. TV, it has no purpose."

"Are you being serious?"

"TV, it is a masturbation. *Mais oui?* It is not a piece of music, a painting, a book, a film. It is not as real as a newspaper, a photograph, or even a souvenir. All your work, it is now in outer space, *non?*"

"Monsieur Boda, I think perhaps you have been watching too much French television."

"Oh, yes, our TV sucks. But I think we take a certain pride in making very bad TV."

"It does seem that way."

"What do you zink is ze problem?"

"Talking heads."

"Talking heads?"

"One head yapping at another head. You don't have shows. You have people who like to hear themselves talk."

"Zo, we talk too much."

"You asked me what the problem was."

"I see. . . . Zo, would you like some of my wine?"

At this point, Caesar, Pascal, and Boda had been drinking for hours, on tiny stools circled around a tiny table.

"I . . . I love your wine."

"I know you love my wine. Everyone loves my wine. But I ask if you want to buy eet."

Caesar turned to Pascal, uncertain. He wasn't supposed to make any reference to buying this much treasured product, except Boda had already lured him into conversation. Maybe this was a trick.

"Yes, I would like to buy your wine."

"Sorry," said Boda, "too late. I only ask you once. Pascal, it is time to go."

"That's it?" said Caesar.

"Take this *Américain* away, Pascal."

"I sit here for three hours drinking your piss and kissing your ass, and that's it?"

"*Au revoir*. Bye-bye."

"No wine?"

"No wine for you."

Pascal scolded Caesar when they emerged into the shrinking daylight.

"I zink maybe you are a big talking head *aussi*."

Though he left empty-handed from Boda's cave, the week in Sancerre—long walks, quiet nights, sumptuous, marathon meals with Pascal's family—was otherwise an antidote to the preceding

177

parade of profound decadence in Cannes. It began with the super-model show, the stated purpose being to select the world's most gorgeous swizzle stick. More correctly, it was a dating service for the show's creator and producer, David Griffin, who propositioned each of the twenty-five supermodels on-site.

The timing of the show was smart. During the film festival, Cannes attracted humanity's most handsome. Virtually all the supermodels were looking for a career change, weary of agencies run by hags or perverts, weary of strange, imperious photographers, bitchy makeup artists tormented by too much creativity, fed up with the leering of aging, closet lesbians who attended so many of the shows. The ideal career change for all of the supermodels was the same. They all wanted to act. And Cannes was a place to be discovered.

So David Griffin lied to them. Said he'd introduce them to his many Hollywood friends, Marty, Stephen, Arnold, Tom. He had invitations to all the big parties—the various sheik-sponsored yacht bashes, Paramount's at the Carlton, the famous annual orgy of a famous ancient French film star. He just needed a couple of days of their time, and they had to pay their way and find their own accommodations. This was treachery on a scale unknown even to Caesar. Griffin was going to pocket most of the network's money. The talent was free, the crew was local, travel costs were zero.

On day one, shooting never got started. They were to meet at Griffin's hotel suite, but he didn't answer their knocks. Telltale audio followed shortly, treble screams and bass moans, so everyone assumed the schedule had been revised, and left. Griffin apologized by leaving a cereal bowl half-full of cocaine at the crew's chateau, outside Cannes.

"I'm in the middle of a difficult transition, Caesar," Griffin told him at breakfast the next morning. "I was a Buddhist monk until last year. No money, no meat, no sex. And since I left the monastery, I've been overindulging. Can you blame me? I denied these urges for so long."

On day two, shooting ended prematurely. He told the supermodels he needed an artistic opening for the show. This meant asking them to drop their pants, bend over, and have an egg cracked and dripped on their behinds. Model One said no. Model Two said yes. Model Three called the police. She was seventeen. On the morning of day three, Griffin was in Paris after catching the overnight, high-speed train.

Caesar remained at Cannes for the X d'Or, which immediately followed. His *Love or Lust* had been nominated in the soft-core category, which meant no penises were on display. Among the other categories were Largest Cock and Best Orgasm. The night of the show, his date was one of Griffin's supermodels. She accepted the X d'Or trophy on his behalf.

"Mr. Fortunato, a very nice man, is very pleased to win this very special award. And I will be available after the show if anyone wants me to be in their next film. But I don't do kinky stuff. Thank you."

The next day, with the end of the festivals, the people of Cannes returned from hiding. For a few weeks of every spring, the city belonged to the young, real and imagined; otherwise, it was a sanctuary for seniors drinking pastis and playing *petanque*. Caesar took one more stroll along the beach promenade and found the merriment in fast retreat, as if a giant eraser were being used, the sand being swept, so efficiently, of tents and tables and chairs, billboards and lights, cups and bottles. The sun was just starting to yawn, and the beach was nearly clean. He walked by a girl, fifteen or sixteen, borderline attractive, her mascara smudged. It looked as though she had slept on the bench from which she was staring. She was not a supermodel. There would be no agency waiting in some international capital to pay her serious money for standing and smiling. She made him think of the hollowness in his heart, of growing old alone.

"You know how we make foie gras, yes?"

"No."

"We feed the goose with corn for six months, and this makes the liver very, very big."

"Right."

"It's so good, but it's not very nice. It's a de-seeze. You understand?"

"Okay. Why are you telling me this, doctor?"

Pascal was at a Paris hospital having his stomach pumped. The doctor had just discovered the cause.

"Monsieur Fortunato, for us, McDonald's, it is like a de-seeze. Okay? Just like the making of foie gras."

"Is he going to be all right?"

"It's too early to tell. I think we'll keep him here for a couple of days."

"I promise, I won't ever take him to McDonald's again."

"You know, all of you Americans, you and your food are a curse on the world."

"Hey, we saved you from the Nazis."

"And you gave us factories that make sheet."

A few hours later, Caesar Fortunato was stirred from sleep by an unsolicited kiss from a woman who'd be his second wife in a matter of months.

The Perfect Day

Lynette had wearied of waiting for the train wreck.

"You little bitch."

Her first move was calling the mother-in-law.

"I'm a little bitch? Do you have any idea what is going on?"

"Oh, stop your nonsense."

"We're going to lose the house, okay?"

"Dear, my son's spending is not the problem."

"You're clueless, aren't you?"

"You must be very good in bed."

"What?"

"Otherwise, I can't imagine how he would tolerate you."

"He's got no fucking money left, you stupid old woman."

"I'm going to hang up. This really is nonsense."

"No, no! You're not going to do that to me again. Listen . . . listen . . . if I find out you have placed another bet for my husband, I will call the fucking police. Okay? I will have you put in jail."

"You're going to have his mother put in jail?"

"Mother? You're the fucking worst mother anyone could ever have. My husband has an illness, do you understand? An illness."

"Oh, you are such a stupid little girl."

"I WILL call the cops."

"You're just a complete bitch, aren't you?"

"Mrs. Fortunato, go fuck yourself . . . really."

Lynette followed up by organizing her next major confrontation. She phoned Gilmartin, Caesar's ancient engineering pal, and Rope, his favorite cameraman, and Beck, the Hall of Fame running back whom she disliked intensely. Lynette suspected Beck was Caesar's chief road pimp, but she asked him anyway because she thought he possessed a trace of goodness and would see the need for immediate, fundamental change. Lynette told Caesar she was throwing a Super Bowl party for him and that all his best chums would be there. It would lift his spirits, she told him.

Actually, his spirits had been on the rise through the month of January 1997. Before the start of the football season, he had left twenty-five thousand dollars with a sports book on a ten to one that the Patriots would win the Super Bowl. The Patriots were coached by Bill Parcells, and in Caesar's mind, Parcells was the best NFL coach since Lombardi. Victory by victory through the playoffs that January, Coach Parcells had been justifying Caesar's confidence. The Patriots had reached the Super Bowl and with a victory would be putting a quarter million dollars in Caesar's pocket.

At halftime, with his Patriots losing 27–14, Lynette began the intervention. He tried to minimize the true damage after the gentle badgering began, but Lynette started pulling out the bank statements and canceled checks. Already annoyed by the score, he progressed shortly to a state of rage.

"Who said you were allowed to embarrass me this way, in front of my friends, you fucking cunt!"

"Goddamn it, Caesar, if you don't get some help, you're going to lose me. I just can't do it anymore. I can't watch this. It's killing me watching you destroy yourself . . . and destroy what we have, or what I thought we had."

Lynette shook her head, defeated, went to the bedroom. Caesar moved rapidly off the couch to get his car keys. Gilmartin and Rope suggested Beck go with him. They took the empty highway east to Las Vegas. Caesar turned on the radio and heard that the Patriots had scored first in the third quarter, making it 27–21. They could win it with one more touchdown. He got that old feeling again, the building, pleasing tension of having a bet down with the real possibility of an impressive payoff.

"You're just a fucking idiot for betting on these games."

"If you're going to start, I'll fucking leave you on the side of the road."

"I played the game, asshole. Right now, some official with money on the Packers could be waiting to fuck the Patriots. Just waiting to flag them at the worst possible time. Who knows? Or Bledsoe could get his knee ripped apart. There are way too many variables."

"You've been out of football for fifteen years. What the fuck do you know?"

"I'll tell you this. The Packers are a better team. And you better prepare yourself to suck it up."

Caesar didn't hear Beck's remark. He was already counting his winnings.

It was Friday morning, June 11, 1982, and he was sitting upright in bed, supported by two fluffy pillows, sipping coffee, speaking with his mom at the conclusion of his room service feast, which was centered around his favorite, a stack of pancakes. His stomach was rumbling, but gently, happily. He was in a Las Vegas hotel suite, about to produce a heavyweight title fight between Gerry Cooney, the latest Great White Hope, and Larry Holmes, one of the least inspiring heavyweight boxers of the twentieth century.

"Okay, Green Hornet. Let's go with the dime bets."

183

"Dimes? On baseball?"

"Sure. They're paying me a lot of money for this fight, Mom. Listen to this. I get paid twice. Once by Don King for the closed-circuit, and then the network has to pay me. It's a Directors Guild thing. I do the job once, get paid twice. How about that?"

"All right, honey. We'll cross our fingers. I've got my pad. Let's go."

"I like Boston at home and California on the road. Reggie's having a good year."

"He was always nice to you, wasn't he, dear?"

"Nickels on the Orioles, the Brewers, Blue Jays, and Royals."

"Wait a minute. The Tigers are having a pretty good year. Are you sure?"

"The Brewers are going to make a run. You'll see. They've got Vukovich pitching tonight. He's a horse."

"Oh yes, he's Cy Young material."

"Right. Very good, Mom."

"Well that's what *Sports Illustrated* said. . . . So we're betting the entire American League slate?"

"And all of the National League."

"You've never wanted this much action before on baseball. Let's see, we've got four grand down right now."

"And we're going to drop another four, Ma. Stay with me. In the National, I like the Cards and the Braves for a dime apiece. . . . What do you think about the Expos?"

"The Cubs are having another awful year, son. You can't lose too much money betting against the Cubs."

"Right. Go with Montreal for a nickel."

"I think that's smart. They have a nice little team up there. And I've always liked their logo."

"Let's go with the Dodgers and Padres. What about our Phillies?"

"For some reason, dear, I don't think this is going to be their year."

"And Carlton isn't pitching."

"Unfortunately, Lefty can't pitch every game for us."

"Pirates for a nickel."

"Listen, dear. If you lose, don't be grumpy, all right? Now what about the fight tonight? When are we going to get something down on that?"

"I'm gonna wait. I always suspect these things are fixed and I might hear something today, you know? I'm leaning toward Holmes, but Cooney's got that big punch. If it was Ali or Frazier, Cooney wouldn't have a chance. But Holmes is going to let him hang around."

"I like this Gerry Cooney. He seems like a nice boy. And he does have the height advantage, doesn't he?"

"And, of course, he's white, too."

"Well, it's been a long time since we've had one of our own."

"Mom, I'll call you about thirty minutes before the bout. All right?"

Scams like this fight, where he could double bill, encouraged his recklessness. By 1982, Caesar Fortunato had long been liberated from worrying about money. Though he lived from paycheck to paycheck, his biweekly grosses were as much as the average Mr. Deskbound-Nine-to-Five-Pencil-Pusher took home over an entire year. And then there were safety nets, like these sorts of jobs, where he'd draw fifty thousand dollars for three days of work. What a wonderful world it was on top of the TV food chain. Though it didn't amount to much, actually his favorite source of easy income was the residual checks, which arrived in the mail steadily, unpredictably, after some show he'd done was replayed or broadcast internationally in places like Sri Lanka or Uruguay. These enchanting pennies from heaven paid for the groceries. As long as his heart was beating, and his brain was functioning, and he stayed out of jail, Caesar Fortunato assumed he'd be a walking, talking cash machine.

After reading the papers in bed, every paper available that morning in Las Vegas, including the *Times* of Los Angeles and of New York, and the *Heralds* from Miami and Boston, Caesar showered in slow motion, enjoying that meditative state usually produced by prolonged exposure to steaming, hot water. He shaved carefully, perfumed himself, deodorized, flossed, rinsed, took unusual care as he circled the can of hair spray about his scalp.

"Beck, who am I betting?"

"Well, I'm hearing Larry is getting too many massages."

"What do you mean?"

"He has this very attractive masseuse, and he's getting like five massages a day."

"Shit."

"I'd still go with Holmes. I mean, Cooney's fought like three times in the last three years. There's no substitute for being in a ring and getting cracked in the head and feeling like you're going to puke every second."

"What do you mean he's getting too many massages?"

"That's what I heard."

"So what?"

"Well, you know, maybe he's losing his focus, getting too much love."

"Rubdowns are for loosening up the muscles."

"Okay. Whatever you say."

"I'm going to put down fifty thousand."

"Oh, stop. Don't be an idiot."

"No, this is my day. It's in the air."

"What if the fight is fixed?"

"Stop fucking with me."

"Caesar, why does Larry Holmes want to win this fight? He loses to the Great White Hope, so he legitimizes Cooney, who is now the heavyweight champion of the world. Then, both of them make twice as much money in the rematch. Then, Holmes wins the rematch and they fight again. Simple."

"That's like a bad *Rocky* movie."

"Oh, by the way, he's here."

"Who?"

"Stallone."

"What's he doing?"

"He's been hanging around Cooney."

"Really? That's it. I don't care about Holmes getting ten massages a day. If Cooney's hanging around with that fucking loser, he's got no shot."

After lunch, they stopped for some prefight craps. At first, Caesar found no proof that this Friday in the month of June 1982, was his lucky day. He lost a grand in ten minutes. Beck was out half as much and starting to excuse himself.

186

"Look," said Beck, alerting Caesar.

"What?"

"Right there."

"Ahhhhh."

Annette Cole, *Sports Illustrated*'s latest swimsuit covergirl, had wedged into a spot at the table, along with another tall, curving, breasty specimen whose virtues had been exploited in the same issue.

"I'm staying."

"Don't you have to work?"

"She's going to help the table. You believe in luck, Beck, don't you?"

"I think you make your own."

"What about being in the right place at the right time? You believe that, don't you?"

"Yes."

"Well, isn't that luck?"

"You are fucking hopeless."

Their eyes met and Annette Cole smiled, this wholesome kind of smile that in itself was a payoff, a dividend for volunteering to live each day in the shadow of ruin. Caesar was going to remain at the table at least until Annette Cole took her turn rolling the dice. Her come-out was a five, his favorite number from childhood. That sealed it. He was going to bet with impunity.

Hawaiian Stanley Fujitake, known as the Golden Arm, once held the dice for three hours, rolled his way to fifty winners in a row. This was known in mathematics as a standard deviation from the norm, an inevitable heavy clustering of winning numbers. There was no way of knowing when it would happen. The bettor had to be at the right place at the right time, like those fortunate souls who were in Las Vegas that night at the California Casino when Stanley Fujitake couldn't lose.

"One more."

Annette Cole also proved the existence of standard deviations. In five minutes, she rolled twenty-three times without crapping out, and Caesar's three grand ballooned to sixty.

"Maybe I should stop," she said with an Australian accent that somehow added to her lustrous wholesomeness.

"Oh, no," Caesar replied, gladly speaking for the table. "No, no. Trust me. You've got more magic in those fingers."

"Oh, really?"

"Come on, I can't even buy a yacht with what I've got here."

"I see."

She looked at the rest of the players.

"Should I stop?"

"No!" they shouted, and laughed as one.

"Told you," said Caesar.

She rolled a five again as her point. Six more rolls and she produced another five, another winner. Caesar had cityscapes of chips all over the felt. Everyone at the table was exploring other bets off the pass line, pressing their luck with each of her rolls, and the cheering had turned into high-fiving.

"I can't take the pressure."

"One more."

"Nooo," she said, laughing. "I've got to get going."

"Please."

"Yes," said another player, "Pleeease."

"I've got to see the fight. I think it's just about to start."

"Look, I'm producing the fight," he said to her, "and I'm still here."

"Well, I'm so sorry, but I've got to go." Her companion assisted in the gathering of Annette's own winnings and they waved good-bye to applause.

The dice were then passed into the hands of a flabby male: He was attired thoughtlessly in a plaid polyester shirt, untucked, and a faded, paint-spotted baseball hat. Certain that the table's luck had vanished with the lady, Caesar slid half his chips to the Don't Pass bar and shortly snake eyes settled on the table for the first time in some thirty minutes, the crapping out by the polyester fatty winning Caesar an additional forty thousand dollars.

"Find her in the crowd."

"We already did the celebrity rundown while you were away . . . Nicholson, Farrah Fawcett, Mr. T. . . . By the way, how much did you contribute to the casino's upkeep?"

"Oh, you are so wrong. Hey . . ."

"What?"

"Turn around."

"I'm trying to direct a fight."

"Look at me."

Jack Allen swiveled left, and Caesar leaned close and whispered.

"No. Really?"

Allen mouthed the number two hundred to confirm.

"Yes, indeedy. Now find Annette Cole."

"All right. You tell Chuck. He probably doesn't know who she is."

Caesar punched up the talent intercom.

"Chuck, next shot, Annette Cole. Big supermodel."

A few seconds later, the stage manager had a message for Caesar.

"What do you want, Barney?"

"Chuck gave me a note. He says he won't be your pimp."

"Barney, you put this on the other side of that note. Are you listening?"

"Yes, sir."

"Write these words: 'Caesar will cut off your vodka.' That's V-O-D . . ."

"Sir, I can spell that, sir. . . . Caesar, he's nodding his head, and he's writing me another note. It says: Don't . . . get . . . greedy . . . you . . . devious . . . little . . . shit."

"Thank you, Barney."

Also at ringside tonight, here in Las Vegas, Nevada, you see the very beautiful Annette Cole, featured not long ago on the cover of the Sports Illustrated *swimsuit issue. . . .*

"I guess he does know who she is."

"Jack, that college professor vocabulary and haughty air of his are just a cover. Believe me, he's a dirty old prick just like the rest of us."

The bout would last thirteen rounds, and Caesar might as well have been in the Holmes corner with Eddie Futch and Ray Arcel. Inside the truck, he was advising the heavyweight champion from moment to moment, exhorting him at high volume on what punch to throw, berating him for lapses in judgment, applauding his successes. He was leaning into the bank of monitors, on the tips of his toes and fingers. In most other environments, he would be thought deranged.

"WHAT ARE YOU DOING, LARRY? WHAT ARE YOU WAITING FOR? STOP CIRCLING AROUND. GET THIS THING OVER WITH. HIT HIM. HIIIT HIIIM!!!"

He had taken half of his winnings from the craps table, one hundred thousand dollars, and deposited it with the casino's sports book: Holmes to win. He had his mom make the same wager, same amount, with their Philadelphia bookie. At first she refused, being a Cooney loyalist. So Caesar had to make up a story about Cooney saying Italians and black people were essentially the same, except blacks got more sun.

"That's terrible."

"Yup."

"Oh, I hope Larry buries a punch in his brain."

"Me too, Mom."

After knocking Cooney to the mat in the second, Holmes was largely effective but unspectacular. He had been trained by throwbacks. Eddie Futch and Ray Arcel liked their boxers to leave the ring with their wits intact and their noses pointed straight. They considered the sport a defensive art, not a game of head-hunting. To these men, veritable doctors of the Sweet Science, the beauty lay in the counterpunch, in letting your opponent swing away, because in doing so, he would sooner or later show you an avenue to victory. Futch and Arcel made Holmes believe that anyone could engage in a slugfest, but it was the greater athlete who exercised caution and patience, who trained his mind along with his arms and legs and lungs, trained himself to retain control, resist temptation after that first thundering punch to the face, all but certain in big-time bouts, when having been struck square and filled fully with rage, the fighter would want to abandon the mission and unleash a vengeful volley and therefore, in his loss of reason, leave himself open to the chief weapon that won most fights: a counterpunch.

Early, a Holmes counter produced a cut under the challenger's left eye and then the champion kept working the area. By the middle of every subsequent round, Holmes had undone the cauterizing by Cooney's corner and Cooney was distracted, futilely dabbing the wound with a glove to wipe the dripping blood. At the opening of the thirteenth and final round, the challenger's face was scourged, puffy. It looked unbalanced, as if it had been redrawn by Picasso.

Caesar was exhausted and hoarse. Every second of every round, he was electrified with a combination of fear and excitement, knowing that he was one punch away from dropping a small fortune. At every second, there was the possibility that Larry Holmes might put his face in the way of a thunderous, already certified left hook from the six-foot seven-inch Cooney.

"How much should I bet?" he once asked a stranger, as they waited to make a wager on a horse race of little significance during a midweek day at Belmont Park.

"That's not the right question," the stranger responded. "The question you should ask yourself is: 'How much excitement do I want?' Do you want two dollars' worth of excitement or two hundred dollars' worth of excitement?"

On June 11, 1982, Caesar was having two hundred thousand dollars' worth of excitement.

It is clear these men have summoned all their resources to this point . . . surely, in this heat, one hundred degrees even under this night sky, the desert still unforgiving, their bodies are telling them to quit . . . but look at them, proceeding, determined . . . Cooney still has that feared left hook, the puncher's chance . . . and Larry Holmes, a splendid champion, but at thirty-two years of age, a champion older than most in this sport's modern history . . . the left side of Cooney's face, gushing once again . . . wrecked by the champion's incessant jabs . . . HOLMES HAS COONEY BACKED UP AGAINST THE ROPES . . . THERE'S A RIGHT . . . COONEY IS SLIDING, ABOUT TO GO . . . THEY'RE CALLING IT OFF . . . THEY'RE CALLING IT OFF . . . HIS CORNER IS CALLING IT OFF.

They had come to a logical pause in the foreplay, after a sufficient amount of deep kissing and groping. It was time to either stop and part, conclude the night, or undress. She got off the bed and stood, eyes still on his, making him comfortable about watching her. Annette Cole slowly unbuttoned her blouse, let it drop to the floor, then quickly unhooked her bra. The revealed breasts, settling, were larger than he expected and as aesthetically pleasing as any he had ever seen. They were like two big teardrops near bursting, the nipples flat, pink, and wide. As she continued stripping with what seemed a pride and pleasure in her movements, he saw that she was fit without being overly muscular. Her belly had not been defeminized into a washboard of muscles. Its softness suggested that Annette Cole enjoyed the occasional dessert.

They were under the influence of a potent marijuana cigarette that smoked without the usual harshness . . . able to inhale deeply. It was the private stock of a rich California wine maker and amateur farmer, one of Annette's many wealthy male contacts around the world. The pot was a welcome additive for Caesar, who was more accustomed to love for money. Most of the hookers worked on his penis with a kind of detached expertise and had no interest in reaching an orgasm of their own. Annette Cole frightened him a little at first because he sensed that she expected him to direct the course of events. The pot made it easier for him to play the leadership role, allowed him to allow himself a long, unmapped night of lovemaking. He began boldly, opening her legs. He was becoming lost in a very complete kind of intoxication, high and naked and facedown in the pussy of one of the world's most beautiful women.

"You should quit, right now. I swear, Caesar."

The next morning, Beck was hearing Caesar total up his winnings. They were sitting at the casino's coffee shop. Every baseball team Caesar picked had won. The whole day, the languorous breakfast in his hotel suite and the magical high-rolling and the splendidly unnerving title fight and the aperitif of sex with a supermodel, was a standard deviation from the norm, a cluster of winning, of indulgences the likes of which few humans ever experience. In twenty-four hours he had sizably increased his net worth, and all the while pursuing his favorite things.

"Look, you won't listen to me, but take some of this money and put it away. I have a broker in New York. He's made me a bunch of money. I'm telling you. Why give all of this to the government? Get some bonds and stuff. Tax-free stuff . . . and stop gambling. This is a sign from God. You hear me?"

"Why don't you come back with me to Rancho Mirage? Richard's picking me up. We'll have a few beers. Come on. I'll tell you what you want to know about Annette Cole."

"I don't think so."

"Hey, you should see her tits."

"All right, but I've got to be back home for a commercial shoot by Tuesday morning."

* * *

192

The drinking began on the ride through the desert and didn't stop. Beck and Caesar had already closed one bar in Rancho Mirage when they tried to get into Chaplin's.

"Sorry, boys, closed," the headwaiter told them.

"But I see some guys over there in the corner."

"They're special guests of the owner."

"Really? Well the owner wouldn't mind some more business, would he?"

"Let 'em in, Ralph."

The voice was Sinatra's, a noted local night owl, but it was the first time he and Caesar had shared the same turf. Frank invited Caesar to sit down. There were five of them at the table all together, including Frank's bodyguard, and the topics were of mutual interest: boxing, drinking, why tipping was important . . . and broads. Beck told Sinatra about Caesar's Las Vegas conquest.

"Where's the piano player?"

"Sleeping, I suspect, Mr. Sinatra," said Manny the bartender.

"Well, wake him up."

"Yes, sir."

Twenty minutes later, there was a private performance by one of the greatest entertainers of the twentieth century. "Caesar," he said, sitting next to the drowsy young pianist, "this one's for you . . . to the guy who got his bird wet but good this weekend in Vegas." Sinatra started with "Lady Is a Tramp."

All Played Out

For serious bettors having subpar years, the Super Bowl was often viewed as a last chance to break even. Or even finish ahead. As he drove with Beck toward Las Vegas on a Sunday afternoon during which his second wife had made a last-ditch effort to salvage their life together, Caesar Fortunato was down many thousands of dollars to his bookie, but a victory by the Patriots was going to take care of that and then some.

Right after the Patriots scored and cut the Packers' lead to six, the Packers responded. They were only twenty miles outside of Rancho Mirage when one of Beck's Heisman successors, Desmond Howard, returned a kick ninety-nine yards for a touchdown. Two hours later, as the game was ending and they were nearing Las Vegas, Howard was being named the Most Valuable Player of Super Bowl XXXI, won by the Packers. And so concluded the worst betting season of Caesar's life, four straight months of losing.

"What are we doing?"

"What does it look like we're doing?"

"Why are we going to the airport?"

"I am going to the airport and you are going to take my car back to Rancho Mirage."

"And where are you going?"

"None of your fucking business."

"I ain't taking your car back to Rancho Mirage unless you tell me where you're going."

"Fine, don't take it back."

Beck was always grateful to Caesar for getting him his first job in TV. He truly enjoyed Caesar's company. And once his celebrity increased, there were few people with whom he was able to enjoy a true friendship. Caesar wasn't dazzled by his stardom and wouldn't hesitate to call him a flaming asshole, if necessary. In return, Beck felt it was his obligation to keep Caesar from bottoming out. When he saw Caesar headed for ridiculous losses at a casino, he'd find some way to make him stop. It was Beck who kept telling him to stop gambling on sports. It was Beck who had convinced him to put a million bucks away with a broker, the remains of which were the only asset keeping Caesar Fortunato from bankruptcy.

"Don't do it."

"Don't do what?"

"Don't be going back to New York and terrorize my friend Sam."

"I'm flying to Cancun."

"No, you're not."

"Listen, what about this film deal you were going to get me? You know, all this lovey-dovey bullshit on the ranch and everything else. When the fuck is that going to happen, big guy? When are you going to come through for me on that?"

"I don't know. Actually, I'm a little pissed off with my buddy Johnny Ray."

"So what am I supposed to live on?"

"Lynette showed us the paperwork, my friend. If you empty out that account, you know it'll be all gone in a couple of months."

"I'm getting a little tired of everyone telling me what to do."

They rode the rest of the way in silence.

At the 1976 Super Bowl, he was finally at liberty. It was his first Super Bowl since getting divorced from Maxine. There would be no annoying, blinking message light greeting him as he returned from dawn patrols. His wired, toxic world had reached its own version of harmony. Caesar rode a weeklong buzz like a surfer negotiating the Bonzai pipeline. The key was a careful maintenance plan: quaaludes by day, cocktails and cocaine by night, and then just before bed, often near sunrise, pancakes and sausages and rye toast and hash browns and scrambled eggs, and maybe a hot fudge sundae. This sunrise special prevented punishing, debilitating headaches and cleansed the bowels.

It was also when Caesar found his soul brother. Charles Beck was a handsome, bubbly, enormously talented black athlete at the peak of his career. Additionally blessed with a beaming smile, he appealed to every single demographic: old and young, male and female, north and south, the God-fearing and the religiously indifferent. Caesar gave Beck his first job in television, Super Bowl sideline reporter. He was available because his team had lost in the first round of the playoffs.

Caesar had hired Beck because of his star quality and his ability to explain football in a simple way. As Caesar quickly discovered that Super Bowl week, Beck could also get laid every hour of the day, if he so desired. As the Super Bowl teams were arriving, a week before the game, Caesar and Beck met Pam and Cathy in the lobby bar. Pam and Cathy worked as secretaries at league headquarters in New York. The foursome had beers at the hotel bar, shared five bottles of sangria at a hospitable, ebullient Cuban restaurant, vacuumed coke in the limo on the way to a jazz club, switched to Champagne, spent more time flinging food than eating it at Caesar's ritualistic poison-sponging fry-fest, then ended up in his suite, where Caesar and Beck alternated with Pam and Cathy.

This was to be the basis of their friendship: goodwill partying. In the ways of getting wasted, they were alike. Their tolerance for drugs and alcohol was largely similar. If one was slurring his speech, so was the other. If one passed out, the other was not far behind.

"What are you going to do after your cuh . . . reer?" Caesar inquired during one of the first of their many late-night ramblings.

"I'll just keep pretending I'm a fu-fucking white guy."

"You're going to be a big star, I'm fucking telling you."

"Hey, we're both gonna be big fucking stars."

"You got the best of both worlds, motherfucker."

"Yeah?"

"You sound like a fucking white guy, but you possess the typical physical attributes of a black man."

"Ain't it wonderful."

The 1976 Super Bowl was a classic, a fair match, football legends in the making, leaping and tackling and passing and catching with fervor and power and precision and intelligence. Every other play made for a great replay. Caesar was sober as he directed the game, adrenaline for once sufficient. Standing, too excited to sit, snapping his fingers to signal each take, he was swept away in the rhythm of making his live movie: cut, cut, cut, dissolve, cut, cut, cut, dissolve. There were fifty monitors in front of him, outputs of cameras, replay machines, graphics. He had full command of this visual smorgasbord, was somehow able to absorb this electronic mosaic, somehow able to see each image on each screen all at once, the game and the broadcast melting into an invigorating flow.

"Rea-dy two . . . take two! . . . rea-dy nine . . . don't lose Swann . . . going deep . . . whoa, he's got it! . . . take nine! . . . he's got it! . . . what a fucking catch! . . . rea-dy ten . . . take ten! . . . rea-dy nine . . . take nine! . . . where's the replay? Is the replay on red? . . . Okay . . . stand by red . . . are you cued up? . . . stand by . . . ROLL RED! . . . What are his numbers? . . . Where's the chyron? . . . Nice, Artie . . . insert chyron!"

Finally, he had the Pete Rose shot, or at least his version of the Pete Rose shot. It was Tommy Vaughn, of course, who got the first-ever Pete Rose shot, which also deeply bothered Caesar. Rounding second on a base hit, suspecting the outfielder's throw would reach third concurrent with his arrival, Pete Rose made like Superman in a telecast directed by Tommy Vaughn. At full sprint, Rose turned himself into a human missile, propelled himself fearlessly toward the bag, both hands stretched in front of him to their fullest, as if he were about to leap a tall building. It became the quintessential image of a player who came to be called Charlie Hustle. Tommy Vaughn's replay showed even more fully the depth of Rose's desire, showed this stocky, half-crazed athlete damning gravity and risking a full-body scab to beat a throw to third. There was a cloud of dirt upon impact and a tag by the fielder one instant too late. Pete Rose was safe because he played the game as if his life depended on it.

Since Vaughn had captured that shot, Caesar had been looking for one of his own. That's why he sometimes installed two cameras in the same position, one for coverage, one for art. One guy would get the facts, the other guy would be looking for the Rose shot. On that Sunday of Super Bowl X, another athlete made a play as if his life depended on it. Lynn Swann's head was still fogged by a concussion administered two weeks before and he had been forewarned by the Dallas defense that they planned a day of aggressive head-hunting, no mercy for the wounded, but Swann saw that he could not catch the fading pass unless he made a leap of faith, a Rose-like leap with a landing most uncertain. Catching the ball wasn't the problem. It was what would happen when he crashed to earth. Caesar's cameras caught the catch and celebrated on several replays the magnitude of Swann's athletic feat, a flying, floating full-body dive that had not been seen before and that in his professional life Caesar would not see again.

He'd been so busy boozing and doping and whoring with Beck before the game, there was no time for betting, which was a good thing, because he didn't give a shit who won. He finished the coverage by lingering on a linebacker from the losing team, head in his hands, seated on his helmet, motionless, disconsolate, a superb snapshot. In the press box, as the trophy presentation started, the reporter from the *New York Times*, the newspaper of record, decided on his lead:

MIAMI — Today, the Super Bowl justified its existence. A game characterized in the past by sluggishness and ennui was instead well played and exciting, unresolved until the last play.

At the very end was the best escape of all. He walked from the truck to a waiting helicopter. He'd remember the awe in the faces of his guys, their hair blown back by the takeoff, waving like little kids, loose papers being thrown about, the deafening *chuk chuk chuk*. As the helicopter followed the interstate to the airport, ten minutes of flying time, Caesar took a quick, maintain-the-high snort and passed the vial to Beck. He would be in a first-class seat on a flight to Los Angeles twenty minutes after the end of the Super Bowl and he would drink for hours and he would flirt with the stewardesses and he would make merry with Beck and when he landed a limousine would be waiting to take him to his new home in the California desert and weeks and weeks of a wholly sybaritic vacation.

"The rest of it, Sam," said Caesar, who had taken the red-eye and slept in his clothes and had spilled coffee on his pants on the way in from the airport. He arrived at JFK well before dawn, 5:41 A.M. Eastern time on January 27, 1997. At a Wall Street diner, waiting for Sam's office to open, he read all three of the New York dailies, plus *Time* and *Newsweek*, and overindulged on jelly-laden bagels, chocolate-frosted donuts, and coffee. "Wired" wasn't even the right word for his chemical state. He should have been wearing a sign that read: DANGER. HIGH VOLTAGE.

"Caesar, you need to get some help," said Sam, starched shirt, pressed suit, recently mouthwashed, aftershaved, and hair-sprayed.

"Sam!"

"Caesar, I gave you almost three quarters of a million six months ago."

"Sam, I want the fucking money!"

"Sit down, Caesar, come on!"

A secretary turned when she heard the yelling and called security when she saw Caesar's hands around Sam's throat.

The next day, his financial advisor now securely alienated, Caesar had half a million in his checking account, all the money he had left in the world. When he landed, Lynette met him at the airport.

"What's up? Why are you here?"

"It's your mom. There was an accident."

"What?"

"I guess she was coming out to see you. She was on a plane, Caesar. There was a sudden storm in the mountains."

"Ah, Lynette. Lynette. She was coming to see me because you cut her off. Fuck, Lynette. Oh my God . . . ah, Jesus."

Talent

"Caesar Anthony Fortunato, television genius, how are you? What a pleasure to hear your distinctive, comforting voice."

He was calling Chuck Holman, once the most hated and most watched broadcaster in sports television history.

"Wife, kids, okay?"

"The girls are great, Caesar, but Wendy's going back to the doctor this week. We hope the cancer hasn't returned."

"Please wish her my best."

After Chuck Holman decided sports was beneath him and began to work games drunk and submitted completely to his dark side, Caesar Fortunato remained his biggest supporter. Holman owed Caesar. He really did. For years, Caesar coddled him, protected him, defended his tart, cruel put-downs, his very public indiscretions, his unwavering, selfish nonsense.

There was the Reggie Jackson story. The Yankees were at home to play the Kansas City Royals, and that morning Reggie was front-page news in all the tabloids. He had the misfortune of being at a nightclub during a shooting. The game producer sent a production assistant to have Chuck find Reggie and ask for an interview.

"Young man, how dare you interrupt me?"

Holman was in the press room relaxing with a cigar, chatting with the only two members of the New York press he had yet to insult. The PA had hovered, unobtrusively, waiting until he sensed a pause in the conversation.

"Who do you think you are, asking me such a thing? Who the fuck do you think you are, young man?" said Holman, gratuitously castigating the polite twenty-four-year-old coworker in front of an audience. "You go back to Ron fucking Dolemeyer and tell him that Chuck Holman does not ask for interviews. When Reggie Jackson wants to speak to Chuck Holman, he will come to Chuck Holman."

The PA returned to the truck and reported Holman's reply.

"Caesar, I am going to strangle that son of a bitch. I've really had enough."

"Ron, here's the deal. He doesn't want to be embarrassed. He doesn't want to go to Reggie and have Reggie turn him down. I'll take care of it."

Caesar found a black associate producer, Reggie was agreeable, and, after the unpleasantness, there was indeed an interview with Chuck that pleased both Chuck and Reggie, because Reggie was able to clear his name before a national audience and Chuck was seen as the guy capable of getting the big stars.

Then there was a football game in Philadelphia in 1977, when Holman visited the team owner before kickoff and allowed one obligatory drink to become a vodka happy hour. As the game started, the owner sent a security guard over to the announce booth with a fire bucket of iced martinis. By the second quarter, Chuck was BWI: broadcasting while intoxicated.

This Washington team is a disgrace. They have neither talent nor adequate will.

They are not deserving of my attention—or for that matter, the attention of our audience.

Chuck, I think you might be jumping the gun a little.

Gil Francis, why are you apologizing for this incompetence?

To Holman, Francis was another half-wit ex-jock handed an announcing job because he was pretty and famous. To Francis, all of Holman's opinions were suspect because he had never played the game.

Chuck, it's not yet halftime.

As always, Gil, you are not prepared to accept the obvious. Have you looked at the scoreboard?

The Philadelphia Eagles were leading, 17–0.

If the Washington Redskins stop turning the ball over, Chuck, they have the offense to get right back in it.

I beg to differ. This team has far too many white players at the skill positions.

Francis knew Holman always drank during the games. But at that point, it was apparent there had been pregame activity.

So, Chuck, he said to America, while making eye contact with Holman, *you're telling me they don't have the RIGHT players on offense.*

The charitable cover-up went unnoticed.

No, no, Gil, you impossible bore. Washington has too many white players. It is well known that they are an organization with a racist past. And this announcer is taking great pleasure in seeing the Eagles integrate their end zone.

In the third quarter, Holman yakked, creaming his colleague's two-hundred-dollar Italian loafers. During the commercial break that followed, Caesar probably saved Chuck's career.

"I will not. That's absurd."

"You want to do this the hard way or the easy way?"

"The most corrupt man in sports television is taking *me* off the air. I'll say it politely, you little guinea: Go fuck yourself."

"Okay, Chuck, listen clearly . . . when we come back from commercial, I'm not going to open your mike. And if you cause any problems, I'll have Barney physically remove you."

Stage manager Barney was definitely in Caesar's camp. For years, Chuck had treated much of the crew, including Barney, like serfs.

"All right, you awful, atrocious little man. I will leafff. But you have no idea what you are doing. I am . . . the most important broadcaster in this country, and I will make everyone aware that it wazzz . . . not my decision. Chuck Holman does not walk out on his responsibility to the American people. Tomorrow morning, the media will know that I was taken off the air by a diss . . . dissolute, half-ass director with a number of serious personal problems, which I will delineate. INHERIT THE WIND, you f-f-fuck," said Holman, throwing his headset to the floor of the booth.

Afterward, as Holman's future was being evaluated, Fortunato called Omar Hawas.

"Chuck's not one to make excuses."

"Uh-huh."

"But he was scared."

"Uh-huh."

"He thought a little vodka would help."

"What scared him into getting drunk, Caesar?"

"Sir, there was a death threat before the game. Guy called his hotel room."

"I wasn't told."

"It's true. Really shook him up."

Chuck Holman was often the subject of death threats, once had FBI agents assigned to protect him, but actually no one expressed an interest in killing him that night in Philadelphia.

"Caesar, you are full of shit, as usual," said Hawas, "but I admire your loyalty. And that means something to me. If you can put up with Chuck's crap, then maybe I can, too. But I think he's running out of second chances, okay?"

"Right, Omar."

"Caesar, do you think if you were in trouble, he'd be making this kind of call? Remember, this is a man who thinks he's bigger than Elvis. We're all just annoying peons in his wonderfully delusional world."

They were never exactly peers. In the beginning, Chuck was definitely more the educator than the equal. In 1967, when Muhammad Ali was prepared to be jailed and lose his title for refusing induction into the U.S. Army, Holman was among the few who pronounced the act courageous. Like so many others in that America,

Caesar viewed Ali as a traitor and a threat. Chuck made Caesar appreciate Ali's incredible gumption. He reminded Caesar that when Ali came home from Rome, the Olympic gold medalist, he still could not eat, shit, or sleep in a white man's establishment.

He also reminded Caesar about the Philadelphia manager who almost made Jackie Robinson quit baseball.

"You don't know what he called him that day in Ebbets Field, do you, Caesar?"

"Chuck, come on. Sticks and stones. How bad could it have been?"

"You have no idea, do you? It was the epitome of cowardice. Do you know the actual words?"

"No."

"Jackie Roosevelt Robinson couldn't fight back, you realize that? He promised Branch Rickey that he would turn the other cheek for two seasons. But his uncommon supreme patience had boundaries, and manager Ben Chapman of the Philadelphia Phillies pushed him to the very edge. The manager of your city's team almost succeeded in ending the great social experiment of Branch Rickey."

Caesar was about to hear, for the first time, all the pertinent details of that day at Ebbets Field, when baseball was still very much divided about the introduction of black players, when Jackie Robinson, unofficially on probation, almost kissed it all good-bye.

"Rachel Robinson hears every word of it, Caesar Fortunato. In the spring of 1947, the Robinsons have a little baby boy and they're living in a hotel, cooking their meals on a hot plate. Everything about their life is precarious. My God, Caesar, they were getting death threats in the mail *every* day! And players in the National League are talking about going on strike unless Robinson is banned.

"So it is a cold, spring afternoon and the Philadelphia Phillies have arrived by train to play the Brooklyn Dodgers and Rachel Robinson is in the stands and she hears her husband mercilessly abused by the manager of the opposition again and again and again. And no one is stopping it! She hears this vile, ignorant man call her husband nigger and jungle bunny. She hears her husband asked by this piece of garbage from Tennessee if he likes white *poontang*, if he's gotten himself some white pussy the night before. The taunting goes on. The rookie second baseman of the Brooklyn Dodgers, who has already endured so much to reach this day, is watching as Ben Chapman stands brazenly on the top step of the visitor's dugout at Ebbets Field and says he suspects that the first black to take the field in Major League baseball has been fucking the wives of all his white teammates."

Chuck's voice rose during this recitation and he maintained a hypnotic rhythm, a staccato, that had become familiar to all of America. He'd also alter the tone of his voice, segue from full forte to pianissimo with the alacrity of a professional musician, as he did that day with Caesar, reducing his voice to nearly a hush as the story continued.

"Jackie Roosevelt Robinson is about to crack up. He wants to go in that dugout and take a bat to this man's face. He suspects his wife can hear this incessant degradation and Jackie Robinson is a deeply proud man. And this is too much! He is ready to lose it. He is ready to knock out someone's teeth in that dugout and walk away from Ebbets Field, walk away from baseball, end the experiment being conducted in front of an entire nation. End the hopes he carries of millions of blacks across the nation in that spring of 1947. But Jackie Roosevelt Robinson resists this natural urge to fight back and he responds in a more productive manner, as he would do again and again and again."

Holman's voice was building to a crescendo.

"In the eighth inning, Robinson singles up the middle. As he steals second, the throw from the catcher bounces into center field and Robinson takes third. Gene Hermanski singles to right, Jackie Robinson scores. Dodgers one, Phillies zero. That's the final. THAT . . . WAS . . . HIS . . . ANSWER."

After the path-blazing early days, when they had the biggest balls and won all the prizes, after Chuck Holman and Caesar Fortunato introduced journalism to sports television, introduced candor to the analysis of sporting events, each grew weary of his station in life. Eventually, Chuck thought he should have been anchoring the evening news or running for senator. Caesar was sure he had booted nobler destinies. Many would suffer for their suffering.

There was a production assistant who nearly killed himself in the middle of a basketball season. It was the kid's first year. Came from Iowa. Rob Fry. An earnest, golly-gee-whiz kid. Dad a farmer. Dean's

List student. Working in New York for a TV network was the answer to his prayers. Caesar and Chuck all but put a rope around his neck.

"Mr. Fry, this is Mr. Fortunato. The desk clerk is telling me that I do not have a suite. I want you to come down here and tell him that I am supposed to have a suite. And I don't want to wait more than ten minutes. Is that understood, Mr. Fry?"

It was one A.M. Caesar had just made his entrance after a long flight from the coast. This violation of standard procedure, no suite for Caesar, put the rookie on immediate probation. The new boy would need a little ass kicking, and it was delivered a day later, during the broadcast. The year was 1986, and Caesar was approaching fifty and he was changing, hardening, finding less and less about life funny or worthy, his sense of wonder ebbing. Even his easy grasp of all matters editorial was suffering from the effects of his prevailing state of boredom.

"It's I-R-V-I-N-G. Not an E. It starts with an I."

Composing the graphics superimposed on the screen—the player names, statistics, and scoring updates—was theoretically Rob Fry's most important job. Caesar was disputing Fry's spelling of basketball legend Julius Erving.

"Caesar, really, it's spelled with an E. I have a poster of Dr. J on my wall at home."

"Change the fucking graphic, Mr. Fry. I am from Philadelphia. Julius Erving plays for Philadelphia. I should know. And don't ever fucking challenge me again, do you understand?"

Fearful and already shell-shocked, Fry consented.

The next day, several papers noted the curious spelling. Rob Fry got a voice mail from the executive producer. The message was left at eight A.M. and it informed Fry that he was now on probation. Another serious error, said the recorded voice, and he would lose his job.

At the following game, Fry was found to be deficient at the *end* of his weekend's work.

"Where is my limo? I'm ready to go, where the fuck is it?"

Caesar had rushed out of the truck to begin the escape. It was still pre–Henry Kapp, when money was no object and creature comforts

207

paramount. As the production assistant, choreographing the escape was another of Rob Fry's many responsibilities.

"Where is Mr. Fry?" Caesar asked to no one in particular. "Someone get Mr. Fry!"

A moment later, the production assistant was in the line of fire.

"You had a good game, everyone was happy, and now you have fucked it up. This isn't some hick operation, son. We do things right, all the time. Where the fuck is my car?"

It would turn out that the limousine had been hijacked earlier by division president Omar Hawas.

That next week, Caesar asked Fry to arrange an interview with Magic Johnson, the reigning superstar in basketball. He was told to have Magic available one hour before the game. Caesar said he would alert the producer so everything would be ready—camera, sound, talent. Fry's one responsibility was to make the arrangements with Johnson. That's what Caesar told him. Magic showed, and so did Chuck Holman. But the crew was on their lunch break.

"Son," said Chuck Holman, "I am here and so is the leading player in all of the NBA. Where's everyone else? This is absurd. This is fucking absurd! I will not ask Mr. Earvin Johnson to wait more than a few minutes."

"Mr. Fortunato said he'd have the producer arrange everything, sir."

"Well, young man, it doesn't look like everything is arranged, does it? And the director of the game is not supposed to be doing your job for you. Jesus! The incompetence I have to put up with! Son, under which rock did we find you?"

Fry, frantic, found Caesar in the midst of a slice of pizza.

"No, this is not my problem, son, it is your problem," said Fortunato, loud enough to be heard by the other pizza eaters surrounding him.

The next morning, there was another voice mail from the executive producer. He wanted to see Fry as soon as possible. Chuck Holman and Caesar Fortunato had both complained about him. There was an issue about an important interview with Magic Johnson. The doomed PA wandered around Manhattan with his impending TV death sentence, his stomach a cauldron, his mind a soup of self-pity and fright. The next day, he was expecting to go into work and be fired and have to move home and milk the fucking cows.

He rode the Staten Island ferry back and forth a few times, went to a movie. That night, he settled at a bar near his tiny midtown apartment. After five beers and three shots of vodka, he weaved his way into another bar, proceeding from typically drunk to seriously disabled. Taking two steps forward and one step sideways, traveling north and then east and then west and then north, he willed himself back to his apartment. On the way up the stairs, he tripped and couldn't break his fall. He felt a warm flow of blood streaming down the right side of his face. After an adventure opening the apartment door, his head throbbing, he groped his way to the bathroom in the darkened apartment. In the mirror, his face blurred and then regained focus, in and out, in and out. He put one hand against the sink but couldn't stop wobbling, and he thought it best to sit down, just for a few minutes. While propped against the tub, he began to slide slowly to the floor, until he passed out, too far gone to be made uncomfortable by the hard, cold, tiled surface.

Returning from his girlfriend's apartment, where he was as yet not welcome to stay over, Ken Coleman discovered his roommate in a puddle of vomit and couldn't tell if he was breathing and he called an ambulance. Emergency measures were required to revive Rob Fry, who was fortunate, in this case, to be a rock-hard farm-boy from Iowa. His heart proved resilient.

Caesar was at Chuck's apartment for some predinner drinking when a *New York Times* reporter called for a comment about the network's hospitalized production assistant.

"Did I have something to do with what? This is ABSURD. How dare you insinuate that I had anything to do with that poor young man's troubles. This is an outrage! Just who do you think you are, asking me such things?"

Chuck winked at his wife and Casear, all parties nursing tumblers of vodka. Wendy picked up another phone.

"If you want a story," she said in her deep, raspy voice, "talk about that cocksucker Fritz Taylor."

Fritz Taylor was the troublesome new color analyst using up too much oxygen in the booth, or so Chuck believed.

"Where did you go to school, young man? Harvard? What an awful institution! And I have even less respect for your newspaper. Red Smith and Dave Anderson—they're hacks! Worthless hacks!"

Both writers were Pulitzer Prize winners.

"You're asking me the same question again? Oh, you are a brazen, obnoxious young man, aren't you? I'm not going to offer any comment, that's what, because this is absurd, totally, absolutely absurd! And if your newspaper prints anything saying or even implying that I had something to do with the troubles of Mr. Rob Fry, I will sue them. And I will sue you, Mr. Reporter. And I will sue your family for having the nerve to release you into the world!"

There was nothing in the paper, because the reporter could not get anyone to speak on the record. Chuck Holman was a big name, and if his name was going to be attached to the near death of a young, vulnerable production assistant, the *Times* editor feared extreme aggravation if the accusers were only anonymous. At the apartment following the call, they all laughed, but not heartily. Chuck and Caesar knew this could have been a problem, and that was the sum of what they were thinking: that the Rob Fry situation could have been a problem for them. Neither was about to send flowers to the hospital. In a short time, Chuck Holman was gone from the network, contract not renewed, although the official word was that he had quit in a huff. That was okay with Hawas, who let people write their own exit stories.

"I need a loan, Chuck."

When they were both working and virtually beyond reproach, Caesar would be the first person Chuck would call during any crisis. But since each was more or less forced into retirement, Chuck had no more need of Caesar and Caesar didn't want to be in a position of needing Chuck.

"Caesar, what are we talking about?"

"I'd liked to scrape together a million for starters, Chuck, not that I'm asking you for a million."

"Let me be frank, Caesar. Is this related to your gambling?"

"What do you mean?"

"The need for this kind of money. Is it still the problem it always was?"

"Of course not. Honestly, I haven't been working that much. I've been waiting on this movie deal. It's about to happen any minute. I just need something to tide me over. I'll have this money back to you in a couple of months."

"Caesar, you are a dear friend, but of course what you are asking is outrageous. . . ."

Upon hearing that word, Caesar rubbed a hand through his hair and silently cursed himself.

"Really, my friend, how could you be making this call to me? . . . I mean, you know my wife has been ill, and I am now a pariah in broadcasting. There is no shame anymore in the industry. No integrity. And right now my first obligation is to my wife and to my children. After all the absurd obligations, after carrying the fucking sports department for years, I am making a belated effort to fully attend to the needs of my family, their needs now and their needs in the future. Caesar, it is not 1968, and we are not working for the free-spending Omar Hawas and drinking liberally from his bottomless well."

The phone call was over, though Chuck continued, uninterrupted, for another five minutes. Twice more he mentioned his wife's illness. Three more times he said the business was shit since he'd left. Again, he cursed the many who had mistreated him. He told Caesar his paltry savings were going to his children, chastised Caesar for panhandling an old man—an old, irascible shit who Caesar knew to have five homes and probably fifty million dollars.

"Caesar, I will do this for you. I will make a phone call. Given your situation, I have a friend you should speak with, and he will not charge for his services. He is the best in his field. I will be my persuasive self, and I will make it clear to my friend that this is a matter of personal importance to me. All right, Caesar? Let me go now, Wendy is motioning to me."

"So you can't give me anything?"

"Can you believe it?"

"What, Chuck?"

"Francis and the wife called up to say they're praying for me. He calls me up to tell me this. Those bastards. Those sick bastards. They should pray for themselves, those sick bastards! She's the one hiring all

211

those children to make her clothes. What a travesty! And he can't keep his pecker in his pants. It's ludicrous! . . . You know, the Baseball Hall of Fame wants to honor me, Caesar."

"That's very nice, Chuck. Listen, I'm gonna get going. My best to Wendy."

"I'm not going to let them do it."

"What, Chuck?"

"I don't want them honoring me. They just want to sell tickets. They just want to use my name to make money. Oh . . . oh! I've just soaked myself. Where is Wendy? You wanted money? That's why you called me, right? This really wasn't a call made out of any lingering affection, or to inquire about my health, was it? Oh, you are a horrible little man. I've always known it. All of you people, horrible little people not worthy of my attention. I must go. Jeez, I'm all wet."

"Talent" was the general term used for the people in front of the camera. The word in TV had no relation to the word in the dictionary. To those who worked behind the camera, most talent were not wonderfully creative creatures but rather ticking time bombs, any moment about to explode in a fit of spectacular petulance. At least half the actors and broadcasters Caesar had known had this kind of acquired disease: Shortly after their anointing, they were possessed by a delusion that the earth was created for the purpose of entertaining their every whim. Further, they believed themselves beyond the confines of normal human propriety.

Caesar had several ways of classifying talent. There were the silly, like Jill Conrad. She was presenting an Emmy with two costars from her hit prime-time soap opera, and it was agreed all the actresses would dress in black gowns. The night of the show, Jill showed up in red and, further, noticeably and unsuccessfully jockeyed for the center position in the threesome. Her taller, peeved costars boxed her out on national television like NBA forwards fighting for a rebound. Later, she denied everything before a highly suspicious press corps.

Then there were the out-of-control substance abusers, like Bob Stein, who became addicted to morphine after losing a leg in a car accident and missed a big football game because he had overdosed.

Sam Piersall was a classic play-by-play announcer who regularly drank himself within reach of a coma. Caesar once saw him impudently pee on the floor of a hotel hallway when he couldn't find his room.

Some required a supply of aspirin, like Stephanie West, who was incapable of admitting a mistake. She would flub a line and blame the stage manager for shuffling his feet, or a cameraman for sniffling, or the food service lady for bringing lukewarm coffee. On a day when her batting average was especially low, she would rival Joan Crawford for sheer venom and blame her way up to the director, and sometimes even the network president.

There were talent who could get you killed, like Pat Maguire. He was doing stand-ups with Caesar for a story about the doping of East German athletes. Their local guide had found a scenic spot, but it was on the fringe of a secret military installation. When the shooting began, Maguire was first to the car. He yelled, "Mush, mush!" to the driver, and left Caesar, crew, and guide behind, in the line of fire.

Caesar reserved his highest level of contempt for two announcers from the country-club sports. In any small space of time, tennis commentator Jimmy Martin could be bratty, cruel, contentious, condescending, insulting, selfish, snooty, whiny, and unreasonable. He also bathed infrequently and wore soup-stained ties on the air. Then there was Kenny Preston, a golf teacher of minimal broadcasting ability who complained almost every hour of every day of every show. Preston rarely experienced anything but a warming sun, skipped from one enthralling landscape to another, from a winter stop at Pebble Beach on California's spectacular northern coast, to the flowering, springtime magnolias at Augusta, to a summer interlude at the majestic, spartan Scottish links used for the British Open. He worked daily enveloped by beauty but moaned if his driver was two minutes late, or his blazer wasn't properly ironed, or if a meeting lasted more than twenty minutes, or if he had to do more than two takes of an on-camera, or if, worst of all, no one had remembered to bring a supply of his favorite beverage: Diet Coke.

Chuck Holman was surely a prima donna, but what he had to say was often courageous and important. He mattered as a broadcaster, and he tried to return Caesar's friendship, at least for as long as they ruled TV. Ten years before, only ten short years before, Chuck Holman was the best man at his Las Vegas wedding to Lynette. They were together gambling when Caesar's father-in-law made his toast—improperly absent but bonding, talent and director. It was a blow that Chuck Holman's reservoir of simpatico, small as it was, had finally dried up. In Caesar's mind, that was the essential difference between talent he could stand and talent he couldn't: Some were capable of a measure of friendship and some were not. For the latter, and there were all too many, it was always about them, as if no one else really counted, and that's where Chuck Holman ended up.

On St. Patrick's Day of 1997, Caesar having run through virtually all of his savings, as predicted by Beck, someone from Dominic's operation called.

"We want it now, now being tomorrow."

Caesar hung up, wondering about the consequences of missing that deadline. His mother had previously handled all dealings with Dominic. This was a new brand of trouble at a very bad time. There was no more money other than a dwindling supply of residual checks that amounted to a couple of hundred a month, and without the Green Hornet, there was no intermediary to tap dance for him.

A week after the call, someone showed up with a shotgun. Lynette was sleeping in another room, halfway out of the marriage. There were three shots, house-shaking blasts. Lynette gasped for air and then shrieked. Caesar froze. When the two finally summoned the courage to get out of their beds, they found the dining area erased.

Caesar later learned that the job was authorized by Fred D. Lite, who had just been released from prison and didn't like the look of his music video, "Increase the Peace." In fairness to Fred, Caesar had defied the singer's orders to shoot the video with a certain kind of reversal film stock. Fred wanted a high-contrast, grainy feel and thought the finished result had the all-too-polished, all-too-middlebrow look of a car commercial. Caesar considered telling Lynette the real story, but he decided it was better that she think the shooting was related to gambling. It was more masculine.

Mexico

"YO, CAE-SAR!"

The hideaway was anything but.

"YO, MY MAN!"

Billy Semple was Caesar's director of photography for *Love or Lust,* though the credits listed him as Barber Stiles.

"Wat you doing down here, my man!"

"Chilling, B.S. . . . Hey, this a friend, Charles Beck."

"Yo, bro."

"And Billy, what the fuck are you doing in Rosarito Beach?"

"Take a look out back."

"What do you mean?"

"If you go out back, and look down the coast, you'll see a very large, turn-of-the-century ocean liner."

"They're doing that here?"

"Yup, built a whole fucking studio for this fucking movie. I think the budget is up to two hundred million. It's sick."

"How long you been here?"

"Like forever. We're done this week. Gonna sink the fucking thing once and for all. And then I'm outta here. No more fucking fish tacos."

After leaving the scene of the crime in downtown Los Angeles, Beck and Caesar cabbed it to the Mexican border: three hours, four hundred bucks. They strolled out of the United States amidst a stream of tourists, a good way to avoid detection, and then jumped in a Tijuana taxi and pushed farther south. This was the first escape engineered by Caesar Fortunato, made necessary because he had assaulted Johnny Ray Thompson on the lot of Triax Pictures.

The chain of events began with Caesar calling Johnny Ray's lawyer to ask about his contract. The lawyer told Caesar he wasn't directing the picture; Caesar called Beck; Beck picked Caesar up and drove him to the lot; both men confronted Johnny Ray Thompson, who was doing the looping work on his most recent film, the process where actors read their lines again because the dialogue recorded while on location had been compromised or could be sufficiently improved. Johnny Ray was in a sound booth and looked none too pretty. In part, this was because he wasn't being filmed. Johnny Ray's face, without the aid of makeup, was kind of a leathery road map, marked by rivers of wrinkles, and tributaries of rivers of wrinkles. He was also cranky, further contributing to his less than luminous appearance. He didn't like ever leaving Texas and certainly hated being in L.A. for any reason.

"You fucking coward," Caesar opened after bursting into the booth.

"I'm working here, son. Someone get this man out of here."

Three security people had made an effort to block the advance of the interlopers, but all fell like bowling pins after being pancaked by Beck.

"You couldn't even pick up the phone and tell me?"

"Johnny Ray," said Beck, now also inside the booth, "I expect people to keep their promises. What the fuck is going on?"

"What the fuck is going on? Well, two dickheads in my midst are interrupting my work. And if either of you have half a brain, which I am doubting, you will get the fuck out of here!"

"I drop good money on you in Las Vegas, supply you with dope, you drag my ass to Texas, tell me you hate Hollywood, and then, after all that, you hire a Hollywood director. And you can't even tell me to my face. What a fucking weasel!"

"Oh excuse me, Mr. Fortunato. When exactly were you going to tell me that you had a FUCKING HEART ATTACK! Maybe my lawyer thinks it's a bad idea to have a cripple directing one of my pictures."

So Caesar hit him, not quite square on the nose, but close.

"Shit!" said the fallen Johnny Ray.

Beck gobbed on his head.

On the way out, a smallish security suit weakly ordered them to stop.

"You want a piece of me!" yelled Beck, bearing down.

"Sir, you are under arrest."

"Get out of the way, fuckhead!"

"Oh . . . oh . . . oh, my God!"

The foolish but brave Triax security man was out for ten minutes. Everyone thought he was dead until a secretary got a vase and drenched his face.

He told Beck they'd head for this place he knew in Mexico, a quaint, lonely, perpetually vacant hotel on a bluff overlooking the Pacific. It had been fifteen years since Caesar had stopped at Rosarito Beach, the customary pissing point on the way back from lost weekends of dedicated drinking in Ensenada. When they arrived, he discovered his quaint hotel had bloated into a double-winged, tacky spa, and the bluff was lousy with new properties, elbow to elbow, none with even a hint of charm, all looking as if they were constructed on a whim in about a week. Adding to the circus of construction, Fox Pictures had built James Cameron a forty-acre studio just down the coast, and he was about to wrap production on the most expensive film ever made.

"The guy is one fucking pain in the ass. I mean, he's on this one-hundred-and-fifty-foot crane with a megaphone, screaming at all of us like sixteen hours a day. I swear, sometimes he thinks he's Jesus, or something. But what fucking balls. I mean, he's got to make four hundred million on this thing just to break even. And he hasn't even started to edit."

217

With nothing to unpack and nowhere else to run, Beck and Caesar retired to the coastal bar and hunkered down. Billy Semple, a compulsive yapper, had joined the fugitives from justice, along with several other survivors of *Titanic*. A platoon of dead beers stood untouched on the table.

"Three weeks into production, we're eating this lobster chowder, and man, we all got so fucking sick. I was barfing all fucking night. You should have seen Cameron. One of the guys said he looked like he'd been sniffing glue. They tested the chowder. How 'bout this: spiked with PCP . . . f-uuu-ck me."

Six months later, after the suspicious food poisoning; after shooting for one hundred and sixty days; after rolling two hundred and eighty-eight hours of film; after dropping two miles below the sea to film the wreck of the real thing using a sub borrowed from Russia; after using the original blueprints from the Belfast shipbuilders to produce a seven-hundred-and-seventy-five-foot replica, the largest set piece in Hollywood history, including the three-story oak staircase; after reproducing the china, four hundred and forty chairs, one hundred and ten tables, and four hundred and fifty sets of silverware; after having BMK Stoddard of England, the original manufacturers, reproduce the carpeting; after hiring four hundred Mexican construction workers, and British plasterers and Seattle welders and architects who normally design suspension bridges; after hiring the production designer for fifteen James Bond films, and fifty electricians and ten first-class camera operators, including Billy Semple, James Cameron was going to wrap production of the most ambitious film ever made by flooding his xeroxed *Titanic* with millions of gallons of water.

"A couple of weeks ago," Semple continued, "one of the Fox executives was down here. He's got a memo with the scenes they want cut. And this is what Cameron is telling the guy: 'If you want to cut my film, you'll have to fire me. And to fire me, you'll have to kill me.' What a fucking piece of work, huh?"

Fifteen years before, the centerpiece of the hotel's backyard was a decaying walled patio with purple inlaid tile, faded by the sea air, chipping. In its place was the steel skeleton of a coming amusement pier. They had vacuumed every last particle of romance from the place where Marilyn Monroe and the Hollywood gang had once come to slum, and in their upgrade were erecting a second-rate Pacific version of the Jersey shore.

Caesar had spent his childhood summers at the Jersey shore, which he knew even as a boy to be the epitome of tackiness. Having just put himself on a most-wanted list in the latest incident of an impressive losing streak, he was expecting Mexico to be a respite from all associations with his all but destroyed life. Yet at a favored retreat where once it was so easy to get lost, he was finding only dreadful reminders, flashbacks to restless childhood vacations, and more evidence that everyone else had found a way to satisfy their ambitions. This was no escape.

"Busted."

The following day, March 29, 1997, another familiar face appeared at the Rosarito Beach Hotel.

"Beck, take a walk."

"And nice to see you, too, Maxine."

She waited impatiently for Beck to make his exit.

"Caesar, what are you doing?"

"It's pretty clear. I'm trying to ruin my life."

"Are you drunk?"

"Not yet."

"Do you mind if I sit down?"

"If you promise you won't stay long."

"Palmer thought you might be here."

"Asshole."

"Speaking of which, do you know about your son?"

"No, dear."

"He's getting a divorce. Or rather, she's about to divorce him."

"What's that all about?"

"Like you don't know."

She looked past him, stared at the calming whoosh of the surf. There was a long pause, a period of silence not unnatural to them. They were accustomed to giving each other the silent treatment. When married, they would often be livid with each other simultaneously. So they would be stewing at the same time, awaiting an apology at the same time. They could be together for a week of dinners, sit at the same table, and not say anything of consequence to each other.

"I could try to talk to her, I guess."

"No, Caesar, I don't think that's going to work. Unless you can tell her of a way they can avoid losing the house. Of course, you've got much bigger problems."

Maxine thought there had been closure when she indulged her rage during the settlement. She demanded custody of the children and generous child support and the Fifth Avenue apartment. About the only thing Caesar retained was the Renoir, which he was prepared to let her have, as well. This was the one material item he really cherished, so he thought the offer to give it away was an important statement: a kind of apology, an admission that he bore some of the blame for the failure of the marriage. Maxine didn't accept it. She considered the gesture a woeful, belated attempt at goodwill that was essentially selfish, designed to ease his own conscience. But that wasn't the truth. Actually, Caesar was being genuine, was genuinely sorry that he had wasted ten years of Maxine's life in a crappy marriage he should have tried to end much sooner. But by that time, Maxine was deeply suspicious of everything the man did, did not really believe the man to be capable of anything approaching kindness.

At five in the morning, Mark was up, wailing with that annoying sound, like a little animal in distress. He waited and let it go on, hoping his infant son would drift back into sleep. It was a ridiculous notion. It never happened. He looked at the clock, his body in revolt at this unspeakable hour, New York in complete hush. Mark would stop for a couple of seconds and then launch into another burst of pathetic yelps. There was no sleeping through it. Oh, no. So Caesar creaked into a sitting position and found his bathrobe and hobbled to the refrigerator. Maxine hadn't left any bottles. Jesus. Cynthia was now awake, building into full cry. This is what he feared, the greatest fear of all who have little children. The domino effect. One starts and wakes up the rest of the house. Shit.

Cynthia got cookies for breakfast and watched TV all morning. He kept trying to put Mark to sleep. Cynthia asked about going to the park, and each time she did he gave her another cookie. Around ten—after Mark, overdosed on milk, finally went off—Caesar was prone on the couch, attempting something of a nap, dozing lightly, every minute or so seeming to remember to check on Cynthia, a few feet away, sitting in her tiny chair, watching cartoons. Maxine was visiting her mother but would be back that afternoon. When she returned, the living room was almost concealed by splattered toys, dolls facedown, overturned cars and trucks, scattered puzzle pieces, a fallen tower of wooden blocks. Mark was still in his pajamas, the top caked with dried milk and wet with little-boy slobber. Cynthia was in her underwear, sobbing.

"Why are you crying?" she asked her daughter.

"I don't know."

"Did Daddy feed you any lunch?"

"No."

"Did you have breakfast?"

"No."

"Did you have some fruit?"

"No."

"Cynthia, did you have any food at all today?"

"Well . . . well, we had cookies, and then, then . . . ice cream!"

"It sounds like you've had a pretty good day with Daddy. So why are you crying?"

"There was a man kicking the ball on TV and I was making noise and Daddy said it was my fault that the man missed."

"What?"

"Daddy said I ruined everything."

"He was watching football, right?"

"I don't know."

"The one where everyone falls down."

"Yes . . . and I-I-I didn't make the man miss."

"Caesar!"

When he was home, the father, husband, and pathetic gambler was a study in contrast, either in suspended animation or in full froth in front of the TV, absorbed watching the consequences of his wagers. While he was away, at another stadium, another arena, another majestic golf course under a glorious sky, Cynthia, then Mark, crawled, walked, and uttered their first coherent sentences. Shortly thereafter, all too many mornings and nights concluded with the children asking their mommy about their father's whereabouts. The first time his son put two words together, they were: "Daddy whurkin."

Caesar was able to run away, but no matter where he went, no matter how long he was absent, there remained a boy and a girl and a wife in wait for his return, three people who would soon begin to measure the distressing distance between the man he was and the man they wanted him to be. After every trip, he'd slouch into the apartment expecting sanctuary but always finding a wife weary of single parenthood, desperately awaiting his help. In an effort to win sympathy and avoid a fair share of the domestic drudgery, Caesar reminded Maxine of his wearying life on the road—how he was left frazzled commanding a wired group of humans judging him second to second, ever alert to detect a weakness. He moaned about bad coffee and cold pizza, about having to fly in bacteria-infested chambers where the recirculated air was contaminated by hours of sneezing and coughing and burping and farting.

Maxine would have traded places with her peripatetic husband any day. America in the sixties was a good time to be out of the house. The kids of Columbia and Berkeley and Kent State, who blithely sacrificed grades and detested anyone with careerist ambitions, were battering the Victorian status quo. Caesar thought them scurvy and self-important, yet benefited, so to speak, from their labors of liberation. A period of extended adolescence had spread across the land, and when he went on the road, every night alone became an opportunity to taste forbidden fruits: a joint, a blot of acid, tequila without reserve, hungry sex with a new body.

In the hazy consciousness of morning, he sometimes was supremely happy. His brain, at the end of its dream state, would fool him for a moment, allow him to think he was untethered. This nirvana was always fleeting. In a few seconds, the facts of his life would tumble into memory. There was a woman snoring next to him and two children who would soon awake scared and hungry and then, with reality having shoved fantasy aside, he'd ask himself: How did I let this happen?

The best thing for him, Caesar Fortunato approaching thirty, was to get himself to an ashram in India, like the Beatles, and spend a couple of months in a lotus position, chewing on leaves. As a director, he was unchallenged. As a husband, he was unfaithful. As a father, he was a dentist's best friend. Somehow he needed to end Maxine's misery and give his children a life with two loving parents. But he had a plane to catch, there was always a plane to catch, and that was where he was stranded, up in the air.

Caesar needed money to gamble as much as he needed water to drink and air to breathe, as much as a vampire needed a monthly bloodletting. He borrowed money from his domestic staff, from Marisol and Richard and the cleaning lady whose name was either Maria or Elena. He borrowed from the Rolex-wearing Mexican guy who trimmed the grass on the golf course, and the guy who ran the Chico pawnshop, and a waiter he knew at Billy Ray's. He took out loans carrying nasty interest rates from three storefront finance operations. He borrowed from a loan shark associated with his bookie. It was the people closest to him who eventually learned that the last thing Caesar needed was money, which was why he stopped asking Beck and Palmer and Gilmartin and the wife of Omar Hawas, and even his estranged daughter. There was, however, one exception to the rule.

Mark Fortunato grew up to write software for a second-tier computer company. He had three children of his own, two in diapers, and the typical, terrifying debt. It included a lingering student loan, abused credit cards, and an albatross of a mortgage on his cruelly overpriced four-bedroom Silicon Valley home.

"Could you borrow a little more from the credit union?"

Caesar had made another long drive north to San Jose.

"I don't know, Dad. We're up to a hundred thousand."

"You're not telling your wife, are you?"

"No, but she's going to start wondering soon."

"I can get the money back to you in two or three months. . . . Here's what you tell your wife. Tell her you're putting it into a special college fund for the kids. Some kind of matching plan with the company."

Following the preachings of his mother, Maxine, Caesar's son fashioned a life in contrast to his dad's: abstemious, responsible. At the same
time, he forgave his father over and over for no good reason, and he went
and kept retrieving money like a zombie in a spell. A check was mailed
to the father in the fall of 1996, another six months later, another after
Caesar failed to pinch Chuck Holman. As Caesar was dropping Johnny
Ray Thompson, Mark was confronted by his wife and revealed the true
nature of the ever larger deductions from his paycheck, and he had to
tell her that the vacation to Hawaii was not going to happen, that little
Gillian's French lessons would have to be put on hold . . . that they might
have to sell the house.

"So, you're going to be a fugitive."

"I guess."

The conversation between the divorcees had circled back and was
near conclusion. Puffs of whistling wind accompanied the sunset, as if
to announce that nightfall was nearing.

"So, that's it. The kids won't ever see you again."

"Maxine, I don't know anything right now."

"What about your son? How could you do that to your son?"

For the first time, she saw the desperation in his eyes.

"Maxine, I'm in really deep this time."

Seoul Survivors

"They're dying."

"So?"

"Caesar, the pigeons are burning."

"I know."

The Games of the twenty-fourth Olympiad were held in Seoul, South Korea. During that fortnight in September 1988, Caesar managed to damage international relations and put everyone's life in jeopardy. His production instincts, generally sound and occasionally brilliant over the years, had been left stateside. There was a good explanation, however. He was hopelessly in love.

"It's disgusting."

"I don't care. Stay with it."

One of the most sacred moments of the Opening Ceremony was turning into a massacre. Pigeons released before the lighting of the flame had settled on the cauldron and were getting barbecued.

"Oh my God, that one just exploded."

"Is this great TV or what?"

The announcers were at first speechless. When the body count increased, millions of viewers having witnessed at least a dozen pigeon immolations, Gary Bryant, the one with the news background, thought it time to issue an advisory.

Some of you may want to turn away. I expect the organizers did not foresee a moment like this.

In the truck, the director, George Acedi, finally defied Caesar and cut to a high, wide shot of the Olympic stadium.

"Georgie!"

"Caesar, there's none left. They're all toast."

"All right . . . Hey, gang, isn't this fun?"

In Seoul, Caesar Fortunato had a big job: coordinating producer. He was expected to sensitively and knowledgeably guide two thousand people over seventeen days and one hundred and fifty hours of coverage. The promotion was a reward from Hawas.

"Do they light the flame again at the Closing Ceremony?"

"No, Caesar, they put the flame out."

"Oh, right. Too bad. No more Korean fried pigeon."

America wanted softness out of its Olympics, the kind of stories that Hawas had always taught his people to find and exploit: the wrestler who fought off cancer to win gold, tales of sportsmanship that transcended borders and faiths and ancient hatreds, uplifting, entrancing competition. America wanted mostly to suspend disbelief for the two weeks of this improbable, quadrennial festival, the world gathered in a truly hopeful gesture. The TV viewers mostly wanted a fairy tale. But Caesar Fortunato, his heart broken and his spirit defeated, wanted to give them a trashy documentary: pigeons flambé, corruption, exploitation.

"Whoa, who is that woman?"

Earlier, during the Parade of Nations, Caesar noticed Camera 8 had a shot of a stunning Italian athlete.

"Hello, people! Who is that woman?"

"Nobody."

"What do you mean, nobody? What the fuck are we paying the researchers for?"

"Caesar, there are ten thousand athletes in the Parade of Nations. Nine thousand of them have no chance whatsoever of winning a medal. That woman is among the nine thousand."

David Crystal, whose duties as vice president of programming included research, managed to convey his contempt without raising his voice.

"Of course, we have identified about seven hundred medal candidates with excellent stories, and for each of them, there are graphics ready to go. But if you must know, the Italian woman in question is Andrea Colichelli, one of the slowest sprinters in the world. We won't see her after the first round of heats."

"Well, build a graphic. I want to know who she is. And Mr. Crystal, if an athlete that gorgeous is not worth our attention, then I have a big problem with our programming philosophy."

Caesar also indulged another infatuation to the detriment of the coverage. He told his director to stay with the fur-coated Mongolians, who looked as if they were ready to leap on horses and reconquer the Asian continent.

"We're going to miss Morocco."

"Who cares? No one likes Arabs."

"The best distance runner in history is from Morocco. He might win three gold medals and set a couple of world records."

"Who?"

"Said Aouita."

"Mr. Crystal, what's better TV? A skinny Arab or menacing Mongolians?"

"Mr. Fortunato, most of the Mongolians are officials. They won't be competing."

"Why don't you leave the truck right now, Mr. Crystal."

"Going to commercial in thirty."

"Stay with the Mongolians. Fuck the runner."

Rebecca Dooley was behind all of it, the real reason why the network had a badly distracted coordinating producer and why America was being subjected to a badly televised Olympics. She was jogging in

Central Park, cutoff T-shirt, caught in a downpour. That's when he first saw her, from the window of his limo. Drenched, somewhat flattered, and by nature adventurous, she accepted the offer of a ride and they were lovers, it seemed, by sunset.

Rebecca Dooley was an outstanding collegiate quarter-miler, long-legged, attractively muscular. Four-hundred-meter runners, as Caesar's vast sporting experience made him aware, were something of a happy medium when it came to their body shapes. They did not need the explosive power of sprinters, who generally had massive legs, no body fat, and no breasts. Quarter-milers also didn't run enough to end up looking like distance runners: stringy and, like sprinters, invariably flat-chested. Rebecca had a discernible figure, and she was twenty-three, and she was Irish.

His first girlfriend made him believe the Irish a superior race. They were not at all like his people in South Philadelphia, in his proud Italian ghetto, domain of a species hot-blooded and all too suspicious. There was a warmth, a joy, a spirited generosity he had never experienced until he met the large, rambunctious family of Catherine O'Hara, the girl who got away, the very good thing he fucked up. Deep down, he had spent the rest of his life looking for another Irish charmer.

Rebecca Dooley, who was treading just above the poverty line working for a medical publisher, accepted Caesar's job offer without hesitation. She was sleeping on a futon in a two-bedroom, one-bath Brooklyn apartment also somehow occupied by two single women and a newly-wed couple. In retrospect, she should have stayed put. As a production assistant, she was actually below secretary in status. Then she soon began doubting her sanity, age twenty-three and dating a tempestuous forty-nine-year-old married man who lived on the West Coast and only came to New York for booty calls.

He fired her. Rehired her. Fired her. They would be in his office for hours, behind a closed door, their words not comprehensible but the volume and tone of their voices effectively documenting the deep trouble that existed in what had become the department's leading affair. As her antipathy increased, so did his desire. Caesar Fortunato wanted what he couldn't have. The release of the revised Olympic personnel list became greatly anticipated. One week, she was going to the Olympics; the next

228

week, her name would be missing. Some weeks, the only change on the list would be her name, added, deleted.

"I just want to tell everyone that they should wear their credentials even when they go out at night. I was at a place last night that got raided by the cops in riot gear and stuff, and if we hadn't been wearing these, I think they would have kicked the shit out of us and thrown us in jail."

Michael Hawas, Omar's son, was working at the Olympics between semesters at Harvard Business School. He was offering this warning at one of the first big production meetings.

"There were these Australians. They were challenging everyone to drinking games, and then something happened with a couple of our soldiers. There were chairs and stuff flying everywhere. Rebecca Dooley told us to show the cops our credentials. Thank God for that, or we'd have ended up like the Australians. They were getting their heads pounded by the cops. So, I mean, I think everyone should know. This is what it's like here, and a credential can save you."

She had come back to the room at four A.M. and refused to explain. After the meeting, after hearing that she was out with the son of the division president and American soldiers and typically riotous, snock-ered Aussies, Caesar told Rebecca to get on a plane and go home, right away. He walked her to the travel office and watched as they changed her ticket.

Two days later, he went back to get her, flew ten thousand miles back to New York. After failing, his plea for forgiveness returned with a deci-sive fuck-you, it took him two days to return because of equipment trouble and dense fog in Anchorage. He arrived back in Seoul, beaten, jet-lagged, and cranky, just hours before the start of the Opening Cere-mony. Omar Hawas, perpetually unflappable, was for the first time in full flap.

"Are you fucking crazy?"

"No."

"Are you fucking crazy?"

"Omar!"

229

"I give you a big job and this is how you repay me?"

"Let me explain."

"Go ahead."

"My wife is very ill."

"And you're going to bullshit me, too. You're fucking the same girl my son is fucking, you idiot. Like I wouldn't know."

"I'm sorry."

"And this girl is fucking everyone. She fucked the pilot who flew her home. I have never gotten into your business, as you know. Your personal life was your personal life. But this IS my business. I demand an honest effort and what I'm getting instead is a lovesick little boy running my Olympics. Wake up, or I'm sending you home for good!"

By the next morning, Hawas was in Tokyo following a heart attack. World-renowned cardiologist Shun Hashimoto was going to perform the necessary repairs on his damaged arterial freeway system, but Dr. Hashimoto never got the chance. A second heart attack in as many days was fatal. Back in Seoul, there was something of a collective shudder. Everyone sensed a less generous future. Hawas had hired Caesar Fortunato and so many other major talents at the network, had coddled them and showered them with understanding and fat contracts. He liked his stars. He liked people with big ideas. He liked people who were not afraid to fail.

"Do you remember why I gave you this job?" Hawas had asked Caesar during their final conversation.

"Because no one else would do it?"

"Why did I ever hire you? I made you coordinating producer because of Los Angeles. That's why. You know that. Because after what you did, you couldn't do any better as a director. You needed a new challenge. So I gave you a new challenge."

At the 1984 Los Angeles Olympics, Fortunato's superb direction at swimming created one of the defining shots of those Games. In the final leg of the men's 4 x 200 meter relay, one of the great races in Olympic history, American Bruce Hayes, an unknown twenty-one-year-old, and six-foot-seven German superstar Michael Gross, the world's most imposing swimmer, were side by side, matching stroke for stroke and about to run out of pool. Hayes had been staked to a lead in the anchor leg, Gross closed the gap with a typically stunning burst of power—making full use of a wingspan that measured almost seven feet—then Hayes unexpectedly answered. With ten meters to go, Fortunato had Drew LaRosa, his main camera, radically change his framing. He wanted to see the hands of the swimmers, only the hands.

"What about third place?" LaRosa worried. "We'll miss the bronze."

"Don't care. Don't care. Zoom in baby, hurry."

"You don't want to see their bodies?"

"Come on, Drew, my boy, only the hands . . . only the hands are gonna matter."

When Drew's coverage was replayed in slow motion, the genius of the shot became even more apparent. There was the right hand of Bruce Hayes emerging out of the spray, his fingers first to the wall, one moment, one tiny but discernible moment before the touch of the giant paw of Michael Gross, the silver medalist by a sliver. The network was asked to make a still photo of Caesar's conclusive freeze frame, and it ran in the next day's *Los Angeles Herald* and in papers across the country.

"Really, I thought you were done as a TV director," Hawas said. "And if you weren't going to leave me, and do something else, and stop making everyone miserable, at least I could give you this new job. What are you going to do, huh? Should I replace you? Or are you going to give me what I expect? Full attention, or more pussy hunting?"

"I'll get it done, Omar."

"Bullshit. After this, do me a favor. Get out. Find something else. Make a movie. Open a coffee shop. Go live in the woods. I've had enough. And, for that matter, you've had enough."

The boxing tournament was an abomination. The Koreans had determined that their athletes had been screwed by the Americans at the 1984 Olympics. Seoul was to be their revenge. Judges from countries less sympathetic to the West, such as Bulgaria, Iran, and Cuba, were asked to fix fights in return for cash and jewelry. The corruption wasn't subtle. Roy Jones, who went on to become the best pro boxer in the world, lost his gold-medal bout despite reducing his Korean opponent to a bloody, woozy mess.

231

By week two, Caesar had turned the network's Olympic coverage into an exposé about the shameless anti-American criminals at the boxing venue. As a devoted gambler, Caesar hated fixes. He had also come to despise the Koreans, or rather he came to despise one particular Korean and then decided he hated all Koreans. The determination followed a night of ungodly drinking with Mr. Lee Bong, a high-ranking Olympic official.

"You sucka," said Mr. Lee, standing on a table at a strip club in Itaewon, the center of nightlife in Seoul. On the stage behind him, naked young women were playing Ping-Pong, using their privates as paddles in a display of astonishing athleticism.

"You sucka, Mr. Caesar. I say you have no balls."

At dinner, Mr. Lee Bong was mostly quiet and hospitable. But the beers flowed at the restaurant, and when the group of American television executives and Korean Olympic officials repaired to the strip club, the drinking continued apace, glasses refilled as soon as they were drained. This was the Korean way. Around the ten-beer mark, Mr. Lee Bong shed his obsequious facade and exposed the true tiger within.

"American soldiers eat bigga shit," he said, his finger pointing downward, accusatorily, from atop his table. "You lose Vietnam. Big joke. Big, big joke. How you lose to Vietnam? Little yellow people always smoking dope. Ho Chi Minh, he kick your ass and good."

Before Mr. Lee could get his own ass kicked by Caesar—and fourteen U.S. Marines within hearing distance, all of their inner tigers also activated—he slipped off the table and cracked his head open. It would be a forty-seven-stitch wound.

The highlight at boxing was another kind of meltdown. After bantamweight Byun Jong-Il was declared the loser by decision, the referee from New Zealand was attacked by Byun's trainer, spectators, and security guards. After the referee was rescued, the loser, mystified and enraged, plopped his butt in the center of the ring and raised his gloves menacingly whenever someone approached him. Caesar covered every second of this pathetic sitdown, and it went on for more than an hour.

He decided to superimpose a clock on the screen. As Byun continued his protest, American viewers saw the minutes accumulating, 56:36 . . . 56:37 . . . 56:38. There were records being set at track and field, the

American basketball team was about to be upset by the Soviet Union, but Caesar stayed at boxing, on a locked-off wide shot. It was as inert as a Warhol art film. Looking to further exploit the episode, Caesar sent his ringside reporter in search of a comment from a Korean boxing official.

Is it true that Byun is upset because he thought he was supposed to win the fight?

Sorry, no English.

What do you mean? You were just speaking English to me two minutes ago.

Sorry, sorry.

Is it true that one of your officials gave a two-thousand-dollar piece of jewelry to the Bulgarian judge?

If you don't watch it, mister, you gonna go home in a box.

The next morning, Fortunato's coverage was front-page news in Seoul. It was bad enough that a Korean boxer had embarrassed the nation. To lose face and have the Americans milk the episode was truly a horror. There were fourteen bomb threats. A memo was issued telling everyone not to wear clothing with the network's logo. The State Department was getting involved.

Caesar did not find the fallout disturbing in the least. He was doing journalism. Proud of it. Let the Koreans blow up his broadcast center. What he did find terribly disconcerting was the reaction of the American press. All boxing all the time was not helping viewership. The ratings were suddenly in a free fall. In general, American TV critics were profoundly ignorant of the medium they were covering, and most of the stories were about the ratings. The ratings they understood. If the ratings were good, they would find a way to praise the broadcasts. If the ratings were bad, then there had to be something very wrong, even if there wasn't. When one writer suggested that Caesar Fortunato was no Omar Hawas, then the rest of the country's TV writers jumped on this conceptual bandwagon. Fortunato wasn't following the famous Hawas formula. He wasn't getting up close and personal with the athletes. He wasn't taking advantage of the great Olympic kaleidoscope. There was not enough poetry, enough celebration, enough humanity. It was five hours every night of the evening news.

Worried for their lives, underwhelmed by the new guy in charge, the studio crew began discreetly distributing a T-shirt. On the front, it read,

ANOTHER UN-FORTUNATO VICTIM. On the back, I WAS PART OF THE WORST-PRODUCED OLYMPICS IN HISTORY. It was about this time that Caesar began to wear sunglasses indoors and blur his reality with quaaludes. It was a more discreet drug than coke, which could announce itself in sniffles, twitches, and bug eyes. The quaalude reinforced Caesar's growing bunker mentality: He was totally right and everyone was out to get him. Eventually, like so many embattled producers and directors, he got around to blaming the writers. This was partly related to a personal situation. One of them, Bruce Something Or Other, was sniffing after his daughter. Caesar issued a memo to the writing staff:

> As you are all aware, our shows have been sloppy and lacking in coherence. As soon as possible, the writing staff must submit a script for each of the remaining ten shows. Use your imagination to determine future medal winners. This should not be viewed as a pointless exercise. It is meant to help you do your jobs better. There is no such thing as too much preparation.

"Where are they, young man?"

Caesar ambushed Bruce Something Or Other as he was sitting with Cynthia in the broadcast center cafeteria.

"Daddy, can we do this some other time?"

"No, Cynthia."

Caesar had brought Cynthia to Korea and assigned her to cut the openings. It was an important job—her experience didn't suggest she deserved it—and there was resentment, which Cynthia surmounted by being good and, unlike her father, a sweetheart. Cynthia had become, without his help, an excellent producer for a syndicated Hollywood entertainment show. Giving her the job at the Olympics was part of a larger plan, recently put into effect, in which he was attempting to compensate for missing most of the first two decades of her life.

"Caesar," said the putative boyfriend, summoning against his will a measure of respect, "do we really have to deal with this *right now?*"

"If I don't have the scripts under my door after tonight's show, young man, then don't bother showing up tomorrow."

"Okay, Caesar, how about this? How about I don't bother showing up at all, tonight, tomorrow, the rest of the Olympics?"

"You're expendable, young man."

"Okay, Mr. Fortunato. You want me outta here? Fine. Like I need this. Like I need to be working for a no-talent psycho."

The writer got up from the table and pushed his chair forward.

"And by the way. Fuuuck you!"

That was two sincere fuck-yous directed his way in the same Olympic fortnight.

"Yeah, Daddy, fuck you!"

And then there were three.

In a matter of weeks, the dark, tumultuous Olympics of Caesar Fortunato were erased in the public memory by a truly wonderful World Series, and Tommy Vaughn was the hero—fucking Tommy Vaughn, a guy Caesar considered lucky, not good. People had begun to call him, affectionately, "TV" Tommy Vaughn. And Caesar, back at home in Rancho Mirage, slumped in his couch on a fourth beer, having lost in a very short span of time a lover, a beloved boss, his daughter's respect, and his once lofty standing in the TV community, saw Tommy Vaughn cutting a masterpiece, about to be credited with the shot of the year, and he wasn't in any way lucky, but very, very good.

Vaughn was directing when Kirk Gibson of the Los Angeles Dodgers, despite a ruined leg, limped to the plate in the World Series and hit a game-winning homer in the ninth off Dennis Eckersley, a relief pitcher who had been as close to perfect as anyone gets in sports. As it was once written, so it was again: Reality had strangled invention.

"TV" had told the story well. He knew Dodgers manager Tommy Lasorda might find a way to use Gibson, even this broken-down version who could barely walk, because Gibson played baseball like the college football star he once was, fearlessly, without compromise, in pain. So at a production meeting the night before, Vaughn had told his camera people to be ready for Gibson. And if he did emerge from the trainer's room, if he decided to unwrap the ice from his knees and limp to the plate, they were going to shoot everything: Gibson pacing, sitting, stretching, twisting. All of it.

So the ninth inning comes and the Dodgers are losing and Gibson is sitting in the trainer's room and he curses to himself and unwraps the ice bags and puts on the uniform and limps down the tunnel that leads to the dugout. And Tommy Vaughn's cameras find him as soon as he makes his appearance, and his cameras watch him pacing, sitting, stretching, and twisting. And Lasorda, down to his last out, sends him out there. Crowd roars. Gibson swings and misses. Eckersley throws another. Gibson swings and misses, almost falling over, pathetic, his heroic intentions and wrecked body completely at odds. Lasorda has his hands on his chin. Opposing manager Tony LaRussa has his hands on his chin. Gibson fouls off pitches. Eckersley's still smoking the ball. Gibson can't catch up to it. Then Eckersley tries to get Gibson to chase some junk low and away. But Gibson's eye is true and his patience extraordinary. The count is full. Lasorda rubs his chin. LaRussa rubs his chin. Eckersley looks into the catcher for a sign. Rears back. Fires. And Gibson swings and the ball is going . . . going . . . going . . . cut to the camera behind home . . . gone!

And then Gibson rounds the bases and Tommy stays with the picture. Stays with the outfield camera and the medium close-up of Gibson rounding the bases, and as Gibson rounds second, about the time another director might have gone high, cut to the camera behind home, or shown the apoplectic crowd, Tommy Vaughn is still with Gibson, rounding the bases as he double pumps . . . makes a fist, pushes the elbow back . . . once, twice, saying, "Yeah! . . . yeah!" And it's one of the shots of all time, sharing that moment with Gibson, the dream come true that everyone can understand so deeply, Tommy Vaughn and Caesar Fortunato and every boy who has ever played the game of baseball. Ninth inning. World Series. Home run. Game over.

Confession

Maxine stayed for some two hours. She wouldn't leave until he told her, for the fifth time, that he would go back, face up to everything, let Palmer get him a lawyer. Beck was going back, too. They would do it in the morning, but first came one last drunk, one more night of carefully paced yet voluminous boozing, one more night to get lost in the alcohol, let it loosen the tongue and diminish the pain and envelop the body in a pleasing numbness.

"You know," said Beck, "I once got a blow job from a guy."

"Come on."

"Best-looking guy I've ever seen. Melons for breasts."

It was a little past nine. The highly decorated television director and nine-time All-Pro were the only ones left on the seaside patio of the Rosarito Beach Hotel.

"Says I can have my money back if I return the favor . . ."

"Uh-huh."

"So I was about to go down on him . . ."

"Right."

"Then he drops his voice into James Coburn range and pulls out his package."

"What did you do?"

"Heaved."

Caesar had to force a laugh. He did not really find the story funny. His brain, feeling freer to express itself after seven Coronas and three tequilas, spit suspicious thoughts into his altered, alcohol-laced stream of consciouness: Maybe Beck was bi . . . maybe his regimen of fucking at least ten females per month was a sort of weird denial of his gayness . . . maybe he was going to end up like that *Rolling Stone* guy, Jann Wenner, deciding to switch teams very, very, very late in the game.

"Caesar, can I ask you a very personal question?"

"No."

"Do you find me attractive?"

"It's not true, is it?"

"Jesus. Of course not. How fucked up are you? You're falling for my bullshit. Come on!"

"Should we go back?"

"Do we have to talk about this right now? Let's get another round while my muchacho is in the vicinity. *Señor!* . . . *Dos mas cervezas y dos mas tequilas. Muy rápido, por favor. Gracias.*"

"Beck, what's the worst thing you ever did?"

"Used a turtle as a baseball."

"You just can't ever be serious."

"I was being serious."

"You grew up in a ghetto."

"We had turtles."

"In the ghetto?"

"Come on, black people have pet stores."

238

"When you were playing, did anybody ever approach you, fix a game, that sort of stuff?"

"Why do you want to know?"

"Because I do."

"Couple of times. Told them to fuck off in no uncertain terms. Besides, I didn't need the money."

"Can I tell you something?"

"I wish you wouldn't."

"Humor me."

"All right. Go on."

His baseball career, the pursuit of which preempted the piano, died on a frosty spring afternoon, the day of tryouts for the freshman baseball team at Resurrection Ascension High School— forty-two kids for twenty spots. The coach slapped grounders to him at second base, and he handled all of those cleanly. Then it was his turn to bat.

He mimicked the major leaguers he had seen—rolled dirt on his hands, scratched a divot in the batter's box with his spikes, tapped the plate, blessed himself before finally peering out at the mound. The pitcher was from the varsity, and he started Caesar with a fastball, which got smacked, whistling into right field. A presumptuous grin erupted on the freshman's face, which changed the pitcher's mood from indifferent to outraged.

The next pitch appeared to be targeted at Caesar's head and instinctively he flinched, bending his body backward, losing his balance, flopping to the dirt. But there was no real danger. As Caesar watched from ground level, the ball abruptly, miraculously changed direction and cut across the plate, a strike. He had been awakened. He had seen his first true curveball and it was one of the most unsettling experiences in his young life. He felt his confidence seeping out of his body in a gush, feeling as if it was puddling around his feet. The pitcher threw him another. Caesar flinched again. He got another curve, and Caesar finally held his ground, but he swung awkwardly, inches above the ball, almost dropping to his rear once again.

Satisfied that the cocky freshman had been sufficiently humbled, the pitcher winked before he threw again. A fastball came fat in front of Caesar's eyes and he hit it deep, a long, high fly headed for the trees at the edge of the field. In the meantime, the coach had walked stealthily over to the batting cage, where his interest in the boy with impressive fielding skills vanished rapidly. As a hitter, the kid with the good glove was typical. This cut was going to be easy. When the varsity pitcher was about to reach back and throw again, Caesar was shaken by a loud bark.

"Next!"

Later, he waited outside to tell his father on the steps of the house. His need to share this crushing disappointment was in conflict with his strong suspicion that Sal Fortunato would not only be unsympathetic, he would in fact be angered. On the stoop, his arms folded against the creeping cold, Caesar kept thinking he should just go back in the house and keep quiet, keep it to himself, but the boy had a greater faith in love than logic, though he didn't know that was why he was waiting outside, that he was waiting to be loved.

He remained in this state of hesitancy for thirty minutes or so. When the evening sky began to drop, Caesar stood up. He had one foot in the door when he heard a car braking at the sidewalk.

"What are you doing, young man?"

"Nothing, sir."

Caesar waited, holding the door open. When he saw his father's face, he couldn't stop it—at first, just a welling of tears at the corners.

"What's this about?"

Caesar detected kindness in his father's voice.

"I . . ."

"Come on, spit it out, son."

"Dad . . ."

His vision was all but blinded as the trickle became a stream.

"Dad, I didn't . . ."

He was trying to restrain his body from seizing into a full, sobbing eruption.

"You got cut."

Sal Fortunato grimaced, looked up, considered his response, then waved his son into the house.

"Well," he said, "maybe you'll listen next time to the old man. Maybe next time, you'll listen."

Three years later, on November 29, 1956, Caesar Fortunato made the headlines for the first time. He had scored sixty-eight points in an exhibition basketball game against the Philadelphia Navy Air Materials Center, an annual warm-up opponent for DeSales University, where Caesar was a brand-new freshman and clearly, as this night proved, a precocious basketball talent.

After his baseball dreams were crushed, he found there to be, in something of a shock, a second chapter in his athletic life. Being able to dribble with both hands, shoot with both hands, as Sergio Palumbo had drilled him to do, placed him far ahead of anyone his age on a basketball court. It made him an offensive machine. No one could defend him, and as he came to enjoy this mastery, he invested in the game his innate creativity.

Playing in the Catholic rec leagues, often on slippery, excessively waxed gym floors that doubled as dance venues, he found it was often difficult to drive to the basket or attempt one of his running hooks without slipping. The solution was something called a jump shot, at the time very much a novelty and entirely unacceptable for at least half the basketball establishment, which was still clinging to the horizontal game of careful passing and earthbound shooting and feared this new verticality. Caesar, however, changed hearts and minds as soon as every coach saw him releasing the ball at the height of his leap with a graceful flick of the wrist and witnessed a subsequent, very audible swish. Developing the use of his once useless left hand so that he could conquer Bach and the rest of Western music, and the ability to improvise and, even more importantly, keep his own counsel, were legacies of a formative youth that had been guided by the unconventional wisdom of a sixty-three-year-old Italian immigrant. Music had made him a hoops star.

"I thought you quit college. Didn't like your coach, or something."

"Got kicked out after my sophomore year. I didn't care as much about it then as I do now."

Beck was about to become the first person to hear Caesar Fortunato's last well-kept secret.

"My freshman year, after I score sixty points against these dopey Navy guys, one of the seniors says he needs to speak with me. Apparently, there's a way to make some extra cash. Good money. Five hundred bucks a week, split among the starters. He made it sound so normal, almost like everyone knew about it. And he made it sound like we were entitled to it. He told me the college was making money off us, and, you know, why shouldn't we get some."

College basketball in the fifties was fundamentally corrupt, utterly compromised. In addition to confirmed stories of recruiters bearing bags of cash, boosters providing no-money-down luxury automobiles, high grades for no-work classes, and excellent pay for no-show jobs, all of which Caesar Fortunato could claim firsthand acquaintance, virtually every major program was tainted, as well, by gambling scandals. The fix was in, everywhere.

It all began with the genius of a prep-school teacher turned bookmaker who, sometime in the forties, came up with the idea of wholesaling odds, or, as it would come to be known, a point spread. In a century of invention, it is possible that no other innovation led to as many broken lives and ruined reputations as the point spread. It meant every single game of almost every single sport, season after season, could be of interest to the gambler. It meant a million more ways for born losers to lose it all, because there was no longer a need to pick a winner.

Suddenly, it was not necessary to bet against all-powerful Notre Dame in football, usually a bad idea, or, in 1958, Caesar Fortunato's run-and-gun DeSales team, which appeared headed to the college championship. It was only necessary to evaluate the credibility of the point spread, to make a commitment based on shades of excellence or lack thereof.

In any given year, sports followed its own bell curve: There would inevitably be a smattering of dominance, teams that were going to win most of their games; a bulk of reliably mediocre, more-difficult-to-assess, so-called .500 teams; and then, a smattering of the reliably hopeless, doesn't-matter-what-they-do, el stinko teams. But no matter what their quality, all were in play, all were of potential interest to the bettor, thanks to the spread. On the night of January 22, 1958, the line out of the Minneapolis Clearinghouse, used by bookies everywhere, had DeSales, at home, favored to beat City University by ten points.

"We knew we had to keep it under ten—we weren't supposed to cover . . . win by nine, that's all. It was easy."

Caesar could see that Beck was listening intently, which was unusual. His friend rarely tolerated monologues, unless it was the telling of a dirty joke. Caesar also sensed that Beck was troubled by what he was hearing, that, in fact, Caesar had tweaked his moral outrage, another oddity, because Beck's moral outrage had been in hibernation for as long as Caesar had known him.

"That's the thing. We weren't dumping games. We never tried to lose. It was just massaging."

The feeling that Beck disapproved put him in justification mode, which is the way all of college basketball sounded in the fifties once confronted by the fact that many of the games had no integrity—that, in fact, on campuses everywhere, in large, brick-encased, smoky fieldhouses, fans were not seeing amateurs engaged in pure competition. Not seeing games played in the interest of a sound mind and body. Witnessing instead, unknowingly, criminal activity often influenced by local mobsters.

"We had the usual deal. The guy's name was Leo. If the team was good, we would try to crush them and make sure we covered. If the team was crappy, like that night against City, we would keep them in the game somehow. Leo knew exactly when we were going to play hard and when we weren't, and he told his friends to bet accordingly. It was a beautiful thing. You could still win, still play hard, still beat the teams you were supposed to beat, just not by too much."

But on January 22, 1958, there was a problem. The other team had a deal, too. City's players were also committed point-shavers, and their fixer, a former player named Jack Molinas, who would later be terminated by shotgun, asked the Lions to make sure they lost to DeSales by at least ten points.

While Caesar Fortunato and his DeSales teammates were trying to keep it close, City's Lions were working to maintain a losing cushion.

"I miss a layup, make it look good. Other end of the court, a City guy misses a layup. I throw a pass into the stands. They throw a pass away. It's like we've all forgotten how to play. It's getting ridiculous. I've got to make the game closer. Two minutes left, we're up by twelve. It's gotta be under ten. I mean, we never had any trouble. But now, it's going to look obvious. And then, in the back of your mind, you start wondering what happens if we can't get it done. Are these wiseguys going to break our arms? I can't score for the other team. At some point, they have to try to score, but they don't want to score. So now we realize, they've got something going, too. We're so fucked. The coach is trying to get me out of the game, because all of a sudden I'm playing lousy, and I keep telling the subs to fuck off. I'm thinking I want to do this and I don't want to do this. Twenty seconds left, we get the ball back. I'm shouting for it so I can dribble it off my foot or something. I don't know what to do. But this kid on the team comes in off the bench, he's not part of this, he won't give it up. He wants to score. He's never scored a point. He sinks a ridiculous twenty-footer. Heaves it. Now we're winning by fourteen. Totally fucked . . . I threw up right after the game."

"So they found out."

"They knew. Everyone knew. Fucking Leo was screaming at us at the end of the game, on the court: 'You little shits. You fucking little shits.' But the school was smart about it . . . they didn't want to attract attention. It wasn't the coach. He knew. Just as long as we were winning, he was hear no evil, see no evil. But the school president was at the game, and he wanted me gone, but not right away. That would make the papers. I was just slowly frozen out. After a few games, I wasn't a starter anymore. The coach had to tell the press I was a better player coming off the bench. Then he tells them I've got some minor injury. When the season was over, I got called into the president's office and I was told to leave. Told me I was lucky they weren't sending me to jail."

As Caesar Fortunato was making his forced exit from the game, college basketball was being saved by acts of individual brilliance, by players who were making athletic fashion statements, comfortable in their own style and proud to show it. Wilt Chamberlain, the greatest Philadelphia basketball product ever, whom Caesar had played against in summer pickup games, left for Lawrence, Kansas, where he proved that a giant could rule with a kind of gentle strength. At the University of San Francisco, Bill Russell demonstrated that a supreme defensive presence could be the most dominating weapon of all. At the University of Cincinnati, Oscar Robertson was a preview of what was to come, a prototype it had taken the game some six decades to produce, a player fully loaded: consummate shooter, passer, rebounder, the one who foretold a day when there would be a Magic and a Michael. And instead of the world knowing about Caesar Fortunato, about his textbook jumper and wondrous dribbling, they would hear of a West Virginian named Jerry West, who had the matching breakthrough skills but also a depth of character Caesar did not possess. Part of his willingness to shave points was about respect, or lack thereof. Caesar respected baseball because it was a game he could not master. Basketball was an afterthought, the runner-up, a game whose skills were dropped in his lap.

There was never a suggestion, not a hint, not a peep of gossip, that Chamberlain or Russell or Robertson or West ever conspired to fix a game—ever played with anything less than an honest effort. This, too, was true about Beck. Though he used all manner of performance-enhancing and pain-relieving drugs available in his era, he would never allow himself to be caught in a conspiracy to fudge the results of a game in which he played. That was his one true creed: The game was sacred. Beck regularly committed all of the seven deadly sins and tolerated complete moral vapidity in others, but he could not countenance someone who would violate the sanctity of competition.

"You know what the worst thing of all was? My old piano teacher was there that night. He was at the game. You don't care about this, do you?"

"Not really," said Beck, who had stopped drinking and was washed with the customary weariness that follows.

"I saw him walking out of the gym. It was strange. He turned his head and looked at me just as I was looking at him. He knew, too. He gave me a look. Boy, it fucking cut. . . ."

Caesar shuddered.

His relationship with Beck had outlasted his two marriages. For that matter, it was the one functioning relationship he had left, with a devoutly hedonistic former pro football player who could no longer help him in any substantial way. Beck's you're-okay-I'm-okay philosophy of life had helped to sustain the friendship. He was always the

245

island of unconditional acceptance in a sea of roiling scrutiny. But he sensed that this might have been the last of their long and mostly agreeable nights addled by some substance, because what he had just revealed to Beck was not okay. And if there was no more Beck, there'd really be no one else to talk to. Caesar Fortunato was at last of no value to anyone—employers, friends, family. And for the first time in his life there was nothing remotely palatable on the horizon, no good reason to wake up the next morning

"Let's see . . . I can be a homeless person in Mexico or become the sex slave of a serial killer with a four-hundred-pound bench press. Remind me, why are we going back?"

"Because you promised Maxine . . ."

"You must have put at least one of those guys in the hospital."

"Yeah, I whacked them pretty good."

"You want me to knock on your door tomorrow?"

"No, that's okay, I'll meet you in the lobby."

The next morning, after he got tired of waiting, he went up to Beck's room. The door was open. The maid was inside, cleaning.

Peace

On April Fool's Day, two miles in the sky, staring out at the California desert, seated on a boulder, he had taken the gun from its position, resting against his right temple, put it on his lap, and reached inside his jacket for the cell phone. The voice was eight thousand miles away and compromised by the wavering quality of the connection. Caesar was able to hear only parts of sentences, but that was still enough.

"Mr. Fortunato . . . *buon giorno* . . . calling . . . Rome . . . are you? . . . a World Prayer . . . show . . . one hundred and eighty countries . . . Can you direct?"

As it turned out, his suicide with a view was interrupted by the Vatican, and less than two months after contemplating a permanent exit strategy, he had certifiably come back from the dead. At the stroke of midnight in Rome, on the third Sunday of May 1997, Caesar Fortunato was handling satellite feeds from fifteen locations around the globe and delivering to billions *A World Prayer for Peace*.

The show opened at the home of the sponsor, at St. Peter's, where the Pope, in Latin, guided a recitation of the Hail Mary from row upon row of his faithful: *Ave Maria, gratia plena, dominus tecum*. . . . Then Caesar cut to London, to the baroque majesty of St. Paul's Cathedral and the echoing voice of the Archbishop of Canterbury. "The Lord is my shepherd, I shall not want. . . ." Then to Mecca, at the Great Mosque, Masjid al-Haram, where a vast, bowing, turbaned multitude raised what seemed like one voice: "Allah!" they proclaimed in Arabic. "To him belongs what is in the heavens and the earth." He cut to Arizona, where it was nearing sunset. At the edge of the Grand Canyon, elders of the Hopi Nation danced in a circle, coated in a festival of colors, their faces covered by scowling and mesmerizing kachina masks.

From Rome to London to Mecca to the Grand Canyon, the sweep was impressive. And there were twelve more sites introduced in the opening minutes. He had a live feed from Jersualem, at the Wailing Wall, men praying to the left, women on the right, divided by a low fence; atop Japan's sacred Mount Fuji, long a beacon for millions of Shinto pilgrims; with the Mormon Tabernacle Choir in Salt Lake City, a wilderness once upon a time where Brigham Young settled his devoted congregation after a withering voyage across the American West; at the ghats in Varanasi, India, center of Hinduism; with the exiled Dalai Lama, cross-legged and chanting at the foot of the Himalayas; beneath Cape Town's signature landmark, Table Mountain, where a purple-robed Desmond Tutu was raising his arms to the sky in adoration; in South America, at the gigantic concrete figure of Brazil's Christ the Redeemer, overlooking a postcard shot of Rio de Janiero and the beaches of Copacabana and Ipanema; among the echoing basso profundo voices of the all-male choir inside the just-built Cathedral of St. Tryphon in Moscow; joining the sick in body but hopeful in spirit at a grotto in Lourdes, France, where Bernadette Soubirous saw a vision of the Virgin in 1858; inside the doors of the Ebeneezer Baptist Church, Atlanta, Georgia, the first pulpit of the Reverend Martin Luther King Jr.; among the privileged at New York's St. Patrick's Cathedral; and amidst the enchanting spires, rising from the surrounding jungle, he was live from Angkor Wat, where among the gathered were the all too many maimed by hidden mines left over from Cambodia's utterly insane civil war.

At each site, the local director would be hearing Rome in one of five languages. Caesar spoke in French to Saudi Arabia because that director had been an exchange student in Paris. In Rio, Spanish, the closest tongue to their native Portuguese. In Thailand, German, because that director's early life included a year of military training, helicopters, at the U.S. base in Wiesbaden. The man who hired him, Father Edward O'Keefe, was a formidable linguist in charge of Vatican Radio. He had instructed Caesar to memorize fifteen or twenty essential production terms he'd need in the designated languages. The coaching began one night over a bottle of smooth, exquisite red wine. Coach O'Keefe's task had been formidable. His student had come to Rome more or less bilingual; he remembered about two phrases in Italian.

"There was cannon fire, and it hit the cockpit area. Then I felt an explosion and the plane was starting to go down."

On the first night he was learning to *parler* and *sprechen* and *hablar,* Caesar also discovered how God's messenger had found him on the mountain. One bottle had already been drained before Father O'Keefe explained, after some prodding, how it was that a war story brought them together for a show about peace.

"I was starting to pull back on the stick and I couldn't do it. And I was wondering why my copilot wasn't helping me."

Father O'Keefe paused a beat.

"He didn't have a head."

Edward O'Keefe left Harvard after his sophomore year because the bombing of Pearl Harbor meant no one was safe, not his mother in Boston, or the Statue of Liberty, or Hollywood. He went first to North Africa, arriving three days after the Germans erased half of the Allied Air Force during a failed raid on Romanian oil fields. He saw planes come apart and men still alive falling to earth. He knew later on, as they were massing planes and munitions for D-day, that he was lucky to climb out of the soupy English fog, because there were always a few

249

who didn't, ill-fated, blinded pilots who would unknowingly send their B-17s and B-24s into head-on collisions. And after a Messerschmitt strafed his bomber and decapitated one of his copilots, he parachuted without breaking a leg and was miraculously rescued by the Belgian underground.

"There was so much wretchedness, so much misery. I thought that there had to be a better way of doing things."

After he broke up with the girl in London, the one who kept him in the Army, kept him in the air for seventy-five missions, all for love, he saw Dachau and that made up his mind. The next army he'd join would be the Pope's.

"Why did you call me?"

"We'd been having some large problems. The show was getting close, and there seemed to be too many loose ends."

"And I'm the guy."

"You're one of the guys. There's very few people who have as much expertise as you doing big live events."

"I'm not much of a Catholic."

"We're not in the business of judging souls."

"You know I haven't been a hot commodity lately."

"Yup, I know."

"You knew about that incident with Johnny Ray Thompson?"

"Yup."

"You still called me anyway."

"It sounded like your typical creative dispute. And the judge seemed to agree."

"I was told the guy didn't like any of Johnny Ray's movies."

"Well, I must confess, you had a pretty good character witness."

"Who's that?"

"Well, I sent a letter to the judge signed by His Holiness. I'm sure he won't mind, if he ever finds out."

"You forged the Pope's signature?"

"Not exactly. It would be better to call it a communication from the Vatican. Look, we needed you here as soon as possible."

"So you had my cell-phone number handy?"

"No."

"So how did you get it?"

"From one of my copilots during the war. He thinks he owes me. My last flight was a milk run back to the States. We were flying a C-46 back to Bradley Field in Hartford. We were drinking on the way back. The Champagne was from a three-star general. He had commandeered us. It was two days after the war ended and we were in Nice and he had us ferry him and his girlfriend to Lake Como. He was very grateful, gave us speedboats to fool around with. His staff would get you anything. Well, on the way back, my copilot has this daring notion. He thinks we should try to fly under the Eiffel Tower."

"Is there enough room to fly under the Eiffel Tower?"

"I didn't think so. Not with a big cargo plane. But my copilot wanted to try. I had to shoot him."

"What? You shot your copilot?"

"I sort of missed. But it made the point. When he sobered up, he forgave me. I believe you know him."

"Really?"

"In fact, he gave up the job and recommended you."

"Uh-huh."

"Yeah, I had this urgent call from Tommy about you . . . Tommy Vaughn."

The broadcast required eighteen satellites, seventy-five cameras, one thousand international television professionals. He had a scientist from AT&T fly over from New Jersey to help wire the Vatican. Caesar was making a worldwide conference call, except he was bouncing pictures and sounds off various pieces of metal orbiting 22,300 miles above the equator. The show was made possible by technical wizardry but designed to be simple. Each site and its significance was introduced. Nothing else. Caesar wanted no interpretive comments from the translators. The viewer was to experience a pure and personal relationship with this global ceremony.

He made two essential contributions, the first calculated, the other inspired. Years before, he had done a high-profile rock concert organized to raise money for famine relief. It was being staged on two continents, and the central problem in organizing people far-flung and resolving technical issues rarely faced was that there was too much talk. People talked about the problems and then expected him to have all the solutions, which he did not. What was needed, in his mind, was to have a clear idea of the problems and then find the people who could solve them. What he insisted on was memos. He wanted everyone writing memos. The problems, in written form, were passed to the problem solvers, who, in turn, articulated the solutions in another memo. Caesar would eventually assemble a manual of memos, and he did so again for the *World Prayer* show, in this case translated into the five agreed languages. The book contained the essential technical and editorial information for all the broadcast locations. This was a way to get everyone literally on the same page.

Having wrestled with the details, he searched for something poetic during the broadcast. He wanted a unifying element and a way to bring the show to a climactic close. Caesar looked up at that most familiar site, a wall full of TV monitors, and he decided to let the viewer see what he was seeing. In that darkened control room, the sixteen sites existed simultaneously for him, all forming a single event, and soon it would seem so to everyone watching.

After he had cut to each of the sixteen sites, one by one, he divided the television screen into four.

And we shall beat our swords into ploughshares . . .

The viewers saw and heard simultaneously Rome, London, Mecca, and Arizona: four languages and faiths and devotions somehow forming a kind of music.

Oh God, lead us from darkness to light . . .

And then Caesar cut to another quad box: Jerusalem, Mount Fuji, Salt Lake City, Varanasi, the rolling rhythm of prayer becoming a blend of Hebrew, Japanese, English, Hindu.

Praise be to the Lord of the Universe who has created us and made us into tribes and nations that we may know each other, not that we may despise each other . . .

Then Dharmsala, Cape Town, Rio, Moscow, believers in the divinity of the Buddha and Jesus unified by a Grass Valley 4,000 switcher.

Almighty God, the Roaring Thunder that splits mighty trees . . . who does not hesitate to respond to our call . . . give us the wisdom to teach our children to love, to respect, and to be kind to each other . . .

After the quad boxes, he created a screen showing eight sites at once, and at last, in the final ten minutes, all sixteen were joined in this remarkable TV mosaic, this spiritual symphony, the many tongues merging into a kind of song, into one, long, soothing, inviting note.

"Oh, sweet Jesus," he whispered to himself.

Caesar walked out later to a wet, cold Roman night. Before he looked for a cab, he turned and faced the dome of St. Peter's, another of Michelangelo's gifts, and in the silence, he put one knee down and dropped his head.

"Oh my God," he whispered, beginning the prayer he considered most important but had not uttered in decades, "I am heartily sorry for having offended thee . . . and I detest all my sins because of thy just punishments . . . but most of all, because they offend thee my God who art all good and deserving of all my love. I firmly resolve with the help of thy grace to confess my sins, do penance, and amend my life. Amen."

The next day, he languished alone over a sumptuous lunch at a trattoria fronting the Tyrrhenian Sea. He had taken the train to Viareggio, the original home to half his ancestry. The meal was almost three hours in the eating, the antipasto followed by the carbonara followed by the *carne* followed by the salad followed by the profiteroles followed by the *caffè*. The sea was relatively serene, and it reminded him of the Gulf Coast in Florida, another spot where baby waves murmured to the shore. He savored the scene just as he had savored the meal, feeling blessed.

On the flight home, Caesar decided he was going to be monastic in the air. He bought some fruit before he boarded, and he vowed to drink water, stretch every hour, ignore any fetching flight attendants, sleep. He was headed to his new home, to a San Diego apartment he had rented unseen. Including the connection at JFK, and another at LAX, it would be another sixteen or seventeen hours before he'd get back. Not long after boarding, he took off his shoes and from the pouch of goodies distributed to first-class passengers pulled out the heavy socks and the blindfold for sleeping. Soon after, soothed by the steady, muted whistling of the jet engines, he closed his eyes and went off.

Generation Ex

Caesar Fortunato stood at the very edge of a pier insufficiently insulated from watery, gusting, bone-chilling winds. The clothes he should have been wearing, the turtlenecks, a fleece he got free at a Winter Olympics, were back home in the closet. While he shivered, teeth chattering, arms folded, bouncing on the balls of his feet, he pictured, peeved, the saving garments left behind, knew exactly the shelf upon which they were neatly folded. He had spent enough summers in San Francisco to know that San Francisco didn't really have summers. It was like the Bay Area had two suns, one for the suburbs, another for the city—one that was baking everyone into raisins down the peninsula and over in the valleys, and a substantially weaker city cousin providing light but little heat. Here it was July 3 and it was fucking cold . . . it was freezing.

Sunset was typically a vision, as it had been every night of the Extreme Games, a revolutionary athletic event of young men and women with a casual interest in their own mortality. So he endured the discomfort and soaked in the busy vista, the postcard bridges, Alcatraz, Oakland in the distance beginning to twinkle. Sailboats were in play everywhere, crisscrossing, their masts bowing toward the sea, their captains attentive, fully engaged, managing a bounty of wind. How he envied those lives, so intelligently ordered. Most of these sailors, he figured, were rich computer guys who always packed the right clothes.

When his nose began to numb, he turned back to the production truck, where he suspected he was doing the last television show of his life. The notion was not troubling, because it was time. He had spent most of the week wishing for an interpreter. It was as if he were a visitor from an ancient civilization, this relic from an analog age who once played music on a phonograph, opposed Communism, remembered when the sporting landscape was baseball and everything else. Remembered when TV production wasn't so oppressively brutish. Even during the cataclysms, when nothing worked or some young producer wanted to bust everyone's balls, there was always time for at least one extended, fabulous, subsidized dinner at a restaurant of high repute and six-dollar desserts. Time to laugh, drink, enough downtime to refresh the brain.

With fourteen shows over six days for three different networks, the undersized production staff in San Francisco labored on eight hours of sleep, total, for the week. Whatever they saw of America's most picturesque city was confined to the view from the window of the van that shuttled between the hotel and the pier. They did not know, or care, about how completely they were being exploited by a very large company with an absurd profit margin, because they had come to San Francisco not for money but for love. Though it was a corporate invention, they perceived the event as an important original statement, athletes of courage on a spiritual quest, displaying their skills in a forum of cooperation, not competition. Further, this doo-ragged, earring-clad, marijuana-partial multitude of new TV blood, with their razored hair of many colors and mumbling monotone of Ex-speak, had the same

255

sickness he'd developed four decades earlier. The work was its own high, and a lot of them would have shown up for free.

Suddenly rehabilitated by the Rome extravaganza, this was his comeback job in sports, a tryout of sorts, with more work promised from the all-sports network if he survived this convocation of children cursed by the Evel Knievel gene, and though he really, *really* needed the money, Caesar was ready to bolt after the Turk Pizano affair. What always remained, despite the many demons he had indulged, the utter callousness and recklessness of his behavior over the years, was his total abhorrence of big-time corporate cowardice.

The Turk Pizano affair began when the fifteen-year-old, in celebration of his victory in freestyle motocross, and with the tacit approval of the Ex producers, launched himself and his 125cc Suzuki into San Francisco Bay. The city police responded to an emergency call about a sunken motorbike and a floating body and then had a conniption. Uninformed of this exhilarating and frightening stunt—a teenager rocketing sixty feet off one of their piers and perhaps inspiring others of commensurate insanity but less skill—their next move was to storm the production compound and confront the suits.

In 1885, German automobile pioneer Gutlieb Daimler put a single-cylinder, four-stroke internal combustion engine on a bicycle and thereby invented the motorcycle. It was not meant to fly then, or ever. A century later, a new generation of bored skiers, skaters, and snowboarders became infatuated with air, burly air, phat air, sick air, and after sending their bodies skyward, off vert ramps, half-pipes, craggy cliffs, they decided to express themselves, created. It started as an aerial ad lib—spinning, flipping, twisting—and one outrageous trick inspired another, and all of this trippy expressing provoked an insatiable need for more air, bigger air, more time for spinning and flipping and twisting. The bikers were late arrivals in this quest, but they were capable of so much more. Unlike the skiers and skaters and snowboarders, they had internal combustion engines.

"Whoa, he's got that Can-Can dialed!"

Larry Stevens, producer of the Freestyle Moto X coverage, always knew of a world with cable and did not remember the Cold War or the attempted assassination of Ronald Reagan. Stevens and Fortunato were inches apart in the truck, producer as always sitting almost elbow to elbow with the director. In all other ways, however, these two were at either end of a time warp.

"Look at that . . . how big can you get! Indian Air off the Superman."

Stevens's head was topped by a pink and purple tie-dyed doo rag, his eyeballs popping from drinking Green Tango, a lightly carbonated, perfectly legal energy drink he had been guzzling since he didn't know when. The liquid amphetamine came in small cans with a warning label: SIDE EFFECTS MAY INCLUDE LONG, PRODIGIOUS BOWEL MOVEMENTS, BEHAVIORAL DISTURBANCES, AND ALTERED SLEEP PATTERNS. On the second or third day of broadcasting, the magic potion was all of a sudden widely available around the compound. The company wouldn't pay for cabs from the airport, had almost everyone sleeping two to a room, housed the production beneath a huge, drafty, catering tent about to be swept off the pier by the lashing gusts, but there were cases of Green Tango everywhere. Caesar, an expert in stimulants, felt obliged to sample the elixir. It had the thick consistency of juice but tasted something like diet soda, not quite appealing but palatable. The mistake was drinking Green Tango with food, which Caesar had done. The drink turned a full stomach into a volcano. Caesar experienced a series of powerful farts, a wave of nausea, and finally the advertised prodigious bowel movement. He went back to coffee and admired Larry's constitution.

"Rodeo Air! This thing is over!"

Fifteen-year-old Turk Pizano was forty feet above the ground and as his Suzuki reached the top of gravity's rainbow, he broke out the Rodeo Air. With one hand on the bars and the other swinging in the air, as if he was riding a bucking bronco, Pizano took his feet off the pegs, brought them over the handlebars, and touched them together, completing a so-called Heel Clicker. That was the easy part. Then he had to land. A year before, Pizano ran out of air two feet short of the landing ramp and dislocated his pelvis from his spine. Doctors were astonished that he lived, expected he'd spend the rest of his days in a wheelchair, then watched in wonderment when he walked out of the hospital.

Though four of the nine riders didn't make it to the finals—each of them suffering injuries that would be considered career-ending in most other sports: destroyed joints, seriously battered brains—Pizano completed his final trick without incident. There wouldn't be a ninth surgery or nineteenth broken bone.

"Okay," Larry said to Caesar, "remember what we talked about before. I think he's still gonna do it."

Stevens had told his director that Pizano was planning a celebratory dunk in the bay. So Caesar was prepared. He made sure there was a camera waiting at the water's edge, on the other side of a berm on the east end of the course.

"There he goes . . . there he goes!"

Pizano took off his chest protector, completed a victory lap, and then accelerated in the wrong direction, right off the pier. He tried to throw a back flip, but when it became apparent to him that he was indeed going to break his neck, he pushed away from the bike. Impetuous teen and his machine splashed down independently. Only the teen floated to the surface. Caesar's camera had photographed the entirety of this outrageous and fully anticipated stunt. In the huge, drafty production tent, there was a loud cheer. At this event, there was no real separation between the athletes and the TV staff. More than one of the paid employees of the all-sports network yelled, "Pizano rules!"

A day later, after the San Francisco Police had interrogated the senior producers about what they knew and when they knew it, after the Environmental Protection Agency started talking about a hundred-thousand-dollar fine for polluting the federally protected bay, after the network's top lawyers back at headquarters told the senior producers to appease anyone with a badge of any kind, there was a notice posted in the huge, drafty production tent: TURK PIZANO'S UNAUTHORIZED JUMP INTO SAN FRANCISCO BAY IS NOT TO BE USED UNDER ANY CIRCUMSTANCES.

Caesar chuckled at how easily the network abandoned the spirit of its so-called revolutionary sporting event. It was okay for Turk Pizano and the other eight riders born without common sense to compete in a new, captivating, insanely dangerous pseudo-sport that was likely to leave half of them with arthritic limbs by the time they were thirty. It was okay that one of the riders was coughing up blood after a wicked crash and remained in the competition, though he should have been having his head examined, literally, at a local hospital. But when the winner of the competition demonstrated his joy in a fashion appropriate to his breed, consistent with the balls-out code of conduct observed by all Ex athletes, and the law started looking for suspects, the network caved, denied, apologized, and blamed the boy. Though the idea was hatched by his parents, and his sponsors arranged for a motorboat to pluck him out of the bay, and producer Larry Stevens was told of the ambitious celebration plans, suddenly the whole thing was a conspiracy of one.

"I regret my actions," said Pizano, a day after the dunk. The senior producers, as part of a deal with the San Francisco Police, had promised to air an interview with a contrite Turk Pizano. "I know it was dangerous, and I guess it would be a bad thing if other kids tried to do something like that. I got a little carried away."

In a concession, the network allowed Pizano to keep his gold medal but decided he should not receive his ten-thousand-dollar first prize, money he was hoping to use for a new pickup truck. Turk didn't have a driver's license yet, but he had been liking the idea that the truck would be waiting when he turned seventeen.

Though Caesar's disgust was profound and he wanted to flee, the long days into nights had sapped his will. So had the effort to understand what the fuck anyone was talking about. He never stopped learning the synonyms for "cool." There was "rad" and "gnarly" and "filthy" and "nasty" and "skanky" and "mint" and "mute." Or you could say, "Word!" Or, "Hot!" Or, Caesar's favorite, "That's tits!"

What had also changed was the role of the director. In the computer age, the director only did half the job. The other half was done by the technical director. Once, the TD was a simple button pusher, taking the director's instructions on camera cuts, tape rolls, and the occasional wipe. The technical directors of the nineties were required to be digital gurus. At the Ex Games, Caesar was working with one of the best, Payton Chadwick, who was really piloting the ship. Spread before Chadwick was an instrumentation panel as cool as any seen in a science fiction film. Chadwick added a sound effect to every graphic. He could align five different pieces of tape to roll back to back to back to back to back. He could instantly reorder reality, altering color, slowing motion, squeezing images, enlarging them, making them explode. Often, Caesar would be little more than an impressed bystander. His day was indeed done.

Then Brett Falcon saved the whole thing, gave Caesar Fortunato a memorable ride into his TV sunset. The greatest skateboarder ever to live became the first to complete a 900. He'd been trying the trick for ten years, had recently cracked a rib and wrenched his back doing it. The 900 was the so-called Holy Grail of the sport, two and a half rotations in the air above the vert ramp. Judged impossible. Even Falcon was having his doubts. But on this night in San Francisco, feeding off the want of a big crowd, a love fest of Ex devotees, he started going for it in the best trick competition. The first fall was nasty. The velocity of the spinning meant Falcon was going to pay in pain for every miss. Caesar started to become involved, getting hypnotized by Falcon like everyone else on the pier, identifying with this lanky, clearly charismatic figure crashing back onto the base of the ramp, wincing but so determined, popping back up, finding the skateboard some twenty feet away, climbing back up the stairs at the side of the ramp.

Falcon would try and fail another nine times, nine more dramatic "yard sales," as Larry described it. Fortunato's voice was rising in the truck, excitement present for the first time that week. There was a rhythm he could feel, and once again he picked up the baton, the five cameras his little orchestra. Wide shot. Falcon's face. Crowd. Falcon's face. Reactions from the other competitors. Crowd. Falcon's face at the top of the ramp. Wide shot. "Eyes, let me see his eyes," Fortunato commanded. When the camera pushed into Falcon's face, the determination was entrancing. He was on the pier and he was not on the pier. He was going to complete the 900 if it killed him.

On the eleventh attempt, Falcon twisted in the air once and then twice and then another half turn, and then he squatted as he rolled back down the ramp, fighting, fighting to keep his balance, and then he stood tall and from all around his fellow competitors slid down the ramp and mobbed him. The shot from the jib showed Falcon from above, arms in the air, in the midst of a pack of his frenzied peers. On his face, a look of astonishment and unadulterated joy.

* * *

He ended up staying an extra day. Larry Stevens invited him to punch some clouds down in Monterey, where they had just finished the sky-surfing competition. He was fifty-eight years old and not sure if his heart could sustain a leap out of an airplane from eighteen thousand feet. But like everyone else, he was still feeling that buzz from Brett Falcon's night of nights, and it awakened his sense of daring.

There was a soupy fog when they took off in the DeHaviland Twin Otter, no seats, everyone on the floor, leaning against each other, looking like fallen dominoes. The worst part was when they opened the large sliding door and there was nothing but three miles of air between him and the ground. Caesar asked God, for the second time that year, that he not end up rotting in hell. He was the third to jump, and in the first seconds he thought his heart had really stopped. Then with his cheeks flapping furiously in the wind, falling at some one hundred and twenty miles an hour, he felt so proud of himself and so happy to be alive and he couldn't remember ever having as big a shit-eating grin on his face.

San Diego

Henry Mandel, who had known him for the shortest period among those present, had the most trouble retaining his composure that Monday morning when they buried Caesar Fortunato, a typically magnificent San Diego morning of unadulterated sunshine and gentle, cooling ocean breezes. There were seven altogether circling the casket, excluding the priest: wife number one, Maxine, son Mark and daughter Cynthia, instant replay co-conspirator Bob Gilmartin, devoted agent Palmer Nash, Heisman Trophy–winner Charles Beck—and Henry. Although Caesar Fortunato had been one tremendous pain in his ass, Caesar's death had Henry Mandel fighting to keep from weeping. Deep down, he had known it was going to happen.

One of the greatest directors in television history

had concluded his career in radio, and Henry Mandel was his producer, and baby-sitter, and his last friend on earth. They had worked together every morning that past year, Caesar the host of a midmorning talk show on the city's all-sports radio station. The career change was Henry's doing. He had seen a feature on Caesar in the local paper. It informed him that a national sports personality with a unique level of experience was out of work and in the neighborhood.

He directed the biggest games and the biggest events. At the top, he was being paid almost a million dollars a year. Now, Caesar Fortunato lives in a small one-bedroom apartment that gets shaken every two minutes by jets landing at nearby Lindbergh Field. And though he is a convicted felon, owes the Internal Revenue Service a million dollars, and is having trouble finding work, Caesar Fortunato claims he is incredibly lucky.

"I had a disease, and I could be in jail," says Fortunato. "But people have been very kind to me. I showed the judge I was willing to reform, and he was very lenient. With the community service, I feel like I'm giving something back. It's helping me, too. And I found out I was a compulsive gambler before it was too late, before somebody found me in a ditch with a bullet in my head."

Fortunato's sentence for assaulting Hollywood star Johnny Ray Thompson requires him to perform one hundred hours of community service, which he is doing here. Yesterday, as part of the San Diego Literacy Project, the 17-time Emmy winner was reading Dr. Seuss to young children at a nursery school in Imperial City.

Fortunato also recently agreed to pay the IRS two million dollars for nonpayment of taxes. Fortunato said the tax issues followed a three-year period during which his gambling was out of control and his finances were left in disarray.

"I've already been able to cut the tax bill in half by selling a painting I owned," said Fortunato. "But I know I'll be paying off the rest of the bill until I die."

So Mandel, enticed by the established name and insider's knowledge and the recent tabloid narrative, gave Caesar another reason to live, and as importantly, a regular paycheck, which probably kept him alive. Since moving to San Diego in search of affordable real estate and then having the IRS figure out, at long last, his tax delinquencies, Caesar's three square meals had been divided among three principal sources: Corn Flakes, peanut butter, jelly.

In a short time, Henry Mandel's discovery, whom he dubbed the Rappin' Roman, developed a loyal following—almost a new family to replace the real one he had all but relinquished. There was Charlie from Solana, a three-hundred-and-fifty-pound ex-Samoan who quoted from the Gospel According to Duke, religious writings allegedly penned by the Hawaiian Olympian and Father of Surfing, Duke Paoa Kahanamoku; and there was Bobby the Flusher, who'd call from inside his bathroom and sign off with a bowl-cleansing blast; and Daisy, a dancer who claimed to have the largest natural breasts in Southern California and campaigned to rid the world of all biology improved by chemistry, such as competing dancers enhanced by silicon or saline, bodybuilders inflated by steroids, and home-run hitters juiced by andro. Charlie and Bobby and Daisy were among dozens of regular callers. They would insist on talking with Caesar every day, and in time there were so many, Henry had to limit each of the regulars to one call per week.

By popular demand, the station held a memorial service for Caesar in the parking lot of Qualcomm Stadium, an occasional site of the Rappin' Roman Show when the Padres and Chargers were at home. "So you're the cocksucker who wouldn't let me talk to him," a venomous Daisy said while confronting Henry after he had delivered an open-air eulogy from a small platform next to one of the station's fully billboarded mobile equipment vans. Charlie from Solana and Bobby the Flusher and the mayor of Hillcrest and Pete from Poway were also in attendance, forming a crowd of some four hundred largely troubled, barely functioning souls whose lives came to revolve around the three-hour broadcasts of a former drinker, junkie, and gambler, twice divorced and once convicted. In Caesar, they found one of their own, an emotional wreck living, somehow, day to day.

I have no one to blame but myself, Caesar Fortunato said on the air during his first broadcast and many thereafter. *I take full responsibility for making a total mess of my life. And that's the day I became liberated. When I stopped blaming everything and everyone else. If you're a drinker, only you can put a stop to it. If you have a drug problem, you have to make a decision to stop. And if you're a gambler, you've got to stop going to the track and hitting the tables and calling the bookie. Please seek help. Don't wait until you've lost your family and your friends and your job, like I did. Don't wait until you're in the gutter, like I was. Don't wait until the law comes after you. Take the blame, then get help.*

264

Henry Mandel traced Caesar's success to the nature of the city. He believed San Diego was a town willing to forget and forgive. Before Caesar's arrival, the city's former mayor had become a successful radio personality despite getting booted from office after four hundred campaign violations and thirteen counts of conspiracy and perjury. Others, less generous, would say that Caesar was succeeding because San Diego was still at heart a dopey little fishing village easily conned.

Hey, Caesar.

Hey, darling. What are you doing?

The dishes.

How's that going?

Well, I just bought this new model from Sears and, you know, it doesn't make as much noise.

That's great. What are you doing after the dishes?

The laundry.

Fabulous. When are we going to get together again?

How about this Friday night? Charlie and I were thinking of going to that grungy bar in Ocean Beach.

I'll see you there.

Some days, half of the show included wholly inane conversations. Charlie was Caesar's dentist, and Kim, the one doing the dishes, was Charlie's wife. Caesar insisted that Kim be allowed on the show as often as she liked, despite Henry's many high-volume protests. Henry determined that Caesar was getting free dental care from Charlie and having some kind of less than traditional affair with Kim—less than traditional because, as Henry knew, sex for Caesar was problematic.

After the heart attack, Caesar told Henry that his erections had been softening year by year. By the time he got to San Diego, a true woody was a thing of the past. Yet, while making appearances around town, Caesar would still be on the prowl, and on several occasions he hijacked the station's van—and stranded Henry—after typically propositioning a middle-aged, large-breasted, somewhat desperate companion willing to have sex by any means available.

"I may not get hard," he explained to Henry Mandel, "but I still bust a nut."

Though his underperforming penis reminded him regularly of his damaged heart, he could not bring himself to exercise much or change

265

his diet. In the first hour of every show, Caesar would order from Gino's Pizza on the air. The restaurant was way up the coast, in Del Mar, a thirty-minute drive from the station, which was in a no-man's-land underneath the I-5 and I-8 interchange at the city's center. When he first arrived, Caesar made a sincere search to find a deli and pizza place up to Eastern standards. It was weeks, after expanding the search from downtown and going north, after stops in Coronado and Point Loma and Ocean Beach and Mission Beach and Pacific Beach and La Jolla, before he found happiness, found the desired sloppy, cheese-and-meat-congested, unpretentious style of pizza that was cooked at Gino's. As for the deli, the search continued.

Caesar, don't worry, I never forget you. The pizza's coming. My boy is bringing it.

The free plug equaled free pizza.

Ham, sausage, salami, super greasy, right, Gino?

Caesar, I also give you some salad today, okay?

Gino, salad is for rabbits.

What do you mean?

It means we don't want salad.

So sorry, Caesar. So sorry. I'll call up my delivery guy. I'll have him bring the salad back.

Gino, make it two pizzas today, since you screwed up.

Yes, Caesar. Absolutely.

Henry and Caesar would often convene for a post-broadcast meal at Perry's, a kind of fifties-style urban truck stop with unrivaled short-order fare. The booths were covered by Naugahyde, so retro they were chic; cheery, uniformed waitresses arrived at the tables already armed with pots of sufficiently hot coffee; the parking lot was inevitably full, eighteen-wheelers side by side with European sports cars, the eclectic mix of vehicles testimony to Perry's preeminence. Henry would watch with a small measure of horror and a larger helping of admiration as Caesar defied fate with certifiably heart-stopping fare gobbled up in single sittings: Mexican omelet, hash browns, sausages, bacon, blueberry French toast.

Henry Mandel had never met someone with such an appetite for living, someone who so avidly sought a way to wrestle a satisfactory portion of excitement out of every hour of every day. From the very start of each broadcast, Mandel felt as if he was chasing a kind of force of nature, a storm with free will and no sense of direction. In other words, anarchy.

* * *

To protect his job, Mandel always made sure he was within striking distance of the dump button, which would erase profanity or entirely inappropriate commentary before it could be heard by the San Diego listeners. Even so, there were days when the technology couldn't counter Caesar's inability to control himself.

Why do you defend Bobby Knight in every single one of your columns?

One morning, Caesar's guest was the city's most famous sportswriter.

Well, Caesar, I think he gets more out of his kids than anyone else.

Yeah, but he does it by abusing them.

That's a little harsh, don't you think?

No. He's a child abuser.

That's ridiculous.

No, it's not. He gets these scared little boys who can't really defend themselves. And then, you know what? He starts calling them cunts . . .

The dump button was activated. Because the broadcast was on a seven-second delay, this meant Henry Mandel had heard Caesar use the "c" word before it was broadcast to thousands of listeners, some of whom would call the station and vigorously complain if it indeed made air. There was also the possibility of heavy fines from the FCC. If Henry was quick, he'd be able to erase all of the offending sentence, because a typical English sentence, subject, verb, and object, took about seven seconds or so to utter. And if the whole sentence was successfully erased, then it would sound like Caesar hadn't been edited at all.

In this case, San Diego heard Caesar talk about "scared little boys who can't really defend themselves," and then a pregnant pause. It was as if Caesar were ruminating.

And when they do something wrong, Knight calls them cunts having a period.

Forced to use the dump button again, Mandel couldn't help clipping the entire sentence. This was less than ideal. It appeared the station was having technical problems, either that or the Rappin' Roman was having a very large brain fart. This had happened before: Caesar's whole show was becoming a dump-out. Mandel tried to get Caesar's attention, waving his arms back and forth with all the subtlety of a sailor flagging supersonic aircraft on the deck of a carrier. With his obstreperous talent secure inside an announce booth, behind a locked door, a chair thrown through the Plexiglas would have been the only other means to reach him quickly.

And then if his kids throw the ball away or miss a shot, he calls them little cunts in front of eighteen thousand people.

Mandel, jittery, hit the dump button too soon. He deleted the first half of the sentence but not the offending latter half. The c-word went airborne and a moment later the station's twenty phone lines were all aglow.

Mandel tolerated such bullshit because Caesar Fortunato was just as often funny and engaging and perceptive and, perhaps more importantly, self-aware. On that night in Rome, when he truly came back and joined the living, Caesar Fortunato felt as if God had allowed him to see himself as others saw him. For the first time, he could see that the reflection in the mirror showed a man drained of love, love of anything. He was every bit as morally vacant as some of the suits and producers and talent he had inscribed on his list of permanently loathed. He may have fought the good fight against some of the most formidable pricks, but he never did it for anyone but himself. He never allowed himself to be recruited for anyone else's good cause.

Henry Mandel admired Caesar mostly for a case of giving at the office. He watched Caesar Fortunato teach Jim Milano how to succeed in broadcasting. The fifty-nine-year-old with forty years of broadcasting buried in his bones taught Milano that he should think of his voice as a musical instrument, with a range of volume and attitude that was worth exploiting; taught him that the art of interviewing started with five words: what, when, where, why, and how; taught him, while watching all manner of games in various sports bars, how to find the edge of difference between the competitors; told him who was important in sports history and why they mattered.

There were areas of his character that Caesar Fortunato had not exactly redeemed since he knelt on the wet cobblestone and genuinely asked to be forgiven. Henry Mandel came to know a man who was intemperate, about his sex life, his language, his eating habits. But about the big things, the things that had really destroyed him, the drugging and the drinking and the gambling, there was clearly an attempt to change. And he said again and again, in private and on the airwaves, that he blamed no one but himself. And, with Jim Milano, there was no expectation of repayment. He taught the newcomer what he knew, even consoled the young man after his mother was swept away in a matter of months by an unstoppable cancer, and he did it out of nothing more than kindness . . . and a restored sense of generosity. At long last, it was time for him to freely share what he knew, in the way that others had once been so generous with him.

That there was indeed nothing in it for Caesar Fortunato was confirmed for Henry Mandel at the funeral. Jim Milano, who had gone off to a better job in L.A., didn't even bother to show up.

A Day at the Races

It was at the Del Mar Racetrack, not far from his preferred pizza joint, that Caesar Fortunato ended his
life in gambling. He had been invited to receive an
award from the Horse Racing Association of America. Tommy Vaughn, Caesar's first choice, made the
presentation. By luck, he was in town directing baseball's Game of the Week.

"I have been watching Caesar Fortunato's work for
a long time because I have been in the business a long
time. And I have been watching Caesar's work
because I am competitive. I wanted to make sure he
wasn't doing anything better than I was doing it. We
are here on this gorgeous day, in one of my favorite
places, to honor Caesar for his contributions to the
coverage of horse racing, the sport of kings. And, in

particular, Caesar will always be known for a broadcast in 1973, the year the great horse Secretariat won the Triple Crown, and doing it in the most impressive fashion possible. Ladies and gentlemen, that day Caesar Fortunato did a very simple thing, and in a way, a not so simple thing.

"No one was prepared for what Secretariat did that day. Everyone knew he was great, but then we found out that he was the greatest ever. That day at Belmont Park, Secretariat shattered the world record for a mile and a half and won the race by the largest margin in history, thirty-one lengths, the distance of a football field.

"Now, as directors, we are paid to understand the moment. Understand what is important about the moment. We are paid to know this without anyone telling us. And without any time to think about it. We are just supposed to know. And on that day, Caesar Fortunato understood what was important.

"He saw that this horse was doing something special. He saw Secretariat's splits at each quarter and saw that he was destroying the rest of the field, forcing them into exhaustion trying to chase him. And so, as this miraculous horse came into the stretch, he told his cameraman, well, maybe yelled to his cameraman: 'Widen out . . . widen out.'

"Our instinct in the truck most times is to be close—to show the athlete's face at the moment of triumph. To show the exertion and the grace. But on this day, the best way to capture the moment was to be wide. Because by being wide, Caesar showed literally and figuratively Secretariat's margin of greatness . . . showed this horse creating an amazing gap of thirty-one lengths . . . a gap the size of a football field. In an instant, Caesar Fortunato made that decision, and it was the right decision, and that is the one shot by which we remember Secretariat. Caesar's great wide shot. That's the shot that still gives us chills. And it was done by a great director who understood the moment."

Later, they sat together outside, over burgers and fries, at the Thoroughbred Club. There were enough distractions— the winning of the award, his first conversation with Tommy Vaughn, exercise-buffed blondes exposing cleavage in peacock-proud fashion statements—to keep him from lining up at the betting windows for each and every race. Del Mar on a summer day—the temperature in the seventies, the Pacific Ocean in view, sombreroed mariachi bands strolling the grounds, the parade of beauty and means—was as inviting a destination as any in the world of sports.

Tommy Vaughn was leaving the business after the next World Series. Like Caesar, he felt himself to be every bit the dinosaur. At some point, he was saying to Caesar, the cost-cutting made it impossible to do the job right, and if it was not possible to do the job right, then it wasn't worth doing at all. He might as well be selling insurance, which is what he had been going to do after the war, before his uncle got him a job at the late Dumont network pulling firehose-sized coaxial cable.

"In the early days, we just tried to stay on the air, you know," said Tommy to a nodding Caesar. "If a show went two hours, maybe half the time all you'd see was a slide with the word 'boxing' or 'baseball.' We were always off the air. Just trying to send a picture from New York to New Jersey was like sending someone to the moon. I remember we were in South Bend, doing the Notre Dame game, when I was with Dumont. And, in those days, we microwaved the picture from the top of the stadium to a relay station, then into Chicago, and then it would hit the network. Well, we're on the air for about fifteen minutes, and we go black. And what happened, they noticed a tube had gone bad. So the engineer had to leave the roof, get in a car, drive into town, go into a radio store, get a tube, come back, and replace it. We were off the air for about an hour."

The first great innovation in sports coverage, before the instant replay, was the centerfield camera. In the fifties, television prospered because of live sports coverage, and the most important live sports event was baseball. Being able to see a baseball game from the pitcher's perspective, in front of the plate, not just behind it, added a vital dimension because that was the center of the game: the ongoing battle between pitcher and batter. All of a sudden, the TV viewer could truly see the curve of a curveball, the wobble in a knuckler, a pitcher painting the corners. And the whole thing was Tommy's idea.

"Where I was brought up in New Jersey," he told Caesar, who had long been curious about Tommy's inspiration, "there was a lot of softball, and the umpire always stood behind the pitcher calling balls and strikes. I always thought that was a great shot, but for a while we were limited, you know, by the length of cable and the type of lenses."

The eighth race was the feature, the Bing Crosby Breeders Cup Handicap. Caesar had a horse he liked. Big Jag had won eight of his last nine races and had been a winner the previous summer at Del Mar. Caesar received further encouragement that morning when he canvased the stables, an old habit, and found Big Jag's groom, who told him the horse was healthy and anxious.

"*Si, si, señor,*" said the teenager, T-shirt blackened, jeans that hadn't been washed in a week, "you win *mucho dinero.*"

Caesar was always a sucker for such inside information, though over the years it had produced very few winning results. Like so many who wagered, he was forever searching for a golden nugget, a tip, a sure thing, a proven system, some manner of making sense out of games of chance. In the eighth race that day at Del Mar, he could have bet with his heart, bet with the amateurs in attendance who had turned up at this heavenly spot for fun, not profit. He could have bet on Son of a Pistol for purely emotional reasons, because he was the son of a cop. Or on Mr. Fortune, being a Fortunato. Or he could have bet on Christmas Boy for reasons of vague coincidence, since he was born two days before Christmas.

Tommy Vaughn, who wished to be part of the solution and not part of the problem, at first tried to discourage Caesar from betting, then relented provided two conditions were met: He, not Caesar, would carry the money to the window, and the limit was fifty bucks. Tommy was betting Christmas Boy because his son was a Christmas baby. Caesar was going with the favorite.

Tommy accepted that life at some point was not worth figuring out. It seemed to him some people were sprinkled with luck and some people were not, but even so, the lucky could become the unlucky instantaneously. He had flown bombers in World War II and had gone into the skies some fifty times, in killing weather, against superior German airpower, piloting a piece of flying metal that was fragile enough without having everyone shooting at it. And for a reason unknown to him, he had lived when so many good men, usually through no fault of their own, had not.

273

Tommy Vaughn's most famous shot was a replay of Carlton Fisk jumping joyously along the first base line after winning the greatest World Series game ever played with a home run over the Green Monster at Fenway Park. "TV" was lucky to get the shot. His cameraman stationed inside the scoreboard, a new angle envisioned by Vaughn, was supposed to be following the ball out of the park, not stuck on Fisk. But Lou Gerard wasn't paying attention as the game was being decided. He was worried about a rat on the floor, and so the camera didn't pan up with the crack of the bat. After hearing the roar, all Lou could do was follow Fisk around the bases, and luckily, that most happy of home run trots became one of the defining images in sports television history.

"Why?"

"Why what?"

"Tommy, I'm calling your house, leaving horrible, threatening messages. Why did you recommend me for the job in Rome?"

"You did seem out of sorts."

"It was charity? Don't tell me it was charity. Don't tell me you helped my out because I was just pathetic."

"No, I wouldn't do that to Father Ed. As you know, I feel a certain obligation to him."

"Right."

"I was going to do the show for him, but then you popped up on my answering machine."

"And you fucking felt sorry for me."

"No, if I felt sorry for you, or concerned about you, or something like that, I would have called the police. Or your agent. The reason I told Father Ed about you was that you were the better person for the job. You were the right guy for the job. I know my limitations. You, on the other hand, don't assume there is any such thing as limitations. It was one of those ridiculous, never-done-before shows. It was made for you. You called at the right time, and, you know, you sounded desperate enough to do great work. It was a psycho call, yes. But the timing was good."

"Tommy, who did the first instant replay? Me or you?"

"Caesar, all the right people know."

274

"Me or you?"

"I know it didn't happen at a Packers game in Los Angeles."

The eighth race was won by Vaughn's pick, the long shot, Christmas Boy, who faded early but then, for the first time in his uneventful racing life, made a late surge. Caesar, swearing to God that he had put down his very last bet after his horse was fourth, remembered feeling like a complete idiot on another day at the track, back in that famous Belmont of 1973, when he was screaming at his cameraman to widen his shot and discover where the fuck the rest of the field was behind the huge chestnut colt about to become the first horse to win the Triple Crown in twenty-five years. He was screaming for the proper editorial reasons, but also because he wanted to see the horse he had bet on, a fine horse born in the wrong year, second in the Derby, second in the Preakness, a horse who challenged Secretariat once again in the Belmont but ultimately faded to last, a horse named Sham.

On the night of his death, in a city at the southwest edge of America, Caesar Fortunato was in week two of what he was hoping would become a nightly ritual. He went to Pacific Beach, a fifteen-minute drive from his condo, and began his walk. He walked near the waves, where the sand had been flattened by the wash of the surf, and periodically glanced down at his wristwatch. He would walk along the beach for twenty-five minutes, then return. The falling sun, orange and large, was cut in half by the horizon. The seagulls squealed, tussling over crumbs from completed picnics. A breeze massaged his face. There was the comforting *shush shush* of the waves, and air thickened by a perpetual mist, diffused salt, and the pungent smell of seaweed and festering, unlucky horseshoe crabs, ocean roadkill.

He liked being a radio celebrity, liked the unwavering admiration of his listeners. He liked radio's simplicity: a microphone, a transmitter, one-on-one contact with the listeners. His television work had a far larger audience, but it was faceless and mute and he never knew if or how he touched anybody. Caesar was surprised how suddenly TV lost its grip on him. Once loosened, the bond rapidly dissolved. It confirmed what he had always suspected. It wasn't so much that he loved

275

TV as he was seduced by it, its pull every bit as compelling and danger-ous as a siren's song.

Half of his money was siphoned to pay his outstanding bill with the IRS, but since taking a forced leave from the land of spectacular indul-gence, he had been able to subsist on what he had left. Even so, his reduced means had not prevented him from starting to repay his son. The first installment was a fifty-thousand-dollar check, the director's fee from the *World Prayer* show, which Father O'Keefe agreeably diverted to Mark Fortunato's address in San Jose. A few months later, while he was in San Francisco at the Ex Games, Caesar had a messenger deliver a large envelope of cash to his son's office. Both devices of repayment pre-vented any bite from the tax man.

"Caesar, can you explain this twenty-five-thousand-dollar miscella-neous expense for salvage?"

A month after the Ex Games, one of the accountants was making a call he'd been expecting.

"You know what that's about, don't you?"

"No. I really need you to explain it."

"Well, I'm surprised none of the senior guys told you about this. When Turk Pizano put his motorcyle in the bay, I was told to get it out of there as fast as possible. You know, the EPA was going to fine you guys a couple of hundred thousand if any oil or gas from the bike spilled in the bay."

"Really. Well, where is the bike now?"

"You're kidding, right? My dredging guys did this in the middle of the night. After they pulled the thing out, they made sure it disap-peared."

"We really need a receipt, Caesar."

"You want a paper trail? Let me tell you, that bike was leaking all kinds of crap into the bay. Your company doesn't want any of this to be traced."

"You wouldn't be making this up, would you?"

"How could I do something like that and still stay in the business, huh?"

After his beach walk, Fortunato drove his Honda back home. He ordered delivery from the local Mexican place. He desperately, desperately wanted a beer, an ice-cold Corona, but on the phone, after a moment's hesitation, he asked for a soda, a Diet Coke. The roaring and tremors from takeoffs and landings at the international airport only blocks away, so maddening when he first moved in, had melted into the larger, unnoticed street mix outside his windows. After the enchiladas arrived, he put on the Padres game and by the third inning dropped off into a sleep from which he would never awaken.

A Killing Frost

The game would be called the Ice Bowl because it was the coldest game in NFL history, sunshine and thirteen below zero. Sustained winds from the Yukon made the afternoon additionally painful. Later, when the wind-chill factor was calculated, it was estimated that the Ice Bowl actually felt like forty-six below. Northern Wisconsin was famous for days like these. It was said to have only two seasons: winter and the Fourth of July. But December 31, 1967, was especially cruel.

On the morning of the game, the Dallas Cowboys needed help getting out of their hotel rooms. There had been an icy snow the night before and the warmth from the rooms had frozen the doors shut. Green Bay free safety Willie Wood couldn't get his car started. He had to call for a tow truck. On the opening play, Norm Schacter, the head of the officiating crew, couldn't separate his whistle from his lips. Then the same thing happened to a line judge, who lost a layer of skin after yanking too hard. After that, the rest of the crew abandoned their whistles and reverted to shouting.

It was a day when thousands chose to defy winter's best shot, when the vaporized breath of the chilled multitude obscured the stands, when the well-equipped were almost too frozen to reach inside their sleeping bags and snowmobile suits for flasks of whisky, when momentarily blinded writers cleared the press box windows by any means available, turning credit cards and wooden coffee stirrers into ice scrapers. All liquids became solids, the stadium's toilets turned into tiny frozen ponds. But nature's brutality would be recalled romantically. It framed a supreme contest.

On the field were archetypal football teams with players whose names seemed to sing of grit and manliness: Herb Adderly, Boyd Dowler, Jerry Kramer, Bob Lilly, Don Meredith, Jethro Pugh, Dan Reeves, Lance Rentzel, Mel Renfro, Bob Skoronski, Bart Starr, Fuzzy Thurston. And guiding these aptly named gridiron warriors were revered commanders: the stern, inscrutable, Bible-belting Tom Landry of the Cowboys, a grand master of the game, and Green Bay's Vince Lombardi, really the quintessential coach, a gap-toothed, eyeglassed block of granite who dressed with all the verve of an insurance agent and ruled his behemoths by intimidation and emotion and neverending mind games, whose totality of commitment would spur thousands of coaches to preach his winning-is-everything gospel, though Lombardi hated the idea that his words had been perverted into a win-at-all-costs mentality. What he had really meant to say was that second place sure is for shit and if you're going to bother to take part in anything, do it right, and do it right all the time.

Lombardi barely tolerated the media, but there was special consideration for Caesar Fortunato. The Packers were always in the big games, and Caesar had become the big-game director. By the Ice Bowl, they were established friends with a standing dinner appointment whenever Caesar was in town. Two nights before the Ice Bowl, they were back at their accustomed spot, Wally Proski's Food and Cocktail Lounge over on Washington Street. In the back room, tucked away from the adoring townsfolk, the respectful young director listened as the seasoned coach waxed on with impunity.

"I may berate players, Caesar, but I never carry a grudge," said Lombardi, filet half-finished, knife and fork moving in the air. "Something happened at practice last week. It involved our young offensive lineman, you know who I'm talking about. I rushed him. He was laughing again. Laughing about getting his ass knocked flat! I just can't stand it. So, I'm flailing away at him with my fists. The guy is eight inches taller, outweighs me by one hundred pounds. It's crazy. I'm a madman. And later, somebody is telling me about it, and I don't even remember. I swear."

Lombardi cut a slice of steak and popped it in his mouth.

"The problem is, he loves everybody. But to play this game, you have to have that fire in you, and nothing stokes that fire like hate. I want him to hate! Hate me! Hate anything! It's a terrible thing, to have to coax this sort of animosity out of someone. What kind of game is it to do that to men? But you've just got to have it, something that keeps you from compromising. It has to be personal for all my players. There has to be emotion. It's got to be there. And then, day of game, you release it. Release that emotion in all its fury. Now it has a purpose. It fuels your desire."

Once, Vince Lombardi had taught physics to high school students, and he was one of those teachers who wanted everyone in his class to understand the subject matter. It wasn't enough for Mr. Lombardi to have half of his juniors understand the workings of the natural universe. He judged himself a failure if anyone failed. It was how he taught the Green Bay Packers, too. He made them run his famous sweep in practice over and over and over, until it became second nature to all eleven starting offensive players, until he could look at the film and see a wholly gratifying and not inconsiderable synchronicity. Vince Lombardi, in a room lit only by the beam of a projector, knew he had succeeded when he paused the machine and saw that every one of his eleven players was moving in unison in the first moments of his famous sweep, every player's right foot raised at the same height at the very same time, as perfectly united as a string of Rockettes at Radio City Music Hall.

* * *

Lombardi's team was at the end of its mythic run of excellence. Aging, bruised, used up, the Packers also were becoming numb to the incessant brimstone of their legendary, tormented coach. The team's stars were massaging, cajoling, medicating bodies that rebounded ever more slowly after Sunday batterings. Lombardi was himself wearied by the demands of success. It was like he was chasing his own tail. There was no final, satisfying resolution, only another season of supreme expectations, which meant new strategies, new ways to motivate players he had pushed to their limitations again and again. His stomach forever unsettled, his heart seemingly on the verge of seizure, Lombardi had been forced into one-hour naps every day after lunch. He had privately resolved that this would be his last season coaching the team.

In the Ice Bowl, on a slippery, concrete-hard field described by one player as a stucco wall laid flat, during a game in which they were outplayed by the Cowboys, at the end of a wonderful run and fast becoming more memory than reality, the Packers had to call upon their guile and their heart, that Lombardi-brewed intensity, and, in the end, they won with a drive, a play that encapsulated the essential nature of their team.

Four minutes left, down by three points, by this time the sun sinking and an even colder night approaching, Starr the quarterback drove them once more despite bruised ribs, an aching shoulder, toes screaming from the frost. Five passes, all complete. There were no fumbles, no interceptions, no penalties. No mistakes. The clock was down to thirteen seconds. The ball was on the one-yard line. Lombardi could have kicked a field goal. Tied the game. Let it go into overtime. That would have been the safe option, but instead, during a seconds-long sideline tête-à-tête, the decision was made to risk the season, roll the dice.

"I'll run it, okay?" said the quarterback hesitantly to the coach.

"All right, then run it!" Lombardi bellowed, "and let's get the hell out of here!"

"What's he going to call?" someone asked Lombardi as Starr trotted back to the huddle.

"Damned if I know!"

Though he may have treated them like dogs during torturous practices that started in the summer's painful heat, on Sundays in the fall his players were coached by a man who regarded them as professionals, as men who deserved his confidence and respect. In the end, Starr would wing it. Lombardi's Packers, to some the epitome of discipline and planning, were about to win by improvisation, by a bold notion about to be exercised under the most extreme circumstances, mental and physical.

"What's he going to do, everyone?"

As Starr was speaking with Lombardi, Caesar polled his announcers.

"Some kind of rollout."

"Yeah, Starr will roll out, probably try a pass to Dowler."

"That sounds right."

On the previous two plays from the one, the Packers had run it up the middle without success. Green Bay's blockers were having trouble with their footing. By now, the completely frozen surface was more like a marble tabletop than a stucco wall, the players making clicking sounds with each step, football that was sounding more like hockey. It made sense that Starr might put it in the air, or at least lull the Cowboys into thinking he might.

Herman Lang was working the field-level camera in the end zone, behind the goalposts. This was a new perspective for TV viewers, another example of Caesar tinkering with the coverage, spending money not exactly allocated, experimenting during a big event when it would have been more prudent to be conservative.

"Herman, you heard all that, right?"

"Yes, sir."

"Be ready to pan over to the wide receiver. Okay?"

"Okay."

In the huddle, Starr called a handoff to his running back. But when he went to the line, he changed his mind, decided to attempt a kamikaze dive over the goal line, right up the middle. The Packers didn't have a quarterback sneak in their playbook. If they were going to win, if they were going to send fifty thousand numbed and largely drunk fans home happy, it would be with a play they had never practiced, a play that the other ten Packers on the field didn't know was coming.

"Ready, Herman?"

"Caesar, I think the camera may be stuck."

If the Packers went left or right, America wasn't going to see it. The end-zone camera had become one of the final casualties, frosted. It was capable of shooting in only one direction: straight ahead. Before Caesar could react, take the safe shot from above, at the fifty, the blue and white of the Cowboys and the yellow and green of the Packers collided, first the bodies rising together, then falling. Green Bay's Jerry Kramer had found a soft spot in the ground, and on the snap, on the very instant of the snap, he launched his two hundred and sixty pounds into Jethro Pugh, an essential piece of the hulking human dike formed by the Cowboys. Next was center Ken Bowman, whose pinpoint thrust sent Pugh flailing backward. Helmet down, Starr wedged his way into the gap, smothering the ball, lunging, scoring, winning it. Caesar's ossified end-zone camera had by accident artfully framed Kramer's historic block and the touchdown that gave the Packers an unprecedented third straight National Football League title.

After this Sunday in Wisconsin, after witnessing the Packers reach their own state of perfection as a team, Caesar Fortunato had a breakdown. It did not happen as an uncontrollable river of tears. It did not manifest itself this time, this first time, as an unreasonable explosion directed at innocents. His breakdown occurred without any apparent dramatics while he was perched on a stool at the bar of the Northland Hotel, as Green Bay's famous coach and his players were smiling themselves into sleep.

He was a December baby, a bittersweet fact. Sometimes, his birthday was submerged by the coming Christmas. Or the entire month could be a parade of presents. Everything was made into a kind of hyperreality. The snow, when there was snow, usually seemed whiter, fluffier. One Christmas Eve, he awoke groggy in the middle of the night and saw Santa Claus landing on the roof of a neighbor's house. Later, it was the season of shouting, collisions with his mother or father. The bad will lingered, the details quickly blurred. Whatever happened around this time had an impact, for better or worse.

A week before the Ice Bowl, he went home to see his parents, who had split up not long after he moved to New York. With Maxine, three-year-old Cynthia, and eighteen-month-old Mark, he cabbed it to Penn Station and caught an empty train on Christmas morning. He was first going to see his father, who had moved to an apartment on the city's fringe, a lower-middle-class neighborhood that was changing its complexion from white to black almost overnight, a profoundly disturbing development for Sal Fortunato. His son was early. Climbing the creaking stairs, Caesar heard the phonograph: Respighi, *The Fountains of Rome*. He thought of his behind numbing on the hard bench, the night when he finally made it from start to finish, note for note, change to change, true to the whole sweep of the work, suddenly not something read from sheets but a part of him. And when he finished, there was a pregnant silence in the house, a silence that was every bit as warming as sustained applause. If his parents weren't talking, it meant they were listening.

As he helped his little daughter up the stairs with his free hand, a shopping bag of presents in the other, he considered the outrageous thought of reconciliation. It was Christmas Day, after all, tidings of great joy, goodwill to all men, a suspension of long-held resolves and regrets—the day that celebrated a homeless boy who came to rule men's hearts for centuries, a day when children the world over waited for presents delivered by one man and eight flying reindeer.

When Caesar rang the bell, the music stopped.

Days later, as the new year dawned, Sal Fortunato's son had a tepid, nearly empty mug of beer before him, and as he was staring at a brigade of vodka and scotch and rye and gin, bottle to bottle, spouted for instant pouring, it hit him. Wham. A welling of despair that buckled him like a sickness. He feared he would never know the depth of satisfaction experienced by Lombardi and his Packers. He had long regretted that he would never be that artist Sergio Palumbo had so generously, so patiently offered to groom. He was in a business he had mastered within years and he could not foresee any transcendent challenges ahead. And Jerry Kramer's block to spring Bart Starr, an instant replay for the ages, didn't bring him any satisfaction. He hadn't composed the shot. If anything, that one belonged to God.

On that New Year's Eve, on a night when even the sunniest of souls can be made melancholy, with the blistering Wisconsin winter seeping through the walls, fifteen minutes after last call, surrounded by an accumulation of fallen confetti, Caesar Fortunato, age twenty-nine, suspected that the best was behind him and wondered for what reason he was staying in the game.

Associated Press, 12/11/98

SAN DIEGO—Caesar Fortunato, who directed many of the biggest events in sports and entertainment, died yesterday at his apartment here. The cause has not been determined. He was 59.

Fortunato was discovered by a friend after he did not report to work at KSBC, an all-sports radio station where he had been hosting a daily call-in show for the last year.

The winner of 17 Emmys, Fortunato was part of the vanguard of young directors in the sixties known for enhancing TV sports coverage with such tools as instant replay and portable cameras.

Born in Philadelphia, he left DeSales University in the middle of his sophomore year to work full time at WBAC. In 1961, only 22 years old, he went to New York and became one of the youngest sports directors in network television.

Fortunato's sports credits include four Olympics, 14 Super Bowls, and six World Series. He directed the Academy Awards, more than a dozen space missions, and a number of critically acclaimed entertainment shows, including specials with Leonard Bernstein, Bob Hope, Michael Jackson, and Christos.

Last year, he was the executive producer and director of "A World Prayer for Peace," broadcast live from 16 major international religious centers and seen in 180 countries.

Just before that program, Fortunato was sentenced to 100 hours of community service for assaulting actor Johnny Ray Thompson. He was later charged with tax evasion for failing to report capital gains on a brokerage account, and ordered to pay $2 million in back taxes and penalties.

Fortunato said he "had surrendered control of his life to drugs, alcohol, and gambling," and that his addictions had "destroyed his judgment."

His agent, Palmer Nash, offered this assessment of Fortunato's four-decade career: "Given the vast reach of television, and considering how many of the major events he directed, it is possible more people have seen Caesar's work than that of any other person in human history."

Acknowledgments

At the start, I said I would give credit where credit was due. Real accomplishments referred to in the book, and attributed to fictional characters, were in fact performed by the people noted below, albeit in honorable ways, completely unlike the actions of the characters in this book.

Joe Aceti directed the Cooney-Holmes heavyweight title fight in 1982. Chet Forte was the producer. Both men were pivotal players in the heyday of ABC Sports, when it could reasonably claim to be the worldwide leader in sports.

The spirit of Caesar's Emmy Award speech was appropriated from the words of Roone Arledge, the ABC executive who is as responsible for the sports TV revolution as any, and whose *Wide World of Sports* included daring broadcasts from the Soviet Union, when such a proposition was as difficult as a moon launch.

Bill Bonnell, Victor Frank, and David Michaels were the producers of the opening tease for the 1992 Barcelona Olympics. Each has been accorded repeated acclaim for his passion and creativity in the edit room.

Harry Coyle is responsible for establishing the centerfield camera on national baseball broadcasts and directed the broadcast of Don Larsen's perfect game in the 1956 World Series. He continued to display his splendid feel for the national pastime, setting up the camera that caught Carlton Fisk's famous home-run trot in the 1975 World Series, and he also captured Kirk Gibson's distinguished trip around the bases in the 1988 World Series.

Terry Ewert was the coordinating producer of the 1988 Seoul Olympics. Michael Weisman was the executive producer. Pigeons did get toasted during the Opening Ceremony, but neither man relished their suffering, nor did either one behave in any other way similar to my character while they were in Seoul.

John Gonzalez was the director of the 1994 Super Bowl, and I would like to make very clear that my version of what happened that day in the truck is entirely fictional.

Marty Pasetta directed the 1977 Oscars telecast. William Friedkin was the producer. My description of what happened in front of the cameras is factual. What happened behind the scenes is not. That is a figment of my imagination.

Roger Englander was associated with much of Leonard Bernstein's groundbreaking television work.

Tony Verna is credited with the first instant replay, which he in fact accomplished at the 1963 Army-Navy game. I do honestly believe it is one of the central inventions of the twentieth century. Verna's credits include all the major events and, in particular, he was the director when Secretariat won the Triple Crown at Belmont by an astonishing margin. He also is known for his ambitious global telecasts, including *Live Aid* in 1985, an entertainment extravaganza that raised millions of dollars for famine relief and was broadcast to 1.5 billion people.

* * *

I dedicated this book to my wife and my agent, who both nursed this project along from its inception. There is also a vital third party who should be immediately acknowledged here, my editor Bob Mecoy. A few times in my life I have been fortunate to have people who decided to roll the dice on my professional prospects. Bob is one of them. My book is about a bad gambler, but I think Bob is gambler of the best kind. Believe me, he had to trust his intuition, considering where this novel started and what it has become. He took the time to show me how one goes about making a credible, unified quilt of words.

Also at Crown, I would like to thank two of my other cheerleaders working closely with Bob, Pete Fornatale and Dorianne Steele; and my thanks to superb designers David Tran and Elina D. Nudelman; production editor Jim Walsh; publicists Katherine Beitner and Stephen Lee; editorial director Steve Ross; and Chip Gibson, Crown's publisher.

I owe a debt of gratitude as well to the remarkable staff at the Linda Chester Literary Agency, which is guided by the benevolent chutzpah of its founder. Linda is in the business of making wishes come true, which generally only happens in Disney movies. Also, I want to extend my thanks to Joanna Pulcini's devoted assistant, Kelly Smith, and to Gary Jaffe, Peter O'Reilly, and Meredith Phelan.

There were a number of generous souls who were kind enough to read my various drafts and who offered vital counsel: Gil Aegerter, Michael Cain, Aaron Cohen, Dave Gabel, Joe Gesue, Mark Kreidler, Patrick Miller, Christianna Nelson, Lindsay Pentolfe, and Nick Worth.

For their kind support and assistance, I would also like to thank the following people: Joe Aceti, Amy Bass, Michael Bass, Gregg Backer, Fred Balzac, Stephen Banyra, Andrew Becker, Jim Bell, Donn Bernstein, Rick Bernstein, Bill Bonnell, Kirby Bradley, Dick Buffington, Pascal Charpentier, Bruce Clark, Bruce Cornblatt, Kevin Cusick, Drew Derosa, Emilie Deutsch, Len Dinoia, Bob Duffy, Rob Dustin, Richard Farrelly, Jeff Freedman, Hugh Fink, Wenda Fong, Cary Glotzer, Ed Givinish, Randy Hahn, Jackie Harris, Steve Hartman, Kelly Hayes, Adam Hertzog, George Hill, Milton Hines, John Hirsch, Steve Horn, Larry Kamm, Artie Kempner, Bob Klapisch, Jay Kutlow, Sal Johnson, Peter Johnson, Steve Lawrence, John Libretto, Chris Lincoln, Maura Mandt, Michael Mandt, Ken Martin, Tom Matthews, Mario Mercado, Steve

Milton, Kevin Modesti, Arnaud Montand, J Moses, Fr. Frank Nugent, Tommy O'Connell, Eddie Okuno, William Patrick O'Malley, Sandy Padwe, Meredith Paige, Maria Pagano, Cathy Recchia, Chris Reynolds, Dr. Ken Rosenberg, Gary Scarpulla, Bill Scheft, Tony Scheinman, Bruce Schoenfeld, Chet Simmons, Jed Simmons, Andrew Smith, Mary Frances Smith Reynolds, Nancy Stern, Phil Tuckett, George Veras, Mike Volpe, Rob Weir, Arnie Wexler, and Paul Zimmerman.

Finally, to the gang who help keep me going, in all endeavors—sisters Brenda, Cathleen, Deirdre, Nadine, Moira, and Ailis, brother Patrick—and the ones who got me started: Tom and Sheelah.